Leif GW Persson

Bäckström: He Who Kills the Dragon

Leif GW Persson has chronicled the political and social development of modern Swedish society in his award-winning novels for more than three decades. He has served as an adviser to the Swedish ministry of justice and is Sweden's most renowned psychological profiler. A professor at the Swedish National Police Board, he is considered the country's foremost expert on crime.

ALSO BY LEIF GW PERSSON

Free Falling, As If in a Dream

Between Summer's Longing and Winter's End

Another Time, Another Life

Bäckström: He Who Kills the Dragon

Bäckström: He Who Kills the Dragon

AN EVERT BÄCKSTRÖM NOVEL

Leif GW Persson

Translated from the Swedish by Neil Smith

VINTAGE CRIME / BLACK LIZARD

VINTAGE BOOKS

A DIVISION OF RANDOM HOUSE LLC

NEW YORK

Library of Congress Cataloging-in-Publication Data
Persson, Leif G. W.
[Den som dödar draken. English]
Bäckström : he who kills the dragon / by Leif GW Persson ; translated from the Swedish by Neil Smith. — First Vintage Crime/Black Lizard edition.
pages cm
1. Detectives—Sweden—Fiction.
2. Murder—Investigation—Sweden—Fiction.   I. Title.
PT9876.26.E7225D4613 2014   839.73'74—dc23   2014010368

Vintage Books Trade Paperback ISBN: 978-0-307-95038-3
eBook ISBN: 978-0-307-90684

Book design by Betty Lew

www.weeklylizard.com

Printed in the United States of America
10 9 8 7 6 5 4 3 2

A wicked tale for grown-up children

Bäckström: He Who Kills the Dragon

1.

A gravy-stained tie, a cast-iron saucepan lid, and a basic upholstery hammer with a broken wooden handle. These were the three most striking things found by the forensics team of the Solna Police during their preliminary investigation of the crime scene. But you didn't have to be a forensics expert to work out that these three things had, in all probability, been used to kill the victim. Anyone with a pair of eyes and a strong stomach could figure that out.

As far as the upholstery hammer with the broken handle was concerned, it became clear relatively quickly that—with, if possible, even greater probability—those initial impressions had been wrong, and that the hammer at least hadn't been used when the perpetrator killed his victim.

As the forensics team got on with their work, the investigating officers had done what they had to. They'd knocked on the doors of people living nearby, asking about the victim and if anyone had seen anything that could be connected to what had happened. One woman, a civilian under contract with the police, had set to work finding out whatever she could from her computer—contracted civilians usually took care of that line of inquiry.

It didn't take long before they had uncovered the tragic story of the most common murder victim in Swedish criminal history during the one and a half centuries that records had been kept. Probably considerably longer than that, since court records from as far back as the early medieval period show the same picture as the legal records of industrialized society. The classic Swedish murder victim, if you like. In today's terminology: "A single, middle-aged man, socially marginalized, with a serious alcohol dependency."

"Your standard pisshead, basically" was how Detective Superintendent Evert Bäckström, head of the preliminary investigation for the Solna Police, described the victim to his boss after the initial meeting of the team on the case.

2.

Even if there was more than enough proof in both the neighbors' statements and the information pulled from various registers, the evidence provided by the two forensics experts had given further support to the argument.

"A typical drunken murder, if you ask me, Bäckström," the older of the pair, Peter Niemi, summarized the case when he presented his and his colleague's findings at the same preliminary meeting.

The tie, saucepan lid, and hammer all belonged to the victim and had been in the flat before the unfortunate sequence of events began. The tie had simply been found around the victim's neck. Under the collar, as per usual, but in this case pulled a couple inches too tight and, just to be sure, tied across his throat with a basic reef knot.

Two people, one of them the victim himself, to judge by the fingerprints, appeared to have spent the hours leading up to the murder eating and drinking together in the same flat. Empty bottles of spirits and export-strength lager, beer and vodka glasses, the remains of a meal on two plates on the table in the living room, together with matching scraps of food found in the small kitchen, all provided evidence that the victim's last meal had consisted of that old Swedish classic, pork chops and kidney beans. The beans were evidently bought as a ready-meal, to judge from the plastic packaging found in the bin, from a local supermarket earlier that day. Then, before they were served, they had been heated up in the cast-iron pan whose lid the killer had used to hit his host repeatedly around the head later that same evening.

The coroner had reached much the same conclusions. He had passed these on to the forensics expert who had been at the post-mortem, since he himself was busy with more important matters when the police team were due to hold their first meeting. His definitive findings would take another week or so to appear in writing, but the usual basic dissection and a trained eye were enough to provide a preliminary oral report.

"Our unfortunate victim was what I believe you gentlemen of the police call a pisshead," the coroner had explained, because, in contrast to present company, he was an educated man who was expected to choose his words carefully.

Taken as a whole, all of this—the neighbors' statements, the sad little notes about the victim in official files, the findings from the scene of the crime, the coroner's initial report—provided the police with all they really needed to know. Two pissheads, previously acquainted with each other, had met for a bite to eat and considerably more to drink, then had fallen into an argument about one of the many pointless matters that made up their private shared history. And one of them had brought their evening together to an end by beating the other to death.

It was no more complicated than that. There was a reasonably good expectation of finding the culprit among the victim's closest circle of like-minded acquaintances, and inquiries were already under way. Cases like this were cleared up nine times out of ten, and the papers were usually on the public prosecutor's desk within a month.

A purely routine case, in other words, and it didn't occur to any of the officers of the Solna Police who participated in that first meeting to call in specialist expertise from outside—from, for instance, the psychological profiling unit of the National Criminal Investigation Department, or even the National Police Board's own professor of criminology, who happened to live just a few blocks away from the victim.

Nor had any of these experts been in contact of their own accord, which was a good thing, since they were bound to have certified that things were exactly as everyone already knew they were. Now at least there was no danger of their being caught with their trousers down in terms of scientific evidence.

But when it came down to it, it turned out that all of the above—everything that had been deduced from the accumulation of criminological evidence, tried and tested police experience, and the good old gut instinct that all real policemen develop over time—was completely and utterly wrong.

"Okay, give me the basics, Bäckström," Anna Holt, Bäckström's boss, the police chief of the Western District, said when Bäckström ran through the case for her the day after the murder.

"Just your average pisshead," Bäckström said, nodding solemnly.

"Okay, you've got five minutes," Holt said, and sighed. She had several other items on her agenda, at least one of which was considerably more important than Bäckström's case.

3.

On Thursday, May 15, the sun had risen over number 1 Hasselstigen in Solna at twenty past three in the morning. Exactly two hours and forty-five minutes before Septimus Akofeli, twenty-five, arrived at that address to deliver the morning newspapers.

Septimus Akofeli was really a bicycle courier, but for about a year now he had been earning some extra money delivering morning papers to a few blocks along Råsundavägen, including the building at number 1 Hasselstigen. He also happened to be a refugee from southern Somalia, from a small village just half a day's walk from the Kenyan border. He had arrived in his new homeland on the day of his thirteenth birthday, and the reason he ended up in Sweden rather than anywhere else was that his aunt, uncle, and a number of cousins had arrived there five years earlier, and all his other relatives were dead. Or murdered, one could say, because very few of them had died of other causes.

Septimus Akofeli wasn't your average Somali refugee, somehow ending up in Sweden at random. He had close relatives who could look after him, and there were strong humanitarian reasons for letting him stay. And everything seemed to have turned out pretty well. Or at least as well as anyone had any right to expect, as far as someone like him was concerned.

Septimus Akofeli had worked his way through school and sixth form in Sweden with decent, not to say good, results in most subjects. Then he had studied for three years at Stockholm University. He had a degree in languages, with English as his main subject. He had a Swedish driving license and had become a Swedish citizen at the age of twenty-two. He had applied for a lot of jobs and had eventually got one of them. As a bicycle courier for Green Carriers—"couriers for people who care about the planet." Then, when the first schedule of repayments on his student loan dropped through the letterbox, he found an extra job delivering newspapers. For the past couple years he had been living alone in a one-room flat on Fornbyvägen in Rinkeby.

Septimus Akofeli took care of himself. He wasn't a burden on anyone. In short, he had accomplished more than most people, regardless of background, and had managed better than almost everyone who shared the same background as him.

Septimus Akofeli wasn't your usual Somali refugee. To begin

with, Septimus was a very unusual first name for a Somali, even among the small Christian minority in Somalia. And his skin was also considerably lighter than that of most of his compatriots. There was a simple explanation for this: A pastor with the Church of England's mission to Africa, Mortimer S. Craigh—*S* as in Septimus—had broken the Seventh Commandment. He had got Septimus's mother pregnant, realized the enormity of his sin, asked the Lord for forgiveness, and returned more or less forthwith to his home parish of Great Dunsford in Hampshire, located in the most pastoral surroundings imaginable.

On Thursday, May 15, at five minutes past six in the morning, Septimus Akofeli, twenty-five, had found the murdered body of Karl Danielsson, sixty-eight, in the hall of his flat on the first floor of number 1 Hasselstigen in Solna. The door of the flat was wide open and the dead body was lying just a meter or so inside the door. Septimus Akofeli had put down the copy of *Svenska Dagbladet* that he was about to put through Danielsson's mail slot. He had leaned forward and taken a good look at the body. He had even squeezed its cheeks gently. Then he had shaken his head and dialed 112 on his cell phone.

At six minutes past six in the morning he had been put through to the emergency control room of the Stockholm Police on Kungsholmen. The radio operator had asked him to stay on the line, then put him on hold while he put the call out, and got a response immediately from a patrol car from the Western District that was on Frösundaleden, just a few hundred meters from the address in question. "Suspected murder at number one Hasselstigen in Solna." And the "male individual" who had called sounded "suspiciously calm and collected," which could be useful to know if it wasn't just someone playing a prank on the police but suffering instead from "more serious mental problems . . ."

What the radio operator did not know, however, was that the fact of the matter was much simpler than that. That Septimus Akofeli was particularly well suited to make the type of discovery he had just made. Even as a small boy, he had seen more murdered and mutilated bodies than most of the other nine million inhabitants of his new homeland.

Septimus Akofeli was short and thin, 167 centimeters tall and weighing just 55 kilos. But he was toned and athletic, the way you are when you run up and down staircases for a couple hours every morning and then spend the rest of the day rushing around on a bicycle taking letters and parcels to anxious customers, the sort of people who care about the planet and who shouldn't be made to wait any longer than strictly necessary.

Septimus Akofeli was good-looking, with dark, olive-colored skin, a classic bone structure, and a profile that could have been lifted straight from an ancient Egyptian vase. And of course he had absolutely no idea of the sort of thing that might be going through the head of a middle-aged Swedish police officer working as a radio operator in the emergency control room of the Stockholm Police, and he had done his level best to forget his childhood memories.

To start with, he had done what he was told and stayed on the line. After a couple minutes he had shaken his head, clicked to end the call—the police had evidently forgotten about him—then had put his bag of newspapers aside and sat down on the staircase outside the door of the flat, remaining in the building just as he had promised.

A couple minutes later he had company. First someone had carefully opened and then closed the front door. Then steps padded up the stairs. Two police officers appeared: first a man in his forties, then, just behind him, his considerably younger female colleague. The male officer had his right hand on the butt of his pistol and was pointing at him with his left arm and outstretched hand. His younger female colleague, standing right behind him, was holding an extended collapsible steel baton in her right hand.

"Okay," the male officer said, nodding toward Akofeli. "This is what we're going to do. First we put our hands above our head, then we get up slowly and calmly, then we turn round with our back toward us, with our legs spread . . ."

Who's this *we*? Septimus Akofeli wondered, doing as he had been told.

4.

Hasselstigen is a short side street off Råsundavägen, only a couple hundred meters long, about half a kilometer from the national football stadium and next to where Svensk Filmindustri's old studio complex, Filmstaden, used to be. These days the studios have been turned into luxury housing for people quite unlike those who live at number 1 Hasselstigen.

The building at number 1 Hasselstigen had been built in the autumn of 1945, six months after the end of the war. Locals used to say it was the building that God, or at least its landlord, had given up on. It was a five-story brick building divided into thirty small apartments, each containing just one or two rooms and a kitchen. It was more than sixty years old and had long been in dire need of external renovation, rewiring, and pretty much everything in between.

Even the tenants had seen better days. About twenty of them were single, and most of those were pensioners. There were eight old couples, all of them retired, and one middle-aged woman of forty-nine who lived in a two-room flat with her twenty-nine-year-old son, who was on disability. The neighbors thought he was a bit odd. Nice, harmless, even helpful when called upon, but he had always lived at home with his mom. Recently he had been living there alone, ever since his mother had a stroke and had spent the last few months in a convalescent home.

Eleven of the tenants had a morning paper delivered, six *Dagens*

Nyheter and five *Svenska Dagbladet,* and for the past year or so Septimus Akofeli had been the person who made sure they got delivered each morning. Regular as clockwork, at about six o'clock every morning—he'd never missed a single delivery.

A total of forty-one people lived in the building on Hasselstigen. Or forty, to be precise, since one of them had just been murdered, and by Thursday afternoon the police in Solna had got hold of a list of everyone in the building, including the victim.

In the hours between that first call being received by the emergency control room and the list being supplied, a fair amount had happened. Among other things, the head of the investigating team from the Solna Police, Detective Superintendent Evert Bäckström, had arrived at the scene of the murder at twenty minutes to ten that morning. Just three and a half hours after his colleagues in "the pit" got the call, and, frankly, a lightning-quick response, considering that this was Bäckström.

There was a very personal explanation for this. The previous day, the staff medical officer of the Stockholm Police had made him promise to make changes in his private life and had listed the medicinal alternatives that—if Bäckström carried on being Bäckström—had scared the life out of even this particular patient. And this had at least led to a sober evening and a sleepless night, after which Bäckström had decided to walk to his new job in the crime unit of the Western District.

An endless road to Calvary, some four kilometers long. Under a merciless sun, the whole way from his cozy abode on Inedalsgatan on Kungsholmen, right out to the main police station on Sundbybergsvägen in Solna. And in temperatures that were beyond human endurance and which would have beaten an Olympic marathon runner.

5.

At a quarter past nine on the morning of Thursday, May 15, the sun was already high in a blue and cloudless sky. Even though it was only the middle of May, it was already twenty-six degrees in the shade when Bäckström, bathed in his own sweat, crossed the bridge over the Karlberg Channel. Being a careful, forward-thinking sort of person, he had dressed for the trials ahead of him. A Hawaiian shirt, shorts, sandals without socks, even a bottle of chilled mineral water that he had put in his pocket so that if it proved necessary he could quickly counteract any looming attack of dehydration.

None of this had helped. Even though he had been voluntarily sober for a whole day for the first time in his adult life—he hadn't touched a drop in twenty-five and a half hours, to be precise—he had never felt worse.

I'm going to kill that fucking witch doctor, Bäckström thought. So much for hangovers. He hadn't touched a drop and was now into his second dry day, and he still felt as lively as an eagle that had flown into a power cable.

At that moment his cell phone rang. It was the duty desk in Solna.

"We've been trying to get hold of you, Bäckström," the duty officer said. "I've been looking for you since seven o'clock this morning."

"I had an early meeting at National Crime," Bäckström lied, because that had been round about the time that he had finally drifted off to sleep.

"What's up?" he asked, to fend off any further questions.

"We've got a murder case for you. Our team on the ground could use a bit of advice and leadership. Someone's killed an old pensioner. I hear the scene looks like an abattoir."

"What have we got?" Bäckström grunted, and felt not the slightest bit better in spite of the good news.

"I don't know much more than that. Murder, definitely murder. The victim's fairly old, apparently, a pensioner—like I said, they reckon he doesn't look too pretty. Perpetrator unknown. We haven't even got a description to put out over the radio, so that's all I know. Where are you, anyway?"

"I've just crossed the Karlberg Channel," Bäckström said. "I usually try to walk to work if it isn't raining too much. It's always good to get a bit of exercise," he clarified.

"I see," the duty officer said, scarcely able to conceal his surprise. "If you like, I can send a car to pick you up."

"Good idea," Bäckström said. "Make sure they know it's urgent. I'll be waiting for them outside that soccer hooligans' hangout on the Solna side of the bridge."

Seven minutes later a patrol car had appeared, blue lights flashing, performed a U-turn, and pulled up by the entrance to AIK Stockholm's supporters' clubhouse. Both the driver and his younger female colleague had got out of the car and nodded amiably at him. Evidently they had an appreciation of the way things should be done, because the driver held open the back door on his side so that Bäckström wouldn't have to sit in the seat behind the passenger seat that was usually reserved for suspects.

"So here you are, Bäckström, waiting in classic criminal territory," the male officer said, gesturing toward the bushes behind Bäckström.

"Holm, by the way," he added, pointing with his thumb at the chest of his own uniform. "That's Hernandez," he said, nodding toward his female colleague.

"What do you mean, classic territory?" Bäckström said once he'd squeezed into the backseat, mainly because his thoughts had already turned to Holm's female colleague. Long dark hair tied up in an artistic knot, a smile that could light up the whole of Råsunda Stadium, and a top deck that was putting her blue uniform shirt under serious strain.

"What do you mean, classic territory?" he repeated.

"Oh, you know, that prostitute. This was where she was found, wasn't it? Well, bits of her, anyway. The old murder that everyone reckons was committed by that coroner and that friend of his, a GP. Mind you, who knows? The head of crime out here, old Toivonen, apparently has an entirely different theory about what happened."

"You must have been involved in that, Bäckström?" Hernandez put in, turning toward him and firing off a brilliant smile. "When was it? I mean, when did they find her? I wasn't born then, but it must have been sometime during the seventies? Thirty-five, forty years ago? Something like that?"

"The summer of 1984," Bäckström said curtly. And one more word from you, you little trollop, and I'll see you get put on traffic duty. In Chile, he thought, glaring at Hernandez.

"Oh, 1984. Okay, I had been born, then," Hernandez said, clearly not about to give up and still showing off her fine set of bright white teeth.

"I don't doubt it. You look a lot older, though," Bäckström said, not about to give up either. Suck on that, you carpet-munching bitch, he thought.

"We've got quite a bit to tell you about this current case," Holm said by way of distraction, clearing his throat carefully as Hernandez turned her back on Bäckström and started looking through her notebook to make sure she got her facts right. "We've just come from there."

"Okay, I'm listening," Bäckström said.

Holm and Hernandez had been the first officers on the scene. They'd just stopped for coffee at the twenty-four-hour gas station behind the Solna shopping center when they heard the call over police radio. Blue lights and sirens, and three minutes later they were at number 1 Hasselstigen.

Their colleague over the radio had advised caution. He thought the "male individual" who had called in wasn't reacting like normal people do when they call with news like that. He showed no sign of losing it and had no trouble controlling his vocal cords. In short, he was suspiciously calm and collected, the way some nuts sound when they call the police to tell them about their latest exploits.

"The guy who called in was delivering papers. An immigrant. Seems a nice lad. I think we can probably forget about him, if you ask me," Holm summarized.

And who the hell would ask someone like you what you think? Bäckström thought.

"What about the victim? What do we know about him?"

"He was the tenant of the flat, name Karl Danielsson. Older man, single, sixty-eight years old. Retired, in other words," Holm clarified.

"We're sure of that?" Bäckström said.

"Quite sure," Holm said. "I recognized him at once. I picked him up for being drunk and disorderly at Solvalla racecourse a few years back. He kicked up a right fuss afterward, reported me and the rest of the team for pretty much anything he could think of. And that wasn't exactly the first time he'd been picked up for that sort of thing. Social problems, alcohol, all that. Socially marginalized, as they say these days."

"Your standard pisshead, you mean," Bäckström said.

"Well, yes. That's another way of putting it," Holm said, and suddenly it sounded as if he wanted to change the subject.

Five minutes later they had dropped Bäckström off outside the door of number 1 Hasselstigen, and Holm had wished him luck. He and Hernandez were heading off to the station to write up their reports, but if there was anything else they could help with, Bäckström was more than welcome to get in touch.

And what the fuck would I want to do that for? Bäckström

thought, as the car pulled away, not bothering to thank them for the lift.

6.

Same as usual, Bäckström thought. Beyond the cordons that had been set up in front of the building crowded the usual collection of journalists and photographers, neighbors, and the generally curious who had nothing better to do. Plus the usual rabble, of course, who had probably ended up there without even wondering how it had happened. Among them were three suntanned youths who took the opportunity to comment on Bäckström's clothing and appearance as he squeezed under the cordon with a certain amount of difficulty.

Bäckström had turned back and glared at them, to register their appearance in his memory for the day when they eventually met in his own place of work. It was only a matter of time, and, when the day finally arrived, he intended to make it a memorable experience for the little shits.

As he passed the young uniformed officer standing by the door of the building, he had given his first order in connection with this new murder investigation:

"Call surveillance and get them to send a couple guys to take some nice pictures of our charming audience," Bäckström said.

"It's already done," his colleague informed him. "That was the first thing the Anchor said to me when she arrived. Our colleagues from surveillance must have been here taking pictures for a couple hours now," he added, for some reason.

"Anchor? What bloody anchor?"

"Annika Carlsson. You know, our tall brunette colleague, used to work in robbery. Nicknamed the Anchor."

"You mean that fucking virago?" Bäckström said.

"I wouldn't like to comment, Bäckström," his colleague said with a grin. "But obviously, you can't help hearing things."

"Such as?" Bäckström said suspiciously.

"Well, it's probably best to avoid getting into an arm-wrestling contest with her," his colleague said.

Bäckström had contented himself with a shake of the head. Where the hell are we heading? he wondered as he stepped inside the door of the building at number 1 Hasselstigen. What the hell is happening to the Swedish Police? Faggots, dykes, darkies, and the usual yes-men. Not a single ordinary police constable as far as the eye can see.

At the crime scene everything looked the way it usually did when someone had beaten an old pisshead to death in his own flat. In short, things looked even worse than they usually did in the home of an old pisshead. This particular example was lying on his back on the hall rug just inside the door, with his feet facing the door, his legs apart, and his arms stretched out above his crushed skull, almost like he was praying. To judge by the smell, his gray gabardine trousers had filled up with excrement and urine when he died. There was a meter-wide pool of blood on the floor. The walls on both sides of the narrow hallway were splattered with blood from floor to ceiling, and there were even traces of blood on the center of the ceiling.

Bloody hell, Bäckström thought, shaking his head. Really, he ought to call *Beautiful Homes* with a tip-off so all those interior designer queers could finally get something serious to chew on, something with the real common touch. A little My-Lovely-Home report from social group seventeen, Bäckström thought. Then his thoughts were interrupted by someone tapping on his shoulder.

"Hello, Bäckström. Good to see you," Detective Inspector Annika Carlsson, thirty-three, said with a friendly nod.

"Hello," Bäckström said, making an effort to sound less rough than he felt.

A woman who was half a head taller than him, even though he was a tall, well-built man in the prime of life. Long legs, narrow waist, irritatingly fit, and with everything in the right place. If she just let her hair grow a bit and put on a short skirt, she could even pass for a completely normal woman. Apart from her height, of course, but it was presumably too late to do anything about that, and with a bit of luck she might have stopped growing by now, even though she was still wet behind the ears.

"Have you got any particular instructions, Bäckström? The forensics team are done with their preliminary checks, and as soon as they've got the body off to the forensics lab you can take a look at our crime scene."

"Later," Bäckström said, shaking his head. "Who the fuck is that?" he asked, nodding toward a slight, dark-skinned figure sitting crouched against a wall at the far end of the shared landing. With a closed, melancholy expression on his face and a cloth bag with newspapers sticking out of it over his shoulder.

"That's our paperboy, the one who made the call," Carlsson said.

"Who'd have thought it?" Bäckström said. "So that'll be why he's got a bag of newspapers hanging from his shoulder."

"No flies on you," Carlsson said with a smile. "To be more precise, he's got five *Dagens Nyheter* and four *Svenska Dagbladet*. The victim's copy of *Svenska* is lying over there by the door," she went on, nodding toward a folded newspaper on the floor by the entrance to the victim's flat. "He'd already delivered one copy of *Dagens Nyheter* to an old woman on the ground floor."

"What do we know about him, then? The paperboy?"

"Well, to start with it looks like he's completely clean," Annika Carlsson said. "Forensics have checked him out and they didn't find any traces at all on his body or clothes. Considering the state of things in there, he'd have been completely drenched in blood if he was the one who attacked our victim. He told us himself that he felt the victim's face, his cheek, to be more accurate, and when he realized he was completely stiff, he knew that the victim was dead."

"So he's studying medicine, is he?" Bloody hell, Bäckström mused. The little sooty clearly wasn't lacking ambition.

"I believe he saw a lot of dead bodies in his former homeland," Carlsson said, this time without smiling.

"Did he take the opportunity to slip anything into his pockets?" Bäckström asked, falling back on old instincts as far as sooties like that were concerned.

"He's been searched. That was the first thing the patrol did when they got here. In his pockets he was carrying a folder containing his driving license, an ID card from the paper that handles distribution of the papers out here, a small amount of money in coins and notes—about a hundred kronor, I think, mostly coins. And a cell phone that belongs to him. And we've made a note of the number, in case you're wondering. If he did take anything, he didn't have it on him, and we've already searched the communal areas of the building, so he didn't hide anything there."

Fucking hell. They're lazy bastards as well, Bäckström thought, not ready to give up.

"Did he make any calls, then?"

"According to what he says, he only made one call. Emergency services, 112. They put him through to our colleagues in the pit. He says the only person he spoke to was the operator there, but obviously we're going to check that out. He's on the list of phone numbers we'll have to investigate."

"Has he got a name, then?" Bäckström said.

"Septimus Akofeli, twenty-five years old, a refugee from Somalia, Swedish citizenship, lives in Rinkeby. We've taken fingerprints and a DNA sample, but we haven't had time to check them yet. But I'm pretty sure he is who he says he is."

"What did you say his name was?" Bäckström said. What a bloody name, he thought.

"Septimus Akofeli," Annika Carlsson replied. "One of the reasons I haven't let him go yet is that I thought you might want to talk to him."

"No," Bäckström said, shaking his head. "As far as I'm concerned, you can send him home. But I thought I might take a look at our crime scene, on the other hand. If those wannabe academics from forensics are going to be finished anytime soon."

"Peter Niemi and Jorge Hernandez, known as Chico," Annika Carlsson said with a nod. "They're part of our forensics team out here in Solna, and we couldn't ask for better, if you ask me."

"Hernandez? Where have I heard that name before?" Bäckström said.

"He's got a younger sister, Magdalena Hernandez; she's one of our uniforms. You've probably seen her about, maybe it's her name you're thinking of." Annika Carlsson smiled broadly for some reason.

"Why do you say that?" Bäckström wondered.

"Sweden's most attractive female police officer, according to the majority of her colleagues. And from my own point of view, I reckon she's a great girl," Carlsson said with a smile.

"You don't say," Bäckström said. I daresay you've been there already, he thought.

Inside the flat, things were just as bad as Bäckström had imagined. First a little cloakroom and narrow hall. On the left a small bathroom and toilet, followed by a small bedroom. On the right a kitchen with a dining table, and straight ahead a living room. All in all, about fifty square meters, and it wasn't exactly clear when the occupant had last done any cleaning. Not this side of the new year, at any rate.

The furnishings were shabby and worn, and the décor likewise. Everything from the unmade bed with the pillow with no pillowcase to the filthy kitchen table and the sagging sofa and armchair in the living room. Yet the things in there bore witness to the fact that the murder victim, Karl Danielsson, had seen better days. A few worn Persian rugs. A sturdy old-fashioned mahogany writing desk with a decorative inlay of some lighter wood. A twenty-year-old television, but it was still a Bang & Olufsen television. And the armchair in front of it was an English leather wing chair with matching footstool.

Drink, Bäckström thought. Drink and loneliness, and he himself had never felt worse since those Neanderthals in the National Rapid-Response Unit had thrown a shock grenade at him some six months ago. He hadn't regained his senses until the next day, and by then they had already had time to shut him away in the psychiatric unit of Huddinge Hospital.

"Anything else you want, Bäckström?" Annika Carlsson asked, and for some reason she looked almost worried as she did so.

A couple large shorts and a pint, Bäckström thought. And if you let your hair grow and put a skirt on, then maybe you can give me a blowjob. But don't start thinking you can get any more than that, he thought, since only twenty-four hours ago he was having serious doubts about earthly desires and spiritual love.

"No," he said, shaking his head. "See you back at the station."

There's something that doesn't make sense, Bäckström thought, as he walked slowly back to the police station. But what was it? And how was he supposed to work it out with a brain that was suffering acute dehydration and was probably already damaged beyond repair? I'm going to kill that fucking witch doctor, he thought.

7.

By three o'clock that afternoon Bäckström had already held his first meeting with the team investigating his new murder case. It wasn't exactly the sharpest team he had led in his twenty-five years in violent crime. Nor the largest either, come to that. Eight people in total, if you counted him and the two forensics officers, who would soon move on to other cases as soon as they had finished the most important work on Karl Danielsson. Which left one plus five, and considering everything he had seen and heard of his colleagues so far, it all boiled down to just one man, Detective Superintendent Evert Bäckström himself. Who else, really? That was what usually happened, after all. Bäckström left standing alone as the last hope of the grieving family. Even if it was most likely that the state-run alcohol monopoly was closer than anyone to Danielsson.

"Okay," Bäckström said. "Well, welcome to this investigation, and for the time being that goes for all of you. If there any changes on that score, I promise to let you know. Does anyone want to kick things off?"

"We do, my colleague and I," the older of the two forensics experts, Peter Niemi, said. "We've hardly had a chance to get started on the flat, so we've got loads to be getting on with."

Peter Niemi had been with the police for twenty-five years or so and had worked in forensics for fifteen of them. He was over fifty but looked considerably younger than he was. Fair, in good shape, slightly above average height. He had been born and raised in the Torne Valley in the far north of Sweden. He had lived in Stockholm more than half his life but still had his regional dialect. He smiled easily and his blue eyes expressed both friendliness and reserve at the same time. You didn't have to be an idiot to see what he did for a job, and the fact that he hadn't worn a uniform for the past fifteen years was completely irrelevant. It was the message his eyes gave off that made all the difference. Peter Niemi was a police officer, and he was nice and kind as long as you behaved. If you didn't, then Niemi wasn't the sort of man to back down, and there was more than one person who had come to realize that in a rather painful way.

"Fine," Bäckström said. "I'm listening." A fucking Lapp, a bastard Finn, sounds like he's just tumbled off the bus from Haparanda, and the sooner I don't have to listen to him, the better, he thought.

"Well, then," Niemi said, leafing through his papers.

The victim's name was Karl Danielsson. Retired, sixty-eight years old. According to the passport that the forensics officers had found in his flat, he was 188 centimeters tall and weighed something like 120 kilos.

"Heavily built and badly overweight, I'd guess maybe thirty kilos too much," said Niemi, who had himself grabbed the body by the arms when it was loaded onto a cart. "You'll get the exact figures from the medical report."

Whatever the fuck we might need them for, Bäckström thought sourly. We're hardly going to mince him down and make sausages out of our murder victim, he thought.

"The crime scene," Niemi went on. "The victim's own apartment. To be precise, the hall. My hunch is that he'd been to the toilet and received the first blow as he was coming out, still doing up his fly. That matches both the splatter pattern and his half-closed zip, in case anyone's wondering. Then he was struck several times in quick succession, and the decisive blows were struck when he was already lying on the hall floor."

"What was he hit with?" Bäckström asked.

"A blue enameled cast-iron saucepan lid," Niemi said. "It was on the floor beside the body. The saucepan is on the stove in the kitchen, no more than three meters away.

"As well as that," he went on, "the perpetrator also seems to have used an upholstery hammer with a wooden handle. The handle broke off right by the head, and both parts were found on the hall floor. Alongside the victim's head."

"Our perpetrator's a thorough little bastard." Bäckström sighed, shaking his big round head.

"I don't think he's that little. Not to judge by the angle of the blows, at any rate. But he was certainly thorough, even if it was hard to see at first because Danielsson's face and chest were so covered in blood," Niemi said. "He was actually strangled as well. With his own tie. When he was lying on the floor, and by then he must have been unconscious and pretty close to death, the perpetrator tightened his tie and finished the job with a reef knot. Completely unnecessary, if you ask me. But I suppose it's better to err on the side of caution, if you want to be absolutely sure." Niemi shrugged.

"Do you have any ideas about who might have done it, then?" Bäckström asked, even though he already knew the answer.

"A typical pisshead murder, if you ask me, Bäckström," Niemi said, smiling amiably. "But it's worth bearing in mind, Bäckström, that you're asking someone from the Torne Valley."

"What about the timing, then?" Bäckström said. So he wasn't entirely thick after all, he thought.

"I'm getting to that. All in good time, Bäckström," Niemi said.

"Before the victim was killed, he and another individual, someone who left his fingerprints at the scene but who we haven't yet been able to identify, sat in the living room eating pork chops with kidney beans. The host probably sat in the only armchair, his guest on the sofa. They had the meal on the coffee table but had time to clear it away. We've found a number of prints from both of them, if you're wondering, and we should have the answers sometime tomorrow. If we're lucky, the perpetrator will be in the fingerprint register already. With their meal they drank five half-liter cans of export-strength lager and more than a bottle of vodka. We've got one empty bottle and one just started. The usual size, seventy centiliters, and it's probably worth pointing out that they were that esteemed brand, Explorer. Both bottles were found on the floor in front of the television, where they had been sitting and eating, and the evidence suggests that the bottles were unopened when they started. For one thing, the seals are still there. You know, the perforated bit at the bottom of the bottle top. The bit that makes that nice cracking sound when you unscrew it."

Every now and then this bastard Lapp sounds completely normal, Bäckström thought, even though he could feel a great vacuum in his chest. Almost like a near-death experience. Where had that come from?

"Anything else? About the perpetrator, and what happened before the murder?"

"I think the man who did this was physically strong," Niemi said, nodding thoughtfully. "That business with the necktie takes a lot of strength. And he turned the body over as well, because to start with, the victim was on his side, or possibly his stomach—we can tell that because of the way the blood spread—but when we found him, he was lying on his back. I think he turned the victim onto his back when he decided to strangle him."

"And when would that have been?" Annika Carlsson asked suddenly, before Bäckström had a chance to ask that very question.

"If you're asking a medical layman like me—the postmortem on the body won't be done until this evening—I'd probably guess at yesterday evening," Niemi said. "Chico and I got there at almost exactly seven o'clock this morning, and by then the victim had developed complete rigor mortis, but of course we'll know much more about this and a lot more besides tomorrow." Niemi nodded, looked at the others in the room, and made a move to get up from his chair. "We've already sent a whole load of material for analysis to the National Forensics Lab in Linköping, but it'll probably be a few weeks before we get any answers. But I'm not sure it will make too much difference in a case like this. Having to wait, I mean. This perpetrator isn't going anywhere. Our forensics colleagues in the county crime unit have promised to help with the fingerprints, so with a bit of luck that'll be done by the weekend."

"We need the weekend," Niemi repeated as he stood up. "On Monday I think we should be able to give you a decent description of what happened inside the flat."

"Thanks," Bäckström said, nodding to Niemi and his younger colleague. As soon as we lay our hands on Danielsson's dinner partner, this one's done and dusted, he thought. One pisshead killing another pisshead, there's no more to it than that.

As soon as the forensics experts had left the room his lazy and inadequate investigating team started making a fuss about needing to stretch their legs and have a cigarette break. If he'd been his usual self he would have told them to shut up, but Bäckström felt strangely apathetic and merely nodded his consent. More than anything he would have liked to walk out, but in the absence of better options he had headed straight for the toilets and must have drunk at least five liters of cold water.

8.

"Okay," Bäckström said when they had all returned to the meeting room and could finally get going again so that this wretched business might come to an end sometime soon. "Let's look at the victim. Then we can throw some ideas around, and before we leave we'll work out a list of what we've done and what we're going to do tomorrow. Today is Thursday, May fifteenth, and I think we could be finished by the weekend so that we can devote next week to more important cases than Mr. Danielsson.

"What have we got on our victim, Nadja?" Bäckström went on, nodding toward a short, plump woman in her fifties who was sitting at the end of the table and had already surrounded herself with an impressive pile of paperwork.

"Quite a lot, actually," Nadja Högberg said. "I've looked up the usual information, and there are some juicy details in there. And I've spoken to his younger sister—she's his only close relative—and she was able to contribute a fair few extra facts as well."

"I'm listening," Bäckström said, even though his mind was somewhere else entirely and even though the comforting sound of the seal on a bottle top being broken was echoing round his head.

Karl Danielsson had been born in Solna in February 1940 and was therefore sixty-eight years old when he was murdered. His father had worked as a typesetter and foreman at a printer's in Solna. His mother had been a housewife. Both parents long since dead. His closest relative was a sister who was ten years younger than him and lived in Huddinge, south of Stockholm.

Karl Danielsson was single. He had never married and had no children. Or rather, no children according to the various registers the police had access to. He had spent four years in elementary school in Solna, then five years in junior secondary, where he passed his exams and got into Påhlmans Business College in Stockholm, where he spent three years. By the time he was nineteen he had completed a sixth-form economics course. Then he did his military service at Barkarby Airbase. He came out ten months later and got his first job as an assistant in a firm of accountants in Solna, in the summer of 1960, aged twenty.

That same summer he made his first appearance in police records. Karl Danielsson had been apprehended driving while in an intoxicated state and was fined sixty days' wages for drunk driving and lost his driving license for six months. Five years later the same thing happened again. Drunk driving, fined sixty days' wages. Driving license withdrawn for a year. Then seven years passed before his third offense, this time considerably more serious.

Danielsson had been drunk as a skunk. He'd driven into a hot-dog kiosk on Solnavägen and absconded from the scene. In Solna District Court he was found guilty of drunk driving and leaving the scene of a crime, and was sentenced to three months in prison and had his driving license revoked. Danielsson had got hold of a hotshot lawyer and went to the Court of Appeal, where he presented two different medical certificates regarding his problems with alcohol. He managed to get his conviction for absconding overturned, and the prison sentence was commuted to probation. But he didn't manage to get his license back, and he evidently wasn't bothered enough by this to apply for a new license when the sentence expired. For the last thirty-six years of his life Karl Danielsson had gone without a driving license, so there were no more convictions for drunk driving.

But even as a pedestrian he continued to attract the attention of the police. During this period the police had locked him up on five occasions, under the Act on Taking Intoxicated Persons into Custody, and it had probably happened more often than that. Danielsson always used to refuse to give his name, which he was under no obligation to supply. The last time he had been taken into custody, things had gone badly wrong.

It had happened on the day of the Elitloppet trotting race at Solvalla racecourse, in May five years before he died. Danielsson had been drunk and rowdy, and when he was being helped into the police van he had started fighting and flailing about. Resisting arrest and violent conduct against a public official, and merely being taken into custody turned into getting arrested, even if it ended the same as usual, with his being put in a cell in the Solna police station to sober up. By the time he was released six hours later, Danielsson had accused both the arresting officers and the staff at the station of physical abuse, in total three police officers and two custody officers. Another hotshot lawyer turned up, new medical certificates were submitted, and then everything spiraled into a big circus. More than a year passed before the first case went to court, and it had to be adjourned immediately when the prosecutor's two witnesses for some reason failed to appear.

Because Danielsson's lawyer was an extremely busy man, another year passed before time could be found for new proceedings. Once again they had to be postponed because the prosecutor's witnesses failed to appear. The prosecutor lost patience and dismissed the case. Karl Danielsson was an innocent man, at least for that part of his life.

"Considering the fact that the chances of being taken into custody and arrested for crimes of this nature are minimal, he must have been drunk pretty much the whole time," Nadja Högberg said, and she knew what she was talking about. She had been a civilian employed by the police in the Western District for ten years, after being born Nadjesta Ivanova and gaining a doctorate in physics and applied mathematics at Saint Petersburg State University. In the bad old days as well, when Saint Petersburg was called Leningrad and when academic requirements had been considerably stricter than they were in the new, liberated Russia.

"What other fuckups has he made, then? Apart from rolling around when he's been on the bottle, I mean," Bäckström asked, nodding toward Nadja Högberg.

Not that he was remotely interested in the murder victim's dealings with his more or less retarded colleagues in the regular force and traffic division, but mainly to rein her in so that he could put a stop to this interminable meeting. So that he could finally drag himself home to Inedalsgatan and the remnants of what had until yesterday been his home. Get in the shower and put a stop to all the noise in his head. Gulp down a few more liters of ice-cold water. Gorge himself on raw vegetables and then do all the things that remained in a life that had been stripped of all meaning the day before.

Why can't you ever learn to hold your tongue, Bäckström? Bäckström thought five minutes later.

Nadja Högberg had taken him at his word and was giving a detailed account of Danielsson's various financial activities and the interactions with the judicial system that these had, in turn, led to.

The same year that he was first convicted of drunk driving, Karl Danielsson had been promoted from accounts assistant to head of the office's section for "trusts, corporations, economic and charitable societies, estates and probate, private individuals, and miscellaneous affairs." After that things had really taken off. First he moved to the business section as a financial adviser and tax consultant, then after a few years he was appointed head of the whole group and was co-opted onto the board.

The week after his close encounter with the hot-dog kiosk

on Solnavägen, soon after his thirty-second birthday, he was appointed deputy managing director and given a permanent seat on the board. A couple years after that he had taken over the whole company and renamed it Karl Danielsson Consultants Ltd. According to the company's articles of association, the business was involved in "financial, accounting, and auditing consultancy, tax and investment advice," and also "management of property and capital investment," which must have been quite an achievement, since throughout this age of greatness the company never seemed to have had more than four employees. One female secretary and three men with the title of consultant and rather vague duties. Karl Danielsson himself was the owner of the company, its managing director, and the chairman of its board.

As such, he had acquitted himself considerably better than he had as Karl Danielsson, the possessor of a driving license and pedestrian. Over a period of twenty-three years, between 1972 and 1995, he had been investigated for various financial crimes on a total of ten occasions. Four cases of complicity in tax evasion and serious tax fraud, two cases of currency offenses, two cases of so-called money laundering, one case of aggravated receipt of stolen goods, and one case of dishonest dealing. In every instance the charges had been dropped. The suspicions against Karl Danielsson could never be proven, and every time, Danielsson had gone on the counterattack and reported his adversaries to the parliamentary ombudsman and the chancellor of justice, or both, just to be on the safe side.

In this he had also been more successful than his opponents. One of the investigating officers of the financial crime unit of the Stockholm Police had been picked up by the ethics committee of the National Police Board and had received a formal warning and been docked fourteen days' pay. The parliamentary ombudsman had arrested one public prosecutor and one of the Tax Office's auditors. The chancellor of justice had prosecuted one of the evening papers and secured a conviction for grave defamation of character.

After 1995 things had calmed down. Karl Danielsson Consultants Ltd. had changed its name to Karl Danielsson Holdings Ltd. There didn't seem to have been much activity, and the company had never had any employees. Nadja Högberg had requested copies of the most recent annual accounts from the company records division of the Patent and Registration Office, and was planning to spend the weekend going through them.

He did not appear ever to have had a particularly remarkable income. Nadja Högberg had dug out his self-certified income declarations for the past five years, and his taxable income had hovered around 170,000 kronor per year. His state pension and a smaller private pension from Skandia. The apartment he lived in cost 4,500 kronor per month, and after tax and rent there were approximately 5,000 kronor left for other things.

If a person's success can be measured by the titles he or she garners, then Karl Danielsson had lived a successful life and had left this world at the top. At the age of twenty he had started his career by working as an assistant in a firm of accountants with thirty-five employees. Forty-eight years later an as-yet-unknown perpetrator had put an end to it by smashing in his skull with the help of a cast-iron saucepan lid, by which time the company in which he had spent all his adult life had been for all intents and purposes dormant for almost fifteen years. In the phone book he was listed as a director, and according to the business cards the forensics experts had found in his otherwise empty wallet, the victim was both managing director and chairman of the board of Karl Danielsson Holdings Ltd.

A pisshead, a serial litigant, and a pathological fantasist, Bäckström thought.

"You've spoken to his sister," Annika Carlsson said as soon as Nadja Högberg had finished. "What does she have to say about what you've just told us?"

Nadja Högberg said that she had confirmed all the main points. As a young man her brother had been "very fond of girls" and "far too keen on partying." But things had gone well for him until he was approaching forty, after which time the drink seemed to have more or less taken over his life. She had also made it clear that they had never been particularly close. During the past ten years they hadn't even spoken on the phone, and the last time they met had been around the time of their mother's funeral twelve years ago.

"How did she take it when you told her that her brother had been murdered?" Annika asked.

For fuck's sake, Bäckström thought, groaning silently to himself. Maybe we should have a minute's silence?

"Fine," Nadja said. "She was fine about it. She works as a staff nurse at Huddinge Hospital and seems pretty sensible, stable. She said it didn't exactly come as much of a surprise. She'd been worried about something like this happening for years. Considering the life he led, I mean—"

"We'll just have to try to deal with our grief somehow," Bäckström interrupted. "So what do we think about all this?"

Then they had started throwing ideas around. Or one single idea that Bäckström, just to be on the safe side, threw out there all on his own.

"Well, then," Bäckström said, since the others for once seemed to have the good manners to keep their mouths shut and let him start.

"One pisshead has been murdered by another pisshead. If there's anyone here who has any other suggestion, now's the time to pipe up," he went on, leaning forward and resting his elbows heavily on the table, glowering at his colleagues.

No one seemed to have any objections, to judge by the unanimous head shaking.

"Good," Bäckström said. "That's enough suggestions. All that's left is to work out where we are and how to smoke out Danielsson's dinner guest from last night.

"How's the door-to-door going with the neighbors?" Bäckström went on.

"Pretty much done," Annika Carlsson said. "There are a couple of them we haven't got hold of yet, and a few more asked if we could talk to them this evening, since they had to get to work. And there was one who had a doctor's appointment at nine o'clock and didn't have time to talk to us. It should all be done by tomorrow."

"The coroner?"

"He's promised to conduct the postmortem this evening and give us at least an oral report early next week. Our colleague Hernandez will be attending the postmortem, so we should know the basics first thing tomorrow morning," Annika Carlsson said.

"Have we spoken to the taxi companies, have we had any tip-offs that are worth looking at, what about the search of the area round the building, and his social network, how did he spend his last few hours, have we spoken to—"

"Calm down, Bäckström," Annika Carlsson interrupted with a broad smile. "It's all under control. We're well on top of this one, so you can relax."

I don't feel remotely relaxed, Bäckström thought, but he would never have dreamed of saying so out loud. Instead he merely nodded. Gathered together his papers and stood up.

"See you tomorrow," Bäckström said. "One more thing before we go. About the paperboy who made the call. What's his name, Sooty Akofeli."

"Septimus," Annika Carlsson corrected, without the slightest trace of a smile. "His name's Septimus Akofeli. We've checked him out. Our colleagues have already compared the fingerprints they took off him at Hasselstigen with the ones he had to give the Migration Board when he first arrived twelve years ago. He is who he says he is, and, in case you're wondering, he's never been in any trouble."

"I hear what you're saying," Bäckström said, "but there's something about that bastard that isn't right."

"What might that be?" Annika Carlsson said, shaking her cropped head.

"I don't know," Bäckström said. "I'm working on it, so the rest of you can at least spare it a moment's thought."

As soon as he had left the meeting room he had gone straight to his new boss, police chief Anna Holt, and explained the situation to her. Pisshead victim. Perpetrator—with almost absolute certainty—also a pisshead. Case completely under control. It would be concluded by Monday at the latest, and he had finished in three minutes even though he could have taken five. Holt seemed almost relieved when he left. She had another matter to think about, and, compared to that, Bäckström's murder seemed like a gift from above.

That gave the scrawny bitch something to think about, Bäckström thought, as he finally stepped out through the door of his new gulag.

9.

Jerzty Sarniecki, twenty-seven, was a Polish carpenter. Born and raised in Lodz, for the past few years he had formed part of the Swedish migrant workforce. And for the past month he and his workmates had been employed on the complete renovation of a small block of rented flats on Ekensbergsvägen in Solna, about one kilometer from the crime scene at number 1 Hasselstigen. Eighty kronor an hour, straight in his pocket, and free to work twenty-four hours a day, seven days a week if he felt like it. They bought food in a nearby ICA supermarket, they slept in the building they were working on, and everything else could perfectly well wait until they returned to civilization back home in Poland.

Around the time Bäckström was leaving the Solna police station, Sarniecki had made his discovery when he dragged a large plastic sack of rubble from the building to throw it into the trash bin out on the street. He clambered up an unsteady ladder and discovered another bag on top of the pile of rubble that neither he nor any of his workmates had thrown there. In itself, this was nothing unusual, the fact that Swedes in the neighborhood made the most of the opportunity to get rid of their own rubbish, but because experience had already taught him that they often threw away things that were still perfectly usable, he had leaned over and fished out the bag.

An ordinary plastic bag. Neatly tied at the top and full of something that looked like clothes.

Sarniecki had climbed down from the ladder. Opened the bag and taken out the contents. A black synthetic raincoat of the longer variety. It looked almost new. A pair of red washing-up gloves. Intact, scarcely used. A pair of dark leather slippers, which also looked practically new.

Why would anyone throw things like this away? Sarniecki wondered in surprise; then a moment later he discovered the blood on what he had just found. Loads of blood splattered over the raincoat, and the pale soles of the slippers were more or less dripping with it. The gloves were stained with blood even though someone had obviously made an attempt to rinse them off.

He had heard about the murder in Hasselstigen that morning, when their Swedish foreman showed up and told them over coffee. Some poor retiree, evidently, and normal, decent folk hardly dared leave their homes any longer. Think about what you're saying, he had thought, as he'd listened with half an ear. Don't curse the paradise that you Swedes actually live in, because it might be taken away from you, he thought. His Catholic priest back home in Lodz had taught him to think like that.

In spite of this he had wrestled with his conscience for several hours before calling the police. I wonder how many hours this is going to take? he wondered, as he stood and waited for the car the police had promised to send. How many hours at eighty kronor would they take from him and his fiancée and the child they were expecting back home in Poland?

A quarter of an hour later a patrol car had arrived carrying two uniformed officers. They seemed strangely uninterested. They had put what he had found, including the bag it had been in, inside another bag. They had made a note of his name and cell number. Then they had left. But before they went one of them asked if he had a business card. He and his father-in-law were thinking of building a sauna out at the summer cottage they shared out on Adelsö Island and might be needing some help at a reasonable price. Jerzty had given him the card that their Swedish foreman had told them to hand out whenever they received queries of this nature. Then they had left.

Later that evening a tall, fair-haired man, who was obviously a policeman even though he was dressed in a leather jacket and ordinary blue jeans, had knocked at the door of the building where Jerzty was working. He had opened the door to him, since he was working in the entrance hall, nailing up new plasterboard while his workmates were having a late supper a couple floors up in the room where they had set up their makeshift kitchen. The fair-haired man gave him a friendly smile and held out a sinewy hand.

"My name is Peter Niemi," Niemi said in English. *"I am a police officer. Do you know where I can find Jerry Sarniecki?"*

"That's me," Jerzty Sarniecki said, before continuing in Swedish. "I speak a little Swedish because I've worked over here for several years now."

"Then you're in the same position as me," Niemi said with a broad smile. "Is there anywhere we could talk undisturbed? I'd like to ask you a few questions."

10.

Bäckström had walked all the way home. All the way from the police station on Sundbybergsvägen in Solna to his home on Inedalsgatan on Kungsholmen. It was as if his feet and legs had suddenly taken on a life of their own, with his body and head merely tagging along. Entirely involuntarily, and when he shut the door behind him he had hardly any idea of what he had spent the past few hours doing. The inside of his sweaty head was completely blank. Had he met anyone? Had he spoken to anyone? Someone he knew and who had been able to see him in all his misery? Evidently he must have stopped and done some shopping somewhere, because he was carrying a bag full of bottles of mineral water and a plastic pack containing a mass of mysterious vegetables.

What the fuck is this? Bäckström thought, holding up the pack. Those little red things must be tomatoes. He recognized them, and he had even eaten one or two when he was a lad. All that green stuff must be lettuce? But all the other stuff? A mass of weird black-and-brown balls of varying sizes. Hare shit? Elk shit? And something that mostly looked like maggots but which must be something else, since they didn't wriggle when he prodded them.

What the fuck is going on? Bäckström wondered as he headed toward the shower, dropping his clothes on the floor as he went.

To begin with, he had just stood in the shower for a quarter of an hour or so, letting the water run over his well-upholstered and harmoniously proportioned body. The same body that had always been his temple and which a crazy police doctor had now decided to lay to ruin.

Afterward he had carefully toweled himself, put on his dressing gown, and prepared a meal with the pack of vegetables and a bottle of mineral water. Just to make sure, he had first taken a quick look in the fridge to see if there wasn't something nice that had survived the previous day's food massacre when he had followed the doctor's list and cleared out all the dangerous and unnecessary things that had been in there. Bäckström's pantry and fridge had been sparklingly clean, and they were still sparklingly clean.

Bäckström had set about the pack of vegetables. He tried to disconnect both his brain and his taste buds as his jaw chewed and chewed, but even so, he had given up after just half the pack. The only edible bits were actually those little things that looked like maggots.

Bound to be maggots, Bäckström thought, as he put the remnants of his vegetable orgy in his empty fridge. If I'm lucky, they're maggots, he thought. Then at least I've actually consumed a bit of protein over the past few days.

Then he had drunk the bottle of mineral water. One and a half liters. Down in one. That had to be a new world record, Bäckström thought, throwing the empty plastic bottle in the bin under the sink. What the fuck am I going to do now, since it's only seven o'clock? he thought, checking his recently purchased Swiss watch.

There was no point looking for any hidden drink. He had got rid of that as well the previous evening, and on that point in particular the doctor had been absolutely immovable. No spirits, no wine, no beer. Nothing, in fact, that contained the merest whiff of alcohol, like cider, or ordinary juice that just happened to have started to ferment, or an old bottle of cough medicine that had evidently also fallen foul of the splendid doctor and his colleagues.

It had amounted to a fair bit, since Bäckström had been pretty well-off for some time now. Several unopened bottles of malt whiskey and vodka. An entirely untouched liter of French cognac. Almost a whole tray of Czech lager. Even more open bottles containing various quantities. Obviously not a single drop of wine, because only ass bandits and carpet munchers drank that. Certainly not Bäckström, who was a perfectly normal Swedish male in the prime of his life. As well as a legendary murder detective and the obvious answer to every woman's secret dreams.

Bäckström had put all of it in a box and knocked on one of his neighbor's doors. A serious alcoholic who used to be a boss at TV3 before he tumbled over the edge while they were recording a series of *Survivor* somewhere in the Philippines. He was given a golden handshake of several million kronor so that he could drink himself to death before he had time to write a book about his time on the channel and all the years before that when he had hopped between various companies within the same media empire. Considering the life he led these days, it looked as if his erstwhile employers were going to be proved right.

"That's a hell of a lot of goodies, Bäckström," the presumptive buyer said after a quick inspection of the box's contents. "Are you moving, or what? Don't tell me things are so bad that your liver's packed up?"

"Not at all," Bäckström said, smiling amiably even though someone was trying to wrench his heart out of his body. "I'm going away on a long trip and it seemed a shame to offer those thieving bastards a load of drink as well when they break in. They pump enough crap into themselves as it is."

"That's true enough, Bäckström," the former television executive said. "I'll give you five thousand for the lot," he said, throwing out an arm in a gesture that was so generous that it almost made him topple over backward.

The poor sod must have double vision at this time of day, Bäckström thought, since he had estimated the value of the drink at about half of that. Well, at least he won't have to get a taxi to go and get more drink for a few days, he thought.

"Done," Bäckström said, holding out his hand as a sign that the deal was concluded.

He had been paid in cash. Not that he had any idea what he was going to use it for, since he no longer ate or drank and couldn't be bothered to think about women.

In the absence of any better options, he had looked at the DVD that his ever-thoughtful doctor had given him as a sort of extra lifeline. A bit of help in his efforts to strive for a better life. The doctor knew from long, painful experience that people like Bäckström were the most difficult patients of all. Your average heavy drug user, forced to inject himself in his feet in a desperate effort to find a functioning vein, was actually nothing compared to a food-and-alcohol abuser like Bäckström. Bäckström and his ilk were practically incurable and it was all because they didn't give a flying fuck about what they were doing. They just ate and ate and ate. And drank and drank and drank. And felt on top of the world.

In an American medical journal the doctor had happened upon an extremely interesting article about attempts in a private clinic in Arizona to use electroshock therapy on people like Bäckström. The doctor had applied for funding from the state authorities, had been given more than he had asked for, and had set off for the United States to spend several months studying how they managed to alter the behavior of people who were eating and drinking themselves to death.

It had been extremely interesting, and when he came home he brought with him a load of visual material. Including the DVD that he had shown Bäckström and told him to take home with him.

Bäckström had put the disc in the DVD player. He had taken three deep breaths, his heart thudding like a jackhammer in his chest, then had pressed play. He had already seen it once, of course, and if it got too bad he could always cover his eyes. Just like the time when he was four and his crazy dad, a sergeant in the Maria district of central Stockholm, had dragged him along to a matinee at one of the cinemas near their home on Södermalm, and the big bad wolf had spent a whole hour hunting and trying to eat the three little pigs. Little Evert had howled like a banshee the whole time, and it wasn't until he wet himself that he was released from his torment.

"This little crybaby will never make a decent officer," his dad had said when he returned his only begotten son to his gentle mother and her tender ministrations—hot chocolate with whipped cream and freshly baked cinnamon buns.

And now it was time. A thirty-minute report from a rehabilitation clinic in the Southwest for patients suffering from relatively mild strokes and blockages in their hearts and brains, where they were going to be brought back to life.

Most of them were very similar to Bäckström. Apart from the fact that they needed walkers to get around and had drooling mouths, dead eyes, and slurred speech. One of them—who was so like Bäckström that they could have been identical twins—was heading away from the camera when his already low-slung trousers slid down to his ankles to reveal the huge blue diaper that he was wearing underneath. Then he had turned to face the camera, smiling happily with wet lips, grabbed the diaper, and summarized what had happened to him.

"No panties," the patient slurred, then the soft voice of the narrator took over and talked about this particular patient, who was apparently only forty-five in spite of the way he looked. He had abused high-cholesterol food for many years and had also drunk large quantities of beer and bourbon, out of some absurd notion that the latter counteracted the effects of the former. The patient had suffered a relatively benign stroke a couple months ago. That was the way it was, but Bäckström already had his eyes closed and had a good deal of trouble locating the off switch.

After that he had quickly pulled on an old tracksuit bearing the force's logo. He had been given it when he attended a course together with all the Neanderthals because some bright spark in management had decided that they needed to learn to cooperate in case something really serious happened.

Who the fuck would turn to people like them? Bäckström thought, as he tied the laces on his freshly bought sneakers with some difficulty, fully intending to walk right round Kungsholmen.

Two hours later he was back, and just as he was putting the key in the lock he had a revelation.

I've worked it out, Bäckström thought. That bright spark in the white coat had got it all wrong, and if there was any justice in the world he ought to hang himself with his own intestines. Only drink, no grub. Then his blood vessels would get rinsed through like a mountain stream in spring, he thought. You didn't have to be a doctor to work that out. Every single intelligent person knew perfectly well that alcohol was the best solvent that had ever been discovered.

No sooner said than done, and two minutes later he was knocking on his neighbor's door, the former television executive.

"I thought you were going on holiday, Bäckström," his neighbor slurred as he gestured defensively with a glass of Bäckström's excellent malt whiskey.

"I've had to postpone it for a few days," Bäckström lied, "so I was wondering if I could buy back some of the drink I sold you the other day. One bottle will do fine. Ideally some malt whiskey, if you've got any left," he said, glancing at the glass in the man's hand.

"You can't go back on a deal," the television executive slurred, shaking his head. "You don't get back what you've sold." And he had abruptly shut the door and turned the safety lock.

Bäckström had tried to make him see sense through his mail slot but only succeeded in getting his neighbor to slam the internal door as well.

At that point even Bäckström had been forced to give up. He had lumbered back to his own apartment. Showered once more, brushed his teeth, and took three of the pills that the crazy doctor had prescribed for him, one brown, one blue, and one pink. Then he had crept into bed. Turning out the light, with no intention of writing a farewell letter, he fell asleep as if someone had whacked him over the head with a saucepan lid.

When Bäckström woke up it was four o'clock in the morning. A merciless sun was shining in the clear blue sky, and he felt even more wretched than he had when he'd gone to bed the previous evening.

Bäckström had made some black coffee and drank three cups in quick succession, standing in the kitchen. He gulped down what remained of the vegetables and polished off another bottle of mineral water. Then he had set out and walked all the way to the Solna police station.

The same hellish weather as the day before, and the fact that the temperature wasn't registering as more than twenty must be because it was still the middle of the night. He staggered into work just after six o'clock. Dizzy with tiredness and mad from the lack of sleep and food. Alone in the entire building, since all his lazy and incompetent colleagues were at home snoring in their beds.

I've got to find somewhere to sleep, Bäckström thought. In his aimless wandering he finally found his way down to the garage in the basement.

"God, you look wide awake, Bäckström," the garage attendant said, clearly already at his post, as he rubbed his fingers on his overalls and held out a greasy palm.

"Murder investigation," Bäckström snarled. "Haven't had a wink of sleep in days."

"No problem, Bäckström," the garage attendant said. "You can borrow the mobile cabin I put together for the drug surveillance squad last winter."

Then he had opened the doors to a perfectly ordinary blue transit van, and inside was everything that a man in Bäckström's situation required. Among other things, a proper bed.

Two hours later he started to stir because he could smell freshly brewed coffee in his nostrils. As well as something else that had to be a hallucination. The smell of fresh rolls with cheese and butter.

"Sorry to have to disturb you, Bäckström," the garage attendant said, as he put a large tray down on the floor and sat down on the chair opposite the bed, "but those eager little buggers in surveillance are saying they need their van. Apparently they're going to sit and stare at some old junkies out in Rissne. I've brought you some coffee and some rolls in case you're hungry."

Two large cups of coffee with lots of milk, two cheese rolls, all without his even realizing how it had happened. Then he had thanked his savior, perilously close to giving him a hug but coming to his senses just in time, and making do with a manly handshake and a slap on the back.

Then he had gone down to the gym and showered, put on a fresh Hawaiian shirt that he kept in his office, and by half past nine in the morning Superintendent Bäckström was sitting behind his desk in the crime division of the Solna police station. For the first time in two days he felt somewhere close to half human.

11.

At ten o'clock on Friday morning Bäckström had a visitor in his office. It was Niemi's colleague, Jorge "Chico" Hernandez, who asked for an audience with the head of the investigation.

Darkies, darkies, darkies, Bäckström thought, sighing heavily somewhere deep inside. He would never dream of saying it out loud. Not after all the stories he had heard about Peter Niemi, who was also a foreigner, a bastard Finn, and a northern foreigner, to be more precise, and evidently best friends with the twenty-years-younger Hernandez.

"Sit yourself down, Chico," Bäckström said, nodding toward the chair on the other side of the desk as he leaned back in his own chair and knotted his hands over the sad remnants of his stomach. He must have lost at least ten kilos, he thought, as he experienced a certain vague anxiety about what was happening to the body that had always been his temple.

"I'm listening," he went on, smiling and nodding encouragingly to his visitor. Even though darkies shouldn't be allowed to become police officers. Maybe it was because of those cheese rolls, he thought.

Hernandez had a fair amount to report. During the previous evening he had been present when the coroner conducted the postmortem on their murder victim, and he began by confirming his colleague Niemi's estimate of the body's height and weight.

"One hundred and eighty-eight tall, and one hundred and twenty-two kilos," Hernandez said. "Peter's good at that sort of thing."

Why the hell would I want to know that? Bäckström thought.

"Which might be worth bearing in mind when we're thinking about what our perpetrator is capable of," Hernandez concluded. "It takes a fair amount of strength to handle a body that large and that heavy."

Apart from being overweight and having an impressively large liver, Danielsson had been in surprisingly good shape. No significant comments from the coroner about either his heart and lungs or his circulatory system. Normal prostate enlargement and all the other things that come with age. Otherwise not much, considering the life he had led.

"If only he'd stopped drinking for a couple months each year and given his liver a chance to recover in between binges, he'd probably have lived past eighty," Hernandez said.

Like a mountain stream in spring, Bäckström thought, nodding in agreement. Maybe we ought to make sausages out of the bastard after all. Maybe cognac sausages, considering the number of years Director Danielsson had been marinating.

"But we want to amend what we said about the upholstery hammer," Hernandez said. "Judging from the X-rays of the skull, there are no injuries matching the hammer, and that goes for both the head of the hammer and the other side, the curved bit with a split in it that you use to pull out nails. Not only that, but the break in the shaft is on the wrong side. Not on the side you use to hit nails in with. The break's on the other side, the same side as the claw, and that suggests to us that the perpetrator managed to break the shaft when he was trying to pull something out using the claw. The problem is that we can't find any evidence of this inside the flat."

"Something he took away with him?" Bäckström suggested. "A cash box, maybe?" Containing Danielsson's old milk teeth and a two-kronor coin he was left by the kind tooth fairy, he thought.

"Something like that, yes," Hernandez agreed with a nod. "For the time being we're thinking it was probably one of those leather briefcases with a brass lock, hinges, and bolts, or some other gold-colored metal. There are traces on the claw of the hammer that suggest that. A small flake, maybe a millimeter long, that we're pretty sure is leather. Light-brown leather. There's a fragment of something that we think might be brass on the sharpened edge of the claw. It might have got there when the claw scratched the lock. We've sent it to the National Lab, since we don't have the right equipment here to determine exactly what it is."

"But you didn't find the briefcase itself?"

"No," Hernandez said. "If we're right, he probably took it with him to open it in peace and quiet."

"Noted," Bäckström said, making a note in his little black book, just to be on the safe side. "Anything else?"

"To go back to the saucepan lid," Hernandez said. "It's cast-iron, and the outside is covered with blue enamel. It matches a pan found on the stove in the flat. Twenty-eight centimeters in diameter, with a handle in the middle. It weighs almost two kilos. The victim received at least six heavy blows with the lid. The first one hit him high up on the right side of his head. It was administered from behind him, off to one side, and we believe the victim received the blow as he stepped out of the toilet door. Danielsson falls forward with his head toward the living room, his feet toward the front door, ending up on his stomach or possibly his side. Then he receives another two blows to the back of the head. Then the perpetrator must have turned him over and finished him off with three blows to the face—"

"How can you be so sure of the order?" Bäckström interrupted.

"You can never be absolutely certain, but this is the picture that best matches the fractures on his skull and other observations of the part of the hall where it happened. The way the hall looks, the splatter pattern and so on. There are also blood, strands of hair, and fragments of bone on the saucepan lid. And the fact that the lid fits the injuries on the victim's head. Our perpetrator isn't just strong. To judge by the angle of the blows, he's tall as well. And we think he was seriously upset with the victim. The first blow on its own was fatal. He may have administered the two to the back of the head and neck just to be sure, so to speak, so we're prepared to let him get away with those. But the three to the face, at least three blows, just seem to be over the top. Especially as he must have put the saucepan lid down to roll the body over, and then picked it up once more before he started hitting him again."

"So how tall was he?" Bäckström said.

"Danielsson was one meter eighty-six. So at a guess, at least one meter eighty. If you ask me, another ten centimeters on that. One meter ninety."

"Assuming he wasn't a professional basketball player," Bäckström teased. "He could have gone for him with his arm raised above his head, you know, the way they throw the ball? Or a tennis player. Serving a blow with a saucepan lid."

"The concentration of professional basketball players in the immediate vicinity is presumably relatively low," Hernandez stated without the slightest trace of a smile. "The same is probably true of tennis players," he added, puckering his lips slightly.

Funny lad, Bäckström thought. Finally, a darkie with a sense of humor.

Hernandez changed the subject. He started to talk about the Polish carpenter's discovery in the trash bin.

"We're waiting to hear from the National Forensics Lab if the blood matches that of the victim. If it does, then the find is undoubtedly very interesting indeed. But we didn't manage to find any prints. Not on the raincoat, the washing-up gloves, or the slippers. The size of the raincoat and slippers fits Danielsson. Large, broad across the chest, size-forty-four shoes."

"How many months do you think it'll be before we hear back from the lab, then?" Bäckström wondered.

"We've managed to nag them into making this a priority," Hernandez said. "After the weekend, is the latest our colleagues in Linköping have told us. To summarize what we've got so far," Hernandez went on, "we're probably talking about a perpetrator who is physically strong, well above average height, with a serious dislike of his victim. If the clothes turn out to match, and if they belonged to Danielsson like the saucepan lid and the upholstery hammer, he seems to be pretty experienced. He puts on the victim's raincoat to avoid getting blood on his clothes. He takes off his own shoes and puts on the victim's slippers for the same reason. He puts on the victim's washing-up gloves so that he doesn't leave fingerprints. The only thing that bothers us is the behavior of the victim's dinner guest, because at an earlier stage of the evening he left a mass of prints all over bits of crockery, glasses, cutlery. And he doesn't seem to have made any effort to get rid of those at all."

"Doesn't bother me. Not in the slightest," Bäckström said, shaking his head. "Because that's what pissheads are like. First he sits and has a drink with Danielsson. Then he suddenly turns on him and when Danielsson goes to the toilet he kicks off his shoes; grabs a pair of slippers, a raincoat, and washing-up gloves; picks up the saucepan lid; and sets to work as soon as Danielsson steps out of the bathroom and is standing there swaying and trying to do up his fly. He's probably already forgotten everything that went before."

"Peter and I were also thinking along those lines," Hernandez said, nodding. "But we've also been wondering whether this is more than just a question of spontaneous anger—if there's a more rational motive."

"Like what?"

"Like the fact that he stole from him," Hernandez said.

"Exactly," Bäckström agreed with heavy emphasis. "Which just goes to show what a fucking moron he is. Stealing from someone like Danielsson. It's like trying to cut a bald man's hair."

"I'm afraid that probably wasn't the case on this occasion," Hernandez said. "In the top right-hand drawer of Danielsson's desk we found a bundle of winning slips from Solvalla. All of them cashed in and held together neatly in date order with an elastic band. The top slip is from the meeting out at Valla the same afternoon and evening that Danielsson was murdered—the day before yesterday, in other words. He won twenty thousand six hundred and twenty kronor, and the winnings were paid out from the cashier at Solvalla immediately after the race. It was the first race of the V65 coupon, to be precise, at half past six that evening. But we haven't found the money. His wallet, for instance, which was on the desk in his bedroom, was completely empty, apart from a few business cards."

"Well, I never," Bäckström said. "Well, I never," he repeated. Must have been a serious win for someone like Danielsson, he thought.

"A couple more things," Hernandez said. "Things we've found, and things we haven't found but should have."

"I'm listening," Bäckström said, grabbing a pen and his little black book.

"We've found a betting slip but no money, we've found traces of what we think was a briefcase but no briefcase. We've found one open and one sealed carton of Viagra. Written out to Karl Danielsson using a repeat prescription that we've also found. Six pills remaining out of eight. According to the details on the prescription, he's had another eight pills since the start of April. We also found a box of condoms, containing ten originally, but there were only two left."

"So our victim had at least two strings to his bow. Even if he needed help getting his instrument tuned," Bäckström said with a grin.

"We found two keys to a safe-deposit box, but we haven't located the box yet," Hernandez went on. "But we didn't find a cell phone, or a computer, or any credit cards. No bills for any of those either, for that matter. We found an ordinary pocket diary with a few notes in it. But no other diary, no photos, no personal correspondence."

"A typical drunk," Bäckström said. "What would someone like that want a cell for? To call and order home delivery of drink? And who'd give a credit card to an old lush? They're not that stupid, even in Social Services. Anything else?" he added.

"There were several bundles of taxi receipts on his desk," Hernandez said.

"Mobility allowance. I daresay all alcoholics get that in our glorious socialist paradise, and the rest of us have to pay for it."

"No," Hernandez said. "No chance. They're just normal receipts. I have an idea that he used to trade in them."

"What, taxi receipts? What on earth for? Are they edible?" Bäckström said.

"I think he knew a taxi driver, and bought his unclaimed receipts for maybe twenty percent of the amount on them, and then sold them on for fifty percent or so to someone who could claim them as tax-deductible expenses for their business. Presumably something he learned during all those years he spent working as an accountant, and he's bound to have a few contacts left from those days," Hernandez said.

"I thought old drunks collected empty bottles and cans," Bäckström said.

"Maybe not this one," Hernandez said.

Whatever the hell this has to do with anything or the cost of vodka, Bäckström thought with a shrug.

"Was that everything?" he asked.

"Yes. That's pretty much everything so far," Hernandez said, standing up. "You and your colleagues will be getting a written report covering what Peter and I have come up with to date, including a number of pictures of the crime scene and the postmortem later today. You'll get it by e-mail."

"Good," Bäckström said. Astonishingly good, considering it was the result of collaboration between a bastard Finn and a strutting tango dancer, he thought.

12.

Detective Inspector Annika Carlsson had been at work since half past seven that morning, even though she hadn't got to bed before midnight the previous evening.

She had hardly had time to sit down at her desk when Peter Niemi called her cell to tell her about the clothing they had found.

"I've been chasing Bäckström, but he isn't answering," Niemi explained.

"I've been chasing him as well. I suppose he'll show up in due course. I'm worried about him. He doesn't seem well. He looked awful yesterday. I don't know if you noticed."

"Yes, I did, but what the hell," Niemi said. "Since both the Pole and his workmates need to be interviewed, and the sooner the better, I thought I'd call you."

"Well, thanks for that," Carlsson said. Niemi's good, she thought. Really good. Not only good at what he does, but the sort who actually gives a damn.

"Like I said, I've been out to the site and we've been through the trash bin but didn't find anything interesting. And there was nothing in the vicinity either, in case you're wondering. We even took a dog patrol, even though it was the middle of the night. Since then I've spoken to the lad who found the bag containing the clothes. Nice boy. Almost speaks better Swedish than someone like me," Niemi said, his smile audible in his voice. "But because it was all a bit hectic, I didn't get long to talk to him."

"So now you want me to do it properly, with a tape recorder and making notes?" Carlsson said, also smiling so broadly it came through her voice. Why can't all men be like Niemi? she thought.

"Exactly," Niemi said. "That's what we're like, you know."

"I'd better get it sorted, then," Annika Carlsson said. Since it's you, she thought.

Then she had called Bäckström again on his cell, but it was still switched off, even though it was now almost half past eight. Annika Carlsson had shaken her head and gone to find Felicia Pettersson, then took one of the cars and headed down to Ekensbergsgatan to talk to Jerzty Sarniecki and his four compatriots, who were renovating a small block of rented apartments in Solna, a thousand kilometers north of their homeland.

Felicia Pettersson, twenty-three, had graduated from the Police Academy in January that year. Now she was on her first practical placement, with the crime unit in Solna, and after just one week here she was helping with a murder investigation. Felicia was born in Brazil. She had been in a children's home in São Paolo and was just a year old when she had been adopted by a Swedish couple who both worked in the police and lived on the islands of Lake Mälaren, just west of Stockholm. Now she herself was a police officer, like so many police children before her. Young and with no practical experience, but with good prospects. In good shape, calm and sensible, and she seemed to enjoy what she was doing.

She'll turn out to be pretty good, Annika Carlsson had thought the first time she met her.

"You know how to get to Ekensbergsgatan, Felicia?" Annika asked, once she had settled into the passenger seat and fastened her seat belt.

"Yes, boss," Felicia Pettersson said, nodding.

"I don't suppose you happen to speak Polish as well?" Annika asked.

"Yes, boss. Of course. Fluently. I thought everyone could?" Felicia said with a smile.

"Anything else I should know about?" Annika Carlsson asked. She's sharp too, she thought.

"My friends usually call me Lisa," Felicia said. "You can too, if you like."

"They usually call me the Anchor," Annika Carlsson said.

"Do you like being called that?" Lisa said, glancing at her in surprise.

"Not really," Annika Carlsson said, shaking her head. "I mean, what have I got to do with an anchor?"

"Not sure," Lisa Pettersson said, and giggled. "But I think you're pretty cool. And I mean that."

Annika Carlsson and Felicia Pettersson were in luck. It may have been only nine o'clock in the morning, but Jerzty and the others were already eating lunch. They had got up before it was light, had breakfast at four, and had started work at half past. By nine o'clock it was high time for lunch if they were going to have the energy to keep working until the evening.

"Sorry to disturb you in your breakfast," Annika Carlsson said in English, smiling and showing her police ID. *"My name is Detective Inspector Annika Carlsson, and this is my colleague, Detective Constable Felicia Pettersson. By the way, does any one of you speak Swedish? Or understand Swedish?"*

"I speak a bit of Swedish," Jerzty said, as three of his work-mates shook their heads and one nodded hesitantly. "I can interpret, if you like."

"We'd just like to ask a few questions," Annika went on. "Is it okay if we sit down?"

"Sure," Jerzty said, quickly getting up. He removed a toolbox from a spare chair that was already standing beside their home-made table while one of his colleagues went to fetch a stool and offered his own chair to Detective Constable Pettersson.

Two beautiful young women. Who also happened to be Swedish police officers, even though one of them looked like she came from the West Indies. Friendly, cheerful, easy on the eyes, and well worth fantasizing about as you hammered in yet another nail. They would stay for an hour. But what did that matter? Eighty kronor was only eighty kronor, and they missed other things much more than work.

Had they noticed anything during Wednesday evening or early Thursday morning?

They had worked until eight o'clock that evening. Then they had stopped because the neighbors usually complained if they carried on after that. Then they had eaten. Chatted, played cards, went to bed at ten or so. None of them had left the building throughout that time, since it had been raining all evening.

What about during the night, then? Did any of them see or hear anything?

They had been asleep. None of them had any trouble sleeping. None of them had seen or heard anything. They had been lying asleep in their beds. One of them had got up briefly to go to the toilet. That was all.

"Leszek, he's a plasterer," Jerzty clarified, nodding toward the man who had emptied his bladder. "The toilet faces the street, it's got a window," he added, preempting Annika Carlsson's next question.

"Ask him if he knows what time it was."

"He doesn't know," Jerzty said after a few quick sentences in Polish and a shake of the head in answer to her question. "He didn't look at the time. He had taken his watch off and put it beside his bed."

"Was it still raining?" Annika Carlsson asked, having already read the report they had received from the meteorological office. Rain getting lighter though Wednesday evening, stopping half an hour after midnight on Thursday, May 15.

"Not much," Jerzty summarized after a short exchange in Polish. "It was dark as well. As dark as it gets. When we woke up, the weather was beautiful. That was at four o'clock in the morning."

About midnight, Annika Carlsson thought.

"Ask him if he saw or heard anything. People, cars, any sort of noise. Or if he didn't see or hear anything. As you can understand, absolutely everything is of interest to us."

More Polish. Hesitant shakes of the head. Smiles from both Jerzty and Leszek. Then the latter had nodded firmly, said something more in Polish, and shrugged.

"I'm listening," Annika Carlsson said. Watch yourself, Anchor, she thought. You're starting to sound like Bäckström, and you don't do that if you're pretty cool.

"He saw a cat," Jerzty said, smiling happily.

A little ginger cat. They often saw it and presumed that it lived somewhere nearby, even though it didn't have a collar. They'd even given it some milk once.

But no people, no cars, no human sounds. It was dark, it was quiet, it was drizzling. No television or radio on anywhere, no lights in any windows. Not even a dog barking. A solitary ginger cat that had strolled past outside. That was all.

13.

Detective Inspector Lars Alm, sixty, had worked in the crime unit of the Solna Police for about ten years. During the years before he arrived there he had first worked in the old violent crime section in police headquarters on Kungsholmen in Stockholm, and then had moved on to the investigative unit covering the city center itself. Then he had moved out to Solna. He had got divorced and remarried, and he and his new wife, a nurse at the Karolinska Institute, had a nice apartment in the center of Solna. Alm could walk to work in two minutes, so it didn't matter to him if it was snowing or raining cats and dogs.

That was one good reason to move to the Solna force, but there were several others. Alm was burned-out. His years in violent crime in Stockholm had taken their toll. Solna ought to be a bit better, he had reasoned. He could finally escape the waves rippling out from the weekend's nightlife that would wash over his desk every Monday without fail. But his hopes had been dashed on that score. Ideally he would have liked to take early retirement, but after looking at the numbers he had decided to try to hold out until he was sixty-five. A nurse didn't earn much, and neither of them wanted to starve when they got old.

He had tried to organize things as best he could. He had avoided the violent crime unit, the surveillance unit, drugs, and robbery. He had taken over the simpler things like petty crime, crimes that affected ordinary people, break-ins to homes and vehicles, the less serious cases of abuse, fights, criminal damage. Personally, he thought he had succeeded pretty well, and he used to keep an eye on the number of cases expected of him. Tried to slot himself somewhere into the average range for people like him.

On Monday, May 12, a tornado had swept through the Western District. Two as yet unknown individuals had robbed a security van out at Bromma Airport. They had shot and killed one of the guards and came close to killing his partner. Aggravated theft, murder, and attempted murder. Just a few hours later the minister for justice had appeared on every television news program. Their new boss, police chief Anna Holt, had no cause for complacency. One month into the job and this happens.

He had survived the first wave. Even though the head of the crime unit, Superintendent Toivonen, had moved a lot of officers in from other departments and responsibilities, he had spared Alm. But on Thursday morning Alm had been dragged in as well. Toivonen had stormed into his office and explained that it was all hands on deck.

"Someone's beaten an old drunk to death up by Råsundavägen," Toivonen said. "The sort of case any normal officer would clear up before lunch, but considering all the shit that's hit us, I'm going to have to give it to Bäckström."

"What did you have in mind for me, then?" Alm said, realizing that this wasn't up for discussion.

"Make sure that little fat nightmare doesn't miss an open goal," Toivonen said, before walking out abruptly.

So that was how things stood. After a gap of more than ten years, Alm had another murder round his neck, and because he was more than aware of who Evert Bäckström was, he'd certainly had better days.

Alm knew Bäckström from long ago. Toward the end of the eighties they had both worked on the murder squad in the old violent crime section in Stockholm. A few years later Bäckström had suddenly got a job with the murder unit of the National Crime Division. Completely incomprehensible. Someone high up in National Crime must have had a stroke or been bribed by the head of crime in Stockholm. Alm and all his more sensible colleagues had taken the ferry to Åland and spent twenty-four hours celebrating. Fifteen years later vengeance had struck with full force.

In his hour of need he had talked to Annika Carlsson. She was a woman, and she was generally very competent. He had offered to put together a profile of the victim, his social life, and what he was doing during the hours before he died. As long as he could sit in his office and didn't have to see Bäckström more than was strictly necessary.

"Sounds like an excellent suggestion," Annika Carlsson said with a nod. "So what's he like? I've heard all the usual stories about Bäckström, but I'd never met him before this morning. And that was only in passing, when he came down to look at the crime scene."

"If you'd met him properly you'd remember it," Alm said with a sigh.

"Is he as crazy as everyone says? A lot of those stories have to be urban myths."

"He's worse," Alm said. "He's much worse. Every time I turn on the news and see that an officer has been shot, I pray to God that it's Bäckström. If we have to suffer something as awful as that, why not start with Bäckström and spare all the normal, decent officers? It never helps," Alm said, shaking his head. "That fat little idiot is immortal. He's entered into some sort of pact with Beelzebub. The rest of us are stuck with him to atone for our sins, and I don't understand what on earth we could have done to deserve him."

"I understand what you mean," Annika Carlsson said, nodding thoughtfully. Well, this is going to be fun. If it comes to it, I suppose I can always drag him down to the garage and break his arms, she thought.

Alm had got off to a flying start with his profile of the murder victim, Karl Danielsson. As soon as people who knew the victim heard rumors of his unexpected demise, the news had spread like wildfire, and they had contacted the police. For once, the police hotline had worked, the tip-offs had come streaming in, and by the time Alm went home on the evening of the first day, he knew that he had a good grasp of the situation.

He had names and full details of about ten people in the victim's closest circle of acquaintances. All of them men, and without knowing for certain, Alm had got the impression that they all shared the same great interest in life as their murdered "friend" and "comrade-in-arms." He had spoken to several of them over the phone. From them he had obtained the names of other friends of the victim who hadn't yet been in touch, and he had already interviewed a couple of them. As Alm walked home at seven o'clock that evening, to a meal of stuffed cabbage leaves and lingonberry sauce with his wife, he was as happy as he could be, considering he was being forced to have anything at all to do with Detective Superintendent Evert Bäckström.

If only Bäckström could do his civic duty and drop down dead, there'd be nothing to worry about with this investigation, Alm thought.

14.

Bäckström had spent the morning trying to bring some order to the murder investigation that his colleagues were already in the process of messing up beyond all reason. He also felt considerably better than he had for a long time, because his sensitive nostrils kept smelling the heavenly scent of fresh rolls with lots of cheese and butter.

Those bloody weight watchers can fuck off, Bäckström thought. You can pretty much eat like a normal person as long as you don't swill it all down with a load of liquid goodies. Then you stop for a while, fasting, drink like a fish and rinse out all the little blood vessels, and then you're back to square one again.

Just after eleven his stomach had started grumbling in that pleasant and familiar way that told him that it was high time he got a bit more nutrition.

So he had gone down to the staff canteen in order to compose a well-balanced lunch that was completely in harmony with his own observations and conclusions.

First he had stopped at the salad bar and put together a pleasant little heap of grated raw carrot with a few sticks of cucumber and some pieces of tomato. He avoided all the elk and rabbit shit, and they didn't seem to have any maggots, even though those had tasted almost like real food the only time he had tried them. Then he had sniffed at the various jugs of oils and dressings and eventually made up his mind. Rhode Island dressing it would be, Bäckström thought. He knew from experience that it was perfectly edible. He even used to buy it for himself, to pour over his homemade hamburgers with loads of cheese and mayonnaise.

Once he got to the counter he spent a long time choosing between the dish of the day, steak with fried potatoes, gherkins, and cream sauce; pasta of the day, carbonara with pork and a raw egg yolk; and fish of the day, fried plaice with boiled potatoes and gherkin mayonnaise. His strong and resolute character had won out and he had chosen the fish even though it was mostly faggots, dykes, and leftists who ate fish. Might still be worth trying anyway, Bäckström thought, feeling suddenly calm and strangely tranquil.

Which just left the choice of drink: tap water, juice, mineral water, or low-alcohol beer? He went for a small glass of low-alcohol beer as a simple and self-evident concession to the restraint he had already so convincingly displayed. Besides, it tasted so disgusting that it had to be good for you.

A quarter of an hour later he was finished. Which left coffee, and the chance to celebrate his triumph with a small almond cake. And maybe one of those little green marzipan cakes dipped in chocolate as well.

Think, Bäckström, think, Bäckström thought, and with almost stoical calm he put the marzipan cake back and made do with just a single almond one on his little plate. He had taken his coffee and gone and sat in a secluded corner to finish off his frugal meal in peace and quiet.

15.

An hour later he had held his second meeting with his investigating team. Bäckström had felt well focused, balanced, and that he was finally in complete control of the situation. He didn't even feel any rise in blood pressure when he asked Detective Inspector Lars Alm to open the meeting by reporting what he had found out about their victim and how he had spent the last few hours of his so tragically pissed-away life.

"Perhaps you'd like to begin, Lars?" Bäckström said, smiling amiably at the man in question. Old Woodentop from crime in Stockholm. How the fuck someone like that ever got to be a police officer was a mystery that even he couldn't solve, he thought.

Detective Inspector Lars Alm had interviewed Seppo Laurén, one of the murder victim's youngest neighbors, at home in the apartment he shared with his mother at number 1 Hasselstigen. The fact that Alm bestowed this honor on him was explained by the fact that ten years before, Laurén had been fined sixty days' income for violent conduct. He had been one of a total of seven AIK supporters who had beaten up a supporter of the opposing team after a match at Råsunda, in an underground station in the center of Solna. That was the only time he appeared in police records, and Laurén had received the most lenient punishment of the seven. But he was also the only person in the building who had been found guilty of a violent crime and happened to be a neighbor of the victim.

"You or me, Lars?" Annika Carlsson had asked, nodding to Alm.

"I'll talk to him," Alm said.

"Thanks, Lars," Annika replied.

A child in a grown man's body, Alm thought, as he concluded the interview and left Laurén. At least ten centimeters taller than him, at least ten kilos heavier, with broad shoulders and long, gangly arms. A grown man. Apart from the long fair hair that kept falling over his forehead, which he kept pushing back with his left hand and a toss of the head; the naïve look in his eyes—a child's eyes, they were blue as well; his ungainly body, his awkward posture. A child in a grown man's body, a pretty wretched state to be in, Alm thought, as he left him.

At four o'clock on Wednesday afternoon, May 14, Karl Danielsson had returned home to his flat at number 1 Hasselstigen in Solna. He had got out of a taxi, paid, and had bumped into Seppo Laurén, twenty-nine, in the doorway.

Laurén, who was in receipt of a state pension in spite of his young age, was living alone at the time. His mother, who he usually shared his flat with, had suffered a stroke and had been in a convalescent home for a while. Danielsson had told Laurén that he had been in to the city, where he had been to the bank and done a few other errands. Then he had given Laurén a couple hundred-kronor notes and asked him to go and buy him some food. He was heading off to Solvalla that evening and didn't have time to do it himself. Pork chops, two decent packs of ready-made kidney beans in sauce, some cans of tonic, Coke, and soda water. That was all, and he could keep the change.

Laurén had run similar errands for Danielsson for many years. When he returned from the local ICA shop Danielsson was just getting into another taxi and seemed to be in good spirits. He had said something about it being time for "Valla, and some serious money."

"Do you remember what time it was then?" Alm asked.

"Yes," Laurén said, nodding. "I remember exactly. I look at my watch a lot." And he had held out his left arm to demonstrate.

"What time was it, then?" Alm said, smiling amiably.

"It was twenty past five," Laurén said.

"What did you do after that?" Alm asked.

"I hung the bag of groceries on his door, then went up to my place and played computer games. I do that a lot," he explained.

"This all fits well with other information that we've received," Alm stated, leafing through his notes. "Danielsson placed a bet on the first V65 race out at Solvalla, which started at six p.m. It can't take more than fifteen minutes to get there by taxi, and he would have had plenty of time to place his bet before the race started—"

"Hang on, hang on," Bäckström interrupted. "Reading between the lines, I get the impression that this Laurén is a few sandwiches short of a picnic."

"He's got learning difficulties," Alm said. "But he can tell the time. I've checked."

"Go on," Bäckström grunted. What a meeting of minds, he thought. Woodentop's first witness is another nutcase, and they're both saying they can tell the time.

In the first race Danielsson had put five hundred kronor to win on horse number six, Instant Justice. A rank outsider that would pay out forty times the initial stake, and the forensics team had found the winning slip in the drawer of his desk.

"We're absolutely certain of that?" Bäckström went on. The bastard could just as easily have been given it or stolen it, he thought.

Absolutely certain, according to Alm. He'd spoken to an old friend of Danielsson's, who said Danielsson had called to tell him.

He had been the one who tipped him off about Instant Justice. A former rider and trainer out at Valla, now retired, Gunnar Gustafsson, who had known Danielsson since they were at primary school together.

"Apparently Gustafsson is something of a legend out at Solvalla," Alm said. "According to colleagues who know about racing, he's known as Jockey Gunnar, and he's not known for handing out tips, so it's probably true that he was a good friend of Danielsson. Danielsson is known as Kalle the Accountant among his old childhood friends from Solna and Sundbyberg.

"Anyway," Alm went on, as he ticked off points in his notes, "Gustafsson said that he was sitting in the restaurant at Solvalla with a few friends when Danielsson suddenly appeared, in an extremely good mood. That was at six-thirty or thereabouts. Gustafsson invited him to join them but Danielsson declined. He was going to head home. He had asked another old school friend over for dinner later on. And this friend had good reason to celebrate as well, since he and Danielsson had shared the bet."

"So what's his name, then?" Bäckström said. "The one Danielsson had invited to dinner?"

"You and I both know him," Alm said. "He went to the same school in Solna as Danielsson. Exactly the same age as Danielsson, sixty-eight. When you and I knew him he worked in surveillance in the old violent crime division in Stockholm. Roland Stålhammar. Roly-Stoly, Iron Man, or just plain Stolly. Well, we give the things we love lots of names."

There we go, Bäckström thought. Roland "Stolly" Stålhammar, caught as good as red-handed, an iron man with a load of rust in his pants, in Bäckström's opinion.

"Well, then," Bäckström said. He leaned back in his chair, folded his hands on his stomach, and smiled with satisfaction. "Something tells me that this case is finished," he said.

"Why don't you explain for the benefit of our younger colleagues? Tell them about our former colleague Roland Stålhammar," Bäckström went on, nodding benevolently toward Alm.

Alm didn't seem particularly keen, but he told them anyway.

"Roland Stålhammar was one of the legendary figures from the old violent crime division. He worked in the division's own surveillance unit. He knew every single ruffian in the entire county. And even they were fond of him, despite the fact that he must have locked up hundreds of them over the years. He retired in 1999. Taking advantage of the option that older officers had in those days to take early retirement.

"Well," Alm said, sighing for some reason. "What else can I add? He was born and raised in Solna. Lived here all his life. Keen on sport. First as a participant, then as a coach. Extrovert. Dynamic. Found it easy to get on with people. He made things happen, you could say—"

"But that's not all, eh?" Bäckström interrupted with a sly look on his face. "There was quite a bit more to him than that, wasn't there?"

"Yes," Alm said, nodding curtly. "Stålhammar used to be a boxer. One of the best in Sweden in his day. Swedish heavyweight champion several years in a row in the sixties. On one occasion he was up against Ingemar Johansson for a charity gala out in the old Circus building on Djurgården. Ingemar Johansson, Ingo, as he was known," Alm clarified, nodding for some reason toward Felicia Pettersson.

"Hearing you describe what a decent old fellow he was almost brings tears to my eyes," Bäckström said. "I can hardly recognize Roly-Stoly from your description. One meter ninety tall, one hundred kilos of muscle and bone, and with the shortest fuse in the entire force. Used to get reported for violent conduct more than the rest of us put together."

"I hear what you're saying," Alm said. "But it wasn't quite as simple as that. Stålhammar made things happen, like I said. He'd saved a lot of young kids who were on the slide from getting themselves into serious trouble. If I'm not mistaken, he was the only one of us who did voluntary work as a probation officer on his own time."

"When he wasn't drinking like a fish, because that was still his best event," said Bäckström, who could feel his blood pressure rising. "And still is, from the looks of it. . . ."

"Maybe I can elaborate on this," Sergeant Jan O. Stigson, twenty-seven, said with a cautious hand gesture. "In light of the current case, I mean."

"Are you an old boxer as well, Stigson?" Bäckström asked, now starting to get seriously annoyed.

A radio-car officer for the modern age. Shaved head, bodybuilder, IQ like a golf handicap, and for some reason brought in from the patrol cars to help on a murder investigation. Only a stupid Finnish joker like Toivonen could come up with something like that, Bäckström thought. And it sounded like the poor bastard came from Dalarna as well. Sounded like a packet of crispbread when he talked. One of those folk-dancing cretins with scarves tied around his knees who just happened to have wandered into a murder case. Christ, what the hell is happening to the Swedish police? he thought.

"Go ahead," Annika Carlsson said with a decisive nod. "So the rest of us don't have to listen to Bäckström and Lars arguing about an old friend. Because I don't think any of us really wants to hear that."

Who the hell does she think she is? Bäckström thought, staring crossly at her. I'm going to have to have a word with her about respect and authority after this meeting, he thought.

"We got quite a bit of information going door-to-door yesterday," Sergeant Stigson said. "I think a couple details might be extremely relevant in light of what Alm has just told us about our former colleague Roland Stålhammar."

"I'm listening," Bäckström said. "What are we waiting for? Is it a secret or what?"

"Stina Holmberg, seventy-eight, widowed," Stigson said, nodding to Bäckström. "She lives in a flat on the ground floor of number one Hasselstigen. Nice old thing. She's a retired teacher, seems alert, still got all her marbles, and nothing wrong with her hearing. Her flat's directly below Danielsson's, and because the walls are quite thin, she had some interesting information to add to the investigation."

Stigson nodded to emphasize his words and looked at Bäckström.

Oh, for fuck's sake, this can't be happening, Bäckström thought. This bastard folk dancer must be related to that witness, Laurén. Half-brothers, probably, since they've got different surnames.

"I'm still waiting," Bäckström said, throwing out his hands in a despairing gesture.

There had been some sort of party in Danielsson's flat on Wednesday evening, May 14. According to Mrs. Holmberg it had started at nine o'clock in the evening, with loud voices, laughing, and shouting, and about an hour later it had got seriously rowdy. Danielsson and his guest had been playing records at top volume, nothing but Evert Taube, according to Mrs. Holmberg, and they sang along to the choruses.

"'The Stoker's Waltz' and 'The Brig Bluebird of Hull,' and 'Fritiof and Carmencita' and lots more, it just went on and on," Mrs. Holmberg elaborated.

It wasn't the first time something like this had happened, but because she was a bit scared of Danielsson, she called another of her neighbors and asked for help. Britt-Marie Andersson, a younger woman who lives on the top floor.

"That Danielsson could be a bit of a handful," Mrs. Holmberg explained. "Even if it's not a nice thing to say about someone who's just died. A big, rough man who used to spend all day drinking. I remember one occasion when he was trying to help me in through the front door and he was so drunk that he fell over, almost knocking me and all my shopping flying."

"So you called your younger friend, Britt-Marie Andersson, and asked her for help?" Sergeant Stigson confirmed. He had conducted and recorded the interview himself and was now reading from the transcript.

"Yes, she's a sensible girl. And she's not afraid to tell men like Danielsson when they're being a nuisance; it wasn't the first time I'd asked for her help."

"Do you know what Miss Andersson did after that?" Stigson wondered.

"Mrs. Andersson, not Miss. She's divorced, or else her husband went and died. I don't actually know. But I suppose she went down and spoke to him, because a little while later it was nice and quiet once more."

"Do you happen to know what time that was, Mrs. Holmberg? When everything went quiet again, I mean," Stigson clarified.

"It must have been around half past ten in the evening. As far as I can recall."

"What did you do after that, Mrs. Holmberg?"

"I went to bed," Mrs. Holmberg said. "Which was just as well. If I'd stuck my nose outside my door I daresay I'd have been beaten to death as well."

"That younger neighbor, then? The one she asked for help? What does she have to say?" Bäckström asked.

"Britt-Marie Andersson. Hubba-hubba," Sergeant Stigson said with a happy smile.

"What do you mean, *hubba-hubba*?" Bäckström said.

"What a woman," Stigson said with a deep sigh. "What a woman. Blonde, a true blonde, I'm sure of that. What a body. What a chest. Hubba-hubba. Eat shit, Dolly Parton, if I can put it like that," Stigson explained with a blissful smile on his face.

"And could she talk as well?" Bäckström asked.

"Oh, yes," Stigson said with a nod. "She was lovely, and it's a

good thing I had the tape recorder with me, because, well, with
that body—"

"For fuck's sake!" Annika Carlsson interrupted. "Just tell us
what she said!"

Okay, dancing boy had better watch out, Bäckström thought.
Carlsson's got that look in her eyes, and she'll soon rip your arms
and legs off, little Stigson, he thought.

"Yes, yes, of course," Stigson said, his cheeks suddenly ablaze. He
shuffled through his papers nervously, then started to read once
more.

"The following is a summary of information received from witness
Britt-Marie Andersson," Stigson read.

"At approximately ten o'clock on Wednesday evening Mrs.
Holmberg phoned Mrs. Andersson to ask for her help with their
neighbor, Danielsson. Mrs. Andersson went down to Danielsson
and knocked on his door, whereupon Danielsson answered, evidently seriously intoxicated. She told him to keep the noise down,
and if he didn't, she threatened to call the police. Danielsson
apologized and closed the door of his flat. Mrs. Andersson stayed
outside for a couple minutes, listening, but when the gramophone
was switched off she took the lift back up to her own apartment.
Approximately a quarter of an hour later Danielsson phoned Mrs.
Andersson's landline. He started shouting at her and generally
behaved disgracefully. He told her that she shouldn't stick her nose
into things that didn't concern her. Then he hung up. According
to Mrs. Andersson, the time was then approximately half past ten
in the evening."

"That seems to fit," Alm interjected. "I got the first lists of
calls through just before this meeting. According to the list of calls
made from the victim's phone—I haven't received the neighbors'
yet—he made a call from his phone to another landline at 22.27
that evening. Just before half past ten, in other words. Let me see
the interview with Andersson," Alm said.

"There you go," Stigson said, passing Alm a printed sheet of A4.

"Yes," Alm said with a nod, after glancing at the sheet. "It's Andersson's home phone number. That's the last number Danielsson called, in fact."

Because then he was beaten to death and robbed by our old hero Roly Stålhammar, Bäckström thought, finding it hard to conceal his delight.

"There's something else that's bothering me. I might as well mention it now before I forget," Alm said, and for some reason he looked at Bäckström.

"Yes, perhaps that would be best," Bäckström said, smiling amiably.

"When I looked up Stålhammar's details I found out that he lives on Järnvägsgatan in Sundbyberg. That's only a few hundred meters from Ekensbergsgatan, where that Polish bloke found the raincoat and so on, the slippers and gloves. It's more or less on the right route, so to speak. If you want to take the shortest route home from Hasselstigen to Järnvägsgatan, you pass Ekensbergsgatan more or less at the point where the Pole found the clothes."

"Well, I never," Bäckström said with a sly smile. "Who'd have thought it of a onetime youth worker?"

"Stigson," he went on. "That woman, Andersson? She never saw who Danielsson's guest was? Unless you forgot to ask her, what with all the other stuff, I mean?"

"No. Of course I asked," Stigson said, glancing nervously at Detective Inspector Annika Carlsson. "Of course I did. No. She never saw who he was. But when she spoke to Danielsson, she could hear someone else in the living room. But of course she never went inside the flat, so she didn't see who it was."

"I've thought of something else," Bäckström said, for some reason looking at Alm.

"What?"

"You started off by saying that lots of Danielsson's old friends got in touch as soon as they heard that he'd been murdered."

"Yes."

"But not Roland Stålhammar?"

"No," Alm agreed. "He hasn't been in touch."

"Surely he out of all of them should have been? A former policeman and all that. Who was sitting getting pissed with the victim just before he died?" Bäckström elaborated, with evident satisfaction.

"Yes, that's been bothering me too, in case you were wondering," Alm said. "Assuming that he knows Danielsson was murdered, and assuming it was him who was there that evening, because we can't be entirely certain in spite of what Jockey Gunnar says. If that is the case, then it bothers me a very great deal."

"Mmh," Bäckström said, nodding. The net's closing, he thought. I wonder if I've got time to reward myself with a little marzipan cake and some coffee with a splash of cream?

"How about taking a short break to stretch our legs?" Bäckström said, looking at the time. "Shall we say quarter of an hour?" Perhaps now isn't the time to talk about respect and authority, he thought, as Carlsson, her eyes narrowed, stormed out of the room at once.

No one raised any objections.

16.

Right, then, Bäckström thought, once he and his colleagues had settled back down again. Now all we need to do is tie things up, without getting too excited and rushing the job.

"Nadja," Bäckström said, nodding genially at Nadja Högberg, "have you found out anything else about our victim?"

According to Nadja Högberg, most of her work was done now. Apart from Danielsson's old limited company, which she was planning to look into over the weekend. But there also seemed to be a safe-deposit box that she hadn't yet found. The keys fitted a box in a branch of Handelsbanken located on Valhallavägen in Stockholm, that much was straightforward. The problem was that neither Danielsson nor his company, according to the bank, had a box at that branch. The number of the box wasn't clear from the keys, and because there were hundreds of boxes at that branch alone, finding the box wasn't as simple as it seemed.

"The bank and I are still grappling with that," Nadja Högberg said. "We'll get to the bottom of it."

One thing that she had already sorted out was the bundles of slips and receipts that the forensics team had found in Danielsson's flat.

"There are loads of them," Nadja said. "Winning slips from Solvalla totaling more than half a million; taxi receipts, restaurant receipts, and loads of other invoices for everything from office furniture to paintwork in an old storehouse out in Flemingsberg, south of the city. In total, the invoices and receipts come to more than a million, and they're all dated from the last few months."

"The bastard must have been a demon with the horses," Bäckström said. He had been only half listening. Half a million in a few months, he thought.

"I don't believe that for a moment," Nadja said, shaking her head. "Betting on the horses is a zero-sum game. If you're lucky and know a bit about horses, you might just break even in the long run. He was trading in winning slips, that's all. It's no more complicated than that, but I daresay a few of them are his own. He sold them on to someone who needed to explain to the tax office how he had been able to buy a new Mercedes even though he didn't have any income. The same with the receipts. He sold them to people who used them as tax-deductible expenses for their businesses. Presumably he had the contacts from when he was active as an accountant and auditor, but it doesn't really demand any particular skills."

Better than collecting empties like all the other pissheads, Bäckström thought.

"Excuse me," Alm said, with an apologetic gesture as his cell phone started to ring.

"Alm," Alm said, then he sat and mostly listened for a couple minutes as Bäckström glared at him with growing anger.

"Sorry," Alm said when the call was over.

"Not at all," Bäckström said. "Don't let us bother you. I'm sure it was vitally important."

"That was Niemi," Alm said. "I took the opportunity to call him during the break, to let him know about Roly Stålhammar."

"Are Stålhammar's prints in the register?" Bäckström asked. "Why didn't you tell us about this before?"

"No," Alm said, shaking his head. "Stålhammar's prints aren't on file officially, but he did give Niemi a set of prints in conjunction with an old murder in Stockholm years ago. Stålhammar and his partner—wasn't his name Brännström?—had gone to see an old junkie living on Pipersgatan, more or less next door to police headquarters. There was no one home, but they took the opportunity to go through his lodgings, since they were there anyway. Brännström thought there was a funny smell in the flat and pulled out the bottom half of an old sofa bed in the living room. And that's where they found the tenant. Stuffed into his sofa bed with an ice pick in his skull. So when the forensics team arrived, Roly and Brännström had to provide a full set of prints so that theirs could be ruled out from the search."

"So you don't think they were the ones who did it?" Bäckström said with a grin. "I seem to remember that Brännström was fond of long-distance skiing and winter sports." Another fucking idiot, he thought. He and Stålhammar must have made a right pair. The blind leading the blind.

"This was in July," Alm said. "The victim had been lying there for a week, so if you don't mind . . ."

"By all means," Bäckström said.

"To get to the point," Alm said, "Niemi was calling to say that he had just compared Stålhammar's prints with the ones they found on the glasses, bottles, and cutlery in Danielsson's flat."

"And?" Bäckström said.

"Well," Alm said. "They're Stålhammar's prints."

"Would you believe it?" Bäckström said. "Such a nice, decent man as well."

"Okay, this is what we're going to do," Bäckström, who had just finished thinking, said. The fact that it had taken only thirty seconds showed that he was starting to feel like his old self again, he thought.

"Annika," he said, nodding toward Carlsson. "Talk to the prosecutor about what we've got on Stålhammar. It would be great if we could just go and pick him up and lock him away for the weekend. Then we can start on him on Monday morning. Three days in a cell without a drop of alcohol usually works well on old pissheads."

"I'll take care of it," Annika Carlsson said, without pursing her mouth at all.

"Nadja, you keep trying to find the number of Danielsson's bank box. It's probably full of a load of old receipts and shit like that. Sort that out with the prosecutor as well, so we don't have to deal with any crap later.

"The victim's old friends," Bäckström went on, nodding at Alm. "Get photographs of them and we'll do another round of the neighbors and see if we can't winkle out a few eyewitnesses as well. Preferably people who saw Stålhammar rolling round the neighborhood wearing slippers, washing-up gloves, and a blood-drenched raincoat."

"I've done that with eleven of them already," Alm said, digging out a plastic sleeve from his folder. "Driving-license shots or passport pictures of all of them. I've got address lists. We may have to finish that off later, but Stålhammar's picture is already in there."

"Excellent. In that case I think I'm going to start by borrowing your pictures," Bäckström said without explaining why. "Full steam ahead now, Alm. Stålhammar is priority number one now, and everything else is no priority at all. Agreed?"

Alm contented himself with nodding and shrugging. Like all bad losers, Bäckström thought.

"You're coming with me," Bäckström said, pointing a fat finger at Sergeant Stigson. "We're going to take a drive past Stålhammar's house and have a discreet little look at what the bastard's up to. Well, I think that's everything, at least for the time being."

"What about me?" Felicia Pettersson said, pointing at herself just to be sure.

"Yes, you," Bäckström said with extra emphasis. "Have a think about that paperboy. That lad, Soot— Him, Akofeli. There's something about him that doesn't make sense."

"But what could he have to do with Stålhammar?" Felicia looked questioningly at Bäckström.

"Good question," Bäckström said, already heading for the door. "It's worth thinking about, Felicia," he went on. There, that gave the pretty little darkie something to chew on as well, Bäckström thought. What the fuck did Akofeli have to do with their murderer? Not the tiniest little thing, if you ask me, he thought.

"Get a car for us, Stigson," Bäckström said as soon as they had got far enough away from Annika Carlsson's sensitive hearing.

"Already sorted," Stigson said. "I've got Stålhammar's address. Järnvägsgatan number—"

"Later," Bäckström interrupted. "Give that woman, Andersson, a call and ask if we can call in at Hasselstigen."

"Sure, boss," Stigson said. "Are you thinking of showing her the pictures of Stålhammar?"

"I thought I might take a look at her boobs first," Bäckström said. He was starting to feel like his old self again. Everything in its own good time, including pictures of Stålhammar, he thought.

"Boobs," Stigson said, sighing and shaking his shaved head

disparagingly. "I promise you, boss. We're talking melons here. Massive great melons."

17.

Oh, for fuck's sake! Bäckström thought, as soon as she opened the door. Britt-Marie Andersson was an old crone! She had to be at least sixty, he thought. This from a man in the prime of life, who wouldn't be fifty-five until the autumn.

Big blond hair, porcelain-blue eyes, red mouth, teeth that were so white that they probably were porcelain, sunbed brown, her flowery dress a fair way above her knees, a generous neckline, and there was no way she was ever going to sleep on her front. What a fucking fate, Bäckström thought. At least sixty, and as a result she'd missed her chance at the Bäckström super-salami way back before the turn of the millennium.

To complete the picture, she also had a little dog that ran round yapping. One of those Mexican cockroaches that you could drown in a teacup. Just to underline the point, his name was Little Sweetie.

"There, there," his owner said soothingly, picking up the wretched creature and kissing it on the nose.

"Little Sweetie always gets jealous when Mommy has gentlemen callers," Mrs. Andersson explained, blinking and smiling with those red lips.

You should probably take care not to end up in a threesome with him and little Stigson, then, Bäckström thought. He seldom missed a chance to think along those lines.

After that he had quickly pulled out the pictures of Danielsson's friends to put an end to this farce and get away from there.

Their hostess had sat down on a low pink plush armchair and had directed her guests to the flowery sofa opposite. And all the while Little Sweetie ran around yapping until his owner took pity on him and lifted him onto her lap.

The folk dancer had been in a state of bliss. Reverse pedophilia, Bäckström thought, and when old crone Andersson leaned over the table to get a closer look at pisshead Danielsson's pisshead friends, little Stigson's eyes had gone completely vacant.

"I recognize almost all of them," Mrs. Andersson said. She straightened up and took some deep breaths just to make sure, as she flashed a broad smile at her guests. "They're Danielsson's old friends. They've been coming and going all the years I've lived here, and I don't think I've ever seen any of them sober. Isn't that one supposed to be an old policeman?" she asked, putting her long red fingernail on Roland Stålhammar's passport photo.

"That's right," Bäckström said. "Retired."

"I daresay he was the one in Danielsson's flat when all that noise was going on, the evening before he got killed."

"What makes you say that, Mrs. Andersson?" Bäckström asked.

"I saw him when I was out walking Little Sweetie," Britt-Marie Andersson said. "He was walking down Råsundavägen. It was around eight o'clock. He could well have been on his way round to see Danielsson."

"But you never saw the person who was inside Danielsson's apartment?" Bäckström asked, simultaneously giving Stigson the evil eye.

"No, I never saw who it was," Mrs. Andersson said. "But I don't know how many times I've seen that Roly, I think that's his name, coming and going to Danielsson's place."

"Anyone else?" Bäckström said, gesturing toward the heap of photographs.

"That one's actually my ex-brother-in-law, Halvar Söderman," Mrs. Andersson said, pointing at the photograph of a former car dealer, Halvar "Halfy" Söderman, seventy-one years old. "I was married to his older brother, Per Söderman, Per A. Söderman," Mrs. Andersson clarified, placing particular emphasis on the A.

"He was a completely different sort of person to his younger brother; he's a real waste of space. I can assure you of that, but sadly my husband died ten years ago."

Probably died when a heavy weight landed on him, Bäckström thought. He glanced one last time at Britt-Marie Andersson's undeniably remarkable assets, thanked her for her help, got the reluctant Stigson to his feet, and said goodbye. Stigson looked as if Bäckström had just torn his heart out, and against all the rules, he had leaned forward and given the old crone a hug before they finally got out of there.

"What a woman, what a woman," Jan O. Stigson said, and sighed as he got in behind the wheel to drive them to Järnvägsgatan so that they could take a discreet look at where Stålhammar lived.

"It hasn't occurred to you that she's old enough to be your grandmother?" Bäckström asked.

"Maybe my mother," Stigson corrected. "Think about that, Bäckström. Having a mother with a body like that."

"You're obviously very fond of your mother," Bäckström said slyly. The same mother who must have exposed him to incestuous abuse at an early age, he thought.

"Isn't everyone?" Sergeant Stigson said, looking at his boss in surprise. "I mean, doesn't everyone love their mom?"

Definitely a victim of incest. Poor bastard, Bäckström thought, but contented himself with a nod.

18.

Bäckström had done everything by the book. First he got Stigson to do a few turns around the block where Stålhammar lived. No sign of him.

Then they had gone inside the building he lived in and listened to his apartment through the mail slot. Not a sound.

Then Bäckström had called him on his landline. They heard the sound of the phone ringing inside the apartment but no audible human activity in response.

Then he had called him on his cell phone.

"Roly," Stålhammar grunted, but Bäckström didn't say anything. "Hello. Hello?" Stålhammar repeated. Then Bäckström had ended the call.

"I'm convinced he's scarpered," Bäckström said, nodding toward Stigson as Stålhammar's next-door neighbor opened his door and stood there staring at them. A sinewy little old man, circa seventy years old, Bäckström thought.

This sort of thing didn't often happen in the book's versions of events, but naturally Bäckström had solved the situation that had arisen.

"Do you know where Roly's gone?" Bäckström asked amiably. "He's an old friend of ours and we'd like a word with him."

"Yes, you don't have to be a genius to work that out," the old man hissed, and stared at Bäckström's Hawaiian shirt and Stigson's shaved head.

But he didn't have anything he could tell them, and if they didn't get out of there at once, he'd call the police.

On their way back to the station Bäckström had explained all the usual, obvious stuff to Stigson. That he should talk to surveillance and get them to keep an eye on Stålhammar's address, and let Annika Carlsson know at once if he showed up. Then give Stålhammar's cell number to the team who dealt with phone surveillance and see if they could locate the tower closest to Stålhammar when he had taken the call.

"You made a note of when I called?" Bäckström asked.

"Fourteen forty-five and twenty seconds," Stigson nodded. "No worries, boss," he assured him.

When Bäckström got out of the car down in the garage he had bumped into Annika Carlsson, who had asked for a private chat with him and given Stigson the evil eye.

"What can I do for you, Annika?" Bäckström said with a gentle smile.

"I've spoken to the prosecutor. They've given it to Tove. She's good," she reassured him.

So you've been there as well, Bäckström thought. But it would have been unwise to say it out loud. Don't want to start the weekend by getting my skull fractured, he thought.

"Do you want me or you to keep an eye on things over the weekend?" Carlsson went on.

"It would be great if you could," Bäckström said. "Things got a bit out of whack in my last post. I had to put in way too much overtime toward the end, and—because I want to be around if things heat up—I thought I might take this weekend off," Bäckström lied.

No problem, according to Carlsson.

When Bäckström returned to his office to pick up the bare essentials and make his escape, Niemi suddenly stuck his nose in and seemed to have a lot on his mind.

"Can I sit down?" Niemi said, and since he'd already sat down, Bäckström had made do with a nod.

"What can I do for you, then?" Bäckström said. Bastard Lapp, he thought.

Not much, according to Niemi. The question was more what he could do for Bäckström.

"A piece of advice in good faith," Niemi said.

"I'm listening," Bäckström said.

"I think you should take it easy with Roly Stålhammar," Niemi said. "He isn't the type who needs a saucepan lid to put the lights out on someone like Danielsson. And they were friends. He just feels wrong for this."

"Really?" Bäckström said, smiling happily. "Correct me if I'm wrong, but first Danielsson and Stålhammar sit and get blitzed and have a high old time until circa quarter past ten that evening. Then the neighbor comes down and tells them to shut up. Shortly after that, Danielsson is beaten to death. But not by Stålhammar, because he has already lumbered off home to get his beauty sleep. Instead, more or less immediately an unknown perpetrator appears out of nowhere, invisible and soundless and without leaving any evidence, because neither you nor Fernandez seem to have found the tiniest little trace of him, even though he was evidently the one who beat Danielsson to death. Have I got that right?"

"I know it sounds odd," Niemi said, "but—"

"Have I got that right?" Bäckström repeated, glaring sourly at Niemi.

"Yes, because I don't believe Roly would do something like that to a friend, so that must be what happened. However unlikely it might sound."

"Well, I don't happen to believe that," Bäckström said. "Now, you'll have to excuse me."

Niemi had shrugged, wished him a good weekend, and walked out. Bäckström had made do with a curt nod. Then he had left the madhouse that was his current place of work and walked all the way home.

19.

One hour later Bäckström was sitting at the kitchen table in his cozy abode, and as he was sweating off the exertion he pulled out a paper and pen to get some order to his new life.

· Let's see now, Bäckström thought, wetting the pen with his tongue. First two days of fasting, he thought. Absolutely clean living down to the smallest detail: only vegetables, water, and other goodies. Then on to a more balanced dietary program for two days, and, if he had worked this out correctly, he should—according to the Bäckström method—be able to go on a real bender as early as Sunday. Great, I can manage that, Bäckström thought.

It had been somewhat sooner than that, since he had had a revelation as early as Friday evening.

First he had got in the shower, and dried himself carefully afterward, put on his bathrobe, sat down on the sofa, and watched the film the doctor had given him. He watched the whole film. Then he put on his tracksuit, walked halfway round Kungsholmen, and gulped down three low-alcohol beers as soon as he got back in through the door. It hadn't helped. The eagle had once again flown into the power cables.

In a position like that he had had no option. He had taken one brown and one blue, collapsed like a clubbed seal, and somewhere round about then, between drowsiness and sleep, he had had a divine revelation.

———

It had been dark and rather foggy in his bedroom, however that could have happened, when suddenly a tall, thin old man in white clothes, with a beard down to his navel, had stepped forward to his bed, put his veined hand on his shoulder, and spoke to him.

"My son," the old man said. "My son, are you listening to me?"

What do you mean—"Dad"? Bäckström had thought in confusion, since this was a skinny old man with a white beard. Nothing like the red-faced drunken skunk who had been a police sergeant in the Maria district, and who, according to his mad old mother, was the begetter of Bäckström himself.

Lord God, Bäckström thought, suddenly realizing what was going on. Lord God!

"My son," the bearded man repeated. "Do you hear what I am saying?"

"I'm listening, Father," Bäckström said.

"The life you live is no longer whole, but split," the old man had rumbled. "You have wandered onto the wrong path, my son, you have been listening to false prophets."

"Sorry, Dad," Bäckström peeped.

"Go in peace, my son," the old man said, patting him on the shoulder again. "Make sure you find the right path again. Become a whole person again."

"I promise, Father," Bäckström said, sitting up in bed and suddenly wide-awake.

The message he had received had been abundantly clear. He had showered once more, put on a pair of trousers, a clean shirt, and a jacket. When he stepped into the street he had raised his eyes to the boundless blue above his round head and thanked his Lord and Creator.

"Thanks a lot, Dad," Bäckström said, and two minutes later he was sitting at his usual table in his favorite neighborhood bar.

"Where the hell have you been, Bäckström?" the woman behind the bar had said. She was Finnish and occasionally got a serious going-over in Bäckström's sturdy Hästens bed, assuming there was nothing better on offer, of course.

"Murder case," Bäckström said in a masculine and concise way. "I've been hard at it all week, but now I've got the pieces in place at last."

"*Vojne, vojne.* It's a good thing they've got you, Bäckström. Sounds like you deserve a little treat," the woman had said with a maternal smile.

"Goes without saying," Bäckström said. Then he had ordered a pint and a large chaser before eating.

Smoked sausage with beetroot and potato gratin. For safety's sake he had backed this up with a couple side dishes of liver pâté and fried eggs. And he had gone on to celebrate the weekend in the traditional way, and by the time he took a taxi to work at nine on Monday morning he had already thrown the crazy doctor's film in the bin. Besides, you had to look really carefully to see any resemblance at all between him and the bloke in the diaper.

"False prophets," Bäckström said, and snorted.

"Sorry?" the taxi driver had said, looking at him in surprise.

"Solna police station. I won't mind if we actually get there sometime today," Bäckström said, back to being Bäckström again.

20.

When Bäckström arrived in his office he found a note on his desk from one of the cell phone surveillance team. Bäckström's nuisance call to Stålhammar on Friday afternoon had made its way to a phone tower on the other side of the Öresund, in the center of Copenhagen.

"I fucking knew it," Bäckström growled, as he called Annika Carlsson on her cell.

"Good morning, Bäckström," Carlsson said.

"Never mind about that," Bäckström replied in his most polite manner. "It looks like that bastard Stålhammar has run off to Copenhagen."

"Not anymore," Annika Carlsson said. "I've just had a call from reception. Apparently he's sitting downstairs and wants to talk to us."

Ten minutes later Bäckström, Carlsson, and Stålhammar were sitting in one of the crime unit's interview rooms. Stålhammar looked like he'd had a hectic weekend, to judge by his clothes and general appearance. Three days' stubble; sweaty, unwashed clothes; and the smell of old and new drinking. But otherwise he was much the same. A large, thickset man, with sharp, furrowed facial features and without an ounce of fat on his muscular body.

"This is an awful business, Bäckström," Stålhammar said, rubbing the corner of his eye with his right knuckles. "What sort of bastard would go and kill Kalle?"

"We were hoping you might be able to help us with that question," Bäckström said. "We've been looking for you for several days."

"I headed off to Malmö on Thursday morning," Stålhammar said, rubbing his red eyes. "That must have been when it happened, if I've understood correctly?"

"What were you doing in Malmö?" Bäckström asked. I'm the one who asks the questions here, he thought.

"I've got an old flame down there. Damn fine woman, so when Kalle and I picked a winner on Wednesday and I suddenly had ten thousand in my pocket, it wasn't a hard decision. I got the train down. Can't stand planes. Way too fucking cramped. You have to be Japanese with no legs to fit in those seats. And no cart service either. I caught the morning train. Got there just after lunchtime."

"Has she got a name?" Bäckström asked.

"Who?" Stålhammar said, looking at Annika Carlsson in surprise.

"Your old flame down in Malmö," Bäckström clarified.

"'Course she has," Stålhammar said. "Marja Olsson. Lives at number four Staffansvägen. She's in the phonebook. She works as a staff nurse at the hospital down there. She picked me up from Malmö Central. You're welcome to call her if you don't believe me."

"What did you do after that?" Bäckström asked.

"After that we didn't leave the house until Friday, when we went to Copenhagen for a proper lunch. We carried on all day and half the night."

"And then?"

"Well, then we came back. Sometime early in the morning. To Malmö, I mean. Back to Marja's, and we carried on as usual again. Went out and got supplies before the shops shut. Then we got going again."

"You got going again?"

"Sure," Stålhammar said with a sigh. "She's in seriously good shape, that girl, and my dander was up. I don't suppose we got out of bed until Sunday evening when Flash called on my cell to tell me what had happened."

"Flash?"

"Björn Johansson. Another old friend from school. You probably know him? He's fairly well known around these parts. An old Solna character. Used to run Flash Electricals down in Sundbyberg, but now his boy's taken over. So he told me what had happened, and it didn't feel right to hang about in Malmö, so I got the night train up to help you find the bastard who killed Kalle."

"That was kind of you, Roland," Bäckström said. Looks like old Roly did some thinking somewhere in all that drinking and decided to put up a bit of resistance, he thought.

"Well, what the hell. Of course I'm going to help. So here I am," he clarified.

It had taken two hours to work out what Stålhammar had been doing since Thursday morning, when he suddenly headed off toward Copenhagen, until Monday morning, when he showed up in the Solna police station. Then they'd taken a break for lunch.

Bäckström had stocked up seriously because he realized this was going to be a drawn-out business. Meatballs and mashed potatoes, cream sauce, and both almond and marzipan cakes this time. Annika Carlsson had taken a quick pasta salad and a mineral water before going off to make sure that Alm and the others had started to check the information that Roland Stålhammar had given them about his visit to Malmö and Copenhagen. Stålhammar had made do with a sandwich and a cup of coffee that Annika had fetched for him from the cafeteria.

We're getting close, Bäckström thought, when they were back in their seats again. Stålhammar had started sweating in a promising way, and when he raised the coffee cup to his lips he had to use both hands.

"You were at Solvalla on Wednesday last week, Wednesday, May fourteenth," Bäckström said. "What can you tell us about that?"

He had got there at about four o'clock that afternoon to watch the warm-up, and then go round and listen to his old friends for a bit.

"Warm-up?" Annika Carlsson asked. She hadn't said much before lunch.

Stålhammar had explained. When you took the horses out onto the track before the race to get them warmed up.

"Like doing exercises, you know. Warming up. Before you go out and race properly," Stålhammar said.

An hour or so later Kalle Danielsson had turned up. They had talked to Gunnar Gustafsson, who reassured them that the tip he had given them the day before still stood. Instant Justice had behaved impeccably during the first warm-up. His old injury seemed to have healed well.

"According to Gunnar, he was like a completely new horse," Stålhammar said. "Not so impetuous anymore, but still with the same phenomenal physique. If you ask me, he's like a fucking train, Bäckström."

"How did you find each other out at Valla?" Annika Carlsson asked. "Had you agreed where to meet up or what?"

"He must have called me," Stålhammar said, shaking his head. "At least I presume he did," he said.

"So Kalle had a cell?" Annika said.

"Everyone does these days, don't they?" Stålhammar said, looking at her in surprise.

"Have you got his number? The number of his cell phone?" Bäckström specified.

"Don't think so," Stålhammar said, shaking his head. "Why would I? I used to call him at home, or else we just bumped into each other out somewhere. If he wasn't home I used to leave him a message on his answering machine. Then he would call back. Anyway, he had my cell number."

"Hang on a minute, Roland," Bäckström persisted. "You must have had Danielsson's cell number." There's something that doesn't make sense here, he thought.

"No," Stålhammar said. "Aren't you listening to what I'm saying?" he said, glowering at Bäckström.

"Did you ever see Danielsson with a cell phone?" Carlsson asked. "Are you sure about that?" There's something that doesn't make sense here, she thought.

"Now that you come to mention it, I don't think I ever did," Stålhammar said.

Shit, Bäckström thought, exchanging a glance with his colleague and deciding to change tack.

"We'll deal with that later," Bäckström said. "So you and Danielsson won a whole load of money?" he said.

He and Danielsson had put five hundred to win on the born-again Instant Justice, sharing the bet, and two minutes after the race started they were some twenty thousand kronor richer.

"And then?" Bäckström asked.

"Kalle cashed out the money," Stålhammar said, "and then he took a taxi home to get dinner. We were going to meet up back at his for a bite to eat, so I thought that made sense. That way you can't be tempted. When you're close to seventy you have a fair idea of what you're like," he explained.

"It was the right decision too," Stålhammar went on, "because after the very next race I was completely broke. I had to borrow a hundred off an old friend to save me having to walk back to Kalle's. It was already almost eight o'clock, and you don't want to be eating in the middle of the night. Unless we're talking supper, of course."

Shit, Bäckström thought.

"Has he got a name?" he asked.

"Who?" Stålhammar said, shaking his head in surprise. "Kalle?"

"The man you borrowed the hundred from?"

"Flash," Stålhammar said. "I thought I'd already said that. Didn't we talk about him before lunch?"

"You took a taxi back to Danielsson's. To number one Hasselstigen?" Bäckström asked, who had Britt-Marie Andersson's testimony fresh in his mind.

"That's right," Stålhammar said with a nod.

"You're absolutely certain of that?" Bäckström said.

"Well, hell, no, now that I come to think about it. That hundred wasn't enough and the money-grabbing Iraqi who was driving kicked me out on Råsundavägen. Not the end of the world, admittedly, since it was only a couple hundred meters from Kalle's door, but I had to do the last bit on foot."

"Did you get a receipt?"

"I would have," Stålhammar said. "I used to give all my receipts to Kalle. He used to sell them on to some old pal who deals in white goods. But the bastard just drove off."

"So you walked the last bit?" Bäckström clarified. He's not that stupid after all, the old drunk, he thought.

"What happened next?" Bäckström asked.

First they had divided the money. More or less. Stålhammar got 10,300 in his hand, ten thousand-kronor notes and three hundreds, but because Danielsson didn't have any change Stålhammar let him keep the last ten.

"My old mate, it's hardly the end of the world," Stålhammar had said with a shrug.

Then they had eaten, drunk, and talked. They started sometime around half past eight with pork chops and kidney beans, a few lagers and chasers. When the food was finished Kalle had mixed himself a vodka and tonic, whereas Stålhammar preferred his neat. They had talked some more, both of them in an excellent mood, and Kalle had put on some old Evert Taube albums.

"He knew his stuff, that man," Stålhammar said with feeling. "Hell, there hasn't been a decent song written in this country since Evert cashed in his chips."

"How long were you playing music for?" Annika Carlsson asked.

"Quite a while," Stålhammar said, looking at her in surprise. "It was one of those old vinyl things, an LP, and I suppose we played it through a couple times. *'Old Highland Rover, a boat from Aberdeen, she lay off San Pedro and took on gasoline,'*" Stålhammar sang quietly. "You hear how good he was, Carlsson? The words are still in there, like a comfy pair of shoes," he declared.

"How long were you singing for?" Bäckström asked.

"Until some mad old crone knocked on the door and started shouting and yelling. I was standing in the living room listening to Evert, so I didn't see her, but I couldn't help hearing her, the way she was carrying on."

"What time was that?" Bäckström persisted.

"I haven't got a clue," Stålhammar said, shrugging. "But I know what time it was when I got home and called Marja, because I looked at my watch first. You don't want to call people in the middle of the night, after all."

"What time was that, then?"

"Half past eleven, if I remember rightly," Stålhammar said. "I remember thinking that it was a bit too last-minute, but by then I'd got the idea in my head. So I plucked up courage and gave her a call. Mind you, I did a bit of private celebrating at home first. Had a bit left in the cupboard, and I suppose it must have been while I was drinking that I got the idea of heading down south."

"What time did you leave Danielsson, then?" Bäckström said. How the hell do we check that last bit? he thought.

"As soon as the old crone started shrieking I realized it was time to go home and get some sleep. So I said goodbye to Kalle and set off home. It couldn't have taken more than ten minutes, allowing for a couple wrong turns on the way," Stålhammar said, smiling and shaking his head. "The party had fallen a bit flat, if I can put it like that, and Kalle had got the hump and had phoned the old woman who had been down shouting at us. He was standing there arguing with her when I left."

"Danielsson was on the phone shouting at his neighbor when you left?" Bäckström repeated.

"Exactly," Stålhammar agreed. "So it felt like the right time to head home for some peace and quiet.

"God, it's a wretched business," Stålhammar went on, rubbing his eyes with his knuckles again.

"While I was lying there having sweet dreams about Marja, some mad bastard is breaking into Kalle's and beating him to death."

"What makes you think someone broke in?" Bäckström asked.

"That's what Flash said," Stålhammar said, looking in surprise first at Bäckström, then at Annika Carlsson. From what he had heard, the door of Kalle's flat was hanging off its hinges. Some bastard had broken in and robbed him. Beaten him to death as he was lying there asleep.

"When you left," Bäckström said, to change the subject, "do you remember if Kalle locked the door?"

"He always did. Kalle was a cautious man," Stålhammar said. "Not that I gave it a second thought, but I'm absolutely sure he would have done. I used to tease him about it. The fact that he always locked himself in. I never use the safety lock when I'm at home."

"Was he afraid of anyone?" Bäckström asked. "If he always locked the door?"

"I suppose he didn't want anyone to break in and steal his things. He had some valuable stuff, after all."

"Such as?" Bäckström asked. He had been in the flat and had seen it in all its shabby glory. Here we go, he thought.

"Well," Stålhammar said, and it looked like he was thinking hard. "His old record collection must have been worth quite a bit. And that desk he had, that was valuable."

"The one in his bedroom?" Bäckström said. How the hell could anyone ever have lifted that? And how the hell could anyone like Stålhammar ever have made it into the police? he thought.

"That's the one." Stålhammar nodded. "Antiques. Kalle had a few things like that. Genuine old carpets, loads of really nice old things."

"I have a few problems with what you're saying," Bäckström said. "When we found him, the door was unlocked and there were no signs of forced entry on it. From the inside you can lock it either with the key or the catch. From the outside you can only lock it with a key. When our colleagues got there it was wide open, but there were no marks on it. The forensics team think that when the culprit left he pulled the door shut behind him, but because the balcony door in the living room was ajar, the draft pulled the front door open again. How do you explain that?"

"Explain?" Stålhammar said in surprise. "If that's what forensics say, then it must be right. Don't ask me what the hell I think about it. I'm an old detective. Not a forensics expert. Ask Pelle Niemi or one of his guys."

"My colleagues and I are working another line of thought," Bäckström said, with a nod toward Annika Carlsson. "We believe that Kalle Danielsson must have let the perpetrator in because it was someone he knew and trusted." Try that on for size, he thought.

"You're on the wrong track there, Bäckström," Stålhammar

said, shaking his head. "Which one of our old friends would have any reason to murder Kalle?"

"You don't have any suggestions?" Bäckström said. "I and my colleague Carlsson here were rather hoping you might have."

"Well, the only one of our old friends who I can think of would probably be Manhattan. From the old gang, I mean. He was the only one who had a grudge against Kalle."

"Manhattan? Manhattan as in New York?"

"Hell, no," Stålhammar said. "As in that disgusting bloody drink made from whiskey and liqueur. How the hell could anyone ever get the idea of pouring liqueur into whiskey? Ought to be against the law."

"Manhattan," Bäckström repeated.

"Manne Hansson," Stålhammar explained. "Known as Manhattan among his friends. Used to be a bartender at the old Carlton when he was still working. Could be a mean bastard when he'd had a few. He put some money into some company on Kalle's advice and evidently it all went to hell. So he wasn't happy."

"Manne Hansson," Bäckström repeated. "Where can we get hold of him, then?"

"That won't be so easy, I'm afraid," Roland Stålhammar said with a smile. "Your best bet is Solna Cemetery. Apparently his kids scattered his ashes in the memorial grove there to keep costs down."

"And when was that?" Bäckström said. What have I done to deserve this? he thought.

"A fuck of a long time ago," Stålhammar said. "Must be a good ten years, if you ask me."

"There's one thing I'm wondering, Roland," Annika Carlsson said. "You used to be one of us, so you know as much about the whole business of checking phone records as I do."

"I can still remember a few of the old tricks," Stålhammar agreed, looking self-conscious.

"When you left Kalle Danielsson he was on the phone shouting at his neighbor. We've checked that call. He made it just before ten-thirty. Then you say you walked home and that it took you something like ten minutes. Which would mean that you got home at about twenty to eleven."

"That makes sense," Stålhammar said with a nod.

"Then you say you called your friend in Malmö at half past eleven or so."

"Yes, I'm sure of that. Because I looked at the time just before I called. Didn't want to call too late, like I said."

"So what did you do before that? You get home at twenty to eleven, and call her at half past eleven. That's fifty minutes. Almost an hour. So what were you doing?"

"I told you," Stålhammar said with a look of surprise.

"In that case I must have forgotten," Annika Carlsson said. "Would you care to jog my memory?"

"I had a drop or two left in the cupboard. And I had something to celebrate, so I started by drinking that. Then I called Marja. And, well, I suppose the blood started to flow a bit while I was sitting there having a little drink," Stålhammar said with a crooked smile.

"Fifty minutes," Annika Carlsson repeated, exchanging a quick glance with Bäckström.

"Must have been a fairly serious drop," Bäckström said.

"Don't be like that, Bäckström," Stålhammar said. "I suppose I was just sitting there thinking about things."

"On a completely different subject," Bäckström said, "do you happen to remember if Kalle Danielsson had a briefcase or attaché case? One of those smart ones, leather, brass locks?"

"Yes, he did," Stålhammar said, nodding. "Light brown leather. A proper director's briefcase. The last time I saw it was when I was there to eat with him, the evening before he got murdered. I definitely saw it."

"You definitely saw it?" Bäckström said. "How can you be so sure?"

"He'd put it on top of the television," Stålhammar said. "In the living room where we were eating. A fucking weird place to put a briefcase. Okay, I haven't got a briefcase like that, but if I did, I don't think I'd put it on top of the television. Why do you ask?"

"It's missing," Bäckström said.

"Oh," Stålhammar said with a shrug. "It was there when I left. It was still on top of the television."

"When we got there the next morning it was gone," Bäckström said. "You haven't got any ideas about where it might have got to?"

"Come on, Bäckström, give it up!" Stålhammar said, glaring at him with his deep-set eyes.

"I think we'll take a break now," Bäckström said, nodding toward his colleague.

"Fine by me," Stålhammar said. "I could do with going home and getting a shower."

"You're probably going to have to give us a few more minutes, Roland," Annika Carlsson said with a friendly smile. "We're going to have to have a word with the prosecutor before you get out of here."

"Okay," Roland Stålhammar said, shrugging.

One hour later the chief public prosecutor, Tove Karlgren, had decided to remand former detective inspector Roland Stålhammar in custody. Bäckström and Carlsson had persuaded her, and although there had been a fair amount of muttering she had eventually agreed with them. Stålhammar would have had plenty of time to beat Karl Danielsson to death and get rid of the clothes and so on while he was on his way home. He had a lot going against him, and there were still plenty of things to chase up. So he was justifiably suspected of murder, and while the investigating team checked what he had told them and searched his apartment, it was best for all involved if Stålhammar remained behind bars.

Just before Bäckström left for the day, Peter Niemi telephoned him. The first results from the National Forensics Lab about the bloodstained clothes had just come through on Niemi's fax.

"Danielsson's blood," Bäckström said, as a statement of fact rather than a question.

"Yep, no doubt about it," Niemi said.

But nothing that didn't come from Danielsson himself, according to both the lab and Niemi. No fibers, no strands of hair, no fingerprints. There was a possibility that they might find some traces of DNA, but that would take longer to look into.

Who gives a fuck? Bäckström thought, calling for a taxi.

21.

The following day, after lunch on Tuesday, the investigating team held their third meeting, and everyone, including the two forensics experts, was present. Just as the meeting was due to start, the head of the crime unit in Solna, Superintendent Toivonen, walked into the room. He nodded to the others with a grim glare before sitting down at the back of the room.

Nine people, one of whom is a proper police officer, Bäckström thought. Apart from him, one purebred bastard Finn, one idiot Lapp—practically a bastard Finn—one Chilean, one Russian, one pretty little darkie, one attack dyke, one retarded folk dancer, and dear old Lars Woodentop Alm, seriously mentally handicapped from birth. Where the fuck is this force heading? he thought.

"Okay," Bäckström said. "Let's get going. How's the search of Stålhammar's flat going?" Bäckström nodded encouragingly to Niemi.

It was almost finished, according to Niemi. To make a long story short, they hadn't found anything that incriminated Stålhammar. No unexplained amounts of cash, no trousers with traces of blood on them, no briefcase showing any trace of an upholstery hammer.

He must have hidden everything and made sure to clean up after him. He's probably buried the dough under a rock, Bäckström thought. Just what you'd expect from an idiot like him.

"What little we have been able to find actually seems to back up Roly's own version," Niemi said.

"Like what?" Bäckström asked. Who'd have thought it? So now we're calling our suspect Roly, are we? he thought.

In the bedroom they had found evidence from Stålhammar's trip to Malmö and Copenhagen on the bed. A half-unpacked sports bag containing clothes, clean and dirty all jumbled together; a shaving kit; and a half-empty bottle of Gammel Dansk. All the usual things that someone like Stålhammar might be expected to bring home after a short trip to Malmö and Copenhagen.

"Plus a bundle of receipts," Niemi said. "Return train tickets to Malmö, then return tickets to Copenhagen. Receipts from five bars in Malmö and Copenhagen. A dozen or so taxi receipts, along with several others. In total they come to about nine thousand Swedish kronor. The times he gave us all match the evidence pretty well."

"All of which he collected to give to his good friend Karl Danielsson the receipt trader. As soon as he got home," Bäckström said with a grin. How fucking stupid can anyone be? he thought.

"According to what he says," Alm interjected. "I've spoken to him about it, and that's what he claims. But I can see what you're thinking, Bäckström."

"So what did you do after that?" Bäckström said with a smile.

"I spoke to the woman down in Malmö who he was with. Telephone interview," Alm said. "I asked her the same thing. She said spontaneously that she had also noticed and had asked him about it when they were in Copenhagen. Why was Stålhammar suddenly hoarding a load of old receipts? He told her he had an old friend at home in Stockholm that he gives them to."

"Who'd have thought it?" Bäckström said, smiling happily. "Roly-Stoly starts making a fuss about collecting receipts, whereupon his little girlfriend wonders what he wants them for. Because presumably he wasn't saving them for his former employers."

"Like I said," Alm said, "I can see what you're thinking."

"Have you got anything else?" Bäckström asked. Before I roll up my sleeves and beat the shit out of Roly Stålhammar, he thought.

"That business with the timings. Those fifty minutes when he says he was sitting at home thinking before he called Marja Olsson down in Malmö. He definitely made the call. At twenty-five minutes past eleven in the evening he called on his landline to Marja Olsson's landline."

"Leaving forty-five minutes in which to think lofty thoughts," Bäckström concluded. "What have you come up with for them, then?"

"To start with I did a test walk from number one Hasselstigen, via the trash bin on Ekensbergsgatan where the clothes were found, home to Stålhammar's flat on Järnvägsgatan. It takes at least a quarter of an hour unless you want to jog."

"Leaving thirty minutes," Bäckström said. "More than enough to smash Danielsson's skull in. Steal his money and change into clean clothes. Chucking the raincoat, slippers, and washing-up gloves on the way home."

"True enough," Alm agreed. "The problem is his neighbor. If he's telling the truth, then it doesn't fit," he said.

I knew it, Bäckström thought. The group effort to get legendary old Roly off the hook at any cost was evidently well under way.

The neighbor's name was Paul Englund, seventy-three. A retired caretaker at the Naval History Museum in Stockholm, and the same man who had threatened to call the police about Bäckström and Stigson. Englund had one son, who worked as a photographer at the *Expressen* newspaper, and the previous evening he had called his dad and told him his next-door neighbor was being held on suspicion of murder. He didn't suppose that the neighbor in question had just happened to leave a spare key with his dad, so that the son could take some nice pictures of the murderer's pad?

Mr. Englund had dashed his son's hopes. He didn't have a key. Stålhammar was a noisy alcoholic and the worst sort of neighbor. He was delighted with every minute he didn't have to share the same building with him, and early the following morning he had called the Solna Police to share his observations of Stålhammar on the evening of Danielsson's murder. Now that he finally had the chance to get rid of him for good. If he had realized the consequences of what he planned to say, it's quite possible that he would have chosen to stay quiet instead.

"What does he have to say, then?" Bäckström asked.

"That he saw Stålhammar come in through the door of the building they both live in at approximately quarter to eleven on Wednesday evening. He's certain it was Stålhammar he saw, but because he doesn't like him very much and usually avoids talking to him, he waited for a minute or so before going inside himself."

"Okay," Bäckström said. "How the hell can he be so sure, and what was he doing out in the middle of the night? How can he be so sure it was quarter to eleven? And was he even sober?" Bäckström said. "It's probably the same old story. He's got his days mixed up. Or got the time wrong by an hour or so. Or seen someone else entirely. Or he's just making the whole thing up because he wants to seem important, or because he wants to fuck up Stålhammar."

"Let's not get carried away, Bäckström," Alm said, loving every second of this. "If what the witness says is true, then Stålhammar could hardly have murdered Danielsson. At the very least, things can't have happened the way we've been assuming. Not immediately after half past ten that evening.

"To work through this in order," Alm went on. "Every evening after the late news on TV Four, the one that ends with the weather at half past ten in the evening, Englund takes his dachshund out. He always goes for the same walk round the block, and it always takes him and the dog about quarter of an hour. But not that evening, because when he is about to turn right, up onto the esplanade, he gets stopped by a uniformed police officer who more or less shoos him back the way he came. So back he goes. Reluctantly, because he is as curious as the next man. But when nothing happens, he stops again down on Järnvägsgatan and listens for a few minutes, then carries on walking home. When he reaches the block next to his, some twenty meters from his own door, he sees Stålhammar go inside the building."

"What were our uniformed colleagues up to there, then?" Bäckström asked.

"They'd cordoned off the esplanade because they were preparing a raid on a flat a hundred meters down the road. The result of a tip-off about someone who was suspected of involvement in the shootings and armed robbery out at Bromma a couple days before."

"The timings," Bäckström said. "What does this tell us about the timings?"

"To start with, it must have been after half past ten in the evening of Wednesday, May fourteenth. There's no other possibility. The raid started then, with our uniformed colleagues trying to shut the area off."

"He could have stood there gawping with his dog for half an hour," Bäckström said. "How the hell can you be so certain that he didn't?"

"You can never be entirely certain," Alm said. "I just know what he says, and I sat for two hours questioning him about this."

"So what else has he got to say?" Bäckström said. "It would be useful to know." Preferably before Christmas, he thought.

"He says he waited a few minutes, then he went home, saw Stålhammar going in the door—he waited a couple minutes so that he wouldn't have to talk to him, then he went in himself and took the lift up to his flat. As soon as he got through the door he calls his son. Calls from his cell to his son's cell. Simply out of curiosity, and his son is already up on the esplanade when his dad calls, because the paper had received a tip-off about what was going on.

"By then it was ten minutes to eleven, according to the phone records that we checked out this morning," Alm concluded.

"So you say," Bäckström said, glowering crossly at his colleague. "Hasn't the old goat got a landline in his flat?"

"Yes," Alm said, "and I know what you're thinking, Bäckström. I'm only telling you what he told me."

"You can't help wondering why he called on his cell phone," Bäckström said. "A mean old prick like that. Why use his cell?"

"Because he already had it in his hand when he walked into his apartment. That's what he says," Alm said.

"I'm sorry, Bäckström," Alm went on, but didn't seem the slightest bit sorry. "Pretty much everything backs up what Iron Man says. That he left Danielsson at half past ten, went straight home, and was in his apartment at quarter to eleven."

Bäckström suggested taking a break. The forensics experts had to leave. Had important things to get on with. And Toivonen had also taken the opportunity to go. For some reason he seemed considerably more cheerful than he had when he arrived. He even nodded encouragingly to Bäckström as he left.

"Congratulations, Bäckström," Toivonen said. "Good to see that you're back to your old self again."

22.

Another crazy witness, Bäckström thought, a quarter of an hour later, when the investigating team had reconvened. At worst, it just meant that Stålhammar had gone back to Hasselstigen later that night to kill and rob Karl Danielsson. Just what you'd expect from someone like Iron Man. Sitting there thinking at home in Järn-vägsgatan as he drank the last few drops, then suddenly the alcoholic haze inside his head lifted and it dawned on him that twenty thousand is twice as much as ten thousand. Whereupon he rolled back to Danielsson's and suggested that they carry on partying. He dressed himself up in the raincoat, slippers, and washing-up gloves, then whacked him with his own saucepan lid. That could very easily have been what happened, he thought.

"Thoughts?" Bäckström said, looking round at the other five people in the room. Five mental cases, if you asked him. One Russian, one pretty little darkie, one attack dyke, one retarded folk dancer, and one Woodentop. The curse of being in charge, he thought.

"Well, I for one am not prepared to let go of Stålhammar," Annika Carlsson said, smiling encouragingly at her boss.

And it takes a dyke to say it, Bäckström thought.

"I'm listening," he said.

"Wouldn't it be a bit weird if someone entirely new just appeared in Danielsson's flat right after Stålhammar left?" Carlsson said, looking at Alm.

"Maybe he stood and waited for him to go," Alm said. "So that he could be alone with his victim."

"And he was let in too," Detective Inspector Carlsson persisted. "Which surely suggests that it must have been another of Danielsson's old friends? Have we had time to go through them all yet, by the way?" she asked, nodding toward Alm.

"Still working on it," Alm said, shrugging uncomfortably.

"I'm probably inclined to agree with Bäckström and Annika," Nadja Högberg said. "If you grew up in the old Soviet Union like I did, you stop believing in coincidence, and we've got no information that suggests that anyone was watching Danielsson's flat. And I'm not really too keen on our witness either. How can he be so sure that it was Stålhammar he saw? A man he seems to dislike so intensely. Can we really rule out that he was seeing what he wanted to see? And the fact that he called his son just before eleven doesn't have to have anything at all to do with our case. It might well be that he was just curious about all the police he saw up on the esplanade. Maybe he just wanted to tip off his son that something was going on. Considering the son works as a photographer on a newspaper, I mean. And whyever would he phone him on his cell if he was inside his flat? We mustn't forget that. This witness doesn't feel sound."

One dyke plus one Russian, Bäckström thought. Mind you, she's shrewd for a Russian.

"I don't think we're going to get any further with this. Not right now, anyway," Bäckström said. "Was there anything else?"

"That would be Danielsson's other old friends, I guess," Alm said. "Like you were wondering, Annika." Alm nodded toward Annika Carlsson.

"So what do we know about them, then?" Bäckström said.

There were some ten or so "Solna boys," according to Alm. Who had grown up, gone to school, and worked in Solna and Sundbyberg. The same age as Danielsson or even a bit older, and hardly your typical murderers in light of their age.

"We shouldn't forget that a murderer over the age of sixty is extremely unusual," Alm said. "And that applies to the murder of so-called pissheads as well."

"Well, on that point I have no problem at all with Stålhammar," Bäckström said.

"Granted," Alm said. "In a purely statistical and criminological sense, he feels like the best fit."

Coward, Bäckström thought.

"I'm a police officer," he said. "Not a statistician or a criminologist."

"Old men, lonely, drinking too much, their wives have left them, their children never get in touch, some of them have got criminal records, mainly drunk driving or drunk and disorderly, but one of them caused a scene in a bar and was found guilty of actual bodily harm even though he was over seventy when it happened." Alm sighed. He sounded like he was thinking out loud.

"A real firecracker," Bäckström said. "What's that one's name, then?"

"Halvar Söderman, seventy-two this autumn. It was at his local bar, and it looks like he got into a fight with the owner about some food he had there the week before. He claimed they were trying to poison him. Söderman's an old car salesman, known as Halfy. The bar owner was Yugoslavian, twenty years younger, but that evidently didn't stop Söderman from breaking his jaw. Halfy Söderman is a legendary figure among the old Solna drinkers, according to our older colleagues here at the station. He used to be a rocker, sold cars, had a removal company, traded in white goods and pretty much everything else between heaven and earth. He appears in the criminal record register several times. He's been found guilty of most things, from fraud to ABH. I went back in the records, and he's been cropping up in our files for the past fifty years. He's served five stretches in prison. The longest was two and a half years. That was in the mid-sixties when he was found guilty of bodily harm, serious fraud, drunk driving, and a few other things besides. But over the past twenty-five years he's calmed down a lot. Age seems to have mellowed him. Well, apart from the Yugoslavian, that is."

"Well, you see?" Bäckström said with a benevolent look on his face. "If you put a saucepan lid in the hands of someone like Halfy, he could probably bring down a whole riot squad on his own. Just curious: Has he got an alibi for the evening of Wednesday, May fourteenth?"

"He says he has," Alm said. "I've only spoken to him over the phone, but he says he's got an alibi."

"What is it, then?" Annika Carlsson asked, apparently out of genuine curiosity.

"He didn't want to go into it, he said," Alm said. "He told me to go to hell and hung up on me."

"And what were you thinking of doing about that?" Bäckström grinned.

"I was thinking of going round to see him and interview him officially," Alm said, not showing much enthusiasm at the prospect.

"Let me know when, and I'll come along," Annika Carlsson said with a frown.

Poor Halfy, Bäckström thought.

"Anything else?" he asked, mostly to change the subject.

"Most of them have alibis," Alm said. "Gunnar Gustafsson and Björn Johansson, or Jockey Gunnar and Flash, as they're known to their friends, have an alibi, for instance. They were sitting in the restaurant out at Valla until eleven o'clock. Then they went to the home of a third friend and played poker. He lives in a villa out in Spånga."

"Does he have a name?" Bäckström said. "The one who lives in Spånga?"

"Jonte Ågren. Known as Bällsta Jonte. Former metalworker, seems to have had a small business down by the Bällsta River. Seventy years old. No criminal record, but a well-known tough guy. Used to be one of those guys who set about pieces of pipe and sheet metal with his bare hands when he was younger. He's also one of the few who are still married, but on the evening that they were playing poker his wife was away, apparently. Visiting her sister down in Nynäshamn. I'm guessing she's learned from past experience, if you ask me, Bäckström."

"Any others?" Bäckström said, starting to get interested against his own will.

"Mario Grimaldi, sixty-five," Alm said. "An Italian immigrant. Came here in the sixties when he worked for Saab down in Södertälje. Ended up best friends with Halfy Söderman, the car salesman, and with his ten-years-older brother, also a car salesman, for that matter. Mind you, he's been dead for the past ten years, so I think we can rule him out. But Mario's still alive. He left Saab a few years later and opened a pizza restaurant. According to what

I've heard, he's still got a couple pizzerias and a bar out here in Solna and Sundbyberg, but if that's true, then his name isn't on any official paperwork."

"Has he got a nickname, then?" Bäckström wondered.

"Apparently his friends call him the Godfather." Alm shook his head miserably. "I haven't managed to get hold of him yet, but we'll track him down."

"There, you see?" Bäckström said cheerfully. "There are plenty of gray panthers for us to sink our teeth into, and speaking personally, I'm still putting my money on our former colleague, Stålhammar. Anything else?" he added, glancing at the time.

"I've found Danielsson's bank box," Nadja said. "It wasn't easy, but I've found it."

"Well done," Bäckström said. She was a shrewd old thing. Typical Russian. They could be almost uncannily shrewd, those Russian bastards.

"I've left a key to the box on your desk," Nadja said.

"Excellent," Bäckström said, seeing before him a little trip into the city and a nice pint of beer.

23.

On Bäckström's desk lay a safe-deposit box key, a copy of the prosecutor's decision, and a handwritten note from Nadja. Name and telephone number of the female employee at the bank who could help with the practical details.

That was all he needed, but because Bäckström was by nature a curious person, he had taken a stroll past Nadja's office on the way out.

"Tell me how you did it, Nadja," Bäckström said.

It was nothing special, according to Nadja. First she had got hold of a list of customers who had safe-deposit boxes at the branch of Handelsbanken at the corner of Valhallavägen and Erik Dahlbergsgatan in Stockholm. Mostly private customers, and she had chosen to ignore them for the time being, as well as a hundred or so organizations. Private companies, trading companies, limited partnerships, limited companies, a few associations, and a couple estates. She had started with the largest group, the limited companies.

Then she had pulled out the details of people who were on the boards, or in management, or who owned shares—anyone who could be linked to the various companies. No trace whatsoever of a Karl Danielsson.

"But I did find a limited company in which Mario Grimaldi and Roland Stålhammar are on the board and Seppo Laurén, you know, Danielsson's young neighbor at Hasselstigen, is the managing director. Which seemed a bit too strange for my liking," Nadja Högberg said, shaking her head.

"Yes, well, he's retarded, isn't he? Laurén, I mean?"

"Possibly," Nadja said. "Alm suggested that he was, and I haven't met him myself, but he hasn't been declared legally incapable and he's never gone bankrupt, so there are no formal reasons why he shouldn't be a managing director. And that was presumably the whole point for Danielsson."

"This is phenomenal," Bäckström said. Fuck, this Russian ought to be head of the Security Police, he thought. Get the old boys there moving a bit.

"It's a small private company. Dormant for the past ten years or so, so it isn't actually doing anything. And it doesn't seem to have any assets either. It's called the Writer's Cottage Ltd. According to the articles of association, it offers writing help to private individuals and companies. Everything from advertising brochures to birthday speeches. The two women who set up the business evidently worked as secretaries in some advertising agency, and presumably they thought this would make them some extra money. It looks like they never got enough customers, so it was sold after a couple years to the then detective inspector Roland Stålhammar."

"Who'd have thought it?" Bäckström said, looking almost as sly as he sounded.

"If you ask me, I think Stålhammar and Grimaldi were used as fronts by Danielsson. If there's any truth in what I've heard about Stålhammar, I doubt he knows anything about this."

"So what was Danielsson using it for? The Writer's Cottage Ltd., I mean."

"That's what I've been wondering too," Nadja said. "Because it doesn't seem to have been active at all. But on the other hand, it did have a safe-deposit box.

"I called the bank," Nadja went on, "and after a bit of reluctant digging in their customer files they found an old power of attorney giving Karl Danielsson access to the company's deposit box. It turns out that the last time he visited the box was the same day he was murdered, the afternoon of Wednesday, May fourteenth. The last time before that was in the middle of December last year."

"Who'd have thought it?" Bäckström said. "What does he have in the box, then?"

"It's the smallest box you can get," Nadja said. "Thirty-six centimeters long, twenty-seven wide, and about eight centimeters deep. So it can't be very much. What do you think?"

"Considering Danielsson's character, I'd guess at some betting slips and old receipts," Bäckström said. "What about you, Nadja?"

"Maybe a pot of gold," Nadja said with a broad smile.

"Now, where would he have got that from?" Bäckström said, shaking his head.

"When I was a child back home in Russia . . . no . . . When I was a child back in the Soviet Union, and everything was miserable and poor and dull for the most part, and completely terrible far too often, my old father used to try to cheer me up. Never forget, Nadja, he used to say, at the end of the rainbow there's a pot full of gold."

"An old Russian proverb," Bäckström said.

"Definitely not," Nadja said, and snorted. "If you uttered that sort of proverb in those days you ended up with the KGB. But if you like, we could have a little bet, for a bottle of vodka," Nadja said with another smile.

"Then I'm betting my bottle on receipts and betting slips," Bäckström said. "What about you, Nadja?"

"A pot of gold," Nadja said, suddenly seeming all melancholic. "Not because it would ever fit in such a small deposit box, but because hope is the last thing that we Russians let go of."

Shrewd, fucking shrewd, Bäckström thought. But just as mad as all Russians.

Afterward he had asked Annika Carlsson to drive them. Who the hell could bear to listen to an incest victim from Dalarna as he sat and droned on about a fat old blonde? Bäckström thought. Carlsson at least had the good sense to keep quiet as she drove, and just a quarter of an hour after leaving the Solna police station she pulled up outside the bank.

The female official had been very obliging. She had taken a quick look at their IDs, then went with them down into the vault, unlocked the box using her own and Bäckström's keys, took out the little metal tray, and put it on a table.

"One question before you go," Bäckström had said, stopping her with a smile. "Danielsson visited the box about a week ago. I believe you were the person who helped him? Do you remember anything about that visit?"

A hesitant shake of the head before she answered.

"We're under bankers' confidentiality here," she said apologetically.

"In which case you know that we're here because of a murder, and that bankers' confidentiality no longer applies," Bäckström said.

"I know," she said. "Well, I remember the visit."

"Why?"

"He was the sort of customer that you tended to notice, even if he wasn't here very often," she said. "Always rather grand, slightly exaggerated gestures, and he used to smell of drink as well. I remember us laughing about it after he'd been here once. How long it would be before the Financial Crime Unit turned up in our branch."

"Do you recall if he had a briefcase with him at all? An attaché case in light brown leather, with brass detailing?" Annika Carlsson asked.

"Yes, I remember that. He always had it with him. Even last week when he was here to get things out of his box."

"Why do you say that?" Annika Carlsson asked. "That he was here to get things out of the box, I mean?"

"As I was getting the box he opened up his briefcase. It was completely empty. Well, apart from a notebook and some pens."

"Thank you," Bäckström said.

"What do you think about these?" Annika Carlsson asked when the official had left them, holding up a pair of plastic gloves.

"What, to look at a little box that's already got a load of bank officials' prints on it?" Bäckström said, shaking his head. "No point. We'll leave that to Niemi and his chums." Betting slips and old receipts, he thought.

"Okay, Annika," Bäckström said, grinning and weighing the box in his hand. "What do you think about a little bet?"

"A hundred, no more," Annika Carlsson said. "I don't usually bet. Okay, I reckon it's betting slips and receipts. What about you, then, Bäckström?"

"A pot of gold. You know, Annika. At the end of every rainbow there's always a pot of gold," Bäckström said, and opened the box.

Fuck, he thought, as his eyes grew as round as his head. Why the fuck didn't I come here alone? I'd never have had to wipe my own ass again for the rest of my life, he thought.

"Are you psychic, Bäckström?" Annika Carlsson said, looking at him with wide-open eyes that were just as round as his.

24.

About six months earlier the head of the National Criminal Investigation Department, Lars Martin Johansson, had called one of his colleagues, police chief Anna Holt, and asked if he could invite her to dinner.

"That sounds nice," Anna Holt had said, trying not to show her surprise. The first time, even though we've known each other for more than ten years, she thought. I wonder what he wants this time. From past experience she knew that Johansson always had a motive for what he did, and almost always a hidden agenda.

"When did you have in mind?" Holt asked.

"Preferably tonight," Johansson said. "Tomorrow at the latest."

"Tonight is fine, actually," Holt said. I wonder what he wants from me this time, she thought. Must be something more than the usual.

"Splendid," Johansson said. "We'll meet at seven o'clock. I'll mail you the address of the place I'm thinking of taking you. Take a taxi and get a receipt, and I'll pay you back."

"Don't worry," Holt said. "One question, though, out of curiosity. What do you want me to do this time?"

"Anna, Anna," Johansson said with a sigh. "I want you to have dinner with your boss. I hope you'll have a nice time. In answer to your question, no, I'm not going to ask a favor of you. But I am thinking of telling you a secret. And it's not about anyone apart from me, so you don't have to worry."

"I'm not worried," Holt assured him. "It'll be nice to see you."

He'd make a good salesman too, she thought, as soon as she had hung up.

I wonder what he really wants, she thought, as she got into the taxi to go and meet him. In spite of his assurances to the contrary, she couldn't quite let go of the idea that this was about something else other than his telling her a secret about himself. Johansson simply wasn't the type to tell secrets. He had no problems at all keeping them, particularly if they related to him.

Some six months before, he had got her and a growing number of her colleagues to secretly go through the findings of the Palme Inquiry to see if they could find anything that everyone else had missed.

Considering that the amount of material was immense and that the whole project should have been declared dead from the outset, something that could only be described as a miracle had occurred. They had discovered two previously unknown but highly likely suspects. One who had planned the murder and one who had held the weapon. The former had been dead for many years, but the second seemed to be alive still. His whereabouts were unknown, since he had seemed to be lying low. But they had suddenly come up with a narrative of what had really happened.

They had found a number of troubling circumstances that counted against their two suspects. They had even found witnesses and technical evidence that supported their suspicions. And eventually they had located the suspect who was still alive. During the hours before they were going to arrest him he had suffered an inexplicable accident. He had been blown to pieces on his boat in northern Majorca, and everything that Holt and her colleagues had deduced had followed him into the depths. In the real world where Anna Holt, her colleagues, and her boss actually lived, the investigation of the murder of the prime minister was now a closed chapter.

If this was what Johansson intended to talk about, then it

was a secret that he shared with other people. The belief that had become their truth but which could never be proved with the evidence at their disposal. And even if they were wrong, they would still never be able to let anyone know.

Reveal a secret about himself? My ass, Anna Holt thought, as she climbed out of the taxi outside the restaurant:

They had met in Johansson's own neighborhood restaurant. A small Italian place that lay just a few blocks from his home on Södermalm. Excellent food, even better wine, and a Johansson who was in his most amiable mood. And staff who treated him like the king he presumably was in that place, and her as if she had been his crowned escort.

He must have told them in advance, Holt thought. That they were colleagues and that it wasn't "some damn lover" that he was taking there.

"I told them before you arrived that we work together," Johansson said with a smile. "So they didn't get any ideas in their little heads."

"I thought as much," Holt said, smiling back. The man who can see around corners, she thought.

"Yes, it's odd, isn't it, Holt?" Johansson said. "That I can see around corners, I mean."

"It's a bit creepy, actually," Holt said. "But right now I'm having a lovely time," she added. Besides, it isn't always true, she thought.

"A wanderer and seer," Johansson said, and nodded. "But it isn't always true, you know. Sometimes I get things wrong."

"Was that the secret you were going to tell me?"

"Definitely not," Johansson said with a hurt expression. "I wouldn't dream of telling you anything like that. Then all my northern Swedish credibility would vanish in a flash." Johansson smiled again and raised his glass.

"You're very entertaining, Lars. When you're in this mood. But because I'm dying with curiosity—"

"I'm leaving," Johansson interrupted. "I'm leaving in a week. I've handed in my notice, with immediate effect."

"I hope nothing's happened?" Holt said. What's he up to now? she thought. What's he saying?

Nothing, according to Johansson. Nothing had happened and he wasn't up to anything. He had simply come to a realization. A purely personal insight.

"I've done my bit," Johansson said. "Really, I should be going in eighteen months, but because I've done my bit, after forty years or so I'm done with my life as a police officer, and there's no point in hanging around just marking time.

"I've spoken to my wife," he went on. "She thinks it's an excellent idea. I've spoken to the government and the national head of police. They tried to persuade me to see out my time. I thanked them for the vote of confidence but declined politely. I've also turned down a number of offers of other jobs and projects."

"When were you thinking of mentioning it at work?" Holt asked.

"It'll be public knowledge on Thursday after the cabinet meeting."

"What are you going to do instead?" Holt asked.

"I'm going to grow cabbages and try to grow old gracefully," Johansson said, nodding thoughtfully.

"Why are you telling me this? Before everyone else at work, I mean."

"Because I've got a question as well," Johansson said.

I knew it, Holt thought. I knew it.

"But because you look the way you look right now, I thought I might start by reassuring you. I haven't asked you here in order to propose to you. Definitely not. By the way, how is your colleague, Jan Lewin?"

"Fine," Holt said. "How is your dear wife, Pia?"

"The best of me, you mean?" Johansson said, suddenly dead serious. "She's like a pearl of gold."

"The question, then," Holt said. "You had a question."

"Ah, yes, that," Johansson said. "I must have some sort of short circuit in my head these days, because as soon as I change the subject . . ."

"Be serious for a minute, Lars. Try to be serious."

"Do you want to be police chief of the Western District?" Johansson said.

Police chief of the Western District? She already had a job. A job that she was happy with. Colleagues she liked, one of whom she had started a relationship with a month previously. This latter fact actually the only reason to change jobs, Holt thought. Workplace relationships took their toll on love, she thought. Took their toll in other ways too, come to that.

Twenty thousand more each month in salary. Walking distance to her new workplace from her home. A well-run police district. One of the best in the county. The challenge would be the chance to lead hundreds of police, some of whom were reckoned among the smartest in the country. But apart from all this, there was just one reason why Johansson was asking her in particular.

"There's only one reason why I'm asking you," Johansson said. "One," he said, holding up his long index finger.

"And what's that?"

"You're the best," Johansson said. "It's no more complicated than that."

"One practical question," Holt said. "Are you really in a position to make this kind of offer? Isn't it the higher-ups in Stockholm Police who decide this sort of thing?"

"These days it's the government," Johansson said. "In conjunction with the National Police Board and, in this case, police officials in Stockholm. The Stockholm County police chief will be contacting you, by the way. Completely independently of anything you say to me here and now. Think about it."

"I promise," Holt said. She knew she was good, and unlike far too many of her sisters, she had no problem saying so if it proved necessary. But as for being the best? And hearing that from Johansson? It's a bit much, considering how much I've argued with him over the years, she thought.

"Good," Johansson said with a smile. "Well, enough of that, we're here to have a good time. No more business. Back to pleasure. You choose the next subject, Anna."

"Tell me," Holt said. "Tell me why you've suddenly decided to stop being a police officer."

"As I said," Johansson said, still cheerful. "It's time to have fun. No more business. But if you like, I could tell you why I became a police officer. How it all started, so to speak."

"Why did you become a police officer?" He hasn't changed, Holt thought.

"Because I like working things out," Johansson said. "That's always been my great passion. That and Pia, of course. The incomprehensible happiness of finding the woman of your life more than halfway through your time on earth."

And now that you know who killed the prime minister, it isn't so much fun finding things out anymore, Anna Holt thought. Which leaves your wife, because, after all, you still love her, she thought.

25.

One week later the Stockholm County police chief had called and asked if he could invite Holt for lunch. Preferably as soon as possible.

"That sounds lovely," Anna Holt said. Because they were both on the board of the same network for female police officers, because they liked each other, respected each other, and because there wasn't the slightest reason to say no.

"That sounds lovely. When did you have in mind?" Holt asked.

"Can you do Friday next week?" the county police chief had asked. "I thought we might eat in my office so we won't have to deal with all those strange men."

"Sounds like an excellent idea," Holt agreed.

Fortunately someone who wasn't the slightest bit like Johansson, she thought, as she hung up.

On Friday the next week she had been asked the same question.

"Would you like to become police chief of the Western District? I'd be very happy if you said yes."

"Yes," Holt said, and nodded. "I'd love to."

"It's a deal, then," said the county police chief, who didn't seem the slightest bit surprised.

Anna Holt's appointment had been made public at the start of January, and on Monday, March 3, she had started her new job. The mills of bureaucracy ground slowly. This time they had ground faster than they usually did.

Considering the job she had chosen, her honeymoon had lasted considerably longer than she had any right to expect. After six weeks as police chief of the Western District the county police chief had contacted her once more.

"We have to meet, Anna," she said. "At once, ideally. I want to ask you for a favor."

Why am I suddenly thinking that you sound almost like Johansson? Anna Holt wondered.

"You wanted to ask me for a favor?" Anna Holt said when she was sitting in the county police chief's office a couple hours later.

"Yes," she said, and looked as if she was getting ready to take the plunge.

"Out with it, then," Holt said with a smile.

"Evert Bäckström," the county police chief said.

"Evert Bäckström," Anna Holt repeated, not even trying to conceal her astonishment.

"Are we talking about the same Evert Bäckström who is currently with the Stockholm Police property tracing department? *The* Evert Bäckström, so to speak?"

"I'm afraid so," the county police chief said with a smile. Well, she made a good attempt at smiling, at any rate. A smile that she had to struggle to achieve.

"You have a vacant superintendent's post in the Western District. I want us to put Bäckström in it," she clarified.

"Considering that we know each other and that I respect you . . ."

"The respect is mutual, you know," the county police chief interjected.

" . . . I can only assume that you have very good reasons."

"I'll say," the county police chief said with feeling. "If only you knew. To deal with the practical side first, I was thinking that we could put him there for the time being, on a temporary placement, which means that we'd avoid any formal difficulties and still have our hands free if it turns out that isn't working. You don't have to worry about that."

"Hang on," Holt said, holding up her hands in a blocking gesture. "Before we do anything, I think I'd like to hear your arguments." A month or so into this new job, Holt thought. Then suddenly Bäckström tumbles from the sky. Right into my arms. Like a fallen angel, or rather a middle-aged, broken-winged, and very fat cherub.

"I've got several arguments if you can bear to hear them," the county police chief said, getting ready to take the plunge again. "If you can bear it?"

"Yes. Of course. I'm listening," Holt said.

To start with, Bäckström had a senior post. After all, he had actually been a superintendent with the National Criminal Investigation Department's own murder unit until his most senior boss had kicked him out and had him transferred back to Stockholm, where he had his basic post.

"For reasons that I've never managed to get entirely clear," the county police chief said. "He isn't a bad detective, after all. He's solved a large number of serious crimes."

"Hmm," said Holt, who had worked with him. "He runs round like a herd of elephants, tearing up everything in his path. Once the dust has settled, his colleagues usually manage to find one or two interesting things. Apart from the way he goes about things, I might actually agree with you. Whenever Bäckström is around, things do at least seem to happen."

"Yes, the man seems to have an inexhaustible amount of energy," the county police chief said with a deep sigh.

"Yes, it's completely incomprehensible, considering the way he lives and the way he looks," Holt agreed.

"His current posting in property was an unfortunate choice. It's not that any of his bosses have come up with anything concrete against him. But there's a huge amount of gossip. I don't actually think enough has been done to try to help him. He's been given work that doesn't interest him. Bäckström feels that he's been unfairly treated. Unfortunately there's a degree of justification in that, and the Police Officers' Association are on my back constantly. He also has excellent references. Outstanding references, actually."

The sort of references you get when your bosses want to get rid of you, Holt thought. How on earth had that happened? she thought, but contented herself with a nod.

"Anna," the county police chief said, with another sigh. "I have a feeling that you're the only person who can handle him. And if you fail, I promise to take him back. Maybe even sack him, although that would have the union demanding my head on a platter."

"I'm still listening," Holt said.

"Over the past six months he's been going round saying that he's uncovered a secret cabal that was involved in Palme's murder. And I was stupid enough to let him present a report about it. I can assure you, Anna . . ."

"I know," Anna Holt said. "I've heard him myself."

"Obviously it's ridiculous, especially when you consider that one of the people he identifies as being part of the cabal suddenly got in touch with me and asked me to help him. Help Bäckström, I mean. A senior member of parliament. He reckons Bäckström's the victim of official maltreatment. Several times over, no less."

"You want to give Bäckström something else to think about?" Holt said.

"Exactly," the county police chief said. "Serious violent crimes seem to be the only thing in his head anyway. And we're not exactly short of those in the Western District."

"Okay," Anna Holt said. "I promise to try my best, but before I make a decision I want to talk to the person who would be his immediate superior and hear what he thinks about it. I owe him that much."

"Go ahead, Anna," the county police chief said. "Just so you know, I've got my fingers crossed."

"Bäckström?" said Superintendent Toivonen, head of the crime unit in the Western District. "We're talking about Evert Bäckström? About him working under me?"

"Yes," Holt said. Toivonen, she thought. A legend within the Stockholm Police. Toivonen, who never backed away, never wasted time on pleasantries. Who always said what he thought and felt.

"Yes," Holt repeated. "I can understand that you might feel a certain reluctance."

"Fine," Toivonen said, shrugging. "I have no problem with Bäckström. If he starts causing trouble, he's the one who's going to have a problem."

"Fine?" Holt repeated. What's he saying? she thought.

"Completely fine," Toivonen said with a nod. "When's he coming?"

At last, Toivonen thought, as he left his boss. It had taken twenty-five years, but now at last it was time. Even though he had almost given up hope of ever having the chance to get even for all their past dealings. Just you wait, you fat little bastard, damn you, Toivonen thought, and the subject of his anger was his new colleague, Detective Superintendent Evert Bäckström.

Toivonen hadn't been up-front with his boss, Anna Holt. More than twenty-five years ago, when he was a young trainee officer—a "fox," as they were known in those days, and still are to officers of Toivonen's generation—he had done three months' work experience on the violent crime unit in central Stockholm. His supervisor had been Detective Inspector Evert Bäckström.

Instead of trying to teach the "fucking fox" anything about detection work, Bäckström had made him into his personal slave. In spite of Toivonen's proud background, generations of peasants and warriors from Karelia, Bäckström had treated him as a Russian serf. Used him to sort the chaos on Bäckström's desk, empty his wastepaper bin, make coffee, buy pastries, drive Bäckström around the city in a police car on mysterious errands that seldom seemed to have anything to do with work, stopping to buy hot dogs and mash for him whenever he got hungry. And he had had to pay with his meager trainee's wages, since Bäckström had always left his wallet in his office. Once, when they had been detailed to help guard an embassy, Bäckström had even made him polish his shoes for him and, when they got there, had presented him to the security staff as "my own fucking fox, a bastard Finn, you know."

Toivonen had been Swedish wrestling champion on several occasions, Greco-Roman as well as freestyle, and he could easily have broken every bone in Bäckström's body without even taking his hands out of his pockets. The thought was constantly there in the back of his mind, but because he had decided to become a police officer, a proper police officer, unlike his supervisor, he had gritted his teeth and resisted the urge. Generations of Karelian peasants and warriors had been adding bark to their bread since time immemorial. Twenty-five years later things were looking brighter. Considerably brighter.

That night Toivonen had had the most delightful dream. First he had softened up the fat little bastard with a standard Lindén hold, then tried both full and half nelsons, plus a few other tricks that used to get you disqualified in the days when he was active. Now that Bäckström was warmed up, he had gone on to a series of flying mares in quick succession. He had concluded with a scissors hold around his fat little neck. And there he lay, twenty-five years later, lilac blue in the face and flailing with his fat little hands while Toivonen panted with satisfaction and squeezed just a bit tighter.

26.

A couple years before he ended up with the Solna Police, Superintendent Evert Bäckström had been expelled from his natural habitat in the National Criminal Investigation Department to the property tracing department of Stockholm Police. Or the lost property store, as all proper police officers, Bäckström included, called this final resting place for stolen bicycles, lost wallets, and wayward police souls.

Bäckström was the victim of evil machinations. His former boss, Lars Martin Johansson, a bastard Lapp, eater of fermented herring and closet socialist, simply hadn't been able to deal with Bäckström's successful battle with increasingly organized crime. Instead he had woven a rope from all the individual slanderous strands, hung it round Bäckström's neck, and kicked the chair from beneath him himself.

The job in the lost property store was obviously a form of punishment. During the two years that followed Bäckström had been forced to look for stolen bicycles, an industrial digger that had disappeared, a yacht that turned out to have sunk in the outer archipelago, various items of environmentally hazardous waste, and barrels of shit. It would have broken the strongest man, but Bäckström had somehow put up with it. He had made the best of things. He had picked up one of his old contacts, a renowned art dealer, and had got a good tip-off, found a stolen oil painting worth fifty million, and made a nice little bit on the side while his cretinous bosses stole the glory from him. He was used to that, and he could live with it.

In the autumn of the previous year the same informant had given him some interesting information about who had killed Prime Minister Olof Palme, and he hadn't hesitated for a second. Fairly soon he had uncovered both the murder weapon and a cabal of four upstanding citizens. All of them undoubtedly deeply involved in the murder. They had shared roots going back many years. Right back to the sixties, when they all studied law together at Stockholm University and spent their free time on various perverse and criminal activities. Among other things, they had a secret society that they called Friends of the Cunt.

When Bäckström had been on the point of questioning one of them, who happened to be a former director of the Public Prosecution Authority and a current member of parliament for the Christian Democrats, the shadowy forces that Bäckström was on the trail of had hit back and tried to destroy him. His archenemy, Lars Martin Johansson, who had spent his whole life as the lackey of those in power, had sent him to the police state's own group of professional killers, the National Rapid-Response Unit. They had done their best to try to get rid of Bäckström, on one occasion throwing a shock grenade at his head. When they failed miserably in their objective, they had locked him away in a mental hospital.

But Bäckström got back on his feet, turned round, and hit back. Against all the odds. He had lined up the Police Officers' Association on his side, as well as powerful forces within the media and evidently one or two influential but anonymous figures who must secretly have sympathized with his struggle for basic justice.

A solitary figure is seldom strong—that was the bitter truth—but Bäckström had shown on more than one occasion that he was stronger than everyone else.

After only a few months he had been back at work. New piles of waste, but at the same time good opportunities to do a bit of work on the side for people who deserved it. All thoughts of finally solving the murder of the prime minister had been temporarily laid aside. Bäckström's victory had had its price, admittedly, but he had a long memory, and sooner or later he would get the chance to call in all outstanding debts.

And it looked like his enemies were starting to back down. That bastard Lapp, Johansson, had suddenly resigned with immediate effect, which is what it was called these days when someone got fired, and just a month ago the head of personnel for Stockholm Police had contacted him and offered him a post as a superintendent in the crime unit of the Western District. Suddenly he was a full-fledged citizen of the force once more, with access to all the goodies kept in police computers. The chance to help one or two old friends in trouble, and forewarned was also forearmed. No more barrels of shit and lost wallets, just your average criminals, people who had chopped their wives' heads off, blasted holes through the babysitter, or had a go at the neighbor's underage daughter.

"I promise I'll think about it," Bäckström told the head of personnel with a serious nod.

"It would be good if you could, Bäckström," the personnel head had said, leafing nervously through his papers. "Don't take too long—they need you, you know. Toivonen, he'd be your new boss, is keen to have you as soon as possible."

Toivonen, Bäckström thought. That Finnish joker, his little "fucking fox" who he had trained to do some neat tricks twenty-five years ago. Couldn't have turned out better, Bäckström thought.

The plan had been for Bäckström to start his new job as a violent crime detective with the Western District Police on Monday,

May 12. That was when his new appointment came into force. But because Bäckström was still Bäckström, he had decided to start by taking some extra time off. He had called the Western District and told them that he was unfortunately unable to come in that day. An old job from his previous posting, concerning the dumping of environmentally hazardous material, was going to court that day and Bäckström was obliged to be there and give testimony.

The following day was impossible as well. He was due to undergo a thorough medical examination with the Stockholm Police staff doctors. It was a thorough check that was expected to take all day. He was therefore unable to appear at his new workplace until Wednesday. Then, the day before that, he had received the news that had almost killed him—from a doctor who turned out to be a latter-day Dr. Mengele—and when he staggered off to the Solna police station on Wednesday, May 14, it was with mortality in his heart.

Now, just one week later, he was himself again.

Bäckström is back, as always, Bäckström thought, because obviously he spoke fluent English. Since he was a discerning and habitual television viewer, on top of everything else.

On Monday, May 12, Anna Holt's honeymoon was definitely over, and it didn't have anything to do with Bäckström.

That morning two thieves had intercepted and robbed a security transport just as it was leaving the gates to the VIP entrance of Bromma Airport. When the criminals had transferred their takings and were about to make off, one of the two guards had used a remote control to detonate the capsules of dye inside the money sack. Then everything had spiraled out of control. The raiders had performed a U-turn and had run down the first guard as he attempted to run off. One of the thieves had jumped out of the vehicle and fired a number of shots with an automatic weapon, killing one guard and seriously wounding the other. Then they had driven off, abandoning the vehicle and the sack of money scarcely a kilometer from the scene of the crime. And then they had vanished without a trace.

That was just the start of Holt's nightmare. That same night a renowned rogue from Finland had been shot outside his girl-friend's flat in Bergshamra when he was about to drive away. It wasn't clear where he was going or why, but in his hand he had been carrying a small suitcase containing everything from clean underwear and a toothbrush to a ten-millimeter pistol and a flick-knife. It was too late to ask him. Two shots to the head, definitely dead.

Toivonen, who was leading the search for the Bromma raid-ers, had long since stopped believing in coincidences of this sort. There was a connection here, and the following day his forensics experts had confirmed it. His latest murder victim had traces of red dye on both wrists. Dye that was difficult to wash off, and whose chemical composition, down to the last molecule, matched the dye that the security company used in their explosive capsules. It was also in the right place, if he had taken part in the raid, between his gloves and the sleeves of his black jacket.

Someone has started cleaning up after themselves, Toivonen thought.

When Bäckström's "pisshead murder" occurred two days later, Anna Holt had felt almost relieved. Finally a normal case, she thought. A gift from above, even. Soon she would have good cause to change her opinion on that matter.

27.

"What the hell do we do now?" Bäckström snarled, staring first at his colleague, then at the safe-deposit box.

"We have to call one of our senior officers at once, to make sure our backs are covered," Annika Carlsson said. "We have to make sure they come down here and seal—"

"Shut the damn box!" Bäckström said, unable to look at the wretched sight any longer. Dragging a literal-minded dyke with him when he had for once been let into Ali Baba's treasure chamber. And he had no signal on his phone either.

"The walls in a vault like this must be extremely thick," Annika Carlsson said. "If you like I can run up and call," she added, taking out her own phone.

"This is what we're going to do," Bäckström said, pointing at her with his short, stubby index finger. "You stay here, don't do anything, and if some bastard comes in, shoot him. And for God's sake, don't lose that damn box."

Then he had gone up into the main bank premises and called Toivonen. He had quickly explained the situation that had arisen and had asked for orders. To cover his back, Bäckström thought. If there had been any justice in the world, he would have been on his way to Rio by now.

"Who have you got with you?" Toivonen asked, not sounding particularly excited.

"The Anchor, Annika Carlsson."

"You've got the Anchor with you," Toivonen repeated. "How much money are we talking about here?"

"Must be millions," Bäckström said, and groaned.

"And you took the Anchor with you?"

"Yes," Bäckström said. Fuck, his voice sounds really weird, Bäckström thought. He can't be drunk, can he? Not at this time of day?

"Okay, then. Ask if you can have a plain paper bag, take the damn box with you, and get yourselves back out here, and I'll talk to Niemi and he can sort out the rest." The Anchor, Toivonen thought. This was all too much.

"But we need to cover our backs," Bäckström said. "I mean—"

"You've done that," Toivonen interrupted. "The Anchor will

stick to the rules until her dying breath, and she's as flexible as an old traffic cop and straight as a die. Just make sure you don't get any ideas, or she'll try out her cuffs on you."

As soon as he had hung up Bäckström got a paper bag from the bank official. He had signed a receipt for the box. And carried it out to the car himself, where he held it in his lap the whole way back to the Solna police station. Annika Carlsson drove and didn't say anything.

As soon as Toivonen had got off the phone he had gone out into the corridor, called his closest and most trusted colleagues into his office, and closed the door behind them.

Then he had explained what was going on in broad strokes, saving the punch line till last in the traditional way.

"Which one of our colleagues do you think the fat little bastard took with him?" Toivonen said, so delighted that he couldn't stand still.

Hesitant head shakes.

"The Anchor, Annika Carlsson," Toivonen said, his smile stretching from ear to ear.

"Poor bastard," Peter Niemi said, shaking his head. "We'll have to take his service revolver away from him so that he doesn't do himself any mischief."

A quarter of an hour later Bäckström had personally placed the paper bag containing the money on Niemi's desk. Annika Carlsson had faithfully clung to his side all the way from the garage to Niemi's office. Was the dyke trying to scare him? Suddenly she was walking like a fucking bodybuilder, thought Bäckström, who by this point hated every single fiber of Annika Carlsson's well-honed body.

"How much money do you think we're talking about, Bäckström? Are we talking millions, or what?" Niemi had asked with an innocent expression.

"I thought you might be able to tell us," Bäckström said. Get hold of some bastard who can count and just give me a receipt for the bastard box. I have to get out of here, Bäckström thought. I have to get out of this building. I need a stiff drink.

Two hours later he was sitting in the bar on his block with his second stiff drink and his second pint of beer. It hadn't helped, at least not yet, and it hadn't got any better when Niemi called him with the news.

"Two million, nine hundred thousand kronor," Niemi said. "Twenty-nine bundles, each worth a hundred thousand, and that was all," Niemi said, sounding as disinterested as if he were reading from a report in front of him. "No prints, and no other evidence either, but he must have been careful and worn gloves when he was touching the money. Anyway, congratulations."

"What?" Bäckström said. Now the bastard Lapp's just making fun of me, he thought.

"On finding all that money. Maybe Danielsson wasn't just your ordinary pisshead after all," Niemi concluded. "Was there anything else I can help you with?"

"Hello? Hello? I can hardly hear you," Bäckström said, switching off his phone and ordering another drink.

"A large one," Bäckström said.

"*Vojne, vojne,* Bäckström," his Finnish bartender said, smiling and nodding maternally.

28.

Another meeting of the investigating team. Arranged at short notice for eight o'clock that morning. Toivonen wanted to be updated about the new state of affairs. Bäckström had been forced to get up in the middle of the night to get there in time. Taxi, crashing headache, stopping en route to take on more fluids and get another pack of cough drops, two more headache pills, and almost a week since Danielsson had been murdered. By now he could have been sitting on the beach at Copacabana with a single malt in one hand and a nice local lass on each knee, Bäckström thought. If it hadn't been for that dyke.

When he was sitting in the taxi the public prosecutor had called and told him that unless some "new, compelling evidence regarding Roland Stålhammar" emerged during the course of the meeting, she was intending to release him after lunch.

"I hear what you're saying," Bäckström said. "The only thing bothering me is that he might have a decent amount of money for his travels when he gets out."

"People like Stålhammar don't usually manage to keep themselves hidden," the prosecutor retorted. "If they go to Thailand, and that's where they usually go, they usually end up coming home of their own accord after a month or so."

"I wouldn't know," Bäckström said. "I don't socialize with people like Stålhammar. But if you say so. Was there anything else?" he asked.

"I think that was everything. By the way, I think you and your colleagues have done a good job so far," the prosecutor said comfortingly.

And what would you know about police work, you tight-snatched little bitch? Bäckström thought, switching off his cell.

At eight o'clock precisely Toivonen had walked into the room, and in contrast to the last time he appeared to be in an excellent mood.

"How's things, Bäckström?" Toivonen said, slapping him on the shoulder. "You look like you're raring to go; hope you had a good night."

Fucking fox, Bäckström thought.

"Perhaps you'd like to start, Nadja?" Bäckström said, nodding in her direction. Not only had he lost almost three million, but the

Russian had won a bottle of vodka off him, and how the hell am I going to get out of that one? Bäckström thought.

Nadja Högberg had spoken to the two women who had set up the Writer's Cottage Ltd. twenty years ago. One of the first things they had done had been to set up a safe-deposit box for the company on Valhallavägen in Stockholm.

"They both worked in an advertising agency nearby," Nadja explained, "so it was a practical solution. The whole thing was only ever supposed to provide them with a bit of extra money."

Which was an idea that hadn't turned out very well. There hadn't been enough customers right from the start, and when their boss at the advertising agency discovered what they were doing, he had objected. Either they resigned from the agency or they gave up the company.

By that point the capital they had got from shares, fifty thousand kronor, was more or less exhausted. They had spoken to the man who looked after their accounting, Karl Danielsson, and asked for his help. Danielsson had done so, selling their business to one of his other clients for one krona. Someone that they had never met, and whose name they didn't even know. Danielsson had prepared all the paperwork. They had met him in his office and signed everything. They had waived the single-krona fee. And that was that.

"But apparently he did offer," Nadja said. "He took out one krona and put it on the desk."

"A nice gesture," Bäckström said. "Anything else, Nadja?"

"Quite a lot more," Nadja said. "Putting aside the two-point-nine million in his safe-deposit box, I think we've got hold of completely the wrong end of the stick as far as our victim is concerned," she said in the colloquial language that she sometimes fell into.

"What do you mean, *putting aside*?" Bäckström said. Two-point-nine million and I could have been in Rio by now, he thought.

"In his other company, Karl Danielsson Holdings Ltd., there seems to be considerably more than that," Nadja Högberg said.

"The pisshead had even more dough? How much more?" Bäckström said suspiciously.

"I was going to come back to that," Nadja said. "First I thought I'd say something about how much he might have got out from the safe-deposit box on the day he was murdered.

"The box is the smallest model, thirty-six centimeters long, twenty-seven centimeters across, and about eight centimeters deep. Space for seven thousand, seven hundred, and seventy-six cubic centimeters, or almost eight liters," she went on. "If you imagine filling it with thousand-kronor notes in bundles of a hundred thousand, it's got room for roughly eight million."

"Eight million, the little foxy bastard," Bäckström said. Fuck, that's criminal, he thought.

"If it had been euros, in the largest denomination of five hundred euros—and they're considerably smaller than our thousand-kronor notes, even though they're worth almost five times as much—there'd be space for something like fifty million," Nadja said with a wry smile. "And if it had been dollars in the highest denomination, five thousand dollars, you know, the one with President Madison on the front—I think they're called Madisons—then there would have been almost half a billion Swedish kronor in Danielsson's safe-deposit box," Nadja said with a broad smile.

"You're pulling our leg, Nadja," Alm said, shaking his head. "What about all those bags our bank robbers haul away with them? How do you explain those?"

"Danielsson must have been the richest pisshead in the world," Bäckström said. He must have been, surely? he thought.

"Low-denomination notes," Nadja said. "Probably hundreds, on average. If you fill our box with hundred-kronor notes, you might get a million in there. If you fill it with twenties, there's hardly room for three hundred thousand."

"So the bastard could have had half a billion in his fucking safe-deposit box?" Bäckström said, completely fascinated in spite of himself.

"I don't imagine so for a second," Nadja said, shaking her head. "I think he had at most eight million in there. To answer your question, Bäckström, I don't think he was the richest pisshead in the world. But on the other hand, I do know that many of the world's richest men are pissheads."

"Which means that he could have taken out five million or so last week," Annika Carlsson said. Back to his flat, she thought. In a case that he placed in his living room, on top of the television.

"If we're talking about a briefcase or attaché case of the most common sort, and—from the descriptions I've seen—that's what we're dealing with here, then it wouldn't have room for five million in thousand-kronor notes," Nadja said. "All these calculations are based on assumptions, of course," she said. "But I've come up with the following calculations, if you want to hear them."

"I'm happy to hear them," Toivonen said with a contented smile.

"Well, to start with, I'm assuming he was there to take out some money," Nadja said. "Obviously he might have removed something else, written notes or something, but I've assumed he was taking out money.

"Then I'm assuming that we're dealing with thousand-kronor notes, in bundles of a hundred thousand, the same as we actually found in the box. And I'm assuming that he put them in a case matching the most common sort of attaché case."

"So how much does it come to?" Toivonen said, for some reason grinning at Bäckström.

"Three million maximum," Nadja said. "But even then you'd have to pack them very carefully, so I think it was less than that. Maybe a couple million," she said with a shrug. "But all this is pure speculation, you understand."

"Has anyone checked if Niemi's bought a new car?" Stigson said, grinning at the others.

"Careful, lad," Toivonen said, glaring at him. "You mentioned his business, Nadja. How much money did he have in there, then?"

"According to the annual accounts, it has a taxable capital sum of about twenty million," Nadja said. "It's worth remembering that this is a limited company with the smallest permitted amount of share capital, a hundred thousand kronor. With Danielsson as its managing director, chairman of the board, and sole owner. The other board member is his old friend Mario Grimaldi, and the co-opted member, Roland Stålhammar."

"Who'd have thought it?" Toivonen said with a crooked smile. "So how much is just hot air?" he went on.

"I've found ten million," Nadja said. "Shares, bonds, other valuable documents in the company's boxes with the SE Bank and Carnegie. The other ten million are supposed to be in foreign accounts, but because I haven't got the paperwork I need from the prosecutor in order to be able to ask them, I don't know. I'd guess that the money's actually there. These annual accounts seem to have been compiled with scrupulous regard to the letter of the law. No, the real problem is something else."

"What's that, then?" Toivonen asked.

"His accounting. We haven't got his accounting records. He's obliged to keep them for ten years, but we haven't been able to find any documentation at all," Nadja concluded with a shrug.

"This almost sounds like something we should hand over to the Financial Crime Unit," Toivonen said.

"That's what I think too," Nadja said. "If you want me to have time to do anything else, we're going to have to."

"Okay, that's what we'll do. Write me a summary and I'll get it sorted at once," Toivonen said. "One more question: When did Danielsson start making all this money?"

"In the last six or seven years," Nadja said. "Before that his company wasn't much to boast about. But six, seven years ago things started to go better and better. It earned a couple million each year on various investments, shares, bonds, options, and other sources, and with interest and the interest on the interest his assets have at least kept up with the rise of the stock market."

"Interesting," Toivonen said, getting up. "It looks like Danielsson wasn't just your average pisshead," he said. For some reason he smiled and nodded toward Bäckström.

29.

"Have we got anything else?" Bäckström asked, glaring at the space left by Toivonen as he went.

"There's the stuff you asked me to look into, boss," Felicia Pettersson said, holding her hand up politely. "The idea that there was something odd about that paperboy. The one who found the body, Septimus Akofeli. I think I've worked out what it is. The odd thing, I mean. I went through his phone list, and I uncovered quite a bit that contradicts what he told us when we interviewed him."

Who'd have thought it? Bäckström thought. So the pretty little darkie had come out of her shell. Even if she was still wet behind the ears.

"What was it, then?" said Bäckström, who wanted to go off to the bathroom and drink a few liters of cold water and take a couple more paracetamol and a little mint mouthwash on top. Maybe he could get away from this madhouse and get back home to his cozy abode, where the fridge and cupboards were once again stocked to their old standard.

"Akofeli had a pay-as-you-go phone," Felicia Pettersson said. "The sort of cell where no one knows who the subscriber is. On Thursday, May fifteenth, when Danielsson was found, he made ten calls in total. The first one was at six minutes past six in the morning, when he calls the emergency number. That conversation lasted about three minutes—one hundred and ninety-two seconds, to be precise," she said, nodding toward the sheet of paper in her hand. "Immediately after that, at nine minutes past six, he calls another number, belonging to another pay-as-you-go cell. The call was ended after fifteen seconds, when the voice mail clicked in. Then he called the same number again, and that call is also terminated after fifteen seconds. Then a minute passes before he dials the same number for a third time. That call is ended after five seconds. At eleven minutes past six, to be precise, and that's what's interesting."

"Why?" Bäckström said, shaking his head. "What is it that makes it so interesting?"

"That's when our first patrol entered the building at number one Hasselstigen. I get the impression that when Akofeli heard someone coming, he ended the call and put his cell away."

"What about the other calls, then?" Bäckström said, making an effort to look as sharp as anyone could with the hangover he had.

"At nine o'clock or so he called his work to say that he was going to be late," Pettersson said, for some reason looking at Annika Carlsson.

"He asked me for permission before he called," Carlsson confirmed with a nod.

"The next call was also to his work. He made the call just before he left Hasselstigen."

First one call to the police, then three to some damn pay-as-you-go cell, then two to work. One plus three plus two makes . . . Yes, what the hell does it make? thought Bäckström, who had already lost the thread.

"The seventh call was made just after lunch," Felicia Pettersson went on. "At twelve thirty-one, to be precise. He calls a business that is a client of the courier service he works for. He's supposed to be picking up a package but has the wrong door code."

"How do you know that?" Bäckström asked.

"Because the customer has gone to lunch. He doesn't answer.

So he then makes his eighth call to the courier company to see if they can find the right door code."

"You've spoken to them?" Bäckström said. "Why did you do that? Was that sensible?" Young shits, he thought.

"I think so," Felicia said with a nod. "But I'll get to that."

What the hell is the pretty little thing saying? Bäckström wondered. We're going to have to have a little chat about respect and authority, he thought.

"He makes the ninth call after he finished work, at seven or so that evening, and the tenth and final call is made four hours later. At quarter past eleven that evening. Both calls are to the same pay-as-you-go cell that he tried to call that morning. He gets no answer, and both calls are terminated after seven seconds, which has to mean that the owner had switched the phone off. So out of a total of ten calls he made that day, five of them were to the same pay-as-you-go number, and we have no idea who owns that phone."

"It doesn't necessarily have to mean anything except that he was calling a friend to tell them what had been happening to him," Bäckström said, sounding as cross as he felt. "Don't all people like that have pay-as-you-go phones? That's the whole point, isn't it? That you can't be traced?"

"Yes, I know. I've got a pay-as-you-go phone myself. It's actually quite practical," she said, looking at Bäckström without seeming the slightest bit bothered.

"Okay," Bäckström said, trying to make his voice softer, since Annika Carlsson's eyes had already narrowed considerably. "I'm sorry, Felicia, but I still don't understand what's so odd about any of this."

"It's because he's disappeared," Felicia Pettersson said. "Septimus Akofeli has disappeared."

"Disappeared," Bäckström said. What's she saying? he thought.

"Disappeared," Felicia went on, nodding. "He's probably been missing since Friday. That morning he delivered the papers as usual, but he never showed up at the courier firm where he works during the day. It's the first time this has happened, and he's actually worked there for over a year. His cell is also completely dead as of Friday. Switched off. The last call from his cell is the one he made at quarter past eleven on Thursday evening, to the pay-as-you-go number with the unknown owner, and since then it's been switched off."

"I'm listening," Bäckström said, nodding encouragingly. So sooty pinched the briefcase, he was thinking.

"They tried calling him from work several times on Friday," Felicia went on. "When he didn't come to work on Monday, one of his colleagues goes round to his home and rings on the door. He lives out in Rinkeby, at seventeen Fornbyvägen, but there was no answer. So he went back outside and looked through the window. He lives in a one-room flat on the ground floor, and the curtains weren't fully closed. The flat looked empty, according to his workmate. So, if he wasn't hiding to avoid having to answer the door, he wasn't home. Later that day the head of the courier firm reported him missing, and because he lives in our police district, this is where the report ended up. I came across it when I was checking him out, and that was when I called his work.

"To answer your previous question, boss," Felicia Pettersson concluded, looking at Bäckström with a perfectly correct expression on her face.

"This isn't good," Bäckström said, shaking his head. "We'll have to try to find . . . find Akofeli. Can you take it, Annika?"

"Felicia and I can," Annika Carlsson said with a nod.

"Good," Bäckström said, getting up with a jerk. "Keep me informed," he said.

"One more thing," Bäckström said, stopping in the doorway and letting his gaze sweep over his colleagues before settling on Felicia Pettersson.

"This business of the calls to that pay-as-you-go number, and the fact that he's gone missing, obviously isn't good. We've got to get to the bottom of this, and it's good that you came up with it,

Felicia. But that still isn't what's bothering me," Bäckström said, shaking his head.

"There's something else bothering me about Akofeli," he repeated.

"Like what?" Annika Carlsson asked.

"Don't know, I'm still working on it," he said, nodding and smiling in spite of his headache. That gave them something to chew on, he thought, as he stepped out into the corridor, since the only thing that was bothering him right now was the lack of a large—very large—and very cold Czech lager.

He could hardly be bothered with people like that sooty. Anyone with a brain ought to be able to work it out, he thought. All the shit that people like that get up to, and I bet he was the one who took that briefcase. If it wasn't Niemi or Hernandez, of course. Any snotty-nosed little kid could see it wasn't Stålhammar. He was probably delighted with the meager amount he'd been able to pinch from the victim's wallet.

Stålhammar beats Danielsson to death. Takes the contents of his wallet and staggers home to Järnvägsgatan. Misses the briefcase containing millions.

Akofeli finds the body. Takes a snoop around Danielsson's flat. Finds the briefcase. Hides it somewhere. Opens it later in peace and quiet. Discovers that he's suddenly become a millionaire. And sets off for Tahiti. Nothing more to it than that. And if it wasn't him, then it was probably Niemi and his little Chilean friend. Okay, high time to get a bite to eat, he thought.

30.

Green Carriers had their offices on Alströmergatan on Kungsholmen. On the way there Annika Carlsson and Felicia Pettersson had discussed the new state of affairs. Anything else would have been peculiar, and almost a dereliction of duty for a couple of proper police officers.

"So what do we think about all this, Felicia?" Annika Carlsson said.

"I hope I'm wrong," Felicia said, "but the most likely scenario is unfortunately that Akofeli nicked the briefcase and hid it somewhere nearby before he called the emergency desk. After all, we've only got his word for it that he called as soon as he found Danielsson."

"Yes, I'm afraid that might be what happened. It doesn't seem unlikely, at any rate."

"Which probably means that Akofeli is out of the country by now," Felicia concluded.

"I've already spoken to the prosecutor," Annika Carlsson said. "As soon as we're done with the couriers we can go on to Akofeli's flat."

"We'll have to arrange to get a set of keys," Felicia Pettersson said.

"I've already spoken to the property management company," Annika Carlsson said with a smile. "What do you take me for?"

"I take you for the kind of person I like," Felicia said. "Just teasing, that's all."

Green Carriers were on the ground floor, with a sign over the door and half a dozen cycles lined up right across the pavement.

"If you were coming down here with a pushchair, you'd have to step onto the road," Annika Carlsson said with a frown.

"*Cool it, babe,*" Felicia Pettersson said in English, flashing her a broad smile. "Maybe deal with that at the end?"

"You can do the talking," Carlsson said. "This is your lead."

First they had spoken to Akofeli's boss, a Jens Johansson—"call me Jensa, everyone who works here does"—who looked like your standard Swedish computer nerd, and who seemed to be considerably older than Akofeli. Most of all he seemed worried. You could see it in his eyes in spite of his thick glasses.

"This isn't like Mister Seven," he said. "Septimus, in other words. We call him Seven, since that's what his name means in Latin," he explained, at the same time shaking his head to emphasize what he said. "He hasn't missed a day since he started working here, and that's eighteen months ago now."

"What's he like as a person?" Annika Carlsson asked, in spite of the promise she had made five minutes before.

"Brilliant," his boss said. "Excellent cyclist, in great shape, always happy to take on a job, even if the roads are like a winter rally circuit out there. Honest, decent, good with customers. Loads of energy. Cares about the environment. That's important here. We're big on that. Everyone who works here has to care about the environment."

"So what do you think has happened?" Felicia Pettersson asked. I'm the one asking the questions here, she thought.

"It must have something to do with that damn murder. Maybe he saw something he shouldn't have. At worst, someone might have wanted him out of the way. That's what the talk round here is saying, anyway."

"Did he seem at all worried when he got here on Thursday?"

"No. He didn't really want to talk about it. Everyone kept asking him, of course. I mean, how often do you come across a body that's just been murdered? It's never happened to me, anyway," Jensa said, polishing his glasses agitatedly. "Nor to anyone else working here, or anyone I know. And then he just disappears. That's got to be too much of a coincidence. In terms of the timing, I mean."

"I hear what you're saying," Felicia said. "Who was his best friend here at work?"

"Lawman," Jensa said. "Nisse Munck. A law student. His dad's supposed to be some hotshot lawyer. He's here now, by the way. Sitting down in the basement, polishing his own racing bike. He rides in races. Mind you, he isn't exactly Girot or Touren, if you ask me," Jensa said, lowering his voice. "Would you like to talk to him?"

"Please," Felicia said. "If he can spare the time out of the saddle."

Lawman was remarkably similar to his boss, complete with glasses and all, and apart from his long, muscular legs, he didn't look much like a professional racer.

"Of course I asked," Lawman said. "Criminal law's my thing. I'm going to set up my own practice doing that as soon as I've graduated. Criminal case lawyer, own firm," Lawman clarified.

"What did he say, then?" Felicia Pettersson asked.

"Said he didn't want to talk about it," Lawman said. "I can understand that. Can't have been nice. I went online and looked as soon as I got home on Thursday—it sounds like a whole chainsaw-massacre thing. Well, they mentioned an ax in the article."

"But the two of you didn't talk about what he'd been through?" Annika Carlsson repeated.

"I tried," Lawman said. "Mister Seven didn't want to talk. Okay, okay. Work to do. New jobs all the time. And we don't exactly ride tandems here, you know?"

"That was all?" Annika Carlsson nodded to him.

"Yes, I think so."

"He didn't say anything else? Didn't ask anything?"

"Now that you come to mention it," Lawman said. "He did have one question. It was just before I went home. It was a bit of a weird question, but everyone here asks me stuff all the time."

"What, about legal matters?" Felicia said.

"Yes," Lawman said with a nod. "Never-ending unpaid consultations. Mostly family law. What happens if my girlfriend kicks me out into the street and my name's not on the lease? What about the fridge we paid for together? That sort of thing. Even though I keep telling them that criminal law's my thing."

"The weird question?" Felicia reminded him.

"He asked about the right of self-defense," Lawman said. "What it was like in Sweden if someone attacked you and you tried to defend yourself. How far you could go, basically."

"So what did you say?"

"First I told him it was a fucking weird question. Then I asked if Seven had beaten the old guy to death because he attacked him for giving him the wrong paper or something. Some customers go a bit far sometimes. But that wasn't it. Seven told me to lay off all that kind of thing. Nothing like that. *No way*," Lawman said.

"Do you remember what his exact words were?" Felicia persisted.

"How far you have the right to go. Suppose someone tried to kill you. Did that give you the right to kill them? That was pretty much it."

"And what did you say in response?" Annika Carlsson repeated.

"Yes. And no. You should know this, shouldn't you? The right to use the level of force motivated by the danger posed by the attack. Plus the extra force necessary to disarm your opponent. I told him he could forget doing anything else. Like that extra kick just for the hell of it when your attacker's already on the ground."

"Did you get the impression that Seven was asking on his own account? That he had ever been the victim of an attack?" Annika Carlsson asked.

"Are you kidding?" Lawman said. "Seven grew up in Somalia. The victim of an attack? Take a look at the Internet. Welcome to planet earth, officer."

"I mean here in Sweden," Annika Carlsson clarified. "Had he been the victim of an attack in Sweden?"

"Yes, I asked him that," Lawman said. "He denied it categorically, as I've already said. Apart from all the racists that someone like Seven has to put up with, of course. Send idiots like that back to live in their cozy Nordic caves, if you want to know what I think."

"Did you get the impression that he was asking on someone else's behalf?" Felicia Pettersson asked.

"I didn't ask him that, actually," Lawman said. "Considering what he'd been through that morning, I suppose it wasn't really that weird. The fact that I assumed he was talking about himself, I mean. That's wasn't weird, was it?"

"No, definitely not," Felicia said with a smile.

After that they had left. Jensa had followed them onto the street and had thus given Annika Carlsson an unsought opportunity to live up to her reputation in the Solna police station.

"Talking about caring about the environment," Carlsson said. "What do you think would happen if you tried to get past here on the pavement with a pushchair?"

"Fixed, fixed, I'll sort it," Jensa said, raising both hands in a gesture of surrender.

"Good," Annika Carlsson said. "I'll expect it to be next time we come by."

"How do we interpret this, then? That business of his question about self-defense?" Felicia said. "The plot thickens, Detective Inspector. It's high time to enlighten a younger colleague."

"The fact that Danielsson died the evening before Akofeli found him is quite clear," Annika Carlsson said.

"The coroner," Felicia agreed with a nod.

"Not just that," Annika Carlsson said. "I was there at seven o'clock, and Niemi and Chico hadn't arrived by then, so I took the opportunity to touch him."

"Tut, tut," Felicia said, smiling broadly. "No looking with your fingers. My lecturer in forensics was always going on about that when I was training."

"Must have forgotten that," Annika Carlsson said. "Anyway, I was wearing gloves."

"And?"

"He was stiff as a board," Annika Carlsson said. "So I have no quarrel with our medical friends at all. Not this time. We're in complete agreement."

"Right, then," Felicia said. "What do you think about getting a bite to eat before heading out to Rinkeby? There's a decent sushi bar in the Solna shopping center."

"Done," said Annika Carlsson, who was already thinking about something else. What's this really all about? Annika Carlsson thought. This is just getting more and more peculiar, she thought.

31.

While his colleagues were presumably running around like headless chickens, Bäckström had paid a visit to a discreet restaurant in the center of Solna. He had eaten pork chops with mushrooms in a cream sauce and potato croquettes, washed down with beer. He had even downed a couple quick shots while he kept a close eye on the door. It was far from out of the question that Toivonen and Niemi might try to do some crafty drinking in working hours, and he wasn't the sort who wanted to be taken by surprise by a couple Finnish bastards.

After a cup of coffee and a little Napoleon cake, and a period of meditation and reflection, he had returned to the police station. Strengthened in both mind and body, he had gone in via the garage and met his good friend, the garage attendant.

"You want to borrow the shack and take the weight off your feet for a while?" his compadre said.

"Well, if it's free," Bäckström said.

"Go ahead. The drugs lads were out all night on a job, so they're at home snoring in their pigsties."

"Wake me in a couple hours," Bäckström said. "I've been at it pretty much for twenty-four hours now, so it's high time I had a bit of a rest."

Two hours later he was sitting in his office. His head clear as glass, his tongue sharp as a razor, and the first one to experience this was their prosecutor, who called to let him know that she had released Roland Stålhammar from custody.

The situation had become more complicated. According to the prosecutor, it didn't look like Danielsson was just an ordinary pisshead. And that was putting it mildly. She would have been delighted if she had just a tenth of the money he had.

The same thing seemed to go for Stålhammar. He didn't look like an ordinary pisshead either. He was also a former colleague of Bäckström's, and given the new facts that had emerged about the victim, it was entirely feasible that the motive and perpetrator were completely unlike those you would expect to see in an ordinary fight between two completely ordinary pissheads.

"Absolutely," Bäckström said. "I completely agree with you. No matter what we might think about pissheads like Stålhammar, we mustn't forget that the vast majority of pissheads don't actually beat anyone to death or even get beaten to death. In fact, the number of pissheads that beat someone to death is pretty much exactly the same as the number of pissheads that get beaten to death."

"How do you mean?" the prosecutor said suspiciously.

"That Stålhammar isn't an ordinary pisshead," Bäckström said. There, that gave her something to chew on, a real Mensa test, he thought, as he hung up.

Then he had taken out a pen and paper and spent the next two hours listing all the main and subsidiary lines of inquiry of his case. He concluded by writing a list of things that his colleagues needed to do. Presumably they had all learned to read by now, Bäckström thought, glancing at the clock. Five o'clock already, and high time he went home, but just as he realized this he was interrupted by a knock on his door.

"Come in," Bäckström grunted.

"Sorry to disturb you," Nadja Högberg said. "I know it's time to go home now, at least that's what I was thinking, but before you go I wanted to give you this," she said, handing over a plastic bag that, to judge by its shape, contained a very large bottle. Vodka, and a whole liter at that—Russian, to judge by the label, a brand that he didn't know and couldn't read either.

"And to what do I owe this honor?" Bäckström said with a cheerful expression. "Come in and sit down, and shut the door so we don't start tongues wagging."

"Our little bet," Nadja said. "I've been feeling guilty about it."

"I thought I was the one who owed you a bottle. I was actually thinking of stopping off on the way home and getting one for you," Bäckström lied. "Feeling guilty? What makes you say that?"

"Even before we made our wager, I was starting to suspect that Danielsson might have a whole lot of money," Nadja said. "I was busy looking into his business affairs, so that idea of the pot of gold wasn't exactly plucked from thin air. So I'm the one who owes you a bottle. You don't owe me anything."

"A little drink, maybe?" Bäckström said with a nod, looking even happier now. "After a hard day at work full of trials and tribulations." Fuck, they're shrewd, these Russians, he thought. The bitch had just sat there, playing it cool, figuring out how to trick me out of the whole bet. Then she gets sentimental. And the next day her conscience gets the better of her and she decides to put things right.

"Well, maybe just a little one," Nadja said. "It's the best vodka you can get, by the way, better that Stolichnaya, Kubanskaya, or Moskovskaya. It's called Standard, and you can't get it in Sweden. My family usually bring a few bottles when they come to visit."

"It'll be interesting to see what it tastes like," Bäckström the connoisseur said. He had already taken two glasses and a bag of cough drops out of his desk drawer. "There we go, glasses and a little something for after," he explained, pointing at the throat sweets.

"I've got a jar of pickled gherkins in the fridge," Nadja said, looking dubiously at the bag of mints. "I think I'll go and get that instead."

Not just gherkins, it turned out. When she returned she had with her a sourdough loaf, smoked sausage, and cured ham.

Probably because of all those world wars they've been through, Bäckström thought. A proper Russian always makes sure they've got supplies within reach in case it all kicks off.

"Cheers, Nadja," Bäckström said, biting into a large slice of sausage and raising his glass.

"*Nazdrovje*," Nadja said, smiling with all her gold teeth, and then snapping her neck back and downing the vodka without so much as a blink.

Fuck, Bäckström thought, a quarter of an hour later, after another sturdy Russian drink, a whole gherkin, and half a sausage. These Russian bastards have a lot of heart. If you just make a bit of effort and gain their trust, he thought.

"What could be better than this, Nadja?" Bäckström said, pouring them a third glass. "All we're missing is a balalaika and some Cossacks jumping about on top of the desk."

"This is good," Nadja said. "I'm happy to skip the Cossacks, but a balalaika might have been nice."

"Tell me about yourself, Nadja," Bäckström said. "How come you ended up here? In the bosom of Mother Svea, here in the High North." A lot of heart, he thought. And he'd never tasted vodka that was anywhere near as good as this. Have to get hold of a crate of this, he thought.

"Are you sure you want to hear it?" Nadja said.

"I'm listening," Bäckström said. He leaned back in his chair and smiled his warmest smile.

So Nadja had told him. How Nadjesta Ivanova had left the disintegrating Soviet empire. How she ended up in Sweden and became Nadja Högberg and had spent the past ten years working as a civilian investigator for the crime unit in the Western District.

Not that it had been altogether straightforward. After graduation she had worked as a risk analyst within the nuclear energy industry and had worked at several nuclear power stations in the Baltic region.

The first time she applied for permission to leave her homeland was 1991, two years after the liberation of 1989. At that time she was working at a nuclear power station in Lithuania, not far from the Baltic coast. She never got a reply. One week later she was summoned by her boss, who told her she was being transferred to another nuclear power station some thousand kilometers farther north, just above Murmansk. Some taciturn men had helped her pack her meager belongings. They had driven her to her new workplace and hadn't left her side for a moment during the two days the journey had taken.

Two years later she didn't bother asking for permission. With the help of some "contacts" she had got across the border into Finland. She had been met by new contacts, and the next morning she woke up in a house in the country somewhere in Sweden.

"That was the autumn of 1993," Nadja said with a wry smile. "I spent six weeks there, talking to my new hosts—I've never been so well looked after in my life—and one year later, as soon as I had learned Swedish, I became a Swedish citizen and got my own flat and a job."

Military intelligence. Good lads, not like those idiots in the Security Police, Bäckström thought, feeling his heart swell with patriotic pride.

"What job did you get?" Bäckström said.

"I forget," Nadja said with a wry smile. "Then I got a different one, as an interpreter for the Stockholm Police. That was in 1995, I remember that."

The Security Police, Bäckström thought. Mean bastards who never worked out that Russians are mostly all heart if you know how to deal with them in the right way.

"What about Högberg?" Bäckström asked, curious.

"That's a whole different story," Nadja said with a smile. "We met on the Internet, then I divorced him. He was a bit too Russian for my liking, if you get what I mean," she said, raising her glass.

"Well, cheers, then," Nadja said with another smile.

"Nazdrovje," Bäckström said. Nothing but heart, he thought.

32.

Detective Inspector Lars Alm and Sergeant Jan O. Stigson had spent most of the day interviewing a couple of Danielsson's old friends, Halvar "Halfy" Söderman and Mario "Godfather" Grimaldi. Alm had been hoping that Annika Carlsson would go with him, considering what Söderman had got up to with that restaurant owner, but evidently other more important matters had come up and he had to make do with Stigson.

They had started with Halvar Söderman, who lived on Vintergatan down in Gamla Solna, behind the football stadium and just a few hundred meters from the scene of the crime. They had called him first on his phone. No answer. Then they had gone to his flat and knocked on the door. After a series of unanswered knocks, Söderman had suddenly thrown open the door in the evident hope of hitting Stigson in the head with it. Alm had seen this before and recognized the danger in advance. As soon as he saw someone behind the peephole in the door he had pushed Stigson aside, grabbed the edge of the door, and given it an extra-hard tug. Söderman had landed on his backside in his own stairwell, and he wasn't happy.

"Whoops," Alm said. "That could have been really nasty."

"What the fuck do you want, fucking idiots?" Söderman yelled.

"Police," Alm said. "We'd like to talk to you. We can do it here or we can take you down to the station. We can even lock you up first if you keep messing with us."

Söderman wasn't that stupid. He made do with glaring at them, and two minutes later they were sitting around the table in his little dining room.

"I recognize you, don't I?" he said, staring at Alm. "Don't you work in violent crime in Stockholm?"

"Used to," Alm said. "Now I work here in Solna."

"Ah, you must be an old friend of Roly's," Söderman concluded. "Can't you have a word with those idiots that have him locked up?"

"He was released an hour ago," Alm said, without going into the details.

"Is that so? Really, is that so?" he said with a grin. "Can I offer you anything?"

"Thank you, no," Alm said. "We won't be long."

"But you could manage a quick cup of coffee? I'm going to have a java. The coffee machine's loaded and ready to go."

"Coffee would be good," Alm said.

"What about you?" Söderman said, nodding in Stigson's direction. "I suppose you'd like a banana?"

"Coffee would be good," Stigson said.

"How long is it since you switched?" Söderman said, looking at Alm.

"Switched?" Alm said. "How do you mean?"

"From Alsatians to chimpanzees," Söderman said with a grin.

"It was a while back," Alm said.

Söderman had got out his best china. Sugar, milk, cream, even schnapps in case anyone was in the mood. He always had some in the house. But sadly there was no cognac left. But he did have a splash of banana liqueur in the cupboard.

"In case I have women round," he explained, nodding in Alm's direction. "But it's fine if the monkey wants some," he went on, nodding in Stigson's direction. "If it's okay with his master, it's okay with me."

"Black's good for me, thanks," Alm said. "The monkey will take his black too."

"Yes, there's a lot of black these days," Söderman sighed. "The other day I amused myself by counting them as I headed down to the Solna center to get some shopping. Do you know how many I saw? On a little walk of four hundred meters?"

"Twenty-seven," Alm said.

"No." Söderman sighed, pouring the coffee. "I gave up counting when I got to a hundred. Do you know how old I was before I saw my first proper Negro?" he went on.

"No," Alm said.

"I was born in thirty-six," Söderman said. "I must have been seventeen before I saw my first Negro. That was in 1953, down in the old Solna center, outside Lorry. The bar, you know the one. They'd only just opened earlier that year. It was like a street party. Everyone wanted to go up to him and slap him on the back and talk English—fucking weird English, mind—and ask him if he knew Louis Armstrong. I had a bird with me, name of Sivan. Sivan Frisk, and she wasn't backward in coming forward, if you know what I mean. Fuck, she was wet, right down to her feet before I managed to drag her away from there."

"Another age," Alm said neutrally.

"That's the difference, though, isn't it?" Söderman said with a sigh. "One is fine, two, even. Especially if you've grown up in a place like this. An old working-class district. All the old Solna boys of my generation. But three is too much. One is fine, two is fine, but three is too much."

"A completely different thing," Alm said.

"You want to know what I was doing on Wednesday evening

last week?" Söderman interrupted. "The same evening some fucking madman beat Kalle to death?"

"Yes," Alm said. "What were you doing then?"

"I've already told your lot," Söderman said. "Some fucking simpleton from the cop shop phoned me up, going on and on about it. Yesterday, the day before? Don't remember."

"What did you tell them?" Alm asked, without letting on that he was the one who had called.

"I tried to explain that I had an alibi, but he didn't want to hear it. So I hung up. I told him to go to hell too."

"So tell me, then," Alm said. "Give me the names of people who can support your alibi."

"Sure, I could do that," Söderman said. "But I'm not going to."

"Why not?"

"Two weeks ago I was supposed to be flying up to Sundsvall to visit an old friend who's in a bad way. He's got prostate cancer, and doesn't look too hot. So when I'm standing there, at the gate to the plane, about to get on, the girl at the desk starts going on about wanting to see my ID. And bear in mind, I was sober and smart, so it was nothing like that.

"So I give her my ticket, but she doesn't give up. Wants to see ID. I explain to her, I haven't got any damn ID. Your mates took my driving license away ten years ago. My passport was in a drawer at home. Anyway, who the fuck takes their passport if they're going to Sundsvall? But I try to keep calm. Explain that I've been a full Swedish citizen for seventy years or so. And as long as I'm in Sweden and not causing any trouble, I don't have to show my ID. Not to fly to Sundsvall on an internal flight with a Swedish airline. It's in the constitution if you care to look. But fuck me, two of them turned up," he said, nodding in Stigson's direction. "So there was no trip to Sundsvall."

"What a shame," Alm said, shaking his head. "Those terrorists have really messed things up for us."

"Bullshit," Halvar Söderman said. "How much do I look like fucking Osama bin Laden?"

"Not much," Alm said with a slight smile. "But—"

"That was when I decided," Söderman interrupted. "To play silly idiot right back. If you and your colleagues could find the slightest bit of evidence to say that I was the one who beat Kalle Danielsson to death, then you wouldn't be sitting here going on about my alibi. I'd be sitting up in Crime if you had anything. Not for the first time either, but I'm sure you know that already."

"What makes you think he was beaten to death?" Alm said. "There are other ways to kill someone."

"From what I've heard, someone got hold of a saucepan lid and whacked him in the head with it," Söderman said.

"Who did you hear that from?" Alm asked.

"I'll give you a piece of advice," Söderman said. "I've lived out here all my life. I've hung around Valla and Råsunda and all the bars out here, seven days a week, for as long as I've lived here. I've sold hot cars to policemen, I've sold white goods and television sets to policemen. I've shifted their stuff when their wives have thrown them out or they've just found a new piece of skirt. I've always given them the usual discount. How many cops do you reckon I know in the Solna station?"

"Quite a few," Alm said.

"So I'm afraid we're not going to get a lot further. I didn't beat Kalle to death. Why would I? He had his moments, Kalle, but don't we all? And if I'd wanted to put his lights out, I wouldn't have needed any fucking saucepan lid. Anyway, I've got an alibi, but since I don't have to tell you, I don't feel like telling you. But if you all sort things out so I can get to Sundsvall without having to show my passport, you're welcome to come back. Then we can talk like reasonable people."

Söderman had held his ground. Even though Alm had sat there for another half-hour, they hadn't got any further. When they were sitting in the car, on their way to see Grimaldi, Stigson had broken the silence.

"That's insulting a public official," Stigson said. "Calling someone a monkey."

"Chimpanzee," Alm said with a sigh. "I was the one who said monkey."

"Yes, but we're colleagues," Stigson said, looking at him in surprise. "That's completely different."

"You've never thought about changing your hairstyle?" Alm said for some reason.

"We should have dragged the old bastard to the cells and twisted his arm," Stigson said, apparently not listening.

"If that's what you really think, I suggest you change jobs," Alm said.

Grimaldi had been the exact opposite of Söderman. He answered his phone when they called to make an appointment. Opened the door on the second ring, shook them by the hand, and asked them into his well-kept home.

They had sat down on the three-piece suite in the living room. Faithful to his roots, Grimaldi had offered mineral water, lemonade, Italian coffee, an aperitif. Or perhaps a glass of red wine? He had opened a bottle for lunch and most of it was still there, so it wouldn't be any trouble.

"Thanks, but we won't be long," Alm said.

What had Grimaldi been doing on Wednesday evening last week, when his good friend Karl Danielsson was murdered in his own home? Just one kilometer from Grimaldi's own home?

"I don't remember," Grimaldi said. "If I had to guess, I'd say I was at home. I'm at home most of the time these days."

"You don't remember?" Alm repeated.

"Let me explain," Grimaldi said.

One year earlier he had been diagnosed with early-onset Alzheimer's. Since then he had been on medication to slow the development of the disease. In spite of the drugs, his short-term memory had deteriorated noticeably over the past few months. If they wanted to talk to his doctor, they were welcome to call the health center in Solna. But he had forgotten his doctor's name. But he had the prescription and the pills. They were in his bathroom cabinet, and they were welcome to look.

"You've never thought about keeping any sort of notes, like a diary?" Alm suggested.

He hadn't. If anyone had ever suggested it to him, he would doubtless have forgotten that as well. Would have sat there wondering what he was doing with pen and paper in his hand.

"And there's no one close to you who would know things like that?" Alm said. "How you spend your days, I mean?" he clarified.

"Fortunately not," Grimaldi said with a smile. "Fortunately I am entirely alone in life. Who would want to subject someone they love to the sort of person I've become?"

They hadn't got any further than that. On the way out they looked in his bathroom cupboard and made a note of the names on the boxes of medication and the name of his doctor from the prescription.

"Some Godfather," Stigson said as they were sitting in the car on the way back to the police station. "There's nothing wrong with the old fart's body at all. What was his name, that Mafia boss in New York? The one who tried the same trick, pretending to be crazy? Whatever was his name?"

"Don't remember," Alm said.

33.

When Annika Carlsson and Felicia Pettersson arrived at Akofeli's flat, Niemi and Hernandez were already there.

"Come in, come in. We're as good as finished," Niemi said. "I tried to call you on your cell about an hour ago but it was switched off. Toivonen sent us. He doesn't like it when important witnesses vanish from his murder investigations. Unless he's just getting more human in his old age and is worried because of that."

"We had our phones switched off," Annika said. "Felicia and I wanted to be able to talk in peace and quiet."

"Girly talk, you know," Felicia said, flashing her eyes at Chico Hernandez.

"About me, I presume," Chico said with a self-conscious shrug that didn't seem entirely put-on.

"About the loveliest officer in the whole station," Felicia said with a sigh. "About Magda, your sister. Nice cap you've got there, by the way, Chico. Did you steal it from the supermarket deli?"

The cap in question was disposable, made of white plastic. Obligatory headwear for every responsible forensics officer who didn't want to contaminate the crime scene with his own hair and dandruff. Wearing it under any other circumstances, such as a night out in a bar when you fancied meeting someone, or if you were just taking part in one of all those incredibly popular television series about forensics officers, wouldn't have done anything for either your appearance or expectations. You'd end up going home alone late at night or getting half the usual viewing ratings.

"Well, it's not the cap that's the main attraction," Chico said with an expressive shrug, then returned to examining the innards of Akofeli's fridge.

One room and a kitchen, with a corner table, a small hallway, and an unexpectedly spacious bathroom with room for a toilet, shower, bathtub, washing machine, and tumble dryer. Sparsely furnished and kept clean.

In the single room, scarcely larger than an average student room, there was a bed, neatly made with a striped bedspread from IKEA, a wardrobe, a small sofa, a television and DVD player, a bookshelf that seemed to contain mainly university course books, a couple dozen paperbacks, DVDs and CDs, an exercise bench covered in green PVC, a barbell, a couple dumbbells, and a small stack of weights. But nothing to remind you of Akofeli's African origins: no rugs, no leather, no tapestries, no statuettes, masks, or other ornaments. No posters or photographs on the walls.

Out in the kitchen was a table with two chairs. On the floor beneath the kitchen table was a computer printer, but no laptop, nor a standard PC either. The kitchen table was presumably where he worked, and bearing in mind that the flat was on the ground floor, it would have been stupid to leave the computer on the table when he wasn't at home. The window facing onto the courtyard was at the same level as the table. The only problem was that the computer wasn't there at all.

There had been no trace of a briefcase. Nor Akofeli's phone. And a lot of the things that are usually missing when someone leaves in a hurry were missing. Clothes, shoes, keys to the apartment, money, ID, and credit cards. The only thing that spoiled that theory was that his passport was still there.

"It was tucked behind the shoe rack in his wardrobe," Niemi said. "He evidently kept it hidden there, so he clearly considered it important."

"Do you think he's disappeared of his own accord?" Annika Carlsson asked.

"Most of the evidence supports that," Peter Niemi said. "If anything has happened to him, it didn't happen here. If it did, I'll eat Chico's cap," he added with a wide smile.

"What about the passport, then? And his computer?"

"The passport bothers me," Niemi conceded with a nod. "Of course, he could have had another passport—we'll have to check if he still has his old Somali passport—but a Swedish passport would be worth its weight in gold if he's headed off to Europe. The computer doesn't worry me as much. It was probably a laptop, and he could easily take that with him."

"Say hi to Magda," Felicia said, flashing her eyes at Chico as she and Annika Carlsson left the flat. "Ask her if she fancies a night on the town with the girls."

Chico contented himself with giving her the finger.

"I think Chico's a little bit stupid," Felicia said as they were sitting in the car on the way back. "He doesn't seem to pick up the simplest things. He hasn't got a clue that I'm hitting on him. I bet he thinks I'm a lesbian who's after his sister."

"A lot of guys are like that," Annika Carlsson said with a smile. "Not just guys, come to think of it."

"What do you mean?"

"Oh, you know, a bit slow like that. No radar, saying the wrong things, doing the wrong things. It's so unnecessary."

"Hello, so who's the world champion, then? Are we thinking of the same man, by any chance?" Felicia said.

"Well, I know who you've got in mind," Annika Carlsson said with a smirk.

"I think he's actually a bit scared of you," Felicia said. "He probably isn't as tough as he tries to make out."

"You reckon?"

"You only have to look at him and he straightens up, poor little fatso," Felicia said.

"Remember that you're talking about your boss," Annika said.

"Yes, he should be grateful for that," Felicia said, and snorted. "Otherwise he'd hear a few hard truths."

When Niemi returned to the station, Bäckström had evidently already gone home. So he talked to Toivonen instead and gave him a short summary.

"So you found his passport," Toivonen said. "And his cell, computer, and all the usual are missing. Have I got that right?"

"Yes," Niemi said. "And there are no traces of anything that might have belonged to Danielsson."

"What about his newspaper bag? Or the pushchair or whatever

he uses when he's delivering papers. The lad must have to deliver hundreds of papers each day. I presume he doesn't carry them all under his arm?"

"I didn't think of that," Niemi said with a grin. "There was no bag of that sort, and no cart in the flat. Nor in his storage space either; we looked there and it was completely empty. It doesn't look like he had his own bike. But now that you come to mention it, I do remember that when I spoke to him in Hasselstigen he had one of those cloth shoulder bags with a strap for his papers. And we haven't found it anywhere. I suppose he could have used that as a kind of suitcase when he left. Doesn't look like the lad had many possessions."

"And no larger case on wheels? No old stroller? No cart?"

"No," Niemi said, shaking his head.

"Now what the hell would he want to take that with him for?" Toivonen said. "If he really is heading south, I mean."

"I haven't the faintest idea," Niemi said.

34.

When Bäckström got home from work it was already eight o'clock in the evening. He was in an excellent mood and had with him a half-empty liter of the finest Russian vodka. He and Nadja had consumed the other half in his office, in pursuit of the truth that could be found only at the bottom of the bottle.

The search continues, Bäckström thought, and as a first gesture he had gone into the kitchen and poured another large shot, then took a pilsner out of the fridge and made himself a sandwich with a lot of liver pâté and gherkin mayonnaise. He prepared a tray that he placed on the coffee table in front of the television. I must tell the Russian to take some pilsners to work, he thought.

Then he took off all his clothes and took a shower, then put on some deodorant and brushed his teeth. Often when he brushed his teeth he thought about his mother. It happened again this time, and he never really understood why. Ah, well, Bäckström thought calmly. He went and settled down on the sofa, turned on the television news to enjoy all the domestic and foreign horrors that had occurred over the past twenty-four hours, while partaking of his simple repast.

Then he must have fallen asleep, because when he woke up it was already two o'clock in the morning and someone was ringing his doorbell.

It must be that damn neighbor, who had probably finished all the drink he tricked him out of last week, Bäckström thought. He already knew what he was going to say. He could forget about buying any more, and if he tried to touch his Russian vodka he was a dead man.

It was his colleague, Annika Carlsson. Fully dressed and wide-awake, apparently.

"I'm sorry if I woke you, Bäckström," she said. "But your phone is off and we don't have your home number at work, so I decided to risk it and came round."

"No problem," Bäckström said. "I was about to get up anyway. I usually go for a run early in the morning." But you haven't come round to get my phone number, have you? he thought.

"I realize that you must be wondering—"

"Don't say anything," Bäckström said, interrupting her, raising his hand just to make his point.

"I'm not stupid," he added. "Let me put some clothes on."

35.

Axel Stenberg was seventeen years old. He was 185 centimeters tall, well built, and in good shape. Stronger than most grown men and more agile than most, no matter what age they were. A sporting prodigy who was too lazy to train but still one of the best in his school at football, ice hockey, gymnastics, and swimming. All thanks to abilities he had been born with. He and his sports teacher had a complicated relationship. Why didn't he do something with his great physical prowess and the talent that he had been born with?

Axel had wavy blond hair, blue eyes, white teeth, and a ready smile. Even when he was in primary school, all the girls had asked if they could be his girlfriend, and it had been the same ever since. With all his teachers, apart from the PE instructor, he had a simple and respectful relationship. How could he not care about his studies? He was far from being without talent.

Hanna Brodin was seventeen years old. She was 175 centimeters tall, beautiful, well built, in good shape. She had long dark hair, brown eyes, white teeth, and a broad smile. Because she had been top of her class since primary school, she had a simple and excellent relationship with her teachers. Even though the boys had been asking to be her boyfriend for just as long, and in every conceivable way.

The most recent to have tried was Axel, and because her mom had gone off to a conference with her new workmates, they had ended up back at hers the first time they were alone together, just the two of them. Axel had made the anticipated moves, but she was as familiar as him with the game they had just embarked upon and had blocked all his moves without any problems.

And because they were each equally interested in the other, it had all taken a very long time.

"What about a night swim?" Axel said. "First of the year."

"Won't it be a bit cold?" Hanna said. "Besides, I don't know where my bathing suit is. Mom and I have hardly had time to unpack yet."

"I was thinking of skinny-dipping," Axel said with a smile.

"Well, I don't want to miss that," Hanna said, smiling back. "But if it's too cold, you'll be swimming alone."

Then Axel had taken her to his favorite swimming spot. His and his friends', to be strictly accurate. It was only a couple hundred meters from the house. A large, softly rounded area of rock that tumbled straight into the waters of the Ulvsundasjön. Isolated and discreet, perfect for sunny days, soft crevices with a lot of undergrowth if you wanted to get intimate with someone. Perfect for diving, since the water was four meters deep right up to the rocks.

Axel had kept his promise. He threw off all his clothes and dived into the water from the rocks, headfirst.

Hanna had sat down on the rocks to watch him. Midnight, but bright enough to see, and she could fill in the details herself.

I bet he's done this before, thought Hanna, who still liked what she saw. Boys, she thought. A bit too predictable sometimes.

Axel had done this many times before, and always from the same spot. A suitably large gap in the rock two meters above the water, a couple quick steps, push off hard, body taut, arms outstretched, palms pressed together, then just a ripple on the surface, a scarcely audible splash as he disappeared into the water. Then a big kick with both legs, back arched, arms outstretched—that was all he had to do to complete the perfect dive into the water and come back up to the surface.

But not this time, because suddenly his hand had touched something. Something soft, large, wrapped in cloth or maybe tarpaulin, something swaying and drifting at the bottom, invisible because of the dark water. Axel used his hands. Felt along it, found a handle, then another, reached down, felt a wheel, then another wheel.

A golf bag, thought Axel, who had an uncle who was a dentist but who would rather spend all day playing golf if it were up to him. He used to use his nephew as his caddy, offering him a beer after the eighteenth hole and giving him a few hundred-kronor notes as they parted, winking at him and telling him not to say anything to his sister. And not to waste the money on nonsense like schoolbooks, or any other books either, come to think of it.

Axel had always kept his promises. There were an awful lot of girls in the world, more than there was enough money for if you wanted to do something fun that cost money. What sort of idiot would throw a golf bag in the water? His uncle's bag contained clubs that were altogether worth as much as a secondhand car.

What the hell is he up to? Hanna thought in irritation. He must have been down there for at least a couple minutes now, she thought. Just as she was standing up to take off her top, he had resurfaced, waving to her.

"What the hell are you playing at?" Hanna said, annoyed.

"Some idiot's chucked a golf bag in here," Axel said. "Hang on, I'll show you," he said, and vanished under the surface once again.

It wasn't stuck to the bottom. How could it be, since there was nothing but smooth rock down there until you got twenty meters out? He grabbed the handles and pulled it upward, letting it float under the surface as he swam the ten meters to where the water suddenly got shallower. He didn't really need to go up for air as he did so. Then Hanna had helped him drag the bag up onto dry land. Only now did he realize how heavy the bag was.

"What do you mean, golf bag?" Hanna said. "I think it looks more like one of those carts paperboys drag round with them when they deliver the morning papers."

Shit, Axel thought.

"Congratulations, Axel," Hanna said with a smile. "You are hereby the owner of two hundred waterlogged copies of *Dagens Nyheter*."

Shit, Axel thought. All the pent-up energy, no sex all evening, only a couple gestures in that direction, and now he had made a fool of himself. What was he going to do with the cart now? he wondered. Take a look, he thought, and then drag it up somewhere and dump it in the bushes.

First he undid the bag, opening the fabric lid. Whatever was inside filled the whole bag and was wrapped in black plastic. He felt it with his hands. Hard, round, definitely not golf clubs, nor newspapers either, for that matter. Then he had torn open the plastic to see what it was.

"Will there be a reward?" Hanna wondered, squatting down on the rock. This is all a bit childish, she thought.

"Shit!" Axel shouted, leaping away from the bag. *"Shit, shit, shit!"* he screamed, waving his hands desperately in the air.

"What are you doing?" Hanna said, starting to get really annoyed now. "Practicing for an Oscar or what?"

"Fuck!" Axel said. "There's a body in the bag." Then he ran off to get his clothes. Completely naked as well, he thought.

"What the fuck do we do now?" Axel said, with a nod toward the bag that was still over by the shore. He had no intention of taking another look just to be sure, and the easiest thing would be just to walk away. At least he wasn't naked anymore. But he was so cold he was shivering. Not to mention his johnson, which suddenly looked like he'd spent all winter in icy water.

"Let's just go," Axel suggested. "Let's just go," he repeated.

"Are you mad?" Hanna said. "We have to call the cops, surely you can see that?"

Then Hanna Brodin, seventeen years old, had dialed the emergency number, 112, on her phone and got through to the police control room. There hadn't been any problems, because she sounded just like people like her sounded when they called to say that they'd just found a body in the water.

"Is it floating in the water by the shore?" the female radio operator had asked. Poor girl, she thought. Bodies in the water are never nice; she knew that from personal experience.

"It's in a bag," Hanna said.

"In a bag in the water?" the radio operator clarified. What's she saying? she thought.

"It was in the water. The bag, I mean. But my boyfriend dived in to go swimming, and that's when he found it. And we pulled it ashore and looked inside. He looked. Not me."

"It'll be okay," the radio operator said. "Stay where you are, you and your boyfriend, don't go back to the bag, don't hang up, and I'll get a patrol car to come and help you, and you and I can keep talking until they get there."

"Thanks," Hanna said.

My boyfriend, Axel thought. It didn't look like all hope was lost, in spite of what had happened to his dick and the fact that he was so cold he was shivering.

The first unit on site was a patrol car from the Western District, containing Inspector Holm and Sergeant Hernandez. Neither Hanna nor Axel had been made to put their hands up, spread their legs, or even be searched. Holm had shone his torch on them, nodded amiably, and introduced himself.

"My name's Carsten Holm," he said. "This is my colleague, Magda Hernandez."

Then Holm had gone over to the bag, shone his torch at it, nodded toward Hernandez, and took out his radio.

Hernandez had led Hanna and Axel away with her. She had taken a blanket out of the trunk and suggested that they sit in the backseat.

"You'll be warmer in there," Magda said with a smile. "This will soon be sorted out, and I promise we'll drive you home."

Christ, what a cop, Axel thought. First eleven I've ever seen, he thought.

36.

Annika Carlsson had summarized the situation as she drove: Two seventeen-year-old kids. A girl and a boy. Lived in Jungfrudansen in Solna, at the top of the hill above the shores of Ulvsundasjön. They had gone down for a swim at about half past eleven at night. Their house lay just a hundred meters from their swimming spot.

"Apparently the boy dived in on his own while his girlfriend sat on the rocks watching. He more or less dived straight onto a large bag, as far as I understand it," Annika Carlsson said. "Then he dragged it up to the shore and got it up onto dry land. When he looked in the bag he realized it contained a dead body."

"How the hell do we know that it's Akofeli, then?" Bäckström said. In the middle of the night, black as inside a sack, and a sooty in a bag, Bäckström thought. What do they mean, Akofeli? Hello, out here the place is crawling with sooties, he thought.

"Holm and Hernandez were the first unit on the scene," Annika Carlsson explained. "Holm's pretty sure it's Akofeli. And he says he recognizes the bag. The same bag that Akofeli used when he was delivering papers. One of those big ones on wheels."

"Holm and Hernandez. Second time in a week. A bit much for my liking," Bäckström said, and snorted. "I wonder if we're dealing with a couple serial killers in a patrol car?"

"I doubt it's quite that bad. Mind you, I can see what you're thinking," Annika Carlsson said with a smile. "It's all due to their rotation, and they don't organize that themselves. This month they're working nights every Wednesday to Thursday."

"What's wrong with finding bodies in the daytime?" Bäckström muttered. "Then at least you can see that you've found a body."

"Sorry I woke you," Annika Carlsson said. "But I thought it was probably best that you were in on this one from the very start."

"Very sensible of you, Annika," Bäckström said. And you got a chance to see how I live. Just in case, he thought.

"But you were just about to go for your run anyway," she said with a smile. "I was actually a bit surprised."

"Surprised?"

"At how nice your flat is. Nice furniture, all neat and tidy. Clean."

"I like things to be nice and tidy," Bäckström lied. *Vojne, vojne,* he thought, since he had to pay for every single desiccated dust ball in his Hästens bed.

"Most of the male officers I know who live alone usually live in pigsties," Carlsson said.

"Filthy sods," Bäckström said indignantly. You should be grateful, he thought. Who the hell can be bothered to clean after someone like you has come along and stolen their girlfriend?

"You're a man of hidden talents, Bäckström," Annika Carlsson concluded, smiling at him.

The rest of the drive had passed in silence. Carlsson had crossed the bridge over the Karlberg Channel and carried on beside the shore toward Ulvsundasjön. They must have driven a good couple kilometers along the footpath by the lake. Up a steep, winding hill. Cordons, vehicles, floodlights, the first curious onlookers already in place although it was the middle of the night.

"This is it," Annika Carlsson said as they got out of the car to join the others sent by the emergency control room.

"Is it the same distance from the other side?" Bäckström asked. "If you're coming from Huvudsta?"

"Yes," Annika Carlsson nodded. "I see what you're thinking," she said.

Gravel paths, hills, several kilometers on foot—the perpetrator must have had a car, Bäckström thought. This isn't the sort of place you'd drag a bag containing a body, he thought.

37.

Bäckström had started by looking at the body. That checks out, Bäckström thought, once he had reassured himself that some other, entirely unconnected sooty hadn't turned up in the middle of his murder investigation. The right sooty, Bäckström thought, and he looked even more miserable than he had when Bäckström had seen him sitting on the landing outside Danielsson's flat.

Then he spotted Toivonen, who was standing some way off, staring at him with his hands deep in his pockets. Bäckström walked over to him to give him something to chew on.

"What do you think, Toivonen?" Bäckström said. "Murder, suicide, accident?"

"You talk a lot of shit, Bäckström," Toivonen said. "Try to do something useful for once. Tell me how the lad ended up here," Toivonen said, glaring first at Bäckström, then at the bag containing the body.

"I think you're on the wrong track there, Toivonen," Bäckström said with an amiable smile. "Surely you're not suggesting that our poor victim might have been mixed up in any funny business, possibly even something criminal?"

"What do you think?" Toivonen said, nodding toward the bag down by the shore.

"There's nothing to support that," Bäckström said, shaking his head. "All the evidence suggests that Sooty Akofeli was a decent, hardworking young man. His main job was as a bicycle courier. He delivered papers in the middle of the night to earn some extra money. In spite of his impressive qualifications. You almost get the impression that he had philanthropic tendencies.

"Akofeli could have gone on to do anything he wanted," Bäckström continued. "If he'd only had the chance to carry on for another twenty, thirty years, I bet you anything you like that he could have got himself his own moped to ride around on."

"Unless you feel like taking a swim, Bäckström, I suggest you shut up," Toivonen said. "A young man's been murdered and you're standing here talking shit about him."

"Okay, we've seen all we need to," Bäckström said to Annika Carlsson a quarter of an hour later. "What do you say about driving me home?"

"Of course, Bäckström. I can understand that you're eager to go for your run."

On the way back to his cozy abode they talked about this latest development.

"Get Niemi and Hernandez to take another look at the lad's flat," Bäckström said. "Tell them to do it properly this time."

"I understand what you mean," Carlsson agreed. "Considering that he was found inside his own newspaper bag, you mean?"

"You're smart, Annika," Bäckström said with a grin. "I find it hard to believe that he dragged the cart with him to the courier office. He must have gone home in between and dropped it off."

"That's what I've been thinking too," Annika Carlsson said. "He usually finished delivering papers by about six o'clock. And he started work as a courier at nine o'clock. He could even have had time to get an hour or so's sleep in between.

"So how about inviting me in for a cup of coffee, then?" Annika asked as she pulled up outside Bäckström's door. "Besides, there's something I want to talk to you about."

"Sure," Bäckström said. They're crazy about you, he thought. Even a notorious carpet muncher like Annika Carlsson is trying it on.

38.

While Bäckström was in the kitchen tinkering with his newly acquired Italian espresso machine, Annika Carlsson had asked if she could have a look around the flat.

"Make yourself at home," said Bäckström, who had nothing to fear. Over the weekend his Finnish bartender friend had used her day off to go through his flat like a blond tornado.

"I'll give you the guided tour," Bäckström said.

First he had shown her his freshly tiled bathroom and the new shower cabinet with a steam-bath option, a stereo, and a little folding seat where you could sit and think as the water streamed down and refreshed your body and soul.

"You program the pressure of the water on that panel there," Bäckström said, showing her.

"Not bad," Annika Carlsson said, with an almost envious look in her eyes.

Then he had led her to the holy of holies, the little workshop where he most recently over the weekend had paid for the cleaning by giving the blond tornado a serious going-over in his bed from the Hästens bed factory.

"That's a Hästens bed, isn't it?" Annika Carlsson asked. "They cost a fortune," she said, feeling the mattress just to be sure.

"You've got it really good, Bäckström." Annika sighed when they sat down five minutes later in Bäckström's living room to enjoy freshly brewed cappuccinos and biscotti. "This coffee table alone must have cost an arm and a leg," Annika said, running her hand over the black top. "It's marble, isn't it?"

"From Kolmården," Bäckström said.

"But how on earth can you afford all this on a police salary?" Annika Carlsson said. "A bed from Hästens, a plasma television—two of them at that—and a leather sofa and a Bang and Olufsen stereo. Proper carpets on the floor, and then there's that watch of yours. It's a real Rolex, isn't it? Did you get a big inheritance, or have you won the lottery?"

"Well, if you look after the pennies," Bäckström said—he had no intention of going into the other sources of income he had alongside his monthly salary. Least of all with Annika Carlsson. "There was something you wanted to talk about?" he reminded her, to get her to change the subject.

"Yes, I'm sitting here trying to pluck up the courage to say it," Annika Carlsson said, smiling amiably at him. "Some things are difficult to talk about, as you know."

"I'm listening," Bäckström said, smiling his most masculine smile.

"Just listening to you, it's easy to get the impression that you're another one of those burned-out, prejudiced officers. You know, the way a lot of us sadly end up in this job."

"I understand what you mean," Bäckström said, already aware of what tactics he was going to employ.

"But it can't be that straightforward," Annika Carlsson said, shaking her cropped head energetically. "I've seen you in action. You're the most professional detective I've ever come across. Alongside all the boorishness. Like with Akofeli, for instance. You were the only one of us who realized from the outset that there was something not quite right about him. And when we were down in the bank vault and you opened the safe-deposit box, I got the feeling that you were almost clairvoyant. Is there anything like that in your family, Bäckström?"

"Maybe a bit on my mother's side, if I'm honest," Bäckström lied. At any rate, she was the most mixed-up old bag on Södermalm, he thought.

"I thought so," Annika Carlsson said with a nod. "I thought so."

"But I also have my strong faith in God as well," Bäckström said with a sigh. "Nothing special, you know. Just a simple, childish faith that I've carried with me through life since I was a small boy."

"I knew it, Bäckström," Annika Carlsson said, looking at her host and boss with excitement. "I knew it. That's what gives you strength. That completely unshakable strength that you've got inside you."

"But I understand what you mean, Annika," Bäckström said, raising a hand in an almost pleading gesture to get her to stop. "When you talk about my view of the world, I mean. Sadly it's very true that all of us in this job get burned-out at some point. It's starting to take its toll on me too. That why I sometimes, and all too often, speak without thinking first.

"I'm so glad I managed to see beyond the surface," Annika Carlsson said somberly.

"While we're on sensitive matters," Bäckström said, "there's something I'd like to talk to you about."

"I'm listening," Annika said.

"I don't think you should be so hard on young Stigson," Bäckström said.

"Yes, but you heard what he was like, going on about that woman like that, about her breasts, I mean," Annika Carlsson said, pointing at her own for the sake of clarity.

"I know," Bäckström said. "Pure sexism. One of the worst examples I've heard in the force. But I'm sorry to say that I think there's probably an explanation."

"What do you mean?"

"I'm afraid our colleague Stigson has been the victim of incestuous abuse. At an early age, sadly."

"Good God," Annika said, looking at Bäckström, wide-eyed. "Is this something he's talked to you about?"

"No," Bäckström said. "They very rarely talk about things

like that, you know. But I recognize all the obvious signs, and after hearing him talk to that neighbor of Danielsson's, that Andersson woman, I'm pretty sure that it was his mother who abused him. I wouldn't be the least bit surprised if Stigson's mom turned out to be a carbon copy of our witness, Mrs. Andersson."

"What can we do?" Annika Carlsson asked.

"We hold off," Bäckström said. "We bear it in mind, we stay alert and ready to help, but we hold off."

39.

Where the fuck do they all come from? Bäckström thought, as he closed the door behind his guest. All these crazy women, each one madder than the last.

At roughly the same time as Bäckström was saying goodbye to his colleague Annika Carlsson, Hanna and Axel were seeking solace in each other and had ended up in Hanna's bed.

Axel ejaculated as soon as he entered her. Not because it was the first time, or because Hanna was at the very least an eight. Axel had got past that stage of life when he was thirteen. It was more complicated than that. Even though it was the first time with Hanna, the only thing in Axel's head for the past few hours was a young female police officer called Magda Hernandez. The first eleven he'd ever seen in his life, even though there weren't supposed to be any of those on a ten-point scale.

He had tried to pull himself together for another attempt, but his thoughts of Magda Hernandez and his proximity to Hanna plunged him back into the icy water again.

"I don't get this," Axel said. "It's never happened before," he said, feeling like nothing more than bursting into tears and running away.

"It doesn't matter," Hanna said, running her nails down his naked, sweaty back. "You must still be suffering from shock." Poor thing, she thought, since it wasn't the first time for her either.

"D'you know what?" she went on. "Let's go to sleep now, and we'll do the other stuff in the morning. It's not the end of the world." I wonder how many times that's ever been said, she thought.

Axel had only pretended to sleep, and as soon as Hanna had fallen asleep he crept up, got dressed, and slunk out the front door.

Maybe that was for the best, Hanna thought, as she heard the door click shut. Life would go on, with or without Axel, and she had school to think about in just a few hours' time.

Must remember to call Magda, she thought before she fell asleep. To talk about that debriefing she wanted me to go to.

40.

On Thursday morning, eight days after the murder of Karl Danielsson, Lars "Sneaker" Dolmander got in touch with his confessor, Superintendent Toivonen.

Sneaker had appeared in person in the police station. He refused to talk to anyone apart from "my old friend Toivonen." He had a hot tip to pass on about the armed raid out at Bromma, and Toivonen was the only officer in the entire force whom he trusted.

During the past ten years of the life of an addict in free fall, Sneaker had supported himself as an informant. There wasn't a single criminal in the whole Western District that Sneaker hadn't grassed up more than once, and with that in mind it was fortunate for him that he had taken an early decision not to deal with anyone but Toivonen.

These days he was too run-down to make a living from his own crimes. His pension was usually gone the day after he got it, and if he was going to survive until the next one, he had to sell out other people. New, and always "hot," tips, and since some of them really were as hot as Sneaker claimed they all were, he still had Toivonen's confidence.

"You're looking lively, Sneaker," Toivonen said. Tattooed like a Brussels rug over his whole body. Thirty-three years old, and the fact that he was still alive was a minor miracle, Toivonen thought.

"I've left off the heavy stuff," Sneaker said. "For the past year or so I've done nothing but smoke. Well, that and the drink, of course, but that counts as health food compared to all the shit I've put in my system over the years."

"Is that so," said Toivonen, who mainly subsisted on meat, fruit, and vegetables. When he and Niemi and the other blokes in the Finnish cavalry weren't out asserting their roots, of course. Mind you, that was a while ago now, he thought.

"I'll keep it short," Sneaker said, with a businesslike nod. "You know that raid at Bromma? On Monday last week when they took out those two Securitas blokes?"

"I've heard of it, yes," Toivonen said with a wry smile.

"That evening someone killed Kari Viirtanen out in Bergshamra. Mad Kari, or Tokarev, as he was known. You know, after that Russian gun, Tokarev. The ten-millimeter automatic pistol he was always waving about."

"We have many names for the things we love," Toivonen said.

"Anyway," Sneaker said, "there's a link between Viirtanen's murder and the raid out at Bromma."

"I've heard that too," Toivonen said with a smile. "Come on, Sneaker. Haven't you got anything new for me?"

"Well, it's like this," Sneaker said, not about to give up. "Viirtanen was involved in the robbery out at Bromma. When the blokes from the security firm let off the dye capsules in the bag, he went mad. He told the driver to go back, then he gunned the guards down. Then him and the driver took off, abandoned the car and the money. No red notes to fuck up their lives. The heavies, the ones behind the raid, get mad at Tokarev and get rid of him that same evening. The driver's probably joined him by now, and if I was you I'd have a look at that colored bloke you fished out of Ulvsundasjön last night."

"Yesterday's news, Sneaker," Toivonen said, looking pointedly at the time. And he probably hasn't got a clue who Akofeli was, he thought.

"I thought as much," Sneaker said. "But now I'm getting to the point."

"I can hardly contain myself." Toivonen sighed.

"You know that old accountant who lived on Hasselstigen? Danielsson, that was his name, Karl Danielsson, the one they did the saucepan dance with last Wednesday. There's a connection between his murder and the raid out at Bromma."

"What makes you say that?" Toivonen said. "Anyway, how come you know Danielsson?"

"Met him out at Valla," Sneaker said. "He used to hang out with Roly Stålhammar. Stolly, you know. Your old colleague."

"So you know him?" Toivonen said.

"Do bears fuck in the woods?" Sneaker snorted. "The first time he arrested me I was fourteen years old. I was dealing up on Karlavägen in the middle of town. Suddenly a car stops. And out pops a man big as a house. Grabs fourteen-year-old Sneaker by the ear and chucks me in the car. Ten minutes later I'm sat in Crime in Stockholm waiting for the old hag from Social to come and get me out. Fuck, I had an unlocked car waiting for me out in Östermalm. Mind you, I'd lost my stash, but that was easy enough for someone like me to sort out."

"So you remember Roly Stålhammar?" Toivonen said.

"One of the most decent cops I ever ran into. He even took me boxing a couple times when I was a lad. But that got all fucked up as well," Sneaker said with a shrug.

"So you met Stålhammar and Danielsson out at Solvalla," Toivonen prompted.

"That's right," Sneaker said. "Last Wednesday. At about six o'clock or so. Just a few hours before Danielsson had a close encounter of the third kind with his own saucepan. Stolly told me I looked like shit. That I looked so bad that he didn't even want to introduce me to an old school friend. That was Danielsson, of course. But even then he had a twinkle in his eye. The way he said it, I mean. Stolly and Danielsson seemed to be pretty cheerful, and Danielsson held out his hand and introduced himself.

"'Kalle Danielsson,' the old boy said, and it was pretty obvious that he'd had a few over the course of the day. If I'd been on the wagon myself, I would have fallen off just from him breathing on me. There was a lot of drink inside that man."

"So what did you say?"

"'Sneaker,'" Sneaker said. "What the fuck would you have said? If you were me, I mean?"

"Sorry, stupid question," Toivonen said. "But what's this got to do with the armed raid on the security van? What's the connection between Danielsson and the raid?"

"The blokes behind the raid. I don't mean Tokarev and the one who did the driving. I mean the heavies. The ones who've already got rid of Tokarev and the driver because they fucked up so badly. Have you got any idea who they are?"

"Yes, I daresay we've all got our ideas of who they might be," Toivonen said. "I'm listening."

"Farshad Ibrahim," Sneaker said.

Right, Toivonen thought.

"His crazy little brother, Afsan Ibrahim."

Right again, Toivonen thought.

"And then their fucking nasty cousin. That big bastard, Hassan Talib," Sneaker said. "Farshad Ibrahim, Afsan Ibrahim, Hassan Talib," he repeated.

Three out of three correct, Toivonen thought.

"What makes you think they were behind the raid?" he asked.

"There's talk," Sneaker said. "There's talk, if you're prepared to listen," he clarified, cupping his hand behind his ear.

There's talk, Toivonen thought. He had already heard the same voices and could also work out one or two things for himself.

"I still don't get where Danielsson comes into the picture," he said.

"Him and Farshad knew each other," Sneaker said.

"You're grasping at straws there, Sneaker. What the hell makes you think that?" he said. What the fuck is the fucker saying? he thought.

"I'm getting to that," Sneaker said. "So, when Roly and his mate Danielsson said goodbye, after we'd met out at Valla, I mean, I suddenly remember that I'd seen him earlier that day. Around lunchtime. I was coming down Råsundavägen, minding my own business, thinking I might go and grab a bit of pizza. And who do I see thirty meters down the road, standing talking to some old bloke at the corner of Hasselstigen? Twenty meters from where I'm standing?"

"I'm listening."

"Farshad Ibrahim," Sneaker said.

"And you know him?"

"Do I know him! We've done time in the same place. Shared a corridor in Hall ten years ago. If you don't believe me I'm sure you can look it up on your computer. The very same, Farshad Ibrahim, and there isn't a worse fucker alive than that man."

"So what did you do?"

"I turned on my heel," Sneaker said. "Farshad's the type who kills people just to be on the safe side, and if he was up to his usual shit, then I didn't want to get mixed up in it just because I wanted to get a bit of pizza."

"You're sure the man he was talking to was Kalle Danielsson?"

"A hundred and twenty," Sneaker said, nodding. "A hundred and twenty percent," he clarified.

"How can you be so sure?" Toivonen persisted.

"Because that's how I make my money," Sneaker said.

"I hear what you're saying," Toivonen said. How the hell I am going to escape Bäckström if this is true? he thought.

"What do you say about a thousand?" Sneaker said.

"What do you say about a twenty?" Toivonen said.

"Meet you halfway," Sneaker suggested, apparently not hurt by this.

"That makes two hundred," Toivonen said.

"If you say so," Sneaker said, shrugging.

41.

While Toivonen was having his confidential chat with Sneaker, Bäckström was holding an extra meeting with his investigating team as a result of the murder of Septimus Akofeli.

As usual, Niemi had begun the meeting. He had accompanied the body to the Institute of Forensic Medicine while Chico Hernandez took another colleague back to Akofeli's flat to do the forensic examination. Now they were both in the room.

"He was strangled," Niemi said. "That was the single cause of death. Otherwise there are no injuries to the body. He was completely naked, by the way. Strangled with a noose that was tied at the back of the neck, the marks from the knot are still there. If you ask me, I'd say he was conscious and was taken by surprise when it happened."

"Why do you think that?" Annika Carlsson said.

"He's got marks on his fingers. The sort you get when you're trying to untie a noose. For instance, a couple of the nails are broken, even though he had very short nails."

"What sort of noose do you think it was?" Bäckström said.

"As far as the noose is concerned—and we haven't found it, of course—it seems to have been fairly narrow. It could be anything from a sturdy shoelace, a washing line, maybe a standard electric cable, even the cord from some blinds. Personally I'd say the thinner type of electric cable."

"Why?" Annika Carlsson asked.

"Because that would be best," Niemi said with a wry smile. "Easiest to tighten. You just pull it tight and knot it, and it stays tight, and you're done."

"You mean this was done by a professional?" Alm said.

"Don't know," Niemi said, shrugging. "But I don't really think so. How many professional stranglers have we got in this country? All the commandos and Special Forces, and the Yugoslavs who made such a mess of the Balkans. Well, according to them, anyway, but they seem to be able to keep their fingers under control here at home.

"The perpetrator is seriously strong. He's taller than Akofeli, I can tell you that much," Niemi said.

"Like whoever killed Danielsson," Bäckström said.

"Yes, the same thought struck me," Niemi said.

"What about time of death?" Bäckström said.

"I'd guess the same day he disappeared," Niemi said. "In other words, Friday, May sixteenth, sometime that morning, afternoon, or evening."

"Why do you say that?" Bäckström said.

"Not that we have any evidence on the body to confirm that. But that's the way it usually is these days. When they stop using their phones, when they don't turn up for work, don't use their bank cards, when their usual routine is broken. That's when something's happened. It's nearly always like that," Niemi said, nodding emphatically.

So the bastard Finn isn't entirely stupid, thought Bäckström, who had been using the same rule of thumb for thirty years.

"The body's in good condition," Niemi went on. "Strangled, naked, folded up, wrapped in black plastic and sealed up with ordinary duct tape, then stuffed into his own newspaper cart. The plastic is from three different bags, normal black bin bags. The duct tape is standard issue, about five centimeters wide. I think it all happened at once. Before rigor mortis set in. The bag was also weighted down. Four barbell weights, five kilos each, twenty in total, taped together with the same duct tape. Since Akofeli weighed about fifty kilos, the weights twenty, and the bag about ten—you'll get an exact weight as soon as it's dried out—we're talking about a total weight in the region of eighty kilos."

"Car," Alm said. "The body was driven by car from the scene of the crime to where it was found."

"Anything else is extremely unlikely," Niemi agreed. "I read an interesting little article the other day, in the *Journal of Forensic Science,* about perpetrators who dump their victims in the open. It's very unusual for anyone to carry or drag a body more than seventy-five meters."

"What about if they have a cart or wheelbarrow?" Bäckström asked.

"A few hundred meters at most," Niemi said. "For longer journeys, the cart and body are usually both transported in a vehicle."

"What about the crime scene, then?"

"You mean Akofeli's apartment at seventeen Fornbyvägen?" Niemi said, exchanging a quick glance with Hernandez.

"We were there again this morning," Hernandez said. "We didn't find anything this time either, but considering the way he was killed, it could still perfectly well be the scene of the crime, even though we can't find any evidence. Besides, there are other circumstances that suggest that."

"Such as?" Alm said.

"The newspaper cart, which in all likelihood belonged to the victim, and the weights, which were used as ballast. We're pretty sure they belonged to the victim. He's got one of those exercise benches, a barbell, and a pair of dumbbells. But surprisingly few weights for the barbell."

Bäckström nodded.

"Well, I never."

"Left in the apartment, I mean," Hernandez clarified.

"Distance," Bäckström said.

"From the victim's apartment to where he was found it's about ten kilometers, and you can drive almost the whole way. Right up to those rocks at the edge of the shore. The ones at the top of that hill. From there there's a gravel track down to the shore, thirty meters. A drop of thirteen meters."

"But you aren't allowed to drive there," Annika Carlsson said.

"Not unless you're a police officer or work for the highways agency or the parks authority, or you're a laborer there on a job. But if you come from the southeast—from the direction facing Kungsholmen, that is—driving is permitted almost the whole way to where the body was found. Apart from a walk of a hundred meters. Uphill, admittedly, but even so." Hernandez shrugged demonstratively.

"Have you found any tire tracks, then? Above the spot where he was found, I mean?" Annika Carlsson asked.

"Loads," Chico said with a smile. "So we haven't been able to come up with anything useful there."

"Chico," Bäckström said. "Tell an old dolt like me what you think happened."

That gave you something to chew on, you little strutting tango dancer, thought Bäckström, who had already received a supporting nod from his colleague Carlsson.

Hernandez had some difficulty hiding his surprise.

"You want me to tell you what I think happened?" he asked.

"Yes," Bäckström said with an encouraging smile. *Just as stupid as they always are, always having to ask more than once,* he thought.

"Okay," Hernandez said. "With the proviso that this is only my personal opinion. As far as the way it started is concerned, I agree completely with what Peter said. The victim was taken by surprise, strangled from behind, undressed, folded in half—he's thin and in good shape, and I bet he could stand with both palms flat on the floor without bending his legs. When the body was folded in half, the perpetrator secured it with tape round his ankles, across his back, round his shoulders, and back again. The tape was fastened back where he started, around the ankles.

"Then he was wrapped in plastic cut into sheets from plastic bags, then the parcel was sealed with more of the same silver tape. Then the bundle was stuffed into his newspaper cart. It's a fairly tall cart, two wheels and two handles, held together by a rectangular metal frame. On the front is a large sack made of canvas, a slightly thicker, waterproof fabric, a bit like tarpaulin. There are also laces or straps sewn into the sack, so that it can be fastened shut or held open. At the top there's a lid made of the same material, which is sealed with another strap."

"How long would all this take, then?" Bäckström said. "From when he was strangled to sealing him inside the bag?"

"If you're strong enough and agile enough, and if you've got everything you need at hand, it wouldn't take more than half an hour," Chico said. "If there are two of you or more, then you could do it in a quarter of an hour."

"You think there could be more than one perpetrator?" Alm said.

"We can't rule it out," Hernandez said, shrugging. "One would be enough, two would be twice as quick. Any more than that and you mainly just get in each other's way. But sure, there could be more than one."

Which everyone but a Woodentop could work out perfectly easily, Bäckström thought, giving Alm the evil eye.

"Then what?" he asked.

"First he's taken out of the apartment in the cart. Probably by the elevator to the ground floor. From there to the nearest place you can park in the street is ten meters. Into the car with the cart and off you go. A total of an hour or so, but since this sort of trip is nearly always done at night and Akofeli was probably murdered in the morning—that's when he stops showing any sign of life, isn't it?—then presumably they waited until it was dark before throwing him in the lake. Killed him, wrapped him up, got him ready to go. Then they either put the cart in the car and drove off and waited until it got dark. Or they returned the same evening to fetch him. But I doubt they would have wanted to leave him in his own apartment any longer than necessary."

"When did they dump him in Ulvsundasjön, then? The next night, or what?"

Bäckström looked questioningly first at Hernandez, who shook his head, then Niemi, who merely turned his.

"It's difficult to say," Niemi said. "The body was so well packaged that it's impossible to tell. He could have been dumped on Friday, but it could also have happened considerably later than that. By the way, we've had divers there since this morning searching the bed of the lake. They haven't found anything."

"Anything else?" Bäckström asked.

"Not at present," Niemi said, shaking his head. "We'll let you know as soon as we find anything. Or don't find anything," he added with a thin smile.

"Okay," Bäckström said, desperate for coffee and biscuits. "So we repeat the door-to-door, and this time Akofeli is at the top of the list. The building at number one Hasselstlgen, and Akofeli's place on Fornbyvägen. Everything about Akofeli and any contact he may have had with Danielsson, plus anything else that might be of interest. Have we got enough people?"

"The neighborhood police team in Tensta have said they'll help with Fornbyvägen," Annika Carlsson said. "It's their patch, after all, and they've got good contacts with the people who live there. It looks like we'll have to deal with Hasselstigen ourselves. I thought I could take care of that."

"Good," Bäckström said.

Then he had asked Stigson to stay behind, and as soon as they were alone he had patted him amiably on the arm and pulled another Bäckström classic, the one Carlsson had prompted the previous night.

"Okay, Oedipus," Bäckström said. "No hugs this time, right?"

"You mean her with . . . ," Stigson said, cupping his hands over his chest.

"Her with the melons," Bäckström confirmed.

"I've talked to the Anchor about that," Stigson said, his cheeks already coloring.

"Excellent," Bäckström said. "Just out of interest, is she a lot like your mother?"

"Who? The Anchor?"

"The witness, Andersson," Bäckström said. "You know who I mean. Her with the huge melons."

"Not at all," Stigson said. "My mom's quite slim, actually."

Typical, Bäckström thought. The surest sign of them all. Denial. Complete denial.

42.

The neighborhood police in Tensta and Rinkeby had throughout their history devoted the majority of their resources to fostering good relations with the people living in the area. Ninety percent of them immigrants from every hard-pressed corner of the world. The majority of them were refugees from countries where they were not allowed to think or even live. It hadn't been easy, and the fact that ninety percent of those working for the neighborhood police were ordinary Swedes hadn't made it any easier. Swedes going back generations, or possibly second- or third-generation migrants. Well established in Swedish society, already rooted in Swedish soil.

Crime fighting had got caught in the middle. All the usual

business of policing had slipped behind. Here it was a question of building bridges between people, creating relationships, confidence. A question of the very simplest things, like just being able to talk to another.

"We'll get this sorted," the head of the neighborhood police said when he discussed the situation with Annika Carlsson. "We have good relationships with each other."

Then he and his colleagues had spent two days talking to Akofeli's neighbors. A total of a hundred people. They had put up posters of his face all the way from his flat on Fornbyvägen to the closest underground station. They had put posters up in entrance halls, on walls, lampposts, and notice boards within a wide radius. They even set up their mobile police station in the squares in both Rinkeby and Tensta, with murder victim Septimus Akofeli as special offer of the week.

No one had seen anything, no one had heard anything. The few who had actually talked just shook their heads. Most of them didn't even understand what they were saying.

The door-to-door at number 1 Hasselstigen had gone relatively well in comparison. Pettersson and Stigson, led by Annika Carlsson and with backup from a couple uniformed officers from Solna, had spoken to everyone who lived in the building. With two exceptions, there was no one who recognized Akofeli. No one had seen or heard anything. A lot of them had had questions, a lot of them had been worried. Did they actually dare live in the building anymore?

The first exception was widow Stina Holmberg, seventy-eight.

Stina Holmberg was an early riser. She was convinced it was because of her age. The older you got, the less sleep you needed. The closer to death you got, the more you had to make the most of your time awake. She had seen Akofeli coming and going on a number of occasions over the past year. Between half past five and six o'clock in the morning. Unless something unusual had happened, like sudden heavy snow or problems on the underground.

She had even spoken to him on one occasion. It was the day after her neighbor had been murdered.

"It was because I still hadn't received any copies of *Svenska Dagbladet*," Mrs. Holmberg explained.

The week before Mrs. Holmberg had switched from *Dagens Nyheter* to *Svenska Dagbladet*, and she had been promised her new paper from the Monday of the following week. For the first four days she had continued to receive *Dagens Nyheter*. On that Friday she had got up early to be able to intercept the paperboy and talk to him directly. Naturally, she could have called the subscription departments of both *DN* and *SvD*, but because she didn't have a push-button phone she had never been able to get through, and eventually she gave up.

Akofeli had promised to help her, although he had seemed a little stressed. He said he would talk to them himself. Then he had given her a copy of *Svenska Dagbladet* that he "had in reserve," without going into any details of how he happened to have it.

"And now it's all working splendidly," Mrs. Holmberg concluded.

Mind you, she hadn't received a paper at all over the weekend, but there was evidently something wrong because none of her neighbors had received theirs either, but things had been fine for the past few days. The only criticism she had would perhaps be that the new paperboy usually turned up half an hour later than the one she had spoken to.

"He seemed nice," Mrs. Holmberg said, shaking her head. "That dark-skinned boy, I mean. A bit stressed, like I said, but who wouldn't be with a job like that, and he was so kind and accommodating. I can't imagine that he would have hurt Danielsson," she added.

"What makes you say that, Mrs. Holmberg?" Stigson asked. "That he might have hurt your neighbor, I mean." She doesn't know that Akofeli has been murdered, he thought.

"Well, why else would you be looking for him? Any child

could work that out," Mrs. Holmberg said in a friendly tone, patting him on the arm.

The other exception was Seppo Laurén, twenty-nine.

"He's the one who delivers the papers. He supports Hammarby," Seppo said, handing back the photograph of Akofeli to Sergeant Stigson.

"How do you know that?" Stigson asked. Poor bastard, he thought. Completely retarded, even though he looks entirely normal.

"I had my AIK shirt on," Seppo said.

"You had your AIK shirt on?"

"I was playing a computer game. A football game. So I had my shirt on."

"So how did you meet the paperboy?" Stigson said.

"I was going down to the petrol station to get something to eat. They're open all night."

"And you bumped into the paperboy?"

"Yes, but I don't get a paper. I don't read papers."

"Did you bump into him inside the building?"

"Yes," Seppo said with a nod. "My neighbor gets a paper."

"How do you know he supported Hammarby?" Stigson asked.

"He asked if I supported AIK. He saw my shirt."

"And so you said that you did. That you support AIK, I mean."

"I asked him who he supported."

"And what did he say?"

"That he supported Hammarby," Seppo said, looking at Stigson in surprise. "I told you that was what he said. Hammarby."

"Is that the only time you spoke to him?"

"Yes."

"Do you remember when it was?"

"No," Seppo said, shaking his head. "But there wasn't any snow. Not winter."

"You're sure about that?"

"I would have been wearing a jacket. You can't go out in winter in just a soccer shirt, can you?"

"No, of course not," Stigson said. "Of course you wouldn't."

"No, because then you'd catch a cold," Seppo concluded.

"But you don't remember more precisely? When it was, I mean? When you spoke to him?"

"Must have been fairly recent, because Mom's in the hospital. When she was home I wasn't allowed to play computer games so much. And there was always food in the house."

"I see," Stigson said. "What did you think of him, then? The paperboy?"

"He was kind," Seppo said.

The last person in the building that they spoke to was Mrs. Andersson. Annika Carlsson had provided Stigson with a chaperone, and Felicia Pettersson had gone a step further and said before they knocked on the door that this time she would be asking the questions.

Mrs. Andersson didn't recognize Akofeli. Had never seen him before, which probably wasn't unexpected, since she usually got up late.

"The earliest I ever get up is eight," Britt-Marie Andersson said with a smile. "I usually have a cup of coffee and read the paper quietly for a while, then I take Little Sweetie out for a morning walk.

"What's happened here is so awful," she said. "You start to wonder what's going on, and if you actually dare to carry on living here."

She regarded the idea that her neighbor Karl Danielsson might have had any "dealings" with Akofeli the paperboy as "out of the question."

"Not that I knew Danielsson particularly well, I certainly wouldn't say that—the little we did have to do with each other was more than enough—but the idea that he might have had any dealings with that young man who seems to have been murdered is completely out of the question."

"What makes you say that, Mrs. Andersson?" Felicia Pettersson asked.

"Well, because Danielsson was a racist," Mrs. Andersson said. "You didn't even have to know him particularly well to appreciate that."

Nothing more to add, and she didn't get a hug this time. Felicia Pettersson gave her colleague Stigson a warning glance as their witness held out her hand to him and leaned forward slightly with a big white smile and a heaving bosom.

"Well, thank you so much for all your help, Mrs. Andersson," Stigson said, shaking her by the hand. "Thanks again."

Good boy, Felicia thought, as they left.

43.

While the majority of his colleagues were going door-to-door, Detective Inspector Alm was sitting in his office, worrying about all the red herrings that had suddenly popped up in a murder case. Deep in thought, and behind a closed door for safety's sake.

Unusually, he had taken out a pen and paper and had started sketching out a number of hypothetical chains of events, all of them based on the idea that Danielsson's childhood friends were the perpetrators. One, two, or more of them, although he deeply and fundamentally despised such novelties as profiling and motive analysis.

The results of his interviews with Söderman and Grimaldi were deeply unsatisfactory. The former had simply refused to answer his questions, and the latter couldn't remember what he was doing. Based on a medical condition that in practical terms couldn't be corroborated. At least not by Alm.

He had spoke to one of his older colleagues who knew Grimaldi and had received a broad smile and a wink in response.

"I saw him a couple weeks ago when I took my wife to that new pizza place up in Frösunda, the one everyone says belongs to him even though he's not on any of the official papers. It didn't look like there was anything wrong with his appetite, if you know what I mean."

"What do you mean?" Alm asked.

"Well, he was sat there holding hands with a blonde, and if I say she was half his age I wouldn't be exaggerating much."

We who built Sweden, Alm thought. Wasn't that what those old boys who threatened to bomb the government called themselves? If you could do that, presumably you could beat to death an old friend no matter what the crime statistics have to say about it, he thought.

What complicated the equation was the murder of Akofeli, hence the need for paper and pen.

One of Danielsson's old friends beats him to death. Takes the case with all the money. Even Roly Stålhammar couldn't be ruled out of this, with his shaky alibi. It all hung on a witness who hated him and who would doubtless have sworn the exact opposite if he knew the way things really were. Anything in his eagerness to get rid of a noisy neighbor.

Nor could they rule out the possibility that there had been more than one perpetrator. That Kalle Danielsson had acted as a black-market banker for Grimaldi, for instance. That he hadn't played it straight. That Grimaldi and his pal Halfy Söderman had paid a home visit, beaten him to death, and taken the briefcase containing all the money.

If only it weren't for Akofeli.

Akofeli finds Danielsson murdered. His old friends, who beat him to death, missed the briefcase with the money. They work it out, go back, discover that Akofeli took the case, go round to his, kill him, dump the body in Ulvsundasjön.

Are you kidding? Alm thought, aiming the remark at himself. Then he drew a thick black line through this latest hypothesis.

Akofeli kills Danielsson and takes the case with the money. Danielsson's old friends find this out, go round to Akofeli's, kill him, reclaim the case, and dump the body.

Why? Alm thought. Why would Akofeli kill Danielsson? And how the hell would his old friends find out that it was Akofeli who killed him?

The plot thickens, Alm thought, with a deep sigh, drawing another thick black line over the paper.

Then he had gone home to his beloved wife. Lamb chops with garlic butter, salad, and baked potatoes. Since it was almost the weekend, or Thursday at least, they had celebrated quietly by sharing a bottle of wine.

44.

While his simpler foot soldiers had doubtless been running round like headless chickens in Hasselstigen and out in Rinkeby, Bäckström had spent his time on slightly more demanding mental activities together with his only colleague worthy of the title, Nadja Högberg, doctor of mathematics and physics. Like him, she was also a connoisseur of fine vodka. A worthy conversational partner in a world where he was otherwise surrounded by nothing but idiots, and this was in spite of the fact that she was a woman, Bäckström thought.

When Bäckström returned to the police station after a nutritious and well-balanced meal, Nadja had knocked on his door and asked if she could come in to go through the contents of Danielsson's pocket diary. She had the original in a plastic evidence bag, but to save time she had given him a computer printout containing all the notes in his diary, arranged in date order.

"His notes are both concise and cryptic," Nadja summarized. "During the period from January first this year to May fourteenth, a total of nineteen and a half weeks, he made a total of one hundred and thirty-one different entries. Less than one a day on average."

"I'm listening," Bäckström said, putting down the sheets she had given him, folding his hands on his stomach, and leaning back in his chair. She's got a smart head on her shoulders, this woman, he thought.

"The first note appears on the first day of the year, New Year's Day, Tuesday, January first, and it reads, and I quote: 'gentleman's dinner with the boys, Mario,' end quotes. An early dinner, it looks like, since the diary indicates that it was supposed to start at two o'clock in the afternoon."

"Perhaps they didn't want to take any chances." Bäckström grinned.

"That must be why. They were sharp," Nadja agreed. "The penultimate note is from the same day he died, Wednesday, May fourteenth. '14.30, Bank.' And that's also the only note during the whole period where he mentions going to the bank."

"Considering the size of his withdrawals, presumably he had no need to keep going every day," Bäckström said.

"The most common entry," Nadja went on, "appears thirty-seven times. Practically every Wednesday and Sunday between January and May he wrote 'Solvalla' or 'Valla' or 'Races.' I'm guessing that they all refer to the same thing, going to Solvalla racecourse to gamble, and he went practically every time there was any racing there. The last note in the diary is also from the day he died: '17.00, Valla.' He hadn't made any entries for the coming days, weeks, or months. Seems to live day to day."

"No other racecourses apart from Solvalla?" That fits in well with what we already know, Bäckström thought.

"Not that he's made a note of, anyway," Nadja said, shaking her head.

"Now, who the hell would bother going all the way to Jägersro just to collect a few betting slips?" Bäckström said.

"Sixty-four notes of a miscellaneous nature. One visit to the bank, like I said, two doctor's appointments, and a couple similar entries, then the rest are almost exclusively the names of his old friends. Roly, Gunnar, Jonte, Mario, Halfy, and so on. One, two, or more of them at a time. Several times a week."

"A comprehensive social life." Bäckström laughed. "Anything of interest to us, then?"

"Anything of interest to us, then?" he repeated.

"I think so," Nadja said. "Thirty entries in total."

Now she's got that look again, Bäckström thought. This Russian's as sharp as a fucking razor blade, he thought.

"I'm still listening."

"Five of them recur at the end of each month. The days vary a bit, but it's always the last week of the month, and it's the same entry each time: 'R ten thousand.'"

"What's your interpretation?"

"That someone with a first or last name starting with R receives ten thousand each month from Danielsson."

"A lover," Bäckström said, suddenly remembering the condoms and Viagra they had found in his flat. But remember, some of us get to fuck without paying, he thought self-consciously, even though it was far from true.

"That's what I think too," Nadja said with a smile. "With that in mind, I think R is the first letter of her first name."

"But you have no idea who she might be?" Bäckström said.

"I'm working on it. Only just started," Nadja said, smiling.

"Okay," Bäckström said, grinning happily. So I daresay I'll have the woman's name later today, he thought.

"Then there's an entry from Friday, April fourth: 'SL twenty thousand.'"

"SL," Bäckström said, shaking his head. "If he was buying monthly tickets from Stockholm Local Transport for twenty thousand, he'd have had enough for all his friends and neighbors as well."

"Someone with the initials *SL* received twenty thousand on Friday, February eighth. I'm working on that too," Nadja said.

Good to hear that someone's doing some work, Bäckström thought. He himself had been struggling under a completely unreasonable amount of work for almost a fortnight now.

"But it's after that that it gets really interesting," Nadja said. "Really interesting, if you ask me, Bäckström."

Really interesting?

"Roughly once a week, four to six times each month, in total twenty-four times throughout this period, three acronyms recur: HA, AFS, and FI, always capital letters. They occur with more or less the same regularity and are always followed by a number. Each acronym is always followed by the same number: 'HA five,' 'AFS twenty,' 'FI fifty.' The pattern repeats, with just one exception. On one occasion the acronym FI is followed by the number one hundred, then a *B* and an exclamation mark: 'FI one hundred B!' "

"What's your interpretation?" Bäckström said, sitting and looking at the printout he had been given for simplicity's sake, scratching his round head with his right hand.

"I think HA, AFS, and FI are people's initials," Nadja said. "And I think the numbers five, ten, twenty, fifty, and one hundred refer to the amount of money being paid out. A sort of basic code, in other words."

"Well, he seems to have got off fairly cheaply, dear old Danielsson," Bäckström said, and grinned. Even I could live with a fiver, or a twenty- or fifty-kronor note, Bäckström thought. Maybe even a hundred, as long as it didn't become a habit, of course. But it didn't look as though it had. Just the once.

"I don't think so," Nadja said, shaking her head. "I think they're multiples," Nadja said.

"Multiples?" Bäckström said. *Nazdorovje? Nyet? Da?* What the hell does she mean? he thought.

"That the initials FI, who gets fifty, gets ten times as much as the initials HA, who gets five. Apart from the one occasion when he gets one hundred—in other words, twenty times as much."

"Exactly," Bäckström said. "Obviously," he said. "And this character AFS, who gets twenty each time, gets four times as much as HA, but only half of what FI gets . . ."

"Forty percent as much, except for the time when FI gets a hundred," Nadja corrected.

"Exactly, exactly, that's just what I was about to say. But what about this 'Bea,' then? After every one of these payments it always says Bea," Bäckström said, pointing at the list he had been given. "For instance, 'FI fifty, Bea,' or 'HA five, Bea.' What do you make of that?"

"I think it's code for some sort of payment," Nadja said. "People like Danielsson often used abbreviations like that. For instance *pd* would mean that you've paid. *Bea* might mean that you have to pay a certain amount: only he would have known."

"I see," Bäckström said, stroking his chin and trying to look smarter than he felt. "How much money are we talking about?

"How much money?" he repeated, just to make sure, considering the heavy mathematical calculations they were dealing with here.

"Well, this is all speculation, now, as I'm sure you appreciate," Nadja said.

"I'm listening," Bäckström said, putting his printout down and leaning back. Make the most of it, Nadja, he thought. Now that you're talking to the only person in the entire force who's smart enough to understand what you're saying.

"If we assume that Danielsson took out two million kronor on the day he was murdered, and bearing in mind that it was almost six months since he was last down in that bank vault, and if he took out the same amount on that occasion, then I estimate that every month he was paying circa seventeen thousand to HA, almost seventy thousand to AFS and about one hundred and seventy thousand to FI.

"In other words, circa two hundred and fifty thousand each month," she went on. "Over six months that comes to one and a half million. If we add in the other costs he must have incurred in connection with this activity, plus the hundred and seventy thousand that FI got on the occasion that he received the multiple of a hundred B plus exclamation mark, we end up with about two million. If we're talking ballpark numbers, of course," Nadja concluded, with the linguistic flexibility that had become part of her Swedish personality.

"I understand exactly what you mean," Bäckström said, having at least absorbed the most important points. If I was one of those fucking analysts at Criminal Intelligence, I'd hang my head in shame if I ever met Nadja, he thought.

"So what are we going to do about this?" Bäckström asked. After all, I'm still the boss here, he thought.

"I thought we could add it to what we've made available to Criminal Intelligence," Nadja said. "See if there's anyone there who has anything to offer."

"Go ahead," Bäckström said, nodding eagerly. How on earth could those morons have anything to add at this sort of level? he thought.

"If it comes to it, we'll just have to work it out for ourselves," he added.

Thirty minutes later Superintendent Toivonen stormed into Bäckström's office. His face was deep red and he was waving the latest Criminal Intelligence information that he'd just printed off from his e-mail.

"What the hell are you playing at, Bäckström?" Toivonen snarled.

"Fine," Bäckström said. "Thanks for asking. And how are you?" Fucking fox, he thought.

"HA, AFS, and FI," Toivonen said, waving the printout. "What the hell are you playing at, Bäckström?"

"I get the feeling that you're in a position to tell me that," Bäckström said with a friendly grin. Correct me if I'm wrong, you Finnish bastard, he thought.

"HA as in Hassan Talib, AFS as in Afsan Ibrahim. FI as in Farshad Ibrahim," Toivonen said, glaring at him.

"Doesn't ring any bells," Bäckström said, shaking his head. "So who are these clowns?"

"You never heard of them?" Toivonen said. "You'd think they might be familiar even to people working in the lost property office, where you've spent the past few years. I daresay the guys in the traffic office know who they are. But you don't?"

"If I did, I wouldn't have had to put it up on Criminal Intelligence, would I?" Bäckström said. Are you thick, or what? That was a so-called rhetorical question. Chew on that, my little Finnish joker, Bäckström thought with a broad smile.

"Just you watch yourself, Bäckström," Toivonen said.

And with that, he walked out.

45.

Before Superintendent Toivonen went home for the day he had a meeting with police chief Anna Holt. She had asked for an informal conversation, just the two of them. Without mineral water, minutes, and other unnecessary formalities.

After his encounter with Bäckström he had gone straight to see Nadja. He had explained the situation to her and asked her to keep a close eye on any information that might be connected to the armed raid out at Bromma.

"I'm sorry," Nadja said. "I had no idea there might be a link between our case and the robbery. If I'd known, obviously I would have come to you first."

"Good," Toivonen said, sounding more severe than he had intended. "Tomorrow we're picking up the pace of the whole process against the Ibrahim brothers and their cousin. I don't want it getting out onto the street, and I don't want to read about it in the papers."

"Don't worry about Bäckström," Nadja said, patting him on the arm. "I promise I'll keep an eye on him."

"I've never been the slightest bit worried about you," Toivonen said.

Then he had taken a quick walk round Solna to lower his blood pressure before going to see his boss.

"Sit down," Anna Holt said. "Can I offer you anything?"

"Thanks, I'm fine," Toivonen said, sitting down.

"Tell me," Holt said.

"There's a connection between the raid out at Bromma and the murder of Kari Viirtanen. I believe forensics will be able to prove that when they're finished with their examination of the van used in the robbery. Viirtanen was the one who shot the guards. But we still don't know who was doing the driving for him. We've got several names to choose from, as I'm sure you can imagine. We're working on it."

"So why did he shoot them?"

"Because that poor sod who died set off the dye capsules in the bag. Which made Kari mad because there weren't supposed to have been any capsules in that bag."

"Tell me," Holt said.

The money came from London. Swedish, Danish, and Norwegian notes that had been exchanged in England and Scotland. As well as British pounds that Swedish banks and currency exchange companies had ordered. They had been brought into Bromma from London by private jet, with a two-man crew and four passengers, British businessmen. They had no idea that they had been joined at the last minute by about eleven million kronor in a small cloth bag.

"Security firms are doing that more and more these days. Unless the amounts are extremely large, they improvise and send them with unscheduled flights. For safety reasons there must never be dye capsules in that sort of bag. Apparently changes in air pressure, among other things, can set them off, and obviously that might be a bit tricky if they happened to be on a plane when they went off."

"I can imagine," Holt said.

"Because the guards themselves aren't allowed to open the bags when they arrive, which was a demand pushed through by the unions to stop staff being suspected of theft, what usually happens is that once the money has been transferred to a security van, it's taken to a security depot without dye capsules. They usually use unmarked vehicles, and because the depot they were heading for was just a fifteen-minute drive from Bromma Airport, and because the amount in question was so small, just eleven million, that's what happened on this occasion."

"A small amount? So what counts as a large amount?" Holt said with a smile.

"Three- or four-figure multiples of millions," Toivonen said, smiling back.

"So what went wrong this time?"

"The guard who was shot was sadly too ambitious for his own good. Without asking his boss for permission, he had taken a spare empty bag containing dye capsules along with them, and he put the bag from London inside that. As soon as the raiders had made off with the bag and he felt safe, he set off the capsules by remote control. It has a range of about two hundred and fifty meters, but this time he was clearly too impatient, because the capsules went off when they were just fifty meters away."

"But would that be enough?" Holt interrupted. "To stain all the notes in the inner bag, I mean?"

"No," Toivonen said with a wry smile. "It wasn't, and there wasn't much wrong with the notes we found in the abandoned vehicle. Which they dumped, by the way, just twenty meters from the Hells Angels HQ about a kilometer from the airport. Maybe they wanted to cause trouble for them too before they ran off."

"The problem was that Kari Viirtanen didn't know that," Holt concluded. "That the money was still usable."

"That's right," Toivonen said with a nod. "And he got as mad as Mad Kari often did. The driver did a U-turn. Kari wound down the window and started firing at the guards who were trying to run. The one running on the driver's side was run down as well, so whoever was driving wasn't particularly pleasant either."

"What do we know about the weapon?" Holt asked.

"An Uzi automatic pistol, twenty-two-caliber," Toivonen said. "The weapons experts are fairly sure of that. The smallest magazine contains sixty bullets, and about thirty cartridges have been found at the scene. The guard who died was hit five times in the back, and his padded vest stopped those, and three times in the head, which killed him instantly. The other one was also shot ten times, but none of them was fatal. The remaining ten shots must have missed," Toivonen concluded.

"Sounds like an inside job," Holt said.

"Definitely," Toivonen agreed. "Our British colleagues are looking for him at their end and we're trying to trace his contacts at our end. If we're lucky, something will give, and once one end is sorted, the other usually follows."

"Viirtanen was shot by the people behind the raid?" Holt asked.

"Yes, he wasn't the only one who's furious."

"What about the driver?"

"I daresay he'll turn up in due course," Toivonen said with a wry smile.

"If I understood you correctly at the meeting yesterday, you believe the Ibrahim boys and their unsavory cousin are behind this?"

"There's always a lot of talk," Toivonen said. "Something like this takes a lot of work and the involvement of a lot of people. There are cars to be stolen, then number plates that match the make and model, you need to get hold of caltrops to scatter as you make your escape. There's always someone who talks. The Ibrahim brothers and Hassan Talib have got pretty low odds this time. And you should always put your money on a surefire winner," Toivonen said. He was fond of visiting Solvalla racecourse even outside of his official duties.

"What about the connection to the murders of Danielsson and the paperboy?"

"Well, to take it step by step, everything suggests that there's a connection between Danielsson and the paperboy, the poor boy they fished out of Ulvsundasjön last night. Our colleague Niemi is even prepared to put money on the fact that they were killed by the same person or persons. One, two, possibly more," Toivonen said.

"But have the murders of Danielsson and Akofeli got any connection to our robbery?"

"If you asked me that this morning, I would have said no. But now I think I know better," he said, handing a slim plastic folder to Holt.

"See for yourself," he said. "My conversation with an anonymous informant, plus information that Nadja Högberg has found in Danielsson's pocket diary, along with her own conclusions . . ."

"Okay," Holt said. "Give me five minutes."

"Well, I agree with you," Holt said four minutes later.

"Yes, most people who think like you and me probably would," Toivonen said. "What remains is to slot the details into the right places, but we can probably assume that Karl Danielsson was acting as a private banker to the Ibrahim brothers and their cousin."

"Who just two days after the robbery suffer an acute shortage of funds to the tune of two million kronor," Holt concluded.

"It costs a lot to clean up your own mess," Toivonen said.

46.

After her meeting with Toivonen, Holt had walked home to her flat in Jungfrudansen in Solna, stopping to do some shopping on the way. Her flat was only a couple kilometers from the police station and she liked to walk whenever she got the chance, especially on a day like today. Sun shining in a blue, cloudless sky. Twenty-six degrees and high summer in Sweden, even though it was still only the end of May.

Since she had become police chief of the Western District she had found herself thinking of it more and more often as her own kingdom, or possibly queendom, and of the importance of being a good and enlightened monarch who cared for justice and fairness and all the other people who lived there. Holt County, Holt thought, because presumably that's what it would have been called, at least colloquially, if she had been a female sheriff in the Midwest or southern States.

More than three hundred and fifty square kilometers of land and water between Lake Mälaren to the west and Edsviken and the Baltic to the east. Between the old tollgates of central Stockholm to the south up to North Järva, Jakobsberg, and the outer archipelago of Lake Mälaren to the north. A queendom with some three hundred thousand inhabitants. Half a dozen billionaires, a few hundred millionaires, and maybe ten thousand who couldn't put food on the table each day and lived off social benefits. Plus all the ordinary people in between.

A realm with five hundred police officers, many of whom

could justifiably be reckoned among the finest in the country. And then there was Evert Bäckström, of course. Plus all the ordinary, normal officers in between.

Now the fire-breathing dragon had dug its claws into what was her territory and her responsibility. Five murders within the space of a week. As many as you would normally expect in a whole year in an area that was nonetheless reckoned to be one of the most crime-ridden in the country.

What I need is a white knight on a purebred charger who can kill the dragon for me, Holt thought, starting to giggle as she thought what would happen if she said that out loud in one of the meetings of the network of female police officers where she was on the board.

He who kills the dragon gets the princess and half the kingdom, Holt thought with a smile. And if that role is taken by any of our colleagues out here, then little Magdalena Hernandez stands a good chance of getting the role of princess, she thought. At least she would if their male colleagues got to vote on the matter.

She herself was too old, forty-eight that autumn, Holt thought with a sigh. Besides, she already had a man whose company she was enjoying more and more. She was very fond of him, maybe even loved him, even if up to now she had tried not to think like that. It would be quite good enough if my white knight kills the dragon for me, she thought.

He who kills the dragon gets the princess and half the kingdom, Anna Holt concluded, nodding to herself as soon as she had made the decision.

And I'd prefer it if he could get on with it straightaway, the police chief of the Western District thought.

47.

On Friday Detective Inspector Alm had hoped to be able to get away from work a bit early. It would be the weekend in a few hours anyway, and there was a fair amount to get done before he could enjoy it in peace and quiet together with his beloved wife and two good friends they had invited over for dinner.

Nothing remarkable about that. Their case seemed to be developing at a surprising pace, and more or less without any input from him. Akofeli's unexpected demise had admittedly complicated matters, but it would all sort itself out if only he got the chance to have a really good think. Unfortunately all his hopes on that score had been dashed, and he hadn't even managed to go and get wine like he had promised. Instead he had to call his wife and argue about it before she finally gave in and did all the things he had promised to do.

An hour after lunch, when he had more or less already packed up and prepared his retreat through the most suitable back door the police station could offer, he had received an unexpected visit. By the time he eventually got home his guests were already sitting and waiting in the living room. His wife was standing in the kitchen, clattering crockery and glasses, and the glance she flashed at him was not a kindly one.

"Hello, darling," Alm said, leaning forward to give her a kiss. On the cheek, at least, he thought.

"If the detective inspector would care to look after our guests, I'll try to see to it that they get something to drink," his wife said, twisting her head away.

"Of course, darling," Alm said. What an unbelievably wretched day, he thought.

"How can I help you, then, Seppo?" Alm said, giving Seppo Laurén a friendly nod and taking an involuntary glance at his watch. Maybe it would be best to switch on the tape recorder as well, he thought, as he placed his aide-mémoire on the desk. The lad was far from clearheaded, so you never could tell.

"So how can I help you, Seppo?" Alm repeated with a smile.

"The rent," Seppo said. "What am I going to do about the rent?" he said, handing Alm a payment slip.

"What do you normally do?" Alm said amiably, looking at the payment slip. Just over five thousand kronor, Alm thought. Pretty high for a two-room flat in that building, he thought.

"Mom," Seppo said. "But since she's been ill I've been giving them to Kalle. But now he's been killed. What do I do now?"

"Kalle Danielsson used to help you with the rent?" Alm said. "Since your mom got ill?" he clarified. I'll have to get someone from Social Services, Alm thought, glancing at his watch again.

"Yes, and I used to get money for food as well," Seppo said. "From Kalle, I mean. Since Mom got ill."

"It was nice of Kalle to help you," Alm said. Surely he should be getting some sort of pension or disability benefit? Alm thought.

"S'pose so," Seppo said, shrugging. "He used to argue with Mom."

"He argued with your mom?"

"Yes," Seppo said. "First he argued with her. Then he pushed her. She fell over and hit her head. On our kitchen table."

"He pushed her?" Alm said. "In your home? And she hit her head?" What's the lad saying? he thought.

"Yes," Seppo said.

"Why did he do that?"

"Then she got ill and fainted at work and had to go to hospital. Ambulance," Seppo said, nodding seriously.

"What did you do? When Kalle argued with your mom?"

"I hit him," Seppo said. "Karate. Then I kicked him. Karate

kicks. Then he got a nosebleed. I got cross. I hardly ever get cross."

"What did Kalle do then? After you hit him?"

"I helped him into the lift," Seppo said. "So he could go home."

"And this happened the day before your mom got ill and had to go to the hospital?"

"Yes."

"What happened after that? When your mom was in the hospital?"

"I got a new computer and loads of computer games."

"From Kalle?"

"Yes. He said sorry too. We shook hands and said we wouldn't fight anymore. He said he'd help me until Mom got better and came home again."

"And you haven't hit him again since then?"

"Well," Seppo said, shaking his head, "I did hit him once more."

"Why did you do that?" Alm asked.

"She never comes home," Seppo said. "She's still in the hospital. She doesn't want to talk to me when I'm there."

What's going on? Alm thought. I've got to get hold of Annika Carlsson, he thought.

48.

Nadja Högberg had got three names from Toivonen. Hassan Talib, Afsan Ibrahim, and Farshad Ibrahim. The initials HA, AFS, and FI in Danielsson's pocket diary. That leaves two, she thought, as she started up her computer at eight o'clock on Friday morning. Just over five hours before her colleague Detective Inspector Lars Alm got an unexpected visitor in his office.

SL and R, first and last names, and first name, respectively, she thought.

First she had pulled out their list of everyone connected to the murders of Karl Danielsson and Septimus Akofeli. Victims, family, friends and acquaintances, workmates, neighbors, witnesses, suspects, and anyone else who just happened to be there. She had checked the first and last names of 316 people and had come up with three matches: Susanna Larsson, eighteen; Sala Lucik, thirty-three; and Seppo Laurén, twenty-nine.

Susanna Larsson worked at Green Carriers with Akofeli. Sala Lucik lived in the flat above Akofeli and was on the door-to-door list, but they hadn't been able to contact her because she had spent the past fortnight locked up in Solna, suspected of serious drug offenses. Seppo Laurén was Danielsson's neighbor. The same young man who, according to Bäckström, was "a few sandwiches short of a picnic."

Easy, Nadja Högberg thought, bringing up Seppo Laurén's file. His closest relative was Ritwa Laurén, forty-nine, who had spent the last two months in the hospital after a stroke. Father unknown, Nadja read.

Could it really be that easy? Nadja Högberg thought.

Probably, she thought, as she brought up Ritwa Laurén's passport photograph on her screen five minutes later. She had been forty-two when the photograph was taken. Blond, beautiful, a shy smile in half-profile, didn't look a day over thirty-five when she had the picture taken seven years after that for her new passport.

She had lived in the same apartment on Hasselstigen for almost twenty-nine years. She had moved in with her three-month-old son before she was twenty. By then her twenty-years-older neighbor Karl Danielsson had already lived there for five years. Never trust coincidence, Nadja Högberg thought.

Almost four months ago, on Friday, February 8, "SL" had received twenty thousand kronor from Karl Danielsson. The day before, Thursday, February 7, Seppo Laurén's mother, Ritwa, had been found unconscious in the toilet at work, and had been taken to A&E at the Karolinska Hospital, and within two hours was being operated on in the hospital's neurosurgical department. One month later she had been transferred to a rehabilitation center. No longer unconscious, but not really much more than that.

Five minutes later Nadja Högberg was digging through the pile of receipts that forensics had found in Danielsson's flat. One of them was a receipt for a computer and various accessories and programs, as well as six different computer games, in total 19,875 kronor. They had all been bought from a computer store in the Solna shopping center, paid for in cash on February 8.

Father unknown, Nadja Högberg thought. Men are pigs, she thought. Some men, at least, Dr. Nadjesta Ivanova corrected herself, and this time it had only taken her an hour to find one of them.

She had spent the rest of the day on other matters. Mainly looking for a good place for someone to hide ten years' worth of accounting files. No safe-deposit box this time, Nadja thought, since there ought to be several boxes worth of documents. He had hired storage space somewhere. Not too close, but not too far away either. Danielsson seemed to be both a practical and a lazy man, the sort who organized things to make life easy for himself. Taxi distance, she thought, and started typing at her computer.

Just before five o'clock Annika Carlsson and Lars Alm had burst into her office, breathless. New and previously unknown information had emerged over the course of the afternoon from an interview with Seppo Laurén. Troubling information.

"I'm listening," Nadja Högberg said, leaning back and folding her hands over her little round stomach. I wonder where the hell he is? she thought, since she hadn't seen any sign of Bäckström since that morning.

"He admits that he had previously hit Danielsson. Evidently because he thought Danielsson was responsible for his mother ending up in the hospital. His relationship with Danielsson was also very different to what we previously thought. We can forget the idea that he just used to run little errands for Danielsson. Apparently Danielsson used to pay the rent on their apartment and gave the kid money for food. And much more besides. This reeks of revenge, if you ask me," Alm concluded.

"And he gave him a computer that must have cost a fair few thousand," Carlsson added.

"Perhaps that isn't so surprising when you consider that he was Seppo's dad," Nadja said.

"Sorry?" Annika Carlsson said.

"What the hell are you saying?" Alm said.

"I suggest we do the following," Nadja said, raising her hands to stop them. "Annika, you go and get a sample from Seppo, and we'll soon get this business of paternity sorted out. After all, we've got Danielsson's DNA already. Laurén's will probably take the usual fortnight before the National Forensics Lab get back to us, but I promise to explain how it all fits together as soon as the sample's done.

"Then you and Lars can go to his apartment and pick up the hard drive from his computer," she went on.

"What do you want that for?" Alm asked, looking at her curiously.

"If I remember correctly, he said in one of your interviews with him that he spent all evening and all night playing computer games," Nadja Högberg said. Idiots, suddenly I'm leading a murder investigation even though I'm only an ordinary civilian employee, she thought.

One and a half hours later it was done. First Nadja had told them what she'd found out from her computer about Karl Danielsson and Ritwa and Seppo Laurén. Once she was finished Alm and Carlsson had exchanged a look, then they looked at Nadja and finally they nodded to her. Reluctantly.

"But why did he deny being the father for all those years?" Annika Carlsson wondered.

"To avoid having to pay child care," Nadja said. "That way Karl Danielsson saved himself several hundred thousand kronor."

"But why didn't he even tell his own son? It's quite clear that Seppo hasn't got a clue that Danielsson is his dad," Alm said.

"Maybe he was ashamed of him. He probably wasn't good enough for a man like Karl Danielsson," Nadja concluded. Some men are pigs, she thought.

Then all three of them had gone to Alm's office. And there sat Seppo Laurén, entertaining himself with Felicia Pettersson, drinking Coca-Cola and apparently having a whale of a time.

Nadja had connected his hard drive and together they had worked out what he was doing from the afternoon of Wednesday, May 14, until the morning of Thursday, May 15. Seppo had been sitting at his computer from quarter past six on Wednesday evening until quarter past six on Thursday morning. At three in the morning he had taken a short break of eight minutes. Otherwise he had been playing nonstop for twelve hours in a row.

"I got a bit hungry then," Seppo said. "I took a break for a sandwich and a glass of milk."

"What did you do afterward? When you stopped playing on the computer, I mean?" Alm said, evidently refusing to give up even though Nadja had already given him several warning glances.

"I fell asleep," Seppo said, looking at Alm in surprise. "Why, what would you have done?"

49.

Bäckström had started Friday by going to see his boss, Anna Holt, and asking for reinforcements. Suddenly he had a double murder on his hands, the same strength team as before, and that had been inadequate from the outset.

"I hear what you're saying, Bäckström," Holt said, starting to sound more and more like her old boss Lars Martin Johansson. "The problem is that I haven't got anyone I can give you. Right now we're on our knees out here."

"Toivonen's got thirty men to investigate a robbery with two fatalities. I've got five to take care of two murders. You have peculiar priorities in this station," Bäckström said, smiling amiably. That gave you something to chew on, you scrawny little nightmare, he thought.

"I'm the one who decided the prioritization," Holt said. "So I'm going to stand by it. If any information comes to light that suggests that the people behind the robbery also killed Danielsson and Akofeli, I'll be transferring you and your colleagues to Toivonen's investigation."

"I'm not sure that would be wise," Bäckström said. Not just scrawny, he thought.

"Why not?"

"I find it hard to believe that the Ibrahim brothers would kill the man who helped them hide their money. And I find it even harder to believe that Danielsson tried to rip them off. He may have been a pisshead but he doesn't seem to have had suicidal tendencies. But do you know what I find hardest of all?"

"No," Holt said with a reluctant smile. "What?"

"If they did it anyway—killed Danielsson because he tried to steal their money, I mean—then surely they would have thought about all their money that was left in Danielsson's safe-deposit box?"

"Do you know what, Bäckström? I have a feeling that you may have a point there. Maybe you've even got an idea of who did do it, who killed Danielsson and Akofeli?"

"Yes," Bäckström said. "Just give me another week."

"Well, that all sounds excellent," Anna Holt said. "I look forward to hearing more. Now you'll have to excuse me. I've actually got a lot to do."

Just as well to kill two dykes with one stone, Bäckström thought, and went straight to Annika Carlsson to find out how things were going.

"Not great just now," Carlsson said, and sighed. "The door-to-door didn't turn up anything. Forensics are lying low and we haven't heard anything from the National Lab or forensic medicine. And as for us, we're short on ideas and leads."

"Akofeli," Bäckström said, shaking his round head. "There's something not quite right there."

"But I thought Felicia had sorted that?" Annika Carlsson said, looking at him in surprise. "Mainly thanks to you, actually, since you put her on the trail."

"I wasn't thinking of his phone calls," Bäckström said, shaking his head. "There's something else bothering me."

"But you don't know what it is?" Annika Carlsson said.

"No, I don't," Bäckström said. "It's in here somewhere, but I just can't put my finger on it."

"And you think it might be important to the case?"

"Important?" Bäckström snorted. "When I work out what it is, we'll have this case cracked. Danielsson and Akofeli."

"Fucking hell," Annika Carlsson said, looking at him, wide-eyed.

Thank you and goodbye, Bäckström thought. How fucking stupid can you get?

"You'll have to help me, Annika," Bäckström said, nodding seriously at her. "I have a feeling that you're the only one who can."

"I promise," Annika Carlsson said.

And that gave you something to chew on, while I go off and enjoy the weekend, he thought.

After that Bäckström had followed his usual Friday routine. Switched his phone's message to "official business." Turned off his cell phone. Left the police station. Took a taxi to a safe location on Kungsholmen, where he ate a decent lunch. Then a short walk home to his cozy abode, a well-earned siesta, and, as the final part of his routine Friday program, he had visited his new masseuse.

An unusually body-conscious Polish girl, Elena, twenty-six, who had her health care practice close to his home, and who had Bäckström as her last client each Friday. She always ran through the whole program and usually concluded by giving the Bäckström super-salami a little taste of the delights to come over the weekend.

That evening he was going to have dinner with an old acquaintance. A renowned art dealer, Gustaf Gustafsson Henning, to whom Bäckström was pleased to have been of assistance on a number of occasions, and who had asked if he could take Bäckström to dinner.

"How about the main dining room of Operakällaren at half past seven?" Henning had asked.

Well-to-do, silver-haired, tailored, famous from antiques shows on television, and over seventy. Out and about, and in the circles that mattered, he was known by the nickname GeGurra, and he bore not the slightest resemblance to the notorious teenage gangster Juha Valentin Andersson-Snygg, born in 1937, whose records had disappeared from the archive of the Stockholm Police many years ago.

"How about eight o'clock?" Bäckström said, since he preferred to allow himself plenty of time for important matters of bodily and personal health.

"Let's say eight, then," GeGurra agreed.

50.

Superintendent Toivonen didn't have thirty men to investigate the murder of his security guard, as Bäckström believed. By Friday morning the reinforcements had arrived. He had been authorized to borrow people from National Crime, the National Rapid-Response Unit, and the riot squad. From Stockholm County Crime and from the other district covered by the county. Even the police down in Skåne had sent him three investigators from the county's special armed robbery unit. For the time being he was in charge of almost seventy officers and detectives, as well as his own unit, and he could have had more if he wanted. Nowadays Toivonen got everything he asked for, and he and his group leaders had spent the whole day planning their strategy.

Now the whole operation had to come together. Internal surveillance, outdoor surveillance, monitoring, telephone interception, cell surveillance, bugging, increasing the pressure, stirring up and bringing in the hang-arounds and wannabes in the groups around the Ibrahim brothers and their cousin Hassan Talib. Lock them up, question them, stop their cars, subject them to body searches whenever the opportunity arose, and, if necessary, beat the shit out of them if they said anything inappropriate, made any rapid movements, or simply showed any signs of normal behavior.

"Okay, let's get to it. The Ibrahims are heading for prison," Toivonen said with a stern expression and a nod to all his colleagues.

Starting from six o'clock in the evening, Superintendent Jorma Honkamäki and his colleagues from the National Rapid-Response Unit and the Stockholm Police riot squad had carried out a total of ten raids on homes and premises in Huddinge-Botkyrka, Tensta-Rinkeby, and North Järva. They hadn't asked for permission to enter first. The doors had been uniformly smashed in. Anyone found in the flats and premises had been carried out in handcuffs. Drug-detection dogs, bomb-detection dogs, and ordinary police dogs had been sent in; the furnishings and fittings had been turned upside down; the interior walls of some offices in Flemingsberg were torn down; and money, drugs, weapons, ammunition, explosives, detonators, smoke grenades, caltrops, balaclavas, overalls, handcuffs, loose number plates, and stolen vehicles had all been found. When the sun rose on a new day in the world's most beautiful capital city, thirty-three people were in custody, and the whole thing was only just starting.

Linda Martinez was the recently appointed superintendent of National Crime's surveillance unit, brought in by Toivonen and responsible for the outdoor surveillance of the Ibrahim brothers and their cousin. She had chosen her team carefully and she was well aware of her opponents' weaknesses.

"Not an ordinary Swede as far as the eye can see," Martinez concluded as she surveyed her forces. "Nothing but black, brown, and blue," she said with a delighted grin.

Before Toivonen left the Solna police station he had met with his boss, Anna Holt, to inform her of the latest from the Criminal Investigation Service on possible connections between Karl Danielsson, the Ibrahim brothers, and Hassan Talib. Now that they knew what they were looking for, everything had been much easier to find. Among other things, a nine-year-old report about Karl Danielsson's involvement in money laundering in the wake of the major armed robbery in Akalla, to the north of Stockholm.

Because the tip-off could never be backed up with firm evidence, the case had been put to one side and eventually forgotten.

In March 1999, some nine years earlier, at least six masked and armed men had raided the depot of a security transport company out in Akalla. They drove a fifteen-ton forklift truck straight through the wall of the depot. They forced the staff onto the floor, and when they disappeared five minutes later they took with them some hundred million kronor in unmarked notes.

"One hundred and one million, six hundred and twelve thousand kronor, to be precise," Toivonen said, reading from his notes just to be sure.

"That sounds like a decent day's work," Holt said. "Not your usual shitty little raid, I mean."

"No, although it was complete fuckup for us," Toivonen said.

Not one single krona of the money had been recovered. None of those involved were ever brought to trial, even though everyone had a fair idea of who they were and how the whole thing had been planned and carried out. The only consolation under the circumstances was that none of the staff had been wounded, and that was thanks to the raiders rather than the police.

The kingpin was a well-known gangster of Moroccan descent, Abdul Ben Kader, born 1950, so now approaching sixty. He had lived in Sweden for more than twenty years and popped up regularly in criminal contexts. Everything from illegal gambling and drinking dens, brothels, organized theft, and receipt of stolen goods to insurance scams and armed robbery.

Constantly under suspicion, taken into custody, locked up on three occasions. But never convicted, never obliged to spend a single day as a convicted felon in a Swedish penal institution.

"A couple months after the Akalla raid the bastard retired and went back to Morocco," Toivonen said with a wry smile. "Apparently he now owns a number of bars and at least one hotel."

"So where do the Ibrahim brothers and their cousin come into this?" Holt asked.

All three had taken part in the raid. That was the firm belief of Toivonen and his colleagues. Farshad, who had been twenty-eight at the time of the raid, was the one who led the actual operation. His cousin, who was three years younger, had driven the forklift, and his little brother Afsan, then just twenty-three years old, had grabbed as much money as he could get his hands on, even though he was dressed in overalls, gloves, and a full ski mask.

"Ben Kader could be described as a sort of mentor to Farshad. Farshad was his favorite even though he wasn't from north Africa but Iran. They're both Muslim, by the way, and teetotalers," Toivonen added for some reason.

"Farshad arrived here as a refugee with his family when he was only three years old. His younger brother was born in Sweden. Ben Kader had no children of his own, and because little Farshad was made of the right stuff, he evidently took a liking to the lad. We know that they're still in touch, because only a few weeks ago we received information from our French colleagues via Interpol that they met up on the Riviera as recently as March this year."

"Danielsson," Holt prompted.

"Ben Kader used him as his bookkeeper, accountant, and financial adviser for his legal activities. Among other things, he owned a grocery store in Sollentuna, a tobacconist's and a dry cleaner's out here in Solna. In hindsight, that probably wasn't all that Danielsson did, but because it could never be proved, he was only ever questioned for information.

"When Ben Kader returned to Morocco, Farshad both took over the grocery store and got Danielsson into the bargain. Farshad still owns the shop in Sollentuna. He has relatives working there, but he's listed as the owner. Danielsson, on the other hand, has vanished from the paperwork."

"Akofeli," Holt said. "How does he come into this? He could

hardly have been involved in the Akalla raid, since he would have been, what, sixteen at the time?"

"To be honest, I haven't the faintest idea," Toivonen said, shaking his head. "I don't think he was involved with either Danielsson or the Ibrahim brothers. Maybe he was just in the wrong place at the wrong time and slipped into it all on a banana peel. I think we can forget any idea of him murdering Danielsson."

"What about the Ibrahim brothers and Hassan Talib, then? Could they have murdered Danielsson and Akofeli?"

"No idea," Toivonen said with a sigh.

"Maybe it'll work out," Holt said, smiling. "Bäckström promised that it would be sorted soon. He said he just needs another week."

"I can hardly contain myself," Toivonen snorted.

Then Toivonen had gone home to his row house in Spånga. Prepared a meal for his two teenage sons, since his wife had gone up to Norrland to visit her ailing father. After the meal his boys had disappeared to meet their friends. Toivonen had poured himself a beer and a small whiskey shot and started the weekend in front of the television. When his younger son got home at eleven, his dad was lying on the sofa, dozing in front of the sports channel.

"Aren't you going to go to bed, Dad?" his son asked. "You're looking a bit tired, if you ask me."

51.

Messrs. Bäckström and GeGurra had met in the main dining room of Operakällaren just after eight o'clock in the evening, and an extremely obliging headwaiter had shown them to their discreet table out on the veranda. He had taken their drink order, bowed once more, and hurried away. As was traditional, GeGurra was picking up the tab.

"Marvelous to see you, Superintendent," GeGurra said, raising his large dry martini as he cautiously nibbled at an olive that had been delivered on a saucer alongside.

"Good to see you too," Bäckström chimed in, raising his own ice-chilled double vodka. Even though you're becoming more like a standard ass-bandit every day, he thought.

Then they had ordered. Bäckström had taken the lead and even GeGurra the faggot had gone along with his selection and chosen to eat like a normal person. More or less, at least.

"To start I'd like Skagen toast with a side dish of salt salmon, the steak à la Rydberg with two egg yolks. Beer and schnapps throughout, and I'll get back to you about the rest."

"And what sort of schnapps would *monsieur le directeur* like?" the headwaiter asked, leaning sideways another few inches.

"Czech lager, Russian vodka. Do you have Standard?" What do you mean, *directeur*? Bäckström thought.

"I'm afraid not," the headwaiter lamented. "But we do have Stolichnaya. Both Cristal and Gold."

"Stalichnaya," Bäckström corrected, with his newly acquired knowledge of Russian. "In that case I'll start with a Gold with the fish and Cristal with the steak," he declared, like a true connoisseur.

"Single or double?"

Is he pulling my leg? Bäckström thought. What's he doing, handing out samples?

"Large doubles," Bäckström said. "All the way through. No half-measures."

GeGurra had concurred, and complimented Bäckström on his choice. He had abstained from the salt salmon and the extra egg yolk, and made do with a single shot with the starter and red wine with the main.

"If you have a decent cabernet sauvignon by the glass?"

Naturally they did, according to the headwaiter. They had a

fine American wine from 2003, Sonoma Valley, ninety percent cabernet.

"And just the slightest touch of *petit verdot* to give it a lift."

Queers, Bäckström thought. Where the fuck do they get all that shit from? *A lift.* Shirt lifters, maybe.

But they had a pleasant evening. GeGurra was in an expansive mood. He thanked Bäckström for his latest assistance in informing him most admirably about the developments in the big art racket that the police had spent the whole winter investigating. Naturally Bäckström's half-witted colleagues had made a mess of things again, but GeGurra hadn't even figured on the preliminary investigation.

It had been Bäckström's last contribution as a lost-property cop, and because he didn't himself have access to that sort of material, he had logged in, like so many times before, on a seriously mentally handicapped colleague's computer, a former forensics officer who had had to cut his hours to part-time since he tried to poison his wife. He had taken a couple copies of the files on disc. One for GeGurra and one for himself, just to be on the safe side.

"Don't mention it," Bäckström said modestly.

"And our new payment arrangements are working?" GeGurra said, for some reason. "I hope you're happy with them, my dear?"

"It's all fine," Bäckström said, because in spite of his tragic proclivities, GeGurra was at least a very generous fag. Credit where credit's due, he thought.

"On an entirely different matter, now that I am fortunate enough to have you here," GeGurra said.

"I saw on television about that dreadful armed robbery out at Bromma Airport," he went on. "Where they shot those poor guards. Those robbers seem utterly ruthless. It must have been a professional job, surely? From what I saw on television, one could almost get the impression that one of those military commando units had been involved."

"Not your usual queer bashers," Bäckström agreed, remembering some of Juha Valentin's early efforts in the parks and alleys of Stockholm.

"I was talking to a good friend who owns a large number of shops here in the city center, and every day a number of his employees have to go to the bank with fairly large amounts of cash. He's terribly worried," GeGurra said.

"It's a jungle out there," Bäckström agreed. "He's probably right to worry."

"You don't think you might be able to help him? Take a look at his routines, give him some good advice? I'm sure he'd be immensely grateful."

"Is he the sort who can keep his mouth shut?" Bäckström asked. "This sort of thing can be a bit sensitive, as I'm sure you appreciate."

"Of course, of course," GeGurra said, emphasizing the point by holding up a blue-veined hand in a calming gesture. "He's a most discreet man."

"You can always give him my cell number," Bäckström said. He had a well-developed plan to revitalize his wardrobe before the summer.

"He's also extremely generous," GeGurra added, raising his glass in a toast.

They suddenly had company for the dessert course. GeGurra, true to his proclivities, had chosen fresh berries, whereas Bäckström made do with a good cognac. Their company was "an old and very dear friend" of GeGurra's, and, like him, in the art business.

Old and old, Bäckström thought. Thirty-five at most, and what fucking hooters—it's a good job the retarded folk dancer isn't here, he thought.

After the introductory kisses on the cheek between old friends, GeGurra had taken care of the formalities.

"My very dear friend Evert Bäckström," GeGurra said, "and this is my utterly delightful friend Tatiana Thorén. She used to be married to one of my old business contacts who didn't always know what was good for him," he clarified.

What would people like you want with someone like her? Bäckström thought. He held out his hand for a manly handshake and gave her a taste of his Clint Eastwood smile.

"Are you interested in art as well, Evert?" Tatiana Thorén asked as soon as GeGurra had pulled out her chair for her so that she could position her well-shaped rear at the right height for Bäckström to be able to enjoy her generous cleavage from exactly the right angle.

"I'm a police officer," Bäckström said with a stern nod.

"A police officer, goodness, how exciting," Tatiana said, her big, dark eyes opening wide. "And what sort of police officer are you?"

"Murders, violent crime, superintendent," Bäckström said. "I don't get involved in the other stuff." And Clint can kiss my ass, he thought.

Then they had kept Tatiana company as she satisfied the worst of her hunger with a simple salmon sandwich and a glass of champagne, while devoting at least ninety percent of her attention to Bäckström.

"Goodness, how exciting," Tatiana repeated, smiling with her red lips and her white teeth. "I've never met a real murder detective before. Only seen them on television."

Bäckström had given her the usual selection of heroic deeds from his action-packed career as a legendary police officer. The super-salami had already started to move, and once everything was starting to happen, it all went like clockwork.

GeGurra had made his excuses as soon as he had settled the bill. At his age he needed a good night's sleep. Then Tatiana and Bäckström had looked in on the nightclub Café Opera, next door to the restaurant, where they had had a couple extra drinks to help them warm up. I don't know why I should need those, Bäckström thought, since the super-salami had definitely woken up. A good thing I'm not standing here naked with some damn baseball cap on my head, Bäckström thought, as he leaned against the bar. I'd have looked like a fucking capital *F,* he thought, thrusting out his broad chest and sucking in his stomach.

"Wow, Superintendent," Tatiana said, running her hand over the front of his shirt. "I don't think this is any ordinary six-pack, is it?"

Tatiana lived in a small two-room apartment on Jungfrugatan in Östermalm. The girl's got a sense of humor, living on "Maiden Street," Bäckström thought. He lost his trousers in the hallway and removed the rest of his clothes on the way to her bedroom. He was in fine form once he had tipped her onto the broad bed. There he had given her a serious seeing-to, according to the usual routine for the first patrol on the scene. Bäckström had groaned and grunted and Tatiana had screamed out loud. Then he had shifted position and let her ride the salami lift up and down for at least a kilometer before it was time once again.

Then he had fallen asleep, and by the time he came to again the sun was already high in the blue sky above Jungfrugatan. Tatiana had provided breakfast. Gave him her phone number and made him promise to see her again as soon as she got back from her holiday in Greece.

52.

On Friday afternoon Detective Superintendent Jan Lewin from the National Murder Squad returned from a murder case in Östergötland. He had gone straight home to his partner Anna

Holt, and when he put the key in her door she was standing there waiting for him. She reached out her hand to his.

"Good to have you home again, Jan," Holt said.

Partner and police chief, Jan Lewin thought, as he sat on the sofa and leafed through all the documents she had given him. Murder, attempted murder, armed robbery, the murder of one of the suspects, then the murder of an old alcoholic, and, just for good measure, the murder of the paperboy who found him. And what does this really have to do with Anna and me? he thought.

"What do you think, Jan?" Holt said, moving closer to him.

"What does Toivonen say?" Lewin asked.

"That he hasn't got a clue," Anna Holt said with a giggle.

"He's probably right, then." Lewin smiled at her. "I haven't got a clue either."

"You don't seem particularly interested," Holt said, taking the papers from him and putting them down on the coffee table.

"My mind's on other things," Jan Lewin said.

"Your mind's on other things?"

"Well, I've been at home with the most beautiful woman in the world for almost half an hour now," Lewin said, glancing at his watch to make sure. "I've had a kiss and a hug and a big pile of papers handed to me. We're sitting on the same sofa. I'm reading. She's watching me. Obviously my mind's on other things." Lewin nodded to Holt.

"So what are you thinking, then?"

"That I want to unbutton your blouse," Jan Lewin said.

53.

At eleven o'clock that evening, Farshad and his brother Afsan had left the large detached house in Sollentuna where they lived with their parents, their three sisters, and their youngest brother, Nasir, twenty-five. Right now, though, the youngster seemed to have gone off somewhere. Not a trace of him for the past week, and Toivonen already had a few ideas of why this might be.

They had driven off in Farshad's black Lexus, and things couldn't have been better, since it was already plugged in and ready. Earlier that evening Farshad had been sloppy and left it in the carpark of the NK department store while he and Talib had gone down to the delicatessen in the basement. Just five minutes, to get something nice for his beloved mother, no big deal.

Linda Martinez's colleagues had needed only a minute to attach a GPS transmitter to the car, so now they could follow Alpha 1—a red electronic arrow with the number one—on a computer screen from the peace and quiet of their surveillance vehicle.

Afsan was driving, while Farshad spent most of the time on the phone. Outside a Lebanese restaurant on Regeringsgatan they had stopped to pick up Hassan Talib, who had also been sloppy. Before he got into the backseat of the Lexus he had opened the trunk of a silver-gray Mercedes that was parked in the street to take out a cell phone, which he put in the breast pocket of his jacket.

The automatic cameras in the surveillance car following the Lexus clicked rapidly, keeping an eye on what was going on from behind.

"Bingo," Linda Martinez exclaimed, since they had just discovered a previously unknown car, and when she personally attached the transmitter five minutes later she was a happy woman. Alfa 3, Martinez decided, marking it off on her digital notepad.

This is the life, she thought. What could the office offer compared to the street? Although that was probably where she should have been. Why the hell did I become a superintendent? she wondered. If her boss, Lars Martin Johansson, hadn't already retired, she would have given him the finger, since it had been his idea.

Her colleagues in the second car had followed the target. They ended up down at Café Opera in Kungsträdgården and watched Afsan double-park twenty meters from the entrance. Then saw the hearty slaps on the back that the three of them exchanged with the bouncers before they vanished inside the nightclub.

Proper little ayatollahs. I'm going to hang those camel jockeys by their own balls, thought Frank Motoele, thirty, as he let his camera whirr.

"Frank has a problem with Muslims," Sandra Kovac, twenty-seven, explained to Magda Hernandez, twenty-five, who had nagged her way to a place in the passenger seat once she had obtained the instant approval of Linda Martinez and been transferred from patrol duty to the surveillance team.

"Frank's a proper little racist nigger," Kovac said, nodding to Magda. "Big black man, hates everyone else—if you're wondering why he looks so cross, I mean."

"Not you, Magda," Frank said with a smile. "If you take off that red top I'll show you just how much I like you."

"He's sexist as well," Kovac said. "Did I mention that? And he's got a really tiny one. Africa's smallest."

"If you stay in the car, Sandra, and stop talking shit, Magda and I will follow them," Motoele decided. He really didn't need to listen to that sort of crap, since his colleague Kovac had found out how things stood on that score after a work Christmas party some seventeen months before.

In the world that Linda Martinez inhabited there weren't any officers who could get into a celebrity nightclub just by flashing their badges to the bouncers. She had already dealt with that by other means, but Magda Hernandez hadn't even had to make use of her assistance. She merely smiled her dazzling white smile and swept past the queue in her red top and short skirt.

Frank Motoele, on the other hand, was stopped at the door, and everything went the way it usually did.

"Sorry," the bouncer said, shaking his head. "At this time of the evening we can only admit members." One hundred and ninety centimeters, one hundred kilos of muscle, and eyes that he had fortunately never seen before. And it was all too likely to end up the way it all too often ended up when he was just trying to do his job, the bouncer thought. I'd give a million to have that nigger's girl. She could stand here in slippers and pajamas while the rabble just stood round bowing, he thought.

"Guest list," Motoele said, nodding to the sheet of paper in the other bouncer's hand. "Motoele," Frank Motoele said. On some really cold, miserable day with the rain lashing the windows of Kronoberg jail, we'll doubtless meet again, he thought, since—belying his outward appearance—he spent most of his free time writing poetry.

"He's on here," the other bouncer said after a quick glance at the list.

"I thought I recognized you," the first bouncer said, attempting a smile and stepping aside.

"Once doesn't count," Motoele said, giving him a look as he turned his gaze inward and looked at himself. One day you and I will meet, he thought. Until that day, I will meet many more that are like you.

God, what a creepy fucker, the bouncer thought, watching him as he disappeared into the club.

"Did you see that nigger's girl?"

"I bet you she's one of those ones who eat their prey alive," his colleague declared, shaking his head.

It wasn't particularly difficult to locate the Ibrahim brothers and their cousin. The huge Talib's shaved head shone like a beacon across the packed club.

"Let's split up," Frank said, smiling as if he had said something completely different.

Magda Hernandez smiled back. She tilted her head to one side. Showed the tip of her tongue to tease him.

I could eat you alive, Motoele thought, as he watched her go. Would little Miss Magda like to make a baby with me? he thought.

Five minutes later she was back. She had also put on a large pair of sunglasses even though the club was dimly lit.

"Hi, Frank," Magda said, stroking his arm, as every male gaze in the vicinity wandered over her red top, her red mouth, and her white teeth.

"I think we've got a problem," Magda said, putting her arm round his neck and whispering in his ear.

"Okay," Frank said. "Switch with Sandra. Tell Linda, and see if we can get a decent photographer here."

"See you later, then, darling," Magda said, stretching up on her slender ankles and kissing him lightly on the cheek.

54.

Sandra Kovac, twenty-seven, was the daughter of immigrants, raised in Tensta. Her dad was Serbian, with far too much hair on his chest for his own good, and he left her mom when Sandra was two years old, only to cause problems for his daughter seventeen years later when she applied to the Police Academy in Solna.

"I presume you're aware that Sandra Kovac is the daughter of

Janko Kovac," the assistant commissioner for submissions said with a nervous smile toward the application committee's female chair.

"I've never believed in inherited sin," the female chair had said. "What did your dad do, by the way?" she added, looking curiously at the assistant commissioner.

"He was a rural priest," the assistant commissioner said.

"Really?" the chair said.

The same day that Sandra Kovac finished at the Police Academy, a well-trained man in his forties had knocked on the door of her student room out in Bergshamra. A fellow officer, Sandra thought. A soon-to-be fellow officer, she thought, since such distinctions were important. Even though she was only wearing her dressing gown and was starting to get ready for that evening's party with the other graduates, she had opened the door.

"What can I do for you?" Sandra Kovac said, tightening the belt of the gown a bit just in case she had missed something.

"Quite a lot, I hope," the well-trained man said, smiling amiably at her and showing his ID. "My name's Wiklander," he said. "I work for the Security Police. A superintendent, actually."

"Surprise, surprise," Sandra Kovac said.

A week later she had started work there. Five years later she had gone with her boss to National Crime, seeing as their mutual boss had moved up the chain and been given responsibility for the National Crime Squad, the National Rapid-Response Unit, helicopters, foreign activity, and everything ranging from all the secret stuff that belonged to the Security Police to all the stuff that was still public.

"You're coming with me, Wiklander," Lars Martin Johansson said the day before his promotion was made public. Hadn't even pointed with his whole hand.

"Can I bring Sandra?" Wiklander asked.

"Janko's daughter," Johansson said.

"Yes."

"Couldn't be better," Johansson said, because he could see around corners.

Magdalena Hernandez, twenty-five, was the daughter of immigrants from Chile. Her parents had fled the night that Pinochet seized power and ordered the dictatorship's lackeys to kill the country's elected president, Salvador Allende. A long journey that had begun on foot over the border to Argentina had finally come to an end when they had got as far north as it was possible to get if you come from Valparaíso in Chile.

Magda was born and raised in Sweden. After her twelfth birthday all the men she met stopped looking her in the eye and started staring at her chest instead. All the men between seven and seventy, she thought, as her seven-years-older brother bloodied his hands for her sake on a daily basis for the same reason.

The day of her fifteenth birthday, she had spoken to him.

"I'll get rid of them, Chico," she said. "I promise."

"I want you to keep them," Chico said, nodding seriously. "You have to understand something, Magda," he added. "You're God's gift to us men and it isn't up to any of us to change what He has given us."

"Okay, then," Magda said.

Ten years later she met Frank Motoele, thirty. She had finished her shift at six o'clock in the morning and, even though she needed to sleep in her own bed, she had gone home with him.

"Would Miss Magda like to make a baby with me?" he asked, turning his gaze outward as he lifted her up on his bed so that he could look her right in the eye without having to bend his neck.

"I'd love to," Magda said. "Just promise to be careful."

"I promise," Frank Motoele said. "I'll never leave you," he added. Because my fire burns brightest in the North, he thought.

———

Frank Motoele came from a children's home in Kenya. He had met his parents twenty-five years ago. His dad, Gunnar, a carpenter from Borlänge, had got a job on a hotel project run by Skanska in Kenya, and he had taken his wife, Ulla, and stayed for two years. They picked Frank up from the children's home the week before they were due to go back to Sweden.

"What about all the paperwork?" Ulla wondered. "Don't we have to get all that sorted out first?"

"It'll be all right," Gunnar Andersson the carpenter said. Then he shrugged and took his wife and son home.

At Arlanda they had to spend twenty-four hours waiting, but eventually it had been sorted out and they were allowed to go home to Borlänge.

"That white stuff out there is snow," Gunnar Andersson explained, pointing through the windshield of the rental car. *"Snow,"* he explained in English.

"Snow," Frank repeated, nodding. Like on the slopes of Kilimanjaro, he thought, because the nice lady in the children's home had already told him. She had also shown him pictures, so it was easy to recognize even though he was only five years old. Like white ice cream, tons and tons of it, he thought.

The day of his eighteenth birthday Frank Andersson had spoken to his dad, Gunnar. He had explained that he wanted to adopt his original name. Change Andersson to Motoele.

"If you don't mind," Frank said.

"Not at all," Gunnar said. "The day you deny your roots is the day you deny yourself."

"So it's okay?" Frank asked. Just to be sure, he thought.

"As long as you don't forget that I'm your dad," Gunnar said.

"You fucked Frank, didn't you?" Sandra Kovac said the next day when they were standing down in the garage and waiting for a former children's home child from Kenya who was already a quarter of an hour late for his shift.

"Yes," Magda said, nodding.

"Impressive," Sandra Kovac said with a sigh. "But don't worry, once doesn't count," she said, because she was still Janko Kovac's daughter and probably lived on a different planet to someone like Magda Hernandez.

"He wants us to have a child," Magda said.

"I thought you were going to transfer to us here at surveillance?" Janko's daughter said. "At least that's what Linda said when I spoke to her."

"Well, that's what he said," Magda said. "To me," she said.

"If he said it, then he must mean it," Sandra said. He didn't want to have a fucking kid with me, she thought.

"I told him, all in good time," Magda said.

"How did he take that?"

"Like all romantics," Magda said with a smile. "And sexists," she added, smiling even more.

"Oh, well, then," Sandra said.

55.

On Saturday morning Grislund, thirty-six, had opened his heart to Superintendent Jorma Honkamäki, forty-two, head of Toivonen's surveillance unit and usually the acting head of the Stockholm Police riot squad.

A heart that was already wide-open, since he had opened it three days earlier to his old friend Fredrik Åkare, fifty-one, who was sergeant-at-arms for the Hells Angels out in Solna. The same Åkare who was absolutely livid when he stepped into his workshop—and what real choice had he had, a simple car mechanic and father of two? Grislund thought.

"Okay, Grislund, unless you fancy drinking the oil from your own drip tray, I suggest you tell me where I can find little Nasir," Åkare said, kicking the contents of the tray across Grislund's well-scrubbed concrete floor to underline the seriousness of what he had just said.

Grislund had revealed everything. He was a simple man but even he realized it was time to choose a side. Naturally, Grislund was not his real name: No one would really be called Pigpen. He actually came from a noble family. He was called Stig after his father and Svinhufvud after his mother, a fetchingly old-fashioned name meaning "pigheaded," because she refused to become a Nilsson upon her marriage to Grislund's father. Her happiness meant her son's unhappiness, and sadly, in spite of her fine background, she didn't possess a single krona that could have softened the blows her son had to endure.

Back in nursery school his friends had nicknamed him Grislund, and the only advantage was that he had been able to eat like an ordinary person all his life, and fairly soon he was living up to his own nickname. As a lad his dad had called him Stiglet. Then, when Grislund told his mom that he and a friend were going to open a car repair shop out in North Järva she had stopped talking to him. Dad still called him Little Stiglet. Either because he didn't know any better or because he wanted to wind up his wife. It's probably more to do with Mom, Grislund thought—he had just turned seventeen and had just completed his mechanics course out in Solna.

The repair shop had gone well, and his old friends had done what they could to help. Mostly Farshad Ibrahim, whom he had got to know in secondary school in Sollentuna. Plus all the others that Farshad even then could count among his retinue.

He had met Åkare much later. One day he just turned up and rolled an old van off the back of a truck, telling him to scrap the fucker before sunset. Grislund had done as he was told and had earned yet another customer.

Everything kept on rolling, so to speak. There had been the occasional little hiccup with grouchy cops sniffing around the repair shop, but nothing he couldn't live with. Up until seven o'clock the evening before, when all hell had broken loose.

He was lying happily beneath his labor of love, a Chevy Bel Air from 1956, tightening some old nuts, mainly for the fun of it. Suddenly the repair shop door had flown open and before he even had time to turn his head and look, someone had grabbed his ankles and pulled him out. It was a miracle that he didn't crack his head open on the frame of the Chevy.

"Grislund," Jorma Honkamäki said, smiling at him with his small eyes. "Call your old woman and tell her not to bother getting you any tea, and I'll take you for sausage and mash back at Solna."

Compared with Åkare, Honkamäki had behaved reasonably, and because it was never wrong to get yourself a bit of extra insurance, he had opened his heart one more time.

Admittedly, Honkamäki had started by winding him up. They'd evidently found a few things: steel wire, solder, all the necessary tools, a dozen caltrops that he'd knocked up and then forgotten about, a few old number plates that it was always useful to have in reserve. It didn't really amount to much, if only that had been all.

If only Nasir hadn't asked him to look after that hundred-gram bag when he looked in on Monday last week to pick up a whole sack of caltrops.

"Only until the end of the day," Nasir had assured him. "I'm on a driving job later today, so, in case anything goes wrong." An eloquent shrug of his slender shoulders.

"Okay," Grislund said, because he was a kind, decent man, and as far as possible he liked to keep his customers happy. Especially if they had an older brother called Farshad Ibrahim. Besides, Nasir had promised to pick the bag up later that evening. After he finished the job, he and his girlfriend were heading down to Copenhagen to celebrate. Meet up with a mutual friend of his and Grislund's. Let their hair down, have some fun.

"After all, I don't drink like you and the other Swedes," Nasir had said.

"A hundred grams of coke," Honkamäki said. "We're talking fourteen days per gram, Grislund, your prints on the bag, and what is it that makes me think you've suddenly gone soft in the head?"

Four years, Grislund thought, because he could count perfectly well. It was high time to open his heart.

"Take it easy, Jorma," Grislund said. "You're talking to a simple foot soldier in the great army of organized crime. Where would someone like me get money like that from?"

And all thanks to a fucking springer spaniel, he thought. First she had just run round like all the other dogs people like Honkamäki brought with them. Then she suddenly stopped and howled, almost tying herself in knots in front of the big oil tray he had in the workshop. The one that even someone like Åkare would think twice about before kicking. Still less stick in his hand, like the dog's master had done without a moment's hesitation.

So he had opened his heart one more time and explained the way things were. Compared with Åkare, Honkamäki had at least behaved more or less like a human being. He hadn't started by putting his hands round his neck, sticking his index finger up his nose, and twisting it.

Nasir and Tokarev had taken off after the shooting out at Bromma. They drove five hundred meters. Abandoned their van twenty meters from the entrance to the Hells Angels' holy of holies. Their clubhouse itself, practically next door to the airport.

No explanation as to why. Because red mist was still coming out of the side window? To cause trouble for their rivals? Because they'd just found an empty parking space? Stupidly, Nasir had pulled off his mask as he was running past one of Åkare's many associates just a couple side streets away, as the sirens began to wail in the background.

"Nasir," Grislund concluded. "Drives like a fucking boy racer."

"Little Nasir," Honkamäki said. I wonder how much money his nasty big brother has had to fork out to fix up board and lodging for him this time? he thought.

"He's a fucking little brat," Grislund said. "Do you know what the bastard says when he gets his fucking caltrops and I've promised to look after his fucking coke so he'll leave me alone to get on with my own thing? Do you know what the bastard says to me as he leaves?"

"No," Honkamäki says.

"Oink, oink," Grislund said.

"You don't have it easy, Grislund." Honkamäki grinned.

"No," Grislund agreed. Whoever said we're supposed to have it easy? he thought.

"Have you told anyone else this?" Honkamäki said.

"No," Grislund said, shaking his head. There are still limits, he thought.

"A little bird told me that you had a visit from Åkare," Honkamäki said, sounding as if he were thinking out loud.

"No way," Grislund said. What the hell is he after? he thought.

"It'll get sorted," Honkamäki said.

"What about the prints?" Grislund asked. "On that fucking plastic bag. Nasir's coke," he clarified.

"What fucking prints?" Honkamäki said, shaking his head. "No idea what you're talking about."

Grislund himself had asked to stay in the holding cell. At least until Monday, to prevent any unnecessary rumors from spreading.

"Make yourself at home, Grislund," Honkamäki said.

Then he had called Toivonen to tell him.

"What the hell would the little bastard want with Copenhagen?" Toivonen said. Anyway, weren't the Hells Angels on the city council there? he thought.

"I've already spoken to our Danish colleagues," Honkamäki

said. "They've promised to keep an eye out for him. If we're lucky, he's still alive."

And if he isn't, things will get even worse, Toivonen thought.

56.

Roughly the same time that Grislund was opening his heart to Honkamäki, Alm was down in the center of Solna doing some shopping. He had bumped into a very cross Roly Stålhammar outside the state-owned alcohol shop, and, in spite of the glare he received, he still ventured to ask a simple question.

"How are things, Roly?" Alm said.

"How the fuck do you think?" Stålhammar said.

"Seppo," Alm said. "Seppo Laurén. You know, that lad who used to help Kalle Danielsson," he clarified.

"Einstein," Stålhammar said.

"Einstein?" What's he mean? Alm thought.

"That's what we called him," Stålhammar said. "Nice and kind, but a bit lost, not like normal people. Kalle used to take him to Valla sometimes when he was in the mood. He used to run and place bets for us so we could sit in peace and quiet and enjoy our beer."

"How did that work out?" Alm asked.

"No problems," Stålhammar said. "Never any problems. He's a demon with numbers, that lad. He's not so good at talking."

"He's a demon with numbers," Alm repeated. He must be drunk, he thought.

"I remember once, it was one of the races before the big Elitloppet race and Kalle had dragged Seppo along with him. He can't have been very old. Before one of the races I happened to say that it was completely open. That any of them could win. Ten horses, one favorite and two second favorites. Odds of winning between two and five to one. The other seven would give you better than twenty to one. The one that would give the best return would have paid out more than a hundred to one."

"I see," Alm said. Definitely drunk, he thought.

"The lad, he can't have been more than ten, asked if he could borrow seven hundred off Kalle. Kalle was in a good mood, a bit drunk. He'd won on an outside bet in the previous race. He hands Seppo a thousand-kronor note. Seppo asks me to put one hundred and forty-two kronor and eighty-six ore on each of the seven horses with the longest odds. He was too young to bet then. He could hardly reach the counter in those days. I explained to him that you couldn't bet with the two kronor and eighty-six ore."

"'One hundred and forty, then,' Seppo says. Okay, I did as he said. One of the seven won. Night Runner, that was his name. Paid out eighty-six to one. Do you know what the lad says?"

"No," Alm said. What does this have to do with anything? he thought.

"'Give me my twelve thousand and forty kronor,' he said."

"I don't actually understand what you mean," Alm said.

"That's because you're soft in the head. Seppo isn't soft in the head. He's different. He talks like a muppet and he looks like a muppet. But he's not soft in the head. And why do I suddenly feel like punching you in the face?" Stålhammar said.

"You don't think Kalle might have had something going on with his mother?" Alm said, thinking it was high time to change the subject.

"I've got no ideeeaa about that," Stålhammar said with a grin. "How about asking her? If she had something going on with Kalle, I'm sure she'd remember."

So it's like that, is it? Alm thought.

"You don't think Kalle could have been Seppo's dad?"

"Why don't you ask him?" Stålhammar said, grinning. "Not the lad, because he doesn't say much. But maybe you and Bäckström could ask Kalle. Fix up one of those mediums they have on television. A real window licker who could help you get in touch with the other side. Ask Kalle, why don't you? If you're lucky, maybe you could squeeze him for some back payments of child support."

So it's like that? Alm thought, and before he had time to thank Stålhammar for the conversation, he had already turned on his heels and left.

57.

Early on Monday morning Linda Martinez had told Toivonen how things had gone with their surveillance of the Ibrahim brothers and their cousin Hassan Talib.

It had all gone according to plan, actually better than they had hoped. They had already attached transmitters to three of the Ibrahim family's cars. They had found a previously unknown Mercedes that was evidently being used by Hassan Talib. And if the eagle-eyed god of surveillance was merciful, Martinez reckoned they should be able to crack two of their cell numbers later that day.

"They headed off in different directions. Talib chatted up a girl in Café Opera and went back to hers by taxi. She lives out in Flemingsberg. Farshad and Afsan left the club soon after and went home to Sollentuna. When Talib got out of the taxi outside the girl's house he made a call, and a few seconds later, when Farshad was standing outside the house in Sollentuna, his phone started to ring. The lads in phone surveillance are busy checking the cell tower, and because they know their positions and have got an exact time, they think it's going to work."

"Of course it's going to work," Toivonen said. If this is war, it has to work, he thought.

"Anything else?" he asked.

"We might have a problem," Linda Martinez said. "Take a look at these pictures and you'll see what I mean," she said, handing over a folder of surveillance photographs.

A quick glance at the photograph on top was enough. I'm going to kill that fat little bastard, Toivonen thought.

"Tell me about it," he said.

Farshad and Afsan had left their home in Sollentuna at eleven. They picked up Talib from Regeringsgatan twenty minutes later. Then the three of them drove on to Café Opera.

"At half past eleven exactly they disappear into the club," Linda Martinez said. "Two of my team follow them. Inside, one of them sees our colleague Bäckström standing at the bar with a girl. The Ibrahim brothers and Talib are standing farther inside the club, and according to my guy, Frank Motoele, actually, it was quite obvious that they were checking out Bäckström. Motoele says he got the impression that Farshad was trying to get eye contact with the woman who was with Bäckström. But there's nothing to suggest any contact between Bäckström and our three subjects. Bäckström seems to have been completely oblivious, focusing all his attention on his female companion."

Half a dozen photographs of Bäckström and his companion. Considerably more of their three subjects. Two pictures in which Bäckström and his companion are visible in the background, with Farshad Ibrahim in the foreground, back to the camera.

Bäckström leaning on the bar. Smiling and making extravagant gestures toward the beautiful woman by his side. A broad smile from her, laughter; she seems utterly absorbed by his company.

"Do we know who she is?" Toivonen asked.

"Yes," Martinez said. "Sandra Kovac went in and recognized her immediately from her time with the Security Police. Her name is Tatiana Thorén. Originally from Poland, Swedish citizen, married and divorced Thorén. A kept woman by profession. One of the most expensive, by all accounts. Between ten and twenty thousand per night. Flat on Jungfrugatan on Östermalm. Hardly ever takes clients there. Mostly hotels."

"So what happened next?"

"Soon afterward Thorén and Bäckström leave Café Opera. They take a taxi from the street outside. Go home to Thorén's flat, where they spend the night. Bäckström doesn't leave until ten o'clock the next morning. The minute after Bäckström and Thorén leave the club, the Ibrahim brothers follow suit. They go directly home to Sollentuna. Farshad's car. The black Lexus, and as usual it's Afsan driving. No attempt to follow Bäckström. Talib leaves half an hour later. He has company in the form of a young woman. Takes a taxi back to hers, like I said. We've identified her too, Josefine Weber, twenty-three, works in a shop selling jeans on Drottninggatan. Nothing remarkable about her. She seems to hang about in bars, socializing with people like Talib. It would be great if we could get hold of her phone number. I get the feeling it wouldn't be too difficult."

"So what's your interpretation of this, then?" Toivonen said.

"That they went to Café Opera to take a look at Bäckström. That it was Thorén who made the move on Bäckström, and told them where the two of them were. Looks like a standard recruitment attempt, and if you ask me I think they've already got their hooks into our so-called colleague, Evert Bäckström. It can hardly be a coincidence that they picked him out. Not considering the man's reputation."

"I think pretty much the same as you," Toivonen said. I'm going to kill that fat little bastard, he thought.

58.

Since Bäckström had no idea what was being discussed in Toivonen's office, he was in an excellent mood when he arrived at work. He was also unusually early due to the fact that he had made an appointment that day to pick up his service revolver at last. The very weapon the powerful forces ranged against him had tried to deprive him of in order to be able to kill him the easiest way.

Bäckström hardly ever carried a service revolver. A man with a super-salami like him didn't need a cock extension, and besides, the holster and handle chafed horribly, no matter whether you wore it under you left armpit or by your waist. What changed his mind had been the National Rapid-Response Unit's attempt to kill him during a so-called raid some six months earlier. He had visited the parliament building to question a member of parliament who was deeply involved in the murder of Prime Minister Olof Palme. But instead he had been accused of trying to take the man hostage.

Bäckström was a blameless and irreproachable knight and had no intention of taking his weapon into the Swedish parliament, and he walked with his visor open, which was more than his opponents did. When they attacked him with bombs and grenades, he had only his bare hands to defend himself with.

When he was eventually permitted to leave Huddinge Hospital, he had immediately requested the return of the service revolver that his crafty opponents had taken off him while he was confined to his sickbed. He had also applied for permission to carry his weapon in his free time and had provided a well-composed justification for this.

All he had received was a firm rejection on the most peculiar formal grounds. In their assessment of the matter, his employers had discovered that Bäckström had never attended the annual shooting tests that were a requirement of bearing a service weapon, not since he had left his post at the National Murder Unit three years before. While he was there he had undergone the tests punctually every year, and the fact that it had actually been his old friend and colleague Detective Inspector Rogersson who took care of the practicalities for him was none of his employers' business. It was between him and Rogersson, and as far as their so-called checks were concerned, he knew where they could shove them.

So Bäckström had to do his shooting again. He had passed with flying colors on only the third attempt, just before he moved to the Western District. His employers had nonetheless tried to delay things, and it wasn't until he called in the Police Officers' Association that they backed down. The notification that he was once again a full police citizen, with the right to bear arms and even to kill if the situation demanded it, had arrived the previous week, and Bäckström hadn't delayed for a second. He had called at once and booked a time to collect his revolver, and now the time had come.

He had also made certain preparations. From a gun dealer he had bought a so-called ankle holster with his own money, the same sort his American colleague Popeye had worn in the classic old police film *The French Connection*. Then he got hold of a cool linen suit from his tailor, with a loose-fitting jacket and trousers with wide legs. Wearing shorts went against the whole idea of an ankle holster, and since the summer was expected to be warm and sunny, he didn't want to have to walk around sweating unnecessarily.

Dressed in a well-cut yellow linen suit, his holster already in place below his left calf, he had shown up at the weapons department of the Western District.

"Service revolver, a nine-millimeter Sig Sauer—standard magazine, fifteen rounds—one box of service ammunition, twenty rounds," the assistant said, lining up the items on the counter. "Sign here," he added, sliding over a receipt for him to sign.

"Hang on, hang on," Bäckström said. "Twenty rounds? What sort of crap is that?"

"Standard issue," the assistant said. "If you want more, I'll need written authority from the head of police."

"Forget it," Bäckström said. "And you can keep this piece of crap," he said, handing back the holster. He tucked the pistol, magazine, and ammunition into his jacket pocket, since he had no intention of revealing where he was planning to carry his weapon.

That bastard Bäckström seems completely unstable, the assistant thought, as he watched the yellow linen suit leave. And he dresses like some fucking Mafioso. Maybe I should phone and warn the guys in the rapid-response unit, he thought.

Once he had closed the door of his office Bäckström did some practicing. He holstered his weapon, shook his trousers so that they hung loose, then quickly slid onto his right knee, pulling up the left trouser leg with his left hand as he pulled out his weapon with a well-judged movement of his right hand, aimed, and fired.

Suck on this, motherfucker, Bäckström thought.

Practice makes perfect, he thought, and repeated the process. Quickly down onto one knee, his confused opponents missing and firing over his head, Bäckström draws his weapon, takes careful aim, smiles his most crooked smile.

"Come on, punk! Make my day, Toivonen," Bäckström snarled.

"Christ, you scared me, Bäckström," Nadja Högberg said, coming into his room with her arms full of papers.

"Just practicing," Bäckström said with a manly smile. "How can I help you, Nadja?"

"The papers you wanted," Nadja said, putting the piles on his desk. "About the Ibrahim brothers and their cousin Hassan Talib. And I promised to remind you that we're having a meeting of the team in a quarter of an hour."

"Right," Bäckström said. He slung his left foot onto the desk and holstered his pistol.

Nadja refrained from shaking her head until she closed the door on him. They're like children, she thought.

Before Bäckström went off to the meeting he loaded a full magazine. Fifteen rounds, one in the chamber. The other four were in his right pocket just in case, and as soon as he got the chance he was going to buy a whole case to keep at home.

As he walked past Toivonen's closed door he almost had to stop himself from tearing open the door and firing off a salvo into the bastard's ceiling. Shooting him in the head would probably be going a bit far, but a few shots in the ceiling would at least be enough to make sure the bastard Finn shit himself, and that was no more than he deserved, Bäckström thought.

59.

"Welcome, everyone," Bäckström said, marshaling his troops, smiling his warmest smile, and sitting down at the head of the table.

Still in a very good mood, and now armed as well. Secretly armed, Bäckström thought, seeing as none of his half-witted colleagues would be able to work out what he was carrying under his well-cut yellow trousers.

"I thought we might start by throwing some ideas around," Bäckström said. So that it didn't go to hell from the outset, he gave them a little clue to chew on.

"Connections," Bäckström said. "Is there any connection between the murders of Karl Danielsson and Septimus Akofeli?"

"Of course there is," Nadja Högberg said. "The murder of Karl Danielsson must have triggered the murder of Akofeli," she said.

Nods of agreement from the Anchor, the pretty little darkie, and the retarded folk dancer. More hesitant squirming from the team's very own Woodentop.

"You seem hesitant, Alm," Bäckström said. "I'm listening."

Alm still had some difficulties with Seppo Laurén. He had actually admitted hitting Danielsson on two previous occasions. Then there was their shared background and the obvious violence of Danielsson's murder.

"The perpetrator more or less beat him to a pulp," Alm said. "Like he was trying to wipe out all traces of him. I think Seppo fits that picture very well, especially if he got the idea that Danielsson was responsible for the fact that his mom is in the hospital. A typical case of patricide, if you ask me."

"And then?" Bäckström said with a sly smile. "What happened after that?" Alm must look like a perfect bird feeder if you were a woodpecker, he thought.

"Well, I buy the simplest explanation," Alm said. "Akofeli snoops round Danielsson's flat. Finds the briefcase full of money. Takes it home with him and gets murdered. And you're probably wondering who killed him?"

"Yes, absolutely," Bäckström said with an amiable smile. "Who killed him?" Feeding time all day long, as soon as Woodentop opens his mouth, he thought.

"I don't think we should make it more complicated that it need be," Alm said. "The simplest explanation, considering the area he lived in, which really is crawling with serious criminals, and the calls he made, is that he had an accomplice, if you ask me. They met in Akofeli's flat to share the takings. An argument arose, they fought, Akofeli was killed, the killer dumped the body."

"I see," Bäckström said. Hesitant body movement from one Anchor, one pretty little darkie, and one tragic incest victim from Dalarna, while Nadja Högberg looked at the ceiling and, just to make sure, sighed out loud. "You don't seem too sure, Nadja." The Russian's going to carve his whole head off, he thought.

"I get the impression Akofeli was taken by surprise, from

behind. Besides, Seppo Laurén couldn't have killed Danielsson because he's got an alibi. He was sitting at his computer when the murder was committed. Seppo Laurén has what's known as an alibi. It's Latin, and means 'in another place'—in other words, that Seppo Laurén was sitting in front of his own computer in his and his mom's flat at the top of the building. Meaning that he wasn't in Danielsson's flat on the first floor of the same building."

"A so-called alibi. Which I don't think much of, to be honest," Alm said. "How do we know it was him sitting there? All we actually know is that *someone* was sitting at his computer. Not that it was necessarily Laurén."

"So who else could it have been?" Nadja said. Alm must be a complete idiot, which is a rarity even in this building, she thought.

"Anyone he knows," Alm said. "He planned it in advance, got hold of some friend who could provide his alibi, and here we can't actually rule out that it could have been Akofeli who helped him—"

"He spoke to him once when Akofeli was delivering papers," Nadja interrupted.

"According to him, yes," Alm said. "If we find the person who was sitting at Laurén's computer, then we've solved this," Alm said.

"I'll have a serious go," Nadja said, taking a deep breath to gather her strength.

"I'm listening," Bäckström said. Here goes the whole fucking bird feeder, he thought.

"The only person who could have been sitting at Seppo's computer is him. It's completely out of the question that anyone else might have been sitting there."

"What makes you think that, Nadja?" Bäckström said.

"Because Seppo is unique," Nadja said. "There's probably only one person anywhere who's like him."

What the fuck is she saying? Bäckström thought. The boy's retarded, for God's sake.

"He spent that night solving Sudoku puzzles, you know, those Japanese number puzzles that all the papers are full of. The difference is that the ones he was solving on his computer were three-dimensional, a bit like a Rubik's Cube, you know. From the computer log I know which quizzes he solved and how he did it. He solves them in such a way and at such speed that I believe he has a quite unique intelligence. There's probably only one Seppo in the whole world."

"But the poor lad's soft in the head," Bäckström said.

"No," Nadja said. "I may be no doctor, but I'm guessing he's got a particular form of autism, which means that his speech has fallen behind. We think he talks like a child. In actual fact he says nothing beyond what is necessary to convey his message. Pretty much like young children talk before their parents teach them a load of unnecessary words, irony, sarcasm, and how to lie."

"So the lad's a genius?" What the hell is she saying? Bäckström thought.

"Definitely a mathematical genius," Nadja said. "Socially handicapped? Sure, if we're measuring him in our own terms. When he hit Danielsson in the face the first time he said he did it because he was angry at him for pushing his mother. The next time he does it is when he's angry again, because his mother doesn't want to talk to him. Surely you can't say it any more straightforwardly than that? When he helps Danielsson into the lift after the first time, he says that Danielsson got in the lift and went home. Not that Danielsson pressed to go down in the lift and got out at the first floor, where he lives. And then went into his flat and closed the door behind him. All the things that normal adults would have said without actually having a clue. Read your own record of the interview, Lars. Read it," Nadja said.

"You're absolutely sure, Nadja? About what you're suggesting, I mean?" Annika Carlsson said.

"Absolutely sure," Nadja said. "This morning I e-mailed him a three-dimensional Sudoku, which I've spent the past three weeks grappling with, whenever I haven't had anything better to do.

"I got it back right away," Nadja said. "He even told me what I needed to do. In his own basic, childish language."

"Okay," Bäckström said. "I don't think we're going to get much further. Besides, we've got plenty to do."

"We're listening," Annika Carlsson said, leaning over her notebook.

"We'll have to go door-to-door in number one Hasselstigen for a third time," Bäckström said. "Take some good pictures of the Ibrahim brothers and Hassan Talib and see if anyone has ever seen them there. It would be particularly interesting if anyone has ever seen them have any contact with Karl Danielsson."

"You think there could be a connection between our two murders and Toivonen's investigation?" Annika Carlsson said.

"Don't know," Bäckström said. "But Toivonen seems to think there is," he said. "And because I've always been a nice, accommodating colleague, I thought I'd better look into it."

"Okay, that's what we'll do," Annika Carlsson said, getting up abruptly.

"I thought I might help out this time," said Bäckström, who had been carrying a deadly weapon for several hours now and was longing to get out into the jungle beyond the police station.

"Can I sit down?" Nadja said when she came into Bäckström's office just a couple minutes after the meeting.

"Of course, Nadja," Bäckström said, smiling his friendliest smile. "You should know, my door's always open for you." *I wonder what's happening with that vodka she said she could get hold of?* he thought.

"How can I help you?" he went on.

"You can help me with this," Nadja said, holding up Karl Danielsson's black pocket diary.

"I thought we'd already solved that bit," Bäckström said.

"I'm not so sure anymore," Nadja said.

"Tell me," Bäckström said, as he adopted his favorite position, and, for safety's sake, put his feet up on his desk so that his visitor could at least catch a glimpse of little Siggy's nose.

"There's something that isn't right," Nadja said.

"With your calculations of how much money he gave them?" Bäckström asked.

"No," Nadja said. "There isn't much wrong with those, if the assumptions are correct, and I'm absolutely convinced it's all about money."

"I'm listening," Bäckström said. Like a razor blade, he thought.

"The psychology doesn't fit my picture of Danielsson," Nadja said. "If it really is the case that he paid out money pretty much every week to Farshad Ibrahim, Afsan Ibrahim, and Hassan Talib, in other words, the initials FI, AFS, and HA, I can't understand why he'd take the risk of writing it down in his own notebook."

"Maybe he wanted to give you and me a little clue in case anything ever happened to him," Bäckström said. "A sort of extra insurance."

"I wondered that as well," Nadja said. "But in that case why not give the actual amounts? Why does he say that Farshad gets ten times as much as Hassan, and on one occasion twenty times as much, and that Afsan gets four times as much as Hassan?"

"That's quite natural. Farshad is their leader, Afsan is his younger brother, and Hassan on the other hand is just a cousin from the country who's allowed to pick up a few crumbs."

"The general assumption seems to be that the money came from the Akalla raid nine years ago, that time when they more or less tore a whole security depot apart," Nadja said. "Farshad leads the operation, Hassan gets the heavy work and drives the truck through the wall, and little brother Afsan gets to stuff the bags. I can maybe buy the fact that Farshad gets most, but shouldn't Ben Kader have given a larger share to Hassan Talib than to Afsan Ibrahim?"

"Maybe they deposited different amounts with Danielsson the banker?" Bäckström said, smiling slyly at her.

"Maybe," Nadja said with a shrug. "Another possibility could be that we're completely wrong about it all, in spite of Toivonen and his tip-off."

"What do you mean?"

"That the initials FI, AFS, and HA mean something completely different, other people, maybe not even people, something else entirely," Nadja said, shrugging again to emphasize her point.

"But you only ever give money to people, surely?" Bäckström said. "You said yourself that you're convinced this is about money, and the initials match their names. They're not exactly common names either. I think you're worrying unnecessarily," Bäckström said.

"I've been wrong before," Nadja said, getting up.

"We're going to solve this," Bäckström said, nodding to instill courage and comfort now that his only colleague worthy of the name seemed to be faltering.

"Yes, I don't doubt that," Nadja said.

60.

Before he left the fortress, Bäckström took the chance to leaf through the bundles of paper that Nadja had given him.

Doesn't sound like they were ever in the church choir, Bäckström thought, when he had finished reading.

Farshad Ibrahim was thirty-seven years old and had arrived in Sweden when he was four. Dad, mom, two older sisters, and an aged grandmother. Six people in total, all of them political refugees from Iran.

In Sweden the family was augmented with two younger brothers for Farshad. Afsan, now thirty-two, and little brother Nasir, twenty-five. Grandmother died the year after they came to Sweden. The two older sisters were married and had moved out of the family home. These days five people lived in the big villa in

Sollentuna. The three Ibrahim brothers and their parents, and the real head of the family was Farshad, since his father had suffered a serious stroke three years before.

In any moral sense, he was a highly dubious leader. When he was fifteen Farshad had stabbed and killed a schoolmate of the same age. He was found guilty of manslaughter and handed over to Social Services. This didn't seem to have had any sort of positive effect on his life. Possibly it made him craftier, seeing as it was another ten years before he was sent to prison for the first time. Four years for aggravated robbery, most of the sentence being served in the same secure unit as one of Superintendent Toivonen's most assiduous informants.

A few months before he was due to be released he had been moved to an ordinary prison so that he could be prepared for his future life outside the walls. This too proved to be an ambitious failure.

After just one week, one of Farshad's fellow prisoners had been found strangled with a washing line in the institution's laundry. Everything suggested that Farshad had taken the chance to get rid of a squealing faggot. Everything, that is, except conclusive evidence and a resolutely silent Farshad.

When he finally got out he was almost immediately suspected of the big raid on the security depot in Akalla. He was taken into custody for three months, said nothing, and was released on lack of evidence. Farshad was now a man with a reputation. Ben Kader's heir, even though Ben Kader was Moroccan and Farshad Iranian. A Muslim, teetotaler, no suspicions of drug use. And no casual female contact—in fact, no women at all, apparently, if you didn't count his mother and two sisters. Above all, no parking fines, no speeding offenses, no disorderly conduct. Dangerous, silent, only three people he seemed to trust and had any sort of relationship with: his two younger brothers, Afsan and Nasir; and his cousin Hassan Talib.

Two younger brothers who, judging by their criminal records, were following in Farshad's footsteps, or at least were trying to without quite succeeding. In the eyes of society it was probably Nasir, the youngest, who looked like the black sheep of the family, since he had served three prison sentences in the space of four years, and all by the age of twenty-five. Grievous bodily harm, rape, robbery. According to the notes in police records, he was also well acquainted with both sex and drugs, and didn't seem to care much what form these took. But no alcohol. A dutiful Muslim in that respect. Not your usual Swede, who drank and spilled the beans on everyone and everything to anyone who could be bothered to listen.

Brought in for questioning by the police more than a hundred times over the years. Initially in the company of his mother and Social Services. A silent Nasir.

"My name is Nasir Ibrahim," Nasir said, before rattling off his ID number. "I have nothing more to say."

"You're just like your older brother Farshad," yet another police interviewer would say.

"That's my eldest brother you're talking about. Respect, when you talk about him."

"Of course," the interviewer would say. "Let's start there, and talk about your eldest brother, Farshad Ibrahim. He's well known for showing other people respect."

"My name is Nasir Ibrahim, eighty-three zero-two zero-six . . ."

Never any more than that when there were police officers around. Out on the town was another matter. There were surveillance pictures, bugged conversations, and reluctant witnesses to testify to that. On a couple occasions even Farshad had been forced to discipline his brother in an almost Old Testament way, even though they were both Muslims.

Hassan Talib was the country cousin in both a metaphorical and a literal sense. He had moved to Sweden with his family some years after the Ibrahim family. He spent his first years in his new homeland with his extended family in the house in Sollentuna. Thirty-six years old, thirty-three of them spent in Sweden. Convictions for manslaughter, grievous bodily harm, robbery, making unlawful threats, extortion. Suspected of murder, a number of armed robberies, yet another murder, and one attempted murder. Three prison sentences totaling ten years, of which he served eight. Farshad's bodyguard, muscle, right-hand man. A terrifying figure, two meters tall, one hundred and thirty kilos, shaved head, dark, deep-set eyes, stubble, grinding jaws as if he were constantly chewing something.

The sort whose head little Siggy would like to comb a parting on, Bäckström thought. He got up abruptly and gave his well-cut yellow linen trousers a shake.

"Come on, punks, come on, all of you, make my day!" Detective Superintendent Evert Bäckström snarled.

61.

Door-to-door. The third time around at number 1 Hasselstigen. Now it was all about Farshad Ibrahim, Afsan Ibrahim, Hassan Talib, and any contact they may have had with Karl Danielsson. They also had good pictures: their own recent surveillance photographs, complemented in the name of justice with a number of similar figures who had nothing to do with any of this. Linda Martinez's faithful colleagues. Only the olive-skinned variety, no brown, black, or blue. Even though Frank Motoele had offered his services when he helped his boss put together the material.

Seppo Laurén hadn't seen anything, even though Alm did his best to prompt him.

"I haven't seen them," Seppo said, shaking his head.

"Take another look, just to make sure," Alm cajoled. "The people we're interested are foreigners—immigrants, if you like."

"I don't understand what you mean," Seppo said, shaking his head.

A proper little genius, Alm thought, sighing and taking back his photographs.

"But these pictures are only of foreigners, or immigrants, as I suppose you have to say these days," Mrs. Stina Holmberg said.

"But there's no one here that you recognize, Mrs. Holmberg?" Jan O. Stigson said.

"Out here in Solna it's nearly all immigrants," Mrs. Holmberg said, nodding amiably at Felicia Pettersson.

"Not that that has anything to do with anything," she added.

Most of the neighbors hadn't recognized anyone.

One Iraqi immigrant who lived on the third floor and worked as a ticket collector on the underground had, however, expressed his appreciation of the work of the police.

"I think you're on the right track," the ticket collector said, nodding to Annika Carlsson.

"Why do you think that?" Carlsson asked.

"Iranians, it's obvious," the ticket collector said, and chuckled. "They're crazy, they're capable of anything."

Bäckström had joined in relatively late, and after a preparatory conversation with his colleague Carlsson.

"I think it would be best if you and I talk to that Andersson woman," Bäckström said. "Considering young Stigson," he clarified.

"I understand exactly what you mean," Annika Carlsson agreed.

In actual fact Bäckström hadn't been thinking of their colleague Stigson. He was out on his own investigative business. After his encounter with Tatiana Thorén—which was bound to become a long-term affair, since she seemed to be completely crazy about him—it was high time for a comparative study, to make sure he didn't let himself in for any problems in the future.

Old women get so fucking saggy as they get older, Bäckström thought.

Mrs. Britt-Marie Andersson had provided them with a golden nugget. Or two, to be precise.

She has to have some sort of fucking metal framework up top, Bäckström thought half an hour later when he and his colleague Carlsson were sitting on Britt-Marie Andersson's sofa showing her the photographs. Even though their presumptive witness had the same impressive volume as Tatiana, who was half her age, they still maintained the same elevation.

What the hell does she do when she lets them hang loose? Bäckström wondered. Does she have to lie on her back first, or what?

"I recognize this one," Mrs. Andersson said excitedly, pointing at a picture of Farshad Ibrahim. Just to make sure, she had leaned toward Bäckström, pointing with a red fingernail.

Incredible, Bäckström thought, trying to tear his eyes away and look at where she had put her finger.

"You're quite sure?" Annika Carlsson said.

"Quite sure," Mrs. Andersson said, nodding to Bäckström.

"When did you last see him?" Bäckström asked.

"The day Danielsson was murdered," Mrs. Andersson said. "It must have been in the morning, when I took Little Sweetie outside. They were standing in the road talking to each other. Right outside the door."

"You're quite sure?" Annika Carlsson repeated, exchanging a meaningful look with Bäckström, who had finally got control of himself and was leaning back in the sofa just to be on the safe side. There was no way he could lift his leg, because the old bag would doubtless get turned on if she caught a glimpse of Siggy, he thought.

"And that one," Mrs. Andersson said, putting her finger on Hassan Talib. "He's a really big man, isn't he?"

"Two meters tall," Bäckström confirmed.

"It's him, then. He was leaning against a car on the other side of the road, watching Danielsson and that other one, the one Danielsson was talking to."

"Did you see what sort of car it was?" Carlsson asked.

"Black, I'm sure of that. One of those expensive, low ones. Like a Mercedes, or maybe a BMW."

"Could it have been a Lexus?" Carlsson asked.

"I don't know," Mrs. Andersson said. "I'm not good with cars. I've got a driving license, but I haven't had a car for years now."

"But you remember the big man standing there?" Bäckström said.

"I'm absolutely sure of it," Mrs. Andersson said. "He was standing there staring at me, to put it bluntly. When I happened to look over at him, he . . . well, he gestured to me. With his tongue, I mean," Mrs. Andersson clarified. She was starting to blush.

"An indecent gesture?" the ever-helpful Annika Carlsson asked. "An obscene gesture?"

"Yes," Mrs. Andersson said, breathing heavily. "It really wasn't very nice. So I came straight back in."

Bloody brilliant, Bäckström thought. The old bag must have a good memory, he thought.

"Why didn't you report it?" Carlsson asked.

"Report it? What for? Because of what he did with his tongue?"

"Sexual harassment," Annika Carlsson clarified.

"No," Mrs. Andersson said. "From what I've read in the paper, there's no point."

Abort, abort, abort, Bäckström thought.

"Well, thank you very much indeed for your help, Mrs. Andersson," he said.

"You can calm down, Nadja," Bäckström said half an hour later when he returned to his office. "About that business with the diary, I mean. We've got a witness who's identified both Farshad and Talib, says she saw them talking to Danielsson outside his house the same day he was murdered."

"I hear what you're saying, Bäckström," Nadja Högberg said.

Maybe she isn't always so shrewd, Bäckström thought, giving his trousers a shake just to be on the safe side.

62.

Before he went home for the day Bäckström looked into Toivonen's office to tell him about what Mrs. Andersson had seen. The poor Finnish bastard probably needs all the help he can get, Bäckström thought. Besides, he had his old supervisory role to consider.

Toivonen had been strangely uninterested.

"Yesterday's news," Toivonen said. "But thanks anyway."

"Just let me know if you need any help," Bäckström said, giving him one of his most good-natured smiles. "I heard over lunch that you've got a hundred people working on this, but that you're not making much progress."

"People talk a lot of crap," Toivonen said. "We're doing okay, so don't you worry about the Ibrahim brothers and their little cousin. How are you getting on yourself?"

"Give me a week," Bäckström said.

"I look forward to it," Toivonen said. "Who knows? Maybe they'll give you a medal, Bäckström."

I wonder what the fat little bastard really wanted? Toivonen thought, when Bäckström had left. I must have a chat with Linda Martinez, he thought.

If you give a bastard Finn your little finger he usually tries to take your whole arm, Bäckström thought, as he left Toivonen's office. But not this time. I wonder what he's really up to? he thought.

In spite of all of Toivonen's informants, in spite of Bäckström's witness in Hasselstigen, Nadja Högberg hadn't been able to let go of Karl Danielsson's pocket diary. Besides, she had had an idea.

You don't only give money to people, Nadja thought. You pay for goods and services as well. Almost always without paying any attention at all to who produced or provided them.

It's worth a try, Nadja thought. Just to be on the safe side she knocked on Bäckström's door, in case he was still playing cops and robbers with himself. Empty, and his phone was switched off, as usual.

I'll have to try to talk to him first thing tomorrow, Nadja thought. It'll have to be the first thing I do when he shows up, she thought.

In actual fact it would be almost a week before she had the chance. That evening things would take place in Evert Bäckström's home—in his cozy abode on Kungsholmen—that would shake the whole nation and put Detective Superintendent Bäckström's name on the lips of every man and every woman, and that would almost cost Chief Superintendent Toivonen his life, because, even though he was in perfect shape, he came close to having both a stroke and a heart attack simultaneously.

63.

This time Hassan Talib was there from the start when the black Lexus left the villa out in Sollentuna at eight o'clock in the evening. The surveillance vehicle had kept a couple blocks away and followed them along a parallel road, since they could track the target on the computer screen in their car and had no need to take unnecessary risks.

Only when they had passed the old tollgates in toward the center did they creep closer. The traffic was heavier, Sandra Kovac was driving, and when the black Lexus turned left at the end of Sveavägen she realized at once what was going on. The biggest multistory carpark in the center of Stockholm, she thought. Several blocks of it, with three stories underground. Four exits, and dozens of ways in and out for pedestrians.

"Shit," Sandra swore. "The bastards are going to run."

Magda Hernandez had grabbed a portable radio, jumped out of the car, and stopped by the ramp into the carpark in case they did a U-turn and drove out again.

Kovac and Motoele had chased around the garage trying to locate the black Lexus, and when they finally found it, it was empty, neatly parked on the lowest level beside one of the many exits. By then Kovac was already talking to Linda Martinez on their own encrypted radio channel.

"Calm down, Sandra," Martinez said. "This sort of thing happens. It isn't the end of the world. Take a turn round the area, see if you can't get a glimpse of one of their other cars."

"So what do we think about this?" Toivonen said half an hour later. "Are they planning to go abroad and get a bit of sun?"

"I don't think so," Martinez said. "It's been quiet all day, no increased activity on the two cell phones we cracked yesterday. Since they left the garage it's been completely silent on their phones, which probably means they're together and don't need to call each other. But they're obviously up to something. The question is, what?"

"Airports, ferries, trains?" Toivonen asked.

"Already sorted," Martinez said. "Our colleagues there have been warned and have promised to do what they can."

"Damn," said Toivonen, who had suddenly had an idea. "Bäckström, that fat little bastard, we have to check—"

"Toivonen, you must think I'm soft in the head," Martinez

interrupted. "We've had him under full surveillance since he left the police station four hours ago, four hours and thirty-two minutes, to be precise."

"So what's he doing?"

"He got home at seventeen minutes to five. What he got up to inside the flat isn't clear, but to judge from the noises he seems to have taken a long nap. An hour and a half ago he turned up in his local bar, and he's still there."

"Doing what?" Toivonen said.

"Drinking beer and shots, eating frankly dangerous quantities of vegetable mash and knuckle of pork, all the while hitting on the waitress. A fine blonde, name of Saila, a compatriot of yours if you're wondering."

Life isn't fair, Toivonen thought.

At about half past eleven that evening another call was received on the Stockholm Police emergency number, 112. One of several thousand that had come in over the past twenty-four hours, and sadly all too similar to far too many of its predecessors.

"Hello, here's another call to spoil your quiet evening," the voice on the telephone said.

"So what's your name, and how can I help you?" the operator said. Drunk, he thought.

"My name's Hasse Ahrén," the voice said. "Director Hasse Ahrén, I used to be head of TV Three," the voice explained.

"And how can I help you?" Hammered, the operator thought.

"Someone's shooting like a fucking madman inside my neighbor's flat," Ahrén said.

"What's your neighbor's name?"

"Bäckström. A little fat bastard who's some sort of policeman. Drinks like a fish, so if you're wondering, Constable, I reckon he's responsible for the shooting."

64.

Bäckström had been obliged to postpone on three different occasions until he finally got back the weapon that was his fundamental human right as a Swedish police officer.

The first time he hadn't even had a chance to fire a single shot. Bäckström had taken a taxi out to a firing range south of the city. He met his shooting instructor, the altogether-too-common sort whose furrowed brow naturally merged with a shaved head. He was given his weapon, inserted a loaded magazine, reloaded, and then turned to ask which of the targets he was expected to blow holes out of.

The instructor had thrown himself to one side, suddenly pale as a headache pill, and screamed at him to put his weapon down immediately. Bäckström had done as he was told.

"I would appreciate it, Bäckström, if you didn't wave a loaded weapon with the safety off toward my navel. In fact, I'd be really, really happy," the instructor said, his voice sounding strained.

Then he had grabbed the pistol, clicked the bolt action, removed the cartridge from the chamber, pulled out the magazine, and checked with his finger just to make sure before putting the gun in his pocket.

"Because otherwise you'll shit yourself," Bäckström said, as politely as he could.

It hadn't helped, because he wasn't allowed to shoot. The instructor had merely shaken his head and walked away.

The second time he had a female instructor, and as soon as he caught sight of her he realized what his adversaries were up to.

The bitch had even put on a padded vest and a helmet, and stood behind him the whole time while she told him what to do. Bäckström couldn't be bothered to listen. How could he, since he had already put on the ear protectors like she had told him to. Instead he had tried to focus on his real task, and had raised his gun, carefully taken aim, closed his left eye, and even squinted with the right one before firing a well-aimed salvo at the cardboard cutout in front of him.

Splendid, Bäckström thought, as he looked at the results a minute later. At least half his shots had hit their target, and even though he was no doctor, he could see at once that most of them would have been fatal.

"So where do I pick up my service revolver?" Bäckström asked.

At first she had merely shaken her head, her face the same color as her colleague's had been previously, and, when she finally spoke, her voice sounded exactly the same as his.

"A Swedish police officer who has been attacked and runs the risk of suffering serious violence—in other words, when he is in a so-called extreme situation—is expected to aim at his attacker's legs. Below the knee, since even a shot to the thigh has a high risk of being fatal," she explained.

"Correct me if I'm wrong," Bäckström said. "If some crazy bastard is running at you with a knife and intends to stab you, you try to shoot him in the knee?"

"Below the knee," the instructor corrected him. "The answer is yes, because that's what firearms regulations say."

"Speaking personally, I'd ask him if he'd like a kiss and a cuddle," Bäckström said with a grin. Then he had merely shaken his head and walked away. As soon as he was in the taxi he called a cousin of his who worked at the Police Officers' Association.

"So your employer is still refusing to give you the right to embrace little Siggy?" his cousin said, suddenly sounding as bloodthirsty as Bäckström felt.

"Exactly," Bäckström said. "And what the fuck are you going to do about it?"

Everything necessary, according to his cousin. Including talking to an old and reliable associate who had once been an ombudsman in the association, and who was now working as a shooting instructor out at the Police Academy, and who had the authority to sign all the certificates that might be required.

"I'll talk to him, and get him to call you and arrange a time," his cousin said.

"Is there anything else I need to think about?" Bäckström asked.

"Take a bottle with you," his cousin replied.

To save time Bäckström had handed over a bottle of his finest malt whiskey when he first arrived at the firing range at the Police Academy.

"Thank you very much indeed," the reliable associate said, licking his lips. "Well, it's time to embrace little Siggy," he said, handing over his own Sig Sauer to Bäckström.

"Do you feel it?" he went on, nodding as Bäckström felt the weapon in his hand.

"Feel what?" Bäckström said.

"The only time you get a real hard-on is when you hold little Siggy," the instructor said, looking as happy as he had when Bäckström handed over his gift.

Probably mad, Bäckström thought, checking that he wasn't standing behind him with another gun that he'd had hidden somewhere.

Then he had taken careful aim, closing his left eye just to be sure, squinting with the right, and fired the usual well-aimed shot, which hit where it usually did.

"Bloody hell," his instructor said, finding it hard to conceal his admiration. "That would make him shut up."

Before Bäckström left him, a signed certificate in his pocket, his new friend had given him a few words of advice.

"One thing that's struck me, Bäckström . . ."

"Yes?"

"Even though you're aiming low, you end up hitting just a bit high, if I can put it like that."

"Okay," Bäckström said.

"Maybe you should try aiming at the ground just in front of the target?" the instructor suggested. "Considering all those old women who work in the disciplinary department, I mean."

Forget it, limp dick, Bäckström thought. Now a full citizen and police officer. If anyone so much as raised a hand against me, I would blow their head off, he thought.

65.

Bäckström had left his beloved local bar before midnight. His blond tornado from Jyväskylä had been prevented from accompanying him, since her more routine companion had suddenly shown up in her place of work. He had also glowered at Bäckström. So Bäckström had lumbered home, opened the door to his cozy abode, yawned indulgently, and stepped right in.

I'll just have to make do with squeezing little Siggy, Bäckström thought, at the very moment when he realized he had unexpected company.

"Welcome home, Superintendent," Farshad Ibrahim said, smiling amiably at his host.

His gigantic cousin didn't say anything. Just glared at Bäckström with his black, deep-set eyes. A face that could have been carved in stone, were it not for the slow grinding of his jaw.

"And what can I do for you gentlemen?" Bäckström said. What the hell do I do now? he thought.

"Perhaps I could offer you a little drink?" he suggested, nodding toward the kitchen.

"Neither of us drinks," Farshad Ibrahim said, shaking his head. He was leaning back comfortably in Bäckström's favorite armchair, while his cousin was standing in the middle of the room, glaring.

"Don't worry, Superintendent," he went on. "We've come in peace, and we have a little business proposal."

"I'm listening," Bäckström said, as he shook his yellow linen trousers as discreetly as possible, even though they suddenly felt drenched with sweat and his legs started trembling of their own accord in a mysterious way.

"We're interested in what your colleagues are up to," Farshad said, "and as I see it, there are two possibilities," he continued, sounding like he was thinking out loud.

Then he had put his hand in his pocket, pulled out a bundle of thousand-kronor notes, and put them on Bäckström's coffee table. A bundle that bore a striking resemblance to all the others Bäckström had himself found in a perfectly ordinary pot of gold. Then for some reason he had pulled out a stiletto knife from his inside pocket, unfolded the double-edged blade, and started to pick at his nails.

It'll have to be a Bäckström double, Bäckström decided. And because there wasn't much choice, he gave it his all from the outset.

"Spare me, spare me!" Bäckström exclaimed, his big round face twisting and his clasped hands rising in supplication. Then he had slumped to one knee in front of the gigantic Talib, as if he were thinking of proposing to him.

Talib's jaw stopped grinding and he took a step back, looking down sympathetically at the pleading Bäckström who was on one knee at his feet. Then he had shrugged, turned his head, and looked at his boss. Evidently embarrassed, or so it seemed.

"Act like a man, Bäckström, not a woman," Farshad said in a tone of warning, shaking his head and pointing the knife at him.

And at that moment Bäckström struck.

66.

More or less at the same time as Bäckström had sat himself down in his beloved local bar on Kungsholmen in Stockholm, the police in Copenhagen received a tip-off. An anonymous male individual, a native Dane—middle-aged, to judge by his voice—had called the emergency number and left a message.

At the end of the large carpark on Fasansvejen, a couple of hundred meters from the old SAS hotel and just five minutes from the center of the city, stood a trash can. In the trash can there was now a body wrapped in an ordinary hessian sack that had once contained pig feed. The man in the sack hadn't crawled in there of his own accord, and, to help even the Danish police to find him, the people who had put him in there had left his naked feet sticking out.

"Well, I think that was everything," the man who had called said before ending the call, made from a pay-as-you-go cell phone, impossible to trace and the obligatory accessory for a certain type of call.

Three minutes later the first patrol car had arrived at the scene, and a half hour later the two uniformed officers had the company of a number of their colleagues from the crime and forensics units of the Copenhagen Police.

More or less at the same time as Bäckström ordered a little chaser to go with his double espresso, they reached the point where they could open the trash can and take a closer look at the naked body inside it. A perfectly ordinary address label had been tied round its neck with string: "Nasir Ibrahim, please forward to Stockholm Police." Someone had stuffed a parking ticket down the corpse's throat, and to judge by the wounds on the body, his death had been both drawn out and painful.

As a message to a Muslim robber who had messed up when he abandoned his getaway vehicle, it could hardly have been any clearer, and because the police in Copenhagen had already been alerted in advance they called their Swedish colleague, Superintendent Jorma Honkamäki of the Stockholm riot squad. When Honkamäki took the call he was standing in the street outside the building where Bäckström lived, supervising the aftermath of Bäckström's efforts.

Nasir's eldest brother, Farshad, was being lifted into an ambulance. Two paramedics carrying the stretcher, a female nurse holding a drip, Farshad moaning in a language that Honkamäki couldn't understand, his trousers round his ankles, drenched in blood.

His cousin Hassan Talib had just left in another ambulance. Unconscious, wearing a neck brace, carried by three paramedics, with a doctor and nurse trying to keep him alive.

The one who seemed to be in the best shape was Nasir's other brother, Afsan. Admittedly, his nose was broken, he was covered with blood, his hands were cuffed behind his back, and he didn't seem to want to walk, but otherwise he seemed pretty much the same as usual.

"I'm going to fuck you in the ass, you fucking pigs," Afsan yelled as two of Honkamäki's colleagues put him inside one of the riot squad's vans.

What the fuck's going on? Honkamäki thought, shaking his head.

"What the fuck's going on?" Superintendent Toivonen repeated a minute later as he got out of his car and caught sight of Honkamäki.

67.

As soon as the obviously embarrassed Talib had looked away—such weakness in a man, as weak as a woman—Bäckström had made his move. He grabbed hold of his ankles with lightning speed and pulled as hard as he could.

Talib had toppled backward like a sawn-off fir tree, however that could be possible considering where he was from, Bäckström thought. He just tumbled backward, straight back, his arms flailing, before his neck and the back of his head smashed into Bäckström's coffee table, cracking the slab of finest Kolmården marble.

Bäckström had pulled out Siggy in the twinkling of an eye—getting up with some difficulty, admittedly—before closing his left eye to be on the safe side and taking careful aim.

Farshad had also stood up, raising his hands in a defensive gesture, dropping the flick-knife, point down, onto Bäckström's expensive carpet.

"Take it easy, Superintendent," Farshad said, waving his raised hands.

"Make my day, punk!" Bäckström roared, firing off a proper salvo with not the slightest intention of causing any scratches in his newly laid parquet floor.

68.

Bäckström's neighbor didn't actually need to call the emergency number, since the police had been there all along.

Shortly after eleven that evening the white Mercedes, Alfa 3, had suddenly begun to move on Sandra Kovac's computer screen. Earlier in the evening it had been parked on the top floor of the same multistory as the abandoned Lexus.

The surveillance vehicle containing Kovac, Hernandez, and Motoele had been in the vicinity and just a couple minutes later they were a hundred meters behind the Mercedes, which was evidently heading for Kungsholmen. Afsan was driving, Farshad was in the passenger seat, and Hassan Talib was in full command of the backseat.

Kovac had contacted Linda Martinez over the radio. Martinez had called for assistance from another unit that had been watching Bäckström earlier that evening and that was now taking a break in McDonald's, just a few blocks from Bäckström's local bar.

Detective Inspector Tomas Singh, adopted as a child from Malaysia, and his colleague Detective Sergeant Gustav Hallberg, who in spite of his name had been adopted from South Africa, had thrown themselves into their car and returned to the bar where they had left Bäckström a quarter of an hour before, happily attached to a large cognac. He was still there. Probably with the same cognac, since the glass on the table in front of him was now empty.

"What do we do now?" Hallberg asked.

"We wait," Singh said.

Five minutes later Bäckström had called over a blond waitress, got up, pulled a sizable bundle of notes from his pocket, crumpled up the receipt, peeled off a five-hundred-kronor note, and shook his head when the waitress evidently tried to give him his change.

"It doesn't look like our colleague Bäckström is short of cash," Sergeant Hallberg concluded.

"What the hell do you think we're sitting here for?" Detective Inspector Singh said. He had been in the job five years longer and was already a hardened young man.

As Bäckström stood up to pay, the white Mercedes had stopped twenty meters from the door of the building where Bäckström lived. Farshad and Talib had got out. Afsan had parked, turned off the lights, and stayed inside the car, as his brother and cousin disappeared through Bäckström's door. Kovac pulled up fifty meters farther up the street, switched the engine off, turned off the lights, and rolled to a stop.

"What do we do now?" Magda Hernandez asked.

"Bäckström is evidently on his way," said Kovac, who could hear their colleague Singh through her earpiece. "Tomas and Gustav are following him on foot," she said, nodding to Hernandez.

"There's something not right," Motoele said, shaking his head.

"What do you mean, not right?" Hernandez said.

"Just a feeling," Motoele said. "I've got a feeling that Bäckström doesn't know they want to see him."

"Dirty cop," Kovac said, and snorted. "Of course he knows."

"Bäckström has had his phone switched off since this afternoon," Motoele objected.

"So either he's got another one or they agreed on a time some other way," Kovac said.

Four minutes later Bäckström disappeared through the door of the building he lived in.

"You can forget any ideas about sneaking in and listening through his mail slot," Kovac said, with a warning glance at Motoele. "We're not taking any unnecessary risks."

"It's fucking hot in the car. Is it okay if I open the window, Mom?" Motoele asked as he wound down the rear window.

"I thought people like you liked the heat?" Kovac teased. "Just don't catch a cold, Frank."

"So what do you mean, 'agreed on a time'?" Motoele said, as he heard a muffled crack in the distance. As he leapt out of the car and started running down the street there was a constant stream of cracks. Muffled cracks, the same sound he had heard thousands of times when he had been at the firing range with ear protection on, practicing with his own service revolver.

Afsan Ibrahim neither saw nor heard anything. He was listening to music on his iPod, humming in time to the music, enjoying it with his eyes shut until it all went wrong when someone suddenly yanked open the car door and grabbed him by the throat. He snatched at the knife between the seats out of sheer reflex. A moment later he was on his stomach in the street, with someone standing on his hand, kicking the knife away, and kicking him hard in the side when he tried to get up. The man grabbed his hair, pulling his head up, then broke his nose with a chop of his hand that made Afsan see stars. Then another, and another, then the darkness enclosing him, voices he could hardly hear any longer.

"Stop it, Frank!" Sandra Kovac shouted. "Do you want to kill him?" Then she had pushed her colleague aside. She sat on the small of Afsan's back, twisted his hands behind his back, and cuffed them, first the right, then the left.

"Fucking hell, you're mad," she repeated.

"The Arab bastard was trying to stab me," Motoele said, nodding toward the knife in the gutter on the other side of the street.

"Get a grip on yourself, Frank," Kovac said. "He didn't have a knife on him when you let loose on him."

Frank Motoele didn't seem to be listening. He had just shrugged, drawn his pistol, and vanished through Bäckström's door.

69.

Farshad had crumpled like an empty sack after the first shot. It had evidently hit his left leg, even though Bäckström would never have dreamed of even aiming at such a stupid place.

Bäckström had fired off a few more shots just to be on the safe side, rather randomly, then everything calmed down. Talib was lying motionless on his back, his eyes half open but the light had gone out of them; his jaw was no longer grinding; blood was dripping out of his ears and nose; and his legs were twitching weirdly. Bäckström leaned over and grabbed the black pistol that was tucked in Talib's belt and tucked it into his own.

Then he went over to Farshad, who was lying whimpering on the floor, clutching his left leg with both hands. He was bleeding like a freshly stuck pig all over Bäckström's expensive carpet, noisily lamenting his lot.

"Okay, you're going to shut up now, you fucking crybaby," Bäckström said, and because he was passing he took the chance to give him a hefty kick in the same leg that little Siggy had already had a go at.

Farshad's eyes rolled back and he lost consciousness. Bäckström pocketed the bundle of notes and surveyed the situation. Finally a bit of peace and quiet, he thought, but at that moment the telephone rang.

"Bäckström," Bäckström grunted as he looked at the destruction around him.

"What's the situation, Bäckström?" a woman replied. "This is Kovac from surveillance," Sandra Kovac explained.

"It's okay," Bäckström said.

"I'm standing in the stairwell outside your flat with some colleagues and was wondering if you felt like letting us in," Kovac said.

"No morons from the rapid-response unit?" Bäckström asked. He had no intention of making the same mistake twice.

"Just perfectly ordinary fellow officers," Kovac reassured him.

"Okay," Bäckström said. "Just give me a minute."

Then he put the money away in his secret place. Poured himself a stiff whiskey. And stuck the Sig Sauer under his belt as well, even though it was starting to get a bit crowded there.

I think that's everything, Bäckström thought, looking around at the destruction one last time. Just to make sure, he thought.

Then he opened the door and let them in, and went and sat on the sofa with a stiff drink. He poured another, just to be on the safe side. Where the hell is this force heading? he wondered. Here he was, in mortal danger for at least a quarter of an hour, until eventually he single-handedly managed to restore order and harmony around him. The best his employers could offer him was evidently five snotty-nosed kids who showed up when it was all done and dusted. Two women, two Negroes, and one poor sod who was evidently only a mulatto and probably got bullied by his colleagues. What the hell is happening to the Swedish Police? Bäckström thought.

When Peter Niemi arrived half an hour later he stopped in the doorway to take a deep sigh. This was once the scene of a crime, Niemi thought. In the formal sense, it was still a crime scene, he thought. Even though by that time it had been visited by fifty or so different people, from paramedics to police officers, who had probably moved anything that could be moved and put their fingerprints all over anything that couldn't.

"Okay," Niemi said. "I'll have to ask everyone to leave the apartment so that my colleague and I can get to work."

"Forget it, Niemi," Bäckström said. "I live here."

"Bäckström, Bäckström," Niemi said. Must be in shock, he thought.

"Here's Talib's pistol," Bäckström said, laying it on the tragic remains of what had once been a coffee table with a top made of Kolmården marble. "And here's mine," he said.

"What about the knife on the floor?" Niemi said with a nod.

"Belongs to Farshad Ibrahim," Bäckström said. "Feel free to take it away with you."

"Bullet holes," Niemi said.

"Everything that happened, happened in here," Bäckström said. "The bastards must have picked the lock and were waiting in here for me when I got home. Then all hell broke loose," he said with a shrug. You can work the rest out for yourself, he thought.

"Did anyone apart from you fire any shots, Bäckström?" Chico Hernandez asked.

"I haven't the faintest idea," Bäckström lied. "It all happened so damn quickly, and it got a bit muddled, if I can put it like that.

"Now, you gentlemen will have to excuse me," he went on. "Make yourselves at home. I just need to take a little lie-down."

Then he had gone into his bedroom and closed the door behind him. Niemi and Hernandez looked at each other and shrugged.

One hour later Bäckström got a visit from Anna Holt and his colleague Annika Carlsson.

"How are you feeling, Bäckström?" Holt asked.

"On top form," Bäckström said, even though he had felt better. Besides, he felt peculiarly distant. It was as if none of this was really happening to him.

"Is there anything I can do for you?" Holt said. "A medical examination, debriefing, and I've booked a hotel room for you as well, by the way."

"Forget it," Bäckström said, shaking his head to underline the point.

"Is it okay if I stay and keep an eye on you?" Annika Carlsson said. "Then I can get the worst of the mess in the living room cleared up for you. I've spoken to Niemi and he's okay with it," she cajoled.

"If you like," Bäckström said, looking at her in surprise. An attack dyke offering to clean up for someone like me. Where the hell are we heading? he thought.

"And I promise to sleep on the sofa," Annika Carlsson said with a smile.

"Fine," Bäckström said. What the hell is she saying? he thought.

"There must be at least fifty journalists out in the street," Holt said. "I imagine you won't have anything against me putting some uniforms on the door?"

"Absolutely fine," Bäckström said with a shrug.

"We'll talk tomorrow," Holt said. "Call me if you feel like it."

Bäckström got into the shower. He stood there letting the water run over him. He dried himself, put on his dressing gown, took one brown and one blue from the pill bottles the police's own Dr. Mengele had prescribed for him. Then he went to bed. He fell asleep as soon as his head hit the pillow, and when he woke up it was to the smell of freshly brewed coffee and fresh rolls with cheese and butter.

"Good morning, Bäckström," Annika Carlsson said with a broad smile. "Would you like breakfast in bed or in the kitchen?"

"Kitchen," Bäckström said. Not worth taking any risks, he thought.

70.

On Tuesday morning Anna Holt and Toivonen tried to get an overview of the situation.

Hassan Talib had undergone two operations during the night in the neurosurgical department at the Karolinska Hospital. Severe bleeding in the brain, and the doctors were fighting to save his life. He was now in intensive care.

Hassan Talib was two meters tall, one hundred and thirty kilos of muscle and bone, feared throughout Stockholm's underworld and even among people who looked the same as him. He had tumbled backward and hit his head on a coffee table. If he had been an ordinary crook, in a film or on television, he would have shaken his head, got up, and made mincemeat of Bäckström. But because he belonged in the real world, it was unclear if he was going to survive.

Farshad Ibrahim had also spent the night on the operating table even though the only bullet to hit him had struck exactly where police regulations demanded, just below the left knee. First it had broken both of the bones in the lower leg, the tibia and fibula, which was only to be expected and exactly as intended. Then several unexpected things had happened. The bullet was the new sort that expanded when it hit its target, the intention being to minimize the risk of the bullet going straight through or ricocheting, against the surmountable price of a larger hole in the body of the person who was shot. This time the casing had splintered and a fragment had travelled along the thighbone and damaged the femoral artery. By the time Farshad Ibrahim arrived at hospital he had lost three liters of blood. His heart had stopped twice in the ambulance. Ten hours later he was lying in intensive care. Prognosis unclear.

His younger brother had been subjected to a quick diagnosis on the street outside Bäckström's door. Broken nose, possibly broken bones and fingers in his right hand. Nothing that prison medical staff couldn't handle. During the short journey to police headquarters in the riot squad's van he had fainted and collapsed on the floor. To start with, they thought he was playacting, then decided to take him to Karolinska as well, and within an hour Afsan was also lying on an operating table. Several broken ribs on his right side, a punctured and collapsed lung, but in considerably better shape than his older brother and cousin.

"He's definitely going to make it," the surgeon who spoke to Honkamäki confirmed. "Unless anything unexpected happens, of course," he added, the way doctors usually do.

Nasir Ibrahim was dead, tortured by what looked like an ordinary soldering iron. His skull had been crushed by the classic blunt object, although precisely what sort was used on this occasion was unclear. Just to make sure, he had also been strangled with the cord with which the address label had been tied to his neck. The body was expected to arrive at the Solna forensics lab later that day. In case the Swedish coroners wanted to take a look at what their Danish colleagues at Rigshospitalet's forensics department had already taken care of.

Just to be on the safe side, arrest warrants for Farshad Ibrahim, Afsan Ibrahim, and Hassan Talib had all been issued on the grounds of probable suspicion a couple hours earlier. Two cases of the attempted murder of Detective Superintendent Evert Bäckström and Detective Inspector Frank Motoele, weapons offenses, and more to come. Considerably more.

Even though none of the three could move without help, even in their hospital beds, they were under an impressive amount of police guard. Twenty uniformed officers from the National Rapid-Response Unit, the riot squad, and the ordinary force. Half a dozen detectives who suddenly had time on their hands.

Chief Superintendent Toivonen wasn't happy.

"Explain to me how that fat little bastard managed to shoot an entire police investigation to shreds," Toivonen said, glaring at his boss with bloodshot eyes. "Are we living in Sweden, or what?"

"Well," Anna Holt said, "we're still living in Sweden, and it isn't quite as simple as you're suggesting."

"Nasir has been murdered, Farshad and Talib and Afsan are all in intensive care," Toivonen said, counting them off on his fingers just to underline his point.

"Well," Holt repeated, "to start with, our colleague Bäckström didn't have anything to do with the murder of Nasir."

"It sounds like you should talk to Mr. Åkare and his friends about that," Holt suggested.

Is she fucking with me? Toivonen thought. During a long career in the police he had had a large number of completely meaningless conversations with Fredrik Åkare and his friends in the Hells Angels. The last time, Åkare had even patted him on the shoulder before vanishing in the company of his slick-haired lawyer.

"You're a bastard Finn, aren't you, Toivonen?" Åkare said.

"What's that got to do with anything?" Toivonen said, trying to outstare the visitor's scornful smile.

"You probably know our old chairman," Åkare said. "He's a bastard Finn as well. He sends his greetings, by the way. Get in touch if you fancy a ride and a beer."

Toivonen hadn't got in touch. Now he was obliged to, and he wasn't looking forward to it.

"According to Niemi," said Toivonen, who wasn't going to give in that easily, "Farshad had a key to Bäckström's apartment in his trouser pocket."

"A recently cut copy, if I've understood correctly," Holt said. She too had spoken to Niemi.

"It's still very odd that it just happens to fit Bäckström's apartment," Toivonen said.

"I can see what you mean, and I'm aware of Bäckström's reputation, but if it's simply a case that they were bribing him, then they just had to knock on the door. And if that was the reason why they were there, then the negotiations don't seem to have gone particularly well. And I say that with a great deal of reluctance," Holt said, being a proper police officer.

"Maybe they hadn't got enough money with them," Toivonen said. "According to Niemi, Farshad didn't have a penny on him."

"Yes, yes," Holt said. "Maybe we should take it easy and not get carried away. Everything that has emerged so far suggests that Farshad and Talib, entirely without Bäckström's knowledge, got into his apartment and took him by surprise. To murder him, threaten him, blackmail him, force him to help them. Or to try to bribe him. We just don't know. It looks like Bäckström was fully justified in defending himself. And the shot to Farshad's leg was entirely in accordance with regulations."

"So what about the other five bullets, then? The ones Niemi pulled out of his walls and ceiling?"

"Presumably things were chaotic. According to Bäckström they threw themselves on him as soon as he entered the apartment. Talib with a drawn pistol and Farshad with a knife. Bäckström managed to draw his pistol. Shots were fired. What's the problem?"

"Correct me if I'm wrong," Toivonen said, taking a deep breath to stop the top of his head from blowing off. I'm calm, he thought to himself.

"Bäckström wrestles Talib to the ground, disarms him, and knocks him out. His pistol just happens to go off a few times as he does so. As soon as Talib is out of the picture he shoots Farshad in the leg, a perfect shot, just below his left knee. Because Farshad is trying to stab him with his knife. Have I got that right?" Toivonen asked.

"More or less," Holt said with a shrug. "According to our colleague Carlsson, who had breakfast with Bäckström this morning, he says he felled Talib with some mysterious trick with his legs that he picked up when he was learning judo as a kid. According to Bäckström, he was pretty good at it while he kept up with it. Unfortunately Talib fell backward and hit his head on Bäckström's coffee table, but under the circumstances we can hardly hold Bäckström responsible for that. Then, when Farshad rushes at him to stab him with his knife, Bäckström shoots him in the leg."

"According to Bäckström, that is."

"I've spoken to both Niemi and Hernandez. According to their forensic examination, there's nothing to contradict Bäckström's version. They both accept the bit about Talib without question. The shots in the walls are also distributed in such a way that they couldn't have been fired by someone standing still and shooting. It might well match what Bäckström says."

"Forensic investigation, right," Toivonen snorted. "You saw what it looked like. There must have been at least fifty people traipsing through that flat."

"Including you and me. And the rest of our colleagues who were in there. And that isn't Bäckström's fault either."

"No, heaven forbid," Toivonen said. "Give the little fat bastard a medal and an extra year's salary. By the way, did you happen to notice the furniture that fat little—"

"Hang on, Toivonen," Holt interrupted.

"What? I'm listening," Toivonen said. I'm completely calm, he thought.

"I'm suddenly starting to get the impression that you're jealous of our dear Bäckström," Holt said with a smile. They're like children, just like children, she thought, as Toivonen marched out of her office.

Even on the morning news, Bäckström was the nation's new hero. Several of his colleagues shook their heads and wondered how on earth it could have happened. Most of them chose to keep quiet and go along with it. One or two aired their concerns.

Jorma Honkamäki was one of them. He had bumped into Frank Motoele at the entrance of the Karolinska Hospital.

"You can't help wondering what the hell happened—really, I mean," Honkamäki said, and sighed.

"What do you mean?" Motoele said, looking at him with eyes that were suddenly as black as a winter's night in the savannah.

"That fat little bastard," Honkamäki clarified.

"Think about what you're saying," Motoele said, turning his gaze inward. "That's a hero you're talking about. Respect."

71.

Bäckström and Annika Carlsson had snuck out the back way, through the courtyard. In the street outside the front door there was mayhem, and the uniformed officers had their hands full. Journalists and curious onlookers. Quite a number who tried to get into the building. If only to reassure themselves that Bäckström actually lived there. A stream of letters, flowers, parcels, and a veritable memorial garden of lanterns and banners, even though the weather outside was high summer.

"Two things," Annika said as soon as they got inside the car. "You have to have a debriefing, and you have to talk to our colleagues in internal investigations."

"Why do I have to?" Bäckström sulked.

"The sooner the better, because then it'll be done," Annika Carlsson said. "Where do you want to start?"

"You may as well decide that as well," Bäckström said.

"A very wise decision," Annika Carlsson said. She patted him on the arm and smiled.

The debriefing had gone quickly. It was with a former colleague that Bäckström knew from his time in National Crime, who had burned out, had a crisis, rediscovered himself, and found a new role within a police organization in a process of constant change.

"How are you feeling, Bäckström?" his former colleague asked, tilting his head to one side.

"Great," Bäckström said. "Never felt better. How about you? I heard you hit the wall." You useless sod, he thought.

Five minutes later Bäckström was walking away.

"But what am I going to put in my report?" his debriefer asked.

"Use your imagination," Bäckström said.

His visit to the Stockholm Police Department for Internal Investigations had taken a whole hour. Bäckström had sat there on numerous previous occasions. For considerably longer, while everyone argued and shouted at one another in an openhearted and collegial way. This time they had started by offering coffee, and the superintendent who was in charge of the Rat Squad had personally welcomed him and assured him that he wasn't suspected of having done anything wrong. Bäckström had exchanged a quick glance with Annika Carlsson, who had accompanied him in case he needed a witness, and she was also the Police Officers' Association's representative in the Western District.

Everything that had emerged thus far unanimously supported Bäckström's version of events. The forensics team, Peter Niemi and Jorge Hernandez, had found numerous pieces of evidence to back up Bäckström's story. The first officers to arrive at the scene, Sandra Kovac, Frank Motoele, Magda Hernandez, Tomas Singh, and Gustav Hallberg, had all given testimony in his favor.

"We spoke to Motoele just an hour ago. Evidently he was the first man in, and what he told us was pretty strong stuff. Said it looked like a battlefield in there, and that it's a miracle you're alive, Bäckström. And you've probably heard that another of the perpetrators tried to stab Motoele out in the street a couple minutes before they were able to get inside and help you."

"An awful business," Bäckström said. "That young lad. How is he, by the way?" *What do you mean, help me? Snotty-nosed kids,* he thought.

"Good, under the circumstances," the investigator said, without going into any details. "Well, really we only have four questions."

"I'm listening," Bäckström said, and Annika Carlsson's eyes had already narrowed in a clearly cheering way.

Bäckström had been carrying his service revolver when he went into his flat at half past eleven in the evening. Why?

"I was on duty," Bäckström said. "Considering the current situation, I and my colleagues carry our service revolvers whenever we leave the station. I was home to change my shirt and get a bite to eat before going back to the police station in Solna."

"We're more or less working round the clock at the moment," Annika Carlsson said. "We've got two double murders that both seem to be connected to the armed robbery out at Bromma. We're seriously understaffed. A total of six officers to cover two murder investigations."

Fuck me, Bäckström thought. Surely she can't be falling in love with me?

"Yes, it's terrible," the investigator agreed, shaking his gray hair. "We're on our knees right now."

Farshad Ibrahim had a copy of the key to Bäckström's flat. Did Bäckström have any idea how he might have got hold of it?

"Well, he didn't get it from me," Bäckström said. "I'd never met Ibrahim before he attacked me in my flat. I have two keys, one that I keep in the drawer of my desk at work, and one on my own key ring. And the caretaker has a copy, of course."

"You have no idea how Ibrahim might have got hold of your key?"

"No," Bäckström lied. He had already worked out what had happened, but intended to sort that out with GeGurra and Tatiana Thorén. "I haven't lost a key, if that's what you're wondering. If I had, I would have changed the lock at once."

"The caretaker?" the investigator suggested.

"I've hardly ever spoken to him," Bäckström said.

"The copy you keep in your desk drawer at work. Do you keep the drawer locked?"

"Hang on, now," Bäckström said. "You're not seriously suggesting that one of my colleagues might have given my key to anyone like Ibrahim and Talib?"

"What about the cleaners?" the investigator persisted.

"I don't think we're getting very far," Annika Carlsson said. "Besides, this isn't really our subject, if I can put it like that."

"No, of course not," the investigator agreed.

I must remember to put a key in that drawer, Bäckström thought. Just in case, but how do I get hold of one that looks the same but doesn't actually fit? he thought.

Bäckström had drunk alcohol in his flat. Why?

"I took a whiskey," Bäckström said. "My heart was racing at something like two hundred a minute, so I thought I needed one. I'd already worked out that I wouldn't be doing any more work that night, and I handed my own gun to Niemi as soon as he arrived."

The investigator had complete understanding of this too and would probably have done the same himself.

Back of the net, Bäckström thought.

Bäckström had fired a total of six shots. One of them had hit Farshad Ibrahim. Did he have any idea which of the shots that was?

"The last one," Bäckström said. "Now that I've a chance to think about it for a while, I'm pretty sure of that."

First the gigantic Talib had thrown himself at him, and he had already drawn his pistol. Bäckström had tried to defend himself and managed to draw his own weapon. Several shots had been fired while he was wrestling with Talib, before he managed to bring him down and disarm him with his bare hands.

"Then the other one came at me with his knife, ready to strike," Bäckström said. "So I took aim and shot him in his left lower leg."

"Yes," the investigator said, and sighed. "Well, I think that's everything. Sometimes there really does seem to be someone holding a protective hand over us police officers."

"What do you want to do now, Bäckström?" Annika Carlsson said. "Do you want to go home and get a few hours' rest? And you should probably get something to eat?"

"The station. A burger on the way will do," Bäckström said. "After all, we've got a case to clear up."

"You're the boss, Bäckström," Carlsson said.

72.

Nadja had given him a hug. Whispered in his ear.

"I put the bag in your desk drawer."

Bäckström was almost touched. As always when someone touched his heart.

"Thanks, Nadja," Bäckström said. Russians, sentimental bastards, he thought.

Young Stigson stood up and saluted, even though he wasn't wearing a uniform.

"Welcome back, boss," Stigson said. "Good to see you, boss."

"Thanks," Bäckström said, patting him on the shoulder. Wonder if his dad had a go at him as well? he wondered.

"Lucky it turned out okay, Bäckström," Alm said.

"Thanks," Bäckström said. You slimy bastard, he thought. As if being crazy wasn't enough, you're an ingratiating sod as well.

"I'm so happy you're alive," Felicia Pettersson said, then she gave him a big hug. Just wrapped her arms round his neck and squeezed.

"There, there," Bäckström said. They're crazy about you, he thought.

"Back to business," Bäckström said. "What is there to report?"

Everything was going according to plan. More or less, anyway. The door-to-door out in Rinkeby was unfortunately going slowly, though. Nothing of interest, even though their colleagues in the neighborhood police unit seemed to be putting their backs into it, Annika Carlsson declared.

The plan to map out Danielsson's circle of acquaintances was also proving troublesome. Many of his old friends didn't even seem particularly interested in talking about it, and Alm was starting to have more and more doubts about several of them.

"Our erstwhile colleague Stålhammar really isn't a terribly nice person. Seems to have had a personality transplant, sadly."

"You've changed your tune," Bäckström said, smiling in an extra-friendly way.

"I don't know about that," Alm said. "I've had my doubts all along."

Nadja Högberg was still looking for Danielsson's accounting files. She had identified and checked a number of companies that rented out storage space. So far she hadn't come up with anything.

Toivonen had been onto her in Bäckström's absence, asking how they were getting on following up the connections between Farshad and Danielsson. He had even offered help if it was needed. Was prepared to lend her two people from his armed robbery investigation. Nadja had explained that she thought it would all sort itself out once her boss was back. Besides, it wasn't up to her to take that sort of decision.

"Who did he have in mind?" Bäckström said. "What did he want to palm off on us?"

"Luft from National Crime and Asph, who works in central Stockholm," Nadja said with a sigh.

Airhead and Cardboardhead, Bäckström thought. He knew

them both. And he already had a standard-issue Woodentop, he thought.

"We can manage without them," Bäckström said. Honestly, what can you say? he thought. The minute someone tries to blow my head off they start trying to infiltrate my murder investigation.

"Anything else?" he added.

"Well, I think I might have found something interesting," Felicia Pettersson said.

"I'm listening," Bäckström said.

Felicia Pettersson had been through Akofeli's telephone. She had requested comprehensive lists of his calls over the past three months. The number that he called five times during the last twenty-four hours before he disappeared had been listed practically every day.

"He seems to have called that number on pretty much a daily basis," Felicia Pettersson said. "Often early in the morning. Between half past five and six o'clock, while he was delivering papers. There's no one else that he calls anywhere near as much."

"But we still don't know whose number that is?" Bäckström said.

"No. But it isn't anyone he worked with, because I've spoken to them. And none of his family recognize the number. None of his friends. He doesn't seem to have had many friends, actually. The people he socialized with were mainly people from the courier company or people he used to know at university. A couple of old friends from high school, and one of his neighbors. None of them recognize the number."

"What about the recipient? Location?" Bäckström asked.

"Here in Solna," Pettersson said. "Solna, Sundbyberg. Always the same towers."

"Have you checked police records, then?"

"Of course," Felicia said. "The number isn't listed on the county's cell surveillance register. It's there now, but only because I put it on there."

"Okay," Bäckström said, stroking his chin. "There's something odd about . . . Akofeli."

"You haven't worked out what it is that's been worrying you, boss?" Felicia said.

"I'm starting to get old," Bäckström said. "With a bit of luck, sooner or later the penny will drop. We'll stick to our plan. Sooner or later we're going to crack this. Carry on with Akofeli, Felicia. I've just got a feeling. I wish I could be more precise, but for now it's just a feeling."

That gave them something to chew on, Bäckström thought. He was starting to feel like his usual self again. Honestly, what feeling? And how the hell am I going to get rid of Carlsson so I can have a decent drink? he wondered.

73.

That afternoon the county police chief had held an extraordinary meeting with her staff. The pressure from the media was immense. The people were demanding to see their hero, Detective Superintendent Evert Bäckström. In fact, she couldn't recall anything similar since the murder of Anna Lindh, and then it wasn't her they were after but the head of the county crime unit at the time. Nowadays he had been given other, less public responsibilities, but it had taken a lot of time and effort to ensure that he wasn't plagued by unnecessary exposure in the mass media.

The new head of the human relations department had kicked off the brainstorming session with an interesting suggestion. He had previously worked for the Moderate Party's policy think tank and had once worked as acting press secretary to the prime minister. Only a month ago he had taken part in a confidential and extremely interesting weekend conference at Gimo Herrgård Manor. And within this closed circle he saw no problems with lifting the veil a bit.

The popular demand for ostentation and vanity was immeasurable. A wealth of opinion polls provided evidence of this. In fact, the "self-affirmation coefficient" had never been so high in all of the thirty years that similar polls had been conducted, and the trend was heading inexorably higher.

The military and the police—even ordinary customs officers, coastguards, and firemen—wanted more distinctive grading, more titles, epaulettes, insignia, medals, and awards. Ordinary people wanted the royal family to have a more prominent role in Swedish society; they wanted the reinstatement of the public honors system, and a qualified majority demanded that it be massively expanded to include citizens such as themselves rather than just a load of culture vultures and generals.

And the prime minister, who had attended the last day of discussion, had come up with an extremely interesting suggestion. A daring suggestion worthy of a great political thinker like him, and among the most thought-provoking the HR head had ever heard. Honestly.

"So what was it?" the county police chief asked.

"The nobility. The prime minister wanted to raise the idea that we should reinstate the nobility. Apparently they've already done the number crunching in Finance, and we're talking about billions that could be saved in wages, bonuses, and golden handshakes.

"Today everything is about chasing dreams. And what are fifteen minutes of fame compared with the chance to flash your backside in a reality show?" the head of HR said.

"So what exactly are you thinking, in practical terms?" the county police chief's top legal adviser asked. She was a thin woman of the same age as her boss, who had been well-disposed toward their marketing maestro from the day he first started his new job.

"The Great Gold Police Medal," the head of HR said. "The most prestigious honor in the police force, and largely forgotten about for generations."

The last time there had even been any discussion of awarding it was almost thirty-five years ago. It was after the hostage crisis in the bank on Norrmalmstorg, when the two "heroes of Norrmalmstorg," Detective Inspectors Jonny Johnsson and Gunvald Larsson, had freed the hostage being kept down in the vault and hauled out the perpetrators in handcuffs with perfect timing for the newspapers' print deadlines and the serious evening news broadcasts, to be met by a veritable wall of microphones and pyrotechnic flashbulbs.

Nothing came of it on that occasion. The then chief of police, an old compromise candidate from the People's Party who only got the job in the absence of anyone better, simply didn't have the guts to go through with it.

"It was in the middle of an election campaign, Social Democratic government and all that, Palme was going crazy, and the chief of police bottled it. Didn't have the balls, basically," the head of HR concluded.

The last time the medal had actually been awarded was almost sixty years ago. The recipient was the then police inspector of Stockholm, Viking Örn, and the reason why he was deemed worthy of the honor was his decisive contribution during the so-called Margarine Riots of November 1948.

"The Great Gold Police Medal," the county police chief said, sounding as if she was trying out the taste of the words. She had been thinking of something else entirely but had decided to keep that to herself. For the time being, at least.

"Do you think you could look into this, Margareta?" she asked her legal adviser. "Put together some notes, and we'll have another meeting early tomorrow morning."

"I'd be happy to," the legal adviser said, and for some reason she smiled warmly at the new head of HR. "It'll be a pleasure," she added.

Who was Viking Örn?

What were the Margarine Riots?

74.

Who was Viking Örn?

Viking Örn was born in 1905, in Klippan, down in Skåne. He was the son of mill owner Tor Balder Örn and his wife, Fidelia Josefina, née Markow. A policeman and a legendary wrestler. In the Berlin Olympics in 1936 he had won the heavyweight gold medal in Greco-Roman wrestling, and it was said that he gained his herculean strength as a lad by running up and down the steep stairs of the mill at home in Klippan, carrying ninety-kilo sacks of flour.

When Viking Örn was taken on as a trainee by the Stockholm Police in 1926 there was much grieving in Klippan and throughout Skåne. Klippan was the home of Swedish wrestling. Viking Örn had already brought home countless titles to his club, and now he was going to leave it for the wrestling community in Stockholm.

In the legendary Olympics final of 1936, in the Berliner Sporthalle, he had beaten the Third Reich's great hero, the wrestling baron, Claus Nicholaus von Habenix. After just one minute Örn had forced von Habenix onto the mat, changed his grip, got his opponent in an inverted waistlock, and stood up with the baron hanging upside down in his massive arms. Then the Swedish Viking let out an almighty roar, threw himself backward, and tossed von Habenix into the third row of the audience.

Twelve years later he was awarded the Great Gold Police Medal.

Viking Örn was by this time a police inspector and the acting head of the Stockholm Police riot squad, and when the squad had been set up fifteen years earlier, its first boss had described it as the Swedish Police's equivalent of the German storm troopers, the SA. In the years after the war their work had taken on a new direction and they largely had two tasks: the transportation of particularly dangerous prisoners to and from the country's prisons and other institutions, and the protection of important "buildings, institutions, and other valuables" in the Royal Capital.

They also possessed the police force's first specialist vehicle. It was a black, extended Plymouth V8, which could carry up to ten officers and their driver. Burly officers at that, since Örn recruited almost exclusively from the Stockholm Police wrestling club. Their van was known popularly as the "Black Maria," and those it carried were known as the "Cauliflower Brigade" after the shape of their ears.

On the third day of the Margarine Riots, at a critical moment in the nation's history, when things were hanging in the balance, Viking Örn had finally put an end to a chain of events that could have ended in tragedy. As a reward, he had been awarded the Great Gold Police Medal.

What were the Margarine Riots?

The Margarine Riots were for a long time a neglected chapter of Swedish social history, and it wasn't until much later that the historian Maja Lundgren, in her dissertation about the rationing policies of the Swedish government after the Second World War, was able to provide a thorough analysis of the event (*Fat Fathers and Meager Mothers,* Bonnier Fakta, 2007).

The riots began on Thursday, November 4, 1948. The cause of the demonstrators' anger was that the Swedish government was still rationing margarine even through it was three and a half years since the end of the war in May 1945. The demonstrators were working-class housewives, and to start with the demonstration was extremely modest in size. Fifty or so women, of whom perhaps half a dozen were carrying placards.

For reasons that were initially unclear, they had decided to demonstrate outside the Trade Union Confederation headquarters on Norra Bantorget instead of the government offices in Gamla stan. Prime Minister Tage Erlander and the minister in question, Gustaf Möller, got off lightly, since the demonstrators' anger was directed instead at the chairman of the TUC and his right-hand man, the confederation's treasurer, Gösta Eriksson.

For the first time in Swedish history a working-class party had its own parliamentary majority. Every right-thinking Social Democrat was perfectly aware that the government was now simply the mouthpiece of the TUC. Hence the decision to demonstrate outside the TUC citadel rather than government offices.

The fifty or so women who had gathered outside the entrance to the TUC building handed over a list of their demands to a TUC representative and were told to address their concerns to the government. But generally they had done nothing much apart from stand there.

On the second day the tone had hardened considerably and the number of women had multiplied. A couple hundred mothers demanding "Margarine on the bread of working-class children," "The rich eat butter, we eat rations"—lots of chanting and shouting. On the third day, Saturday, November 6, the situation was critical. "Fat fathers and meager mothers" was the text on one of the most offensive placards, which also depicted both Strand and Erlander enjoying a drink.

The day before the weekend, and also the anniversary of the death of the great warrior king, Gustaf II Adolf. It was a particularly unfortunate choice of day on which to protest in such a fashion.

Working-class women had come by train from the whole Mälar region, and the number of demonstrators passed five hundred that morning. The police of the Klara district of Stockholm had turned to the chief of police, Henrik Tham, and asked for help, since the local force could no longer guarantee public order and safety. Tham had ordered out the riot squad under the command of the legendary Viking Örn, who arrived personally in the Black Maria, accompanied by a number of ordinary patrol cars. He had pushed his way through the angry crowd and stood at the top of the steps of the TUC, surrounded by his awe-inspiring wrestling colleagues. No one had even needed to draw their saber.

"Go home, old women, or else you'll get a thrashing," Örn roared, raising his right hand threateningly, a hand that was as big as the ham served at His Majesty the King's Christmas dinner table.

And because this happened in the bad old days, when practically all women did what their men told them, they had shuffled off. Besides, most of them had children to look after, and on top of everything else it had also started to rain, a cold, lashing November rain.

Overnight Viking Örn became the hero of the ruling middle class, and was awarded the Great Gold Police Medal, and praised by the chief of police and in the leader columns of all the right-wing newspapers in the country. Unfortunately he also made a number of comments that, sixty years later—in the pale glow of history's night light—appear rather questionable.

In a radio interview—Stockholm-Motala—he had even talked down his contribution. Much ado about nothing, whereas the wrestling baron had been quite a different matter. What sort of weaklings were these men who couldn't make a gaggle of hysterical women shut up and do what they were supposed to—cooking, cleaning, washing, and looking after their kids instead of running round the streets causing trouble for him and his men, and for all decent people in general? He at least didn't have any problems with discipline at home.

One dissenting voice had been heard in the otherwise martial tone of the media. The female reporter known as Bang, who declared concisely and in summary that Viking Örn was the natural leader of Stockholm Police's very own Cauliflower Brigade, and if he hadn't existed for real then they would have had to make him up.

The county police chief's staff read the senior legal adviser's memo in silence. For a brief second the county police chief had imagined that Evert Bäckström was tailor-made for this particular honor, then she had come to her senses.

The head of HR had made the usual attempt at saving face.

"What about the others who were awarded the medal in the past?" the HR head asked. "They can't all have been the same as Örn."

"Of course not," the senior legal adviser said in an unusually silky voice. "That particular medal was even awarded to famous figures in world history."

"Really?" the head of HR said. He was fundamentally an optimistic soul and happily took the chance to feel his hopes rise.

Most famous of all was the German SS general Reynhardt Heydrich. In 1939 Heydrich, at the initiative of the Swedes, had been appointed chairman of the International Police Organization. The following year he was awarded the Great Gold Police Medal for his "exemplary contribution to maintaining law and order in a Czechoslovakia hit hard by the winds of war."

"Would you like to hear any other examples?" the senior legal adviser asked with a gentle smile.

We'll have to do what we usually do, the county police chief thought, as she hurried off to her next meeting. There was no way of avoiding a press conference with the little fat disaster, sadly. With a bit of luck, Anna Holt was enough of a woman to keep it within reasonable bounds. Speaking for herself, she knew of at least one person who wouldn't be attending. There'd have to be the customary cut-glass vase, of course, she thought.

75.

That same day Bäckström had held a press conference with his boss, police chief Anna Holt. Also on the podium was his immediate superior, Superintendent Toivonen, as well as the county police chief's own press secretary. Because a large crowd was expected, the county police chief had put the auditorium of police headquarters on Kungsholmen at their disposal.

Regrettably she was unable to attend herself because she was obliged to attend a series of important meetings. At least that was what she told Holt, but in reality, in the world where nothing is ever really concealed from eyes that can see and ears that can hear, she was sitting alone in her office, following proceedings on TV4's live broadcast.

Anna Holt had kicked it off, giving a brief summary of what had happened. Almost no questions, even though the room was packed with journalists.

Then Toivonen had explained what was happening in the investigation into the armed robbery out at Bromma and made it clear that the main suspects were now in custody. Later that day the prosecutor would propose the formal arrest of Farshad Ibrahim, Afsan Ibrahim, and Hassan Talib for murder, attempted murder, and aggravated robbery.

But as far as the two perpetrators of the armed robbery itself were concerned, Toivonen said little. The situation was sensitive and for that reason he didn't want to comment. This was a view that the journalists didn't appear to share, because almost all of their questions had been on that particular subject. They also appeared to know most of the details already.

Kari Viirtanen, Nasir Ibrahim? Did he have anything to say about them?

No comment.

Kari Viirtanen had been shot outside his girlfriend's flat in Bergshamra. The perpetrators were the men behind the armed robbery who wanted to take revenge on him for messing things up and shooting the guards, wasn't that true?

No comment.

Nasir Ibrahim had been driving the getaway car at the raid in Bromma. He had abandoned it outside the Hells Angels' clubhouse, five hundred meters from the scene of the crime. Then he was found murdered in Copenhagen. The Hells Angels getting their revenge?

No comment.

Somewhere around then the press secretary had broken off the questions in order to let Superintendent Bäckström speak. None of the journalists objected.

Could Bäckström tell them what had happened on Monday evening in his own apartment?

Suddenly there was complete silence in the room. The journalists even shushed the photographers who were trying to take pictures of him.

Bäckström surprised everyone who knew him. He was reserved, concise, almost brusque. On the few occasions when his mouth twitched in an approximation of a smile, he looked rather like a Swedish version of Andy Sipowicz, the hero of the television series *NYPD Blue*. Nor did this fact escape either the reporters or the headline writers. But it was still a toss-up. Either Andy Sipowicz or Clint Eastwood's *Dirty Harry* Callahan.

"There's not really much to say," Bäckström said. "They got into my apartment, and the minute I walked in they attacked me and tried to kill me."

Then he nodded and smiled a crooked smile.

His audience took this to be a dramatic pause, and that there was more to come. Bäckström merely shrugged again, nodded, and looked almost uninterested.

"Well, that was it, really," Bäckström said.

His audience didn't seem to share that view. There was a barrage of questions, and when the press secretary eventually restored some order, he invited the reporter from the largest television channel to speak.

"What did you do then?" she shouted, holding her microphone up even though Bäckström was sitting five meters away and had a microphone of his own attached to his lapel.

"What could I do?" Bäckström said. "One of them had a pistol and was trying to shoot me. The other one had a knife and was trying to stab me. So I was just trying to save my life."

"So what did you do?" the national broadcaster's reporter yelled, not prepared to be overlooked a second time.

"I did as I've been trained," Bäckström said. "I disarmed the one with the pistol and rendered him harmless. The other one was trying to stab me, so I shot him in the leg. Below the knee," he added for some reason.

"Hassan Talib," the reporter from *Expressen* panted. "One of the most feared heavies in the country, and a renowned assassin. He tried to shoot you and you say you disarmed him and rendered him harmless. According to information from the Karolinska Hospital, Talib has a fractured skull and is in intensive care, still in a critical condition."

"First I removed his weapon, seeing as he was trying to shoot me, then I brought him down with a judo move I learned when I was a boy. Unfortunately he hit his head on a table, and I'm very sorry about that."

"You disarmed him and brought him down—"

"I think he has to take some of the blame for this," Bäckström interrupted. "What do you think I should have done? Give him a kiss and a big hug?"

No one in the room seemed to think so. There was cheering and applause and Bäckström was praised to the skies, and it could doubtless have carried on through the night if he hadn't put a stop to it himself after just ten minutes.

"Now, if you'll excuse me," Bäckström said, standing up. "I've got a job to do. Among other things, I've got a double murder to sort out."

"One more question," pleaded the female reporter from TV3, and because she was better known for her blond hair and big breasts than her journalistic accomplishments, Bäckström had given her a half-Sipowicz and a benevolent nod.

"Why do you think they were trying to kill you?" she asked.

"Maybe they were more afraid of me that some of my colleagues," Bäckström said with a shrug. Then he pulled off his microphone and walked out. When he passed his colleague Toivonen on the way out, he did so in a way that couldn't escape anyone.

What's good for Bäckström is good for the police, and that's good for me, the county police chief thought, switching off the television. For the time being, she thought.

76.

An unusually quiet hero who, unlike both Andy Sipowicz and Harry Callahan, belonged in the real world. In the absence of Bäckström himself, other people had to talk about him. The *Afton-*

bladet newspaper had a large interview with his shooting instructor, which was practically lyrical.

"The best pupil I ever had . . . one of the best shots in the police . . . ever . . . absolutely phenomenal . . . particularly under pressure . . . Absolutely ice-cold . . ."

Several of his fellow officers had spoken out, and the fact that most of them chose to do so anonymously was simply because Bäckström had always been "a highly controversial figure in the eyes of police management."

There was complete unanimity and every comment was enthusiastic.

"A legendary murder detective."

"He's always right."

"He always sticks up for his fellow officers."

"Completely fearless, never backs down, never stands aside."

"Heads straight for his targets like a train."

And so on, and so on.

Two of his fellow officers had appeared under their own names. First, his old friend and colleague, Detective Inspector Rogersson, himself a "legendary murder detective," who contented himself with saying that "Bäckström is a hell of a guy." And second, one of his former bosses, Lars Martin Johansson, now retired, and the man who fired him from National Crime.

"What do I think about Evert Bäckström?" Johansson said.

"Yes, what do you think about him?" *DN*'s reporter repeated, even though he had done his homework on Johansson and Bäckström's shared history.

"Evert Bäckström is an absolute disaster," Johansson said.

"Can I quote you on that?"

"Absolutely," Johansson said. "As long as you don't call this number again."

For some reason Johansson's comment didn't appear in the paper.

When the press conference was over Holt had provided a simple lunch for those most closely involved. Bäckström had been thanked with a cut-glass vase on which his name had been engraved under the emblem of the Police Authority, as well as with an old-fashioned police badge that was supposed to have belonged to Viking Örn.

As soon as Bäckström got home he knocked on the door of his alcoholic neighbor, the former TV executive, and gave him the vase as a gift.

"What the fuck do I want that for?" his neighbor said, glowering at Bäckström suspiciously.

"I thought maybe you could drown yourself in it, you fucking rat," Bäckström said. During his visit to the internal investigation team he had had the chance to listen to the recording of the call made to emergency control.

He had spent the rest of the evening reading all the letters and e-mails he had received, even replying to some of the most promising. He opened all the parcels and presents and had a few drinks in the process.

The best vodka in the world, Bäckström thought, holding up the little drinking glass that Nadja had put in the bag with the bottle. A lot of heart in that woman, he thought.

77.

On Wednesday, a fortnight after the murder of Karl Danielsson, a fair amount had happened. Bäckström had gone from "police celebrity" to "national celebrity."

Stockholm Police's biggest criminal investigation since the murder of Foreign Minister Anna Lindh had been reduced to ash and ruins, and even though it was the perpetrators who were responsible for the conflagration, Toivonen wasn't inclined to laugh. He and his colleagues were left with the task of trying to mop up the mess, and it didn't look like an easy job.

It was impossible to talk to Hassan Talib at all. His doctors merely shook their heads. Even if the patient survived, he wouldn't be able to contribute much, even in the future. Extensive brain damage. Permanent damage.

"Superintendent, you're going to have to drop any hopes of that," the doctor said, nodding to Toivonen.

Farshad and Afsan Ibrahim could at least talk. The problem was that neither of them wanted to talk to the police.

Fredrik Åkare had already been questioned. He had been good-humored, had brought his usual lawyer, but had been completely uncomprehending. He and his friends were supposed to have murdered Nasir Ibrahim? A person that Åkare had never met, would never dream of meeting? And in Copenhagen? It must be at least a year since the last time he visited the Danish capital to see old friends and acquaintances.

"Sometimes I almost worry about you, Toivonen," Åkare said with a smile. "You haven't started drinking, have you?"

Peter Niemi had submitted a new forensic report, which, in any ordinary case, would have been a breakthrough in the investigation.

"The pistol Bäckström took off Hassan Talib matches the bullets that were pulled out of Kari Viirtanen's skull by the pathologist," Niemi said. "Although fuck knows what we do with that now."

Toivonen had made do with a loud sigh. That fucking fat little bastard, he thought.

"What do we do?" Niemi repeated.

"Make sure the prosecutor gets something to read," Toivonen said. "Preferably before Bäckström holds his next press conference."

"I see what you mean," Niemi said. "Do you want to, or shall I?" he went on.

"What?"

"Strangle the fat fucker with our bare hands," Niemi said with a grin.

78.

Nadja Högberg hadn't gone to the press conference, and had also declined an invitation to attend the lunch, even though Bäckström himself had asked her. She had a lot to do, since earlier that day she had discovered a storage facility run by Shurgard just half a kilometer from the Solna police station. A friendly colleague had snapped at one of the many hooks Nadja had set out. She compared the list of the company's tenants with the list she had got from the crime section of Solna Police, and had found that one of the smaller storage spaces was leased to Flash's Electricals.

Nadja had set off to take a look, taking young Stigson with her. Inside the storage space were ten boxes containing the accounts of Karl Danielsson Holdings Ltd. But not a trace of Flash's Electricals.

In the box at the bottom of the pile she had also found a twenty-nine-year-old handwritten will, signed and witnessed on Christmas Eve 1979. It contained the following:

At the top was one word, in the middle of the lined page, which seemed to have been torn out of an ordinary pad. Ballpoint pen.

Will

Then a double-line space, followed by the text itself.

> I, Karl Danielsson, being of sound mind and body, and on a day
> like today in a damn good mood after a decent lunch, hereby
> declare that it is my last will and testament that everything I
> own should be inherited upon my death by Ritwa Laurén and
> her and my firstborn son, Seppo.

Solna, December 24, 1979.

The will was signed by Karl Danielsson, in grandiose handwriting, and witnessed by Roly Stålhammar and Halfy Söderman.

I suppose they were drunk. Nadja, who had an old-fashioned attitude to matters of this nature, sighed.

Nadja and Stigson had taken the boxes and the will with them back to the police station.

She spent the first couple hours leafing through the bookkeeping files. Mostly statements from various deals, with shares and other certificates, and thick bundles of receipts for costs incurred in the line of business, principally entertainment and travel.

After that she had a fair idea of how Karl Danielsson Holdings Ltd. made all its money. Not because he was a genius at investment, but because someone had most likely handed him a load of black-market money, which he then whitewashed with the help of various financial transactions.

Eight years earlier, the almost penniless company had been granted a remarkably generous loan of five million kronor from a foreign loan company. The only security given to the lender was a personal guarantee from Karl Danielsson, who by then had a taxable income of just two hundred thousand a year. Movements on the world's stock markets had taken care of the rest. The loan had evidently been repaid within three years, and the company now had its own declared capital of just over twenty million and an actual value that was several million higher than that.

Nadja had sighed and called the Financial Crime Unit to remind them of their promise to take over that part of the investigation as soon as she had uncovered the basics. They promised to get back to her. Right now things were a bit chaotic, but things were bound to have improved by next week.

Nadja looked at the clock. High time to go home and prepare the meal that she usually ate on her own in front of the television.

Instead she called Roland Stålhammar on his cell, explained who she was, and asked if she could invite him for a bite to eat. She had some questions she wanted to ask him.

Stålhammar was unwilling to start with. He thought the police had fucked about with him and his friends quite enough by now. Living and dead friends alike, come to that.

"I'm not thinking of fucking about with you," Nadja said. "It's about Karl Danielsson's old will. Besides, I'm a good cook, you know."

"I've always had a weakness for that sort of woman," Stålhammar said.

Two hours later Stålhammar was ringing on the door of her flat on Vintervägen in Solna. The pies were in the oven, the beetroot soup on the stove, and the Russian soused herring already on the kitchen table together with beer, water, and the world's finest vodka.

Nadja herself was flushed from cooking, and Roly Stålhammar had begun by handing her a small bunch of flowers. He was also wearing a smart jacket, smelled of aftershave, and seemed completely sober.

"You're a damn fine cook, Nadja," Stålhammar declared an hour later when they were sitting in the living room drinking coffee and even a small glass of Armenian cognac.

"I'm sorry if I was rude on the phone."

Roly Stålhammar remembered Kalle Danielsson's will very well.

"There must have been half a dozen of us lads who decided to celebrate Christmas together, and Mario was in charge of the food. We all knew about Seppo, that he was his and Ritwa's boy,

I mean. The lad was only a few months old then, of course. So I suppose we started teasing Kalle and asking who was going to pay for his little lad, us or him. Things were up and down for Kalle in those days, and if I remember rightly he was completely broke that Christmas. I'm sure you know better that me what things were like when he died. He still had a few decent things that could probably be sold, but I don't suppose the lad should expect millions. Awful business about his mother, as well."

"What would you say if I told you Kalle Danielsson was good for at least twenty-five million when he died?" Nadja asked.

"I'd say you sounded just like Kalle when he'd been on the drink in the last few years," Stålhammar said, with a wry smile and a shake of the head.

"Kalle was an artistic soul, a bohemian," he went on. "If he had money in his pocket, he was generous to a fault. Okay, he never seemed to want for much. Partly because he had various pensions, some of those private investments too, but he'd also calmed down a lot when he was out at Valla. Things have actually gone fairly well for us this year. We gambled together a lot of the time, as I'm sure you know. We actually had one V65 this spring that came in at almost one hundred to one."

"What about ten years ago?"

"Up and down," Stålhammar said, shrugging. "So how much did he have?" Stålhammar looked at her curiously as he turned his cognac glass between his coarse fingers.

"Twenty-five million," Nadja said.

"And you're sure about that?" Stålhammar said, having trouble concealing his surprise. "Kalle was pretty hot at accounts, you know. I remember Flash's electricals business looked really shaky for a while, but Kalle sorted that out for him. He just had to go down to the bank and get out a fat loan, and he'd sort out the details. You make meringue from egg whites, Kalle used to say."

"Twenty-five million. Not meringue this time," Nadja said.

"Fucking hell," Roly Stålhammar said, shaking his head.

79.

Alm was having trouble letting go of Seppo Laurén and the notion of patricide. He had talked to a friend in National Crime who was good with computers, and according to him there were several ways of creating a false alibi using your computer. You get someone else to sit there instead of you. If you were smart and cunning enough, that person didn't even have to sit there in any physical sense.

"You can connect to another computer, and sometimes it can be really difficult to trace that sort of thing," the expert said.

"Really?" said Alm, who was in the habit of shaking his computer when it didn't do what he wanted.

"Nowadays there's even software that can do the job for you. Then you can go off and do whatever you like. The computer looks after itself, doing whatever the software tells it to."

"Like playing computer games for you, for instance?" Alm asked.

"Yes, for instance."

Nadja wasn't particularly impressed when Alm told her what one of the force's "best computer nerds" had just told him.

"I hear what you're saying, Alm," Nadja said. "But that isn't the problem."

"What do you mean?" Alm said.

"Seppo likes playing computer games," Nadja said. "It's pretty much the only thing he likes doing. So why would he get a piece of software to do it for him? Leaving aside the fact that he could probably put together that sort of software himself."

"Yes, well, there you are," Alm said. "Listen to what you just said, Nadja."

"Drop Seppo," Nadja said. "He didn't kill Danielsson."

"How can you say that? How do you know that?"

"Seppo can't lie," Nadja said. "People like him are incapable of it. If he killed Danielsson, he would have said when you asked him. He would have told you in exactly the same way he's replied to every other question we've asked him."

What a complete idiot, Nadja thought, as Alm left her.

Not only is she a computer expert, but now she's evidently a psychiatrist as well, Alm thought, as he closed her door.

Alm didn't give up, and the next day he finally got his reward. On Wednesday, April 9, about a month before he was killed, Karl Danielsson was admitted to the ER at the Karolinska Hospital. At around eleven o'clock that evening one of his neighbors had found him lying unconscious by the entrance of number 1 Hasselstigen and had called an ambulance.

Because he didn't have any obvious external injuries, the ambulance staff thought at first that he must have suffered a heart attack or a stroke, but the doctor who examined him found other injuries when they undressed him. Someone had knocked Karl Danielsson to the ground from behind. Severe bruising to his body indicated that he had suffered a number of blows to the backs of his knees, his back, and his neck. And had suffered a mild concussion and lost consciousness.

He had come round in the ER. The doctor had asked him whether he could remember what had happened. Karl Danielsson had replied that he must have tripped on the stairs.

"But you don't believe that?" Alm said when he spoke to the doctor.

"No," the doctor said. "It's out of the question. Someone attacked him from behind. Probably began by hitting his knees so that he fell forward. Then set about him when he was on the ground."

"Do you have any idea what his attacker might have used as a tool?" Alm asked.

The doctor had fairly definite views on that matter. He had even put an entry in the notes.

"A baseball bat, an ordinary cudgel, a long baton. The patient looked like people do when they've been attacked by football hooligans and the like. And there was actually a match at Råsunda that evening. AIK versus Djurgården, if I remember rightly."

"You remember that? Are you sure?" Alm said.

"You'd remember too if you'd been on duty that night," the doctor said with a wry smile. "This place looked like a field hospital."

Then he had spoken to Seppo's next-door neighbor. A very striking woman with a shapely and well-preserved figure even though she must have passed fifty several years ago, thought Alm, who had himself hit sixty a few months earlier.

"You mostly just have to feel sorry for the poor lad," Britt-Marie Andersson said. "After all, he's retarded, if I can put it like that."

"Mrs. Andersson, do you have any idea about how he got on with Karl Danielsson?" Alm asked.

"What, apart from the fact that he's his son?" Britt-Marie Andersson said with a faint smile.

"So you know about that?" Alm said.

"Most people who've lived here long enough probably know. But I don't know if the lad himself knows. His mom . . ."

"Yes?" Alm cajoled.

"Well, even though she's in the hospital," Mrs. Andersson said, pursing her lips. "His mom was very young thing. She didn't make any secret of the fact that she and Danielsson were an item, even though he must have been at least twenty-five years older than her. But I'm not sure if Seppo knew about it."

"So how did Seppo get on with Karl Danielsson?" Alm reminded her.

"Mostly he seemed to be Danielsson's errand boy. Do this, do that. And I suppose he usually did as he was told. But sometimes they fought like cat and dog, so in recent years it's been a bit tricky, if I can put it like that."

"Could you give me an example, Mrs. Andersson?"

"Well, there was one time last winter when I got home. I'd been out to let my little darling do his business. There was a terrible commotion in the entrance. Danielsson was drunk and was yelling and shouting, and suddenly Seppo flew at him and tried to strangle him. It was awful," Mrs. Andersson said, shaking her head.

"I yelled at them, telling them to behave themselves, and they actually stopped."

"But before that Seppo had been trying to strangle him?" Alm said.

"Yes, if I hadn't managed to stop them fighting I don't know what would have happened," Mrs. Andersson sighed, her bosom heaving.

Hmm, Alm thought, and merely nodded.

Now the hawk takes the finch, Alm thought. As soon as he had left Mrs. Andersson he called his colleague Stigson on his cell phone and told him to get to Hasselstigen at once. Stigson was there within fifteen minutes. Seppo didn't open the door until they had been ringing on his doorbell for a good two minutes.

"I'm playing computer games," Seppo said.

"You'll have to stop for a while. We need to talk to you," Alm said, making an effort to sound friendly and authoritative at the same time.

"Okay," Seppo said with a shrug.

The second time Seppo hit Karl Danielsson. Did he remember what day that was?

"Don't remember," Seppo said, shaking his head.

"What if I say it was the same day that AIK played a match against Djurgården? Do you remember what day it was now?"

"It was April ninth," Seppo said, nodding happily. "Now I remember. It was a Wednesday."

"You remember that?" Stigson said. "That it was a Wednesday? How come you remember that?"

"Because today is a Wednesday too," Seppo said. "Wednesday, May twenty-eighth. April has thirty days," Seppo explained, holding out his watch toward Stigson to underline what he had just said.

The lad must be completely nuts, Alm thought, and decided to change the subject.

"Do you remember how you hit him?" Alm asked.

"Yes," Seppo said, nodding.

"Did you use karate?" Alm asked.

"No," Seppo said. "I hit him with my baseball bat."

"Seppo, what you're telling us is very serious," Alm said. "You told me before that the first time you hit Karl you used karate, but this time you hit him with a baseball bat? Why did you do that?"

"I told you," Seppo said. "I was very angry."

Alm made a whispered call to the prosecutor on his phone. Then they took his baseball bat but left him there.

"We'll probably have to talk to you tomorrow," Alm said. "So we don't want you to go anywhere."

"That's all right," Seppo said. "I never go anywhere else."

80.

Two days after the press conference Bäckström gathered his strength for another meeting of the investigative team. Alm was sitting there, desperate to start talking, so Bäckström took his time dealing with various formalities before eventually asking Nadja to talk about her big discovery, Danielsson's accounts and will.

Nadja wasn't in any hurry either.

"So you mean that Danielsson was good for twenty-five million?" Bäckström said. A common drunk? Where the hell was Sweden heading? he thought.

"More or less," Nadja said, nodding. "Since we got rid of inheritance tax, that's pretty much the amount that Seppo and his mother will share between them."

"What about the tax office?" Bäckström said. "They're going to want to get their hands on every last krona."

"I can't really believe that," Nadja said. "They'll have a hard job blowing any holes in his bookkeeping—"

"Which surely reinforces my own theories," Alm interrupted, evidently not prepared to sit and listen any longer. "There's more to this than usual paternal hatred. The lad also had strong financial motives for killing Danielsson. I think it's high time we had a serious talk with our prosecutor, so that we can bring the boy in and declare him a formal suspect. Do a thorough search of his flat. And get forensics to take a look at that baseball bat that we brought in yesterday."

For some reason Alm glared at both Bäckström and Nadja as he relieved some of his internal pressure.

"Don't let's get carried away," Bäckström said with a friendly smile. "How are you getting on with the cell phone surveillance, Felicia?"

Absolutely fine, according to Felicia Pettersson. The day before, she got hold of the records of the phone that Akofeli used to ring almost daily during the months leading up to his death. The same phone that he called five times during the twenty-four hours before he disappeared.

"That pay-as-you-go account has only been active for about six months," Felicia said. "It seems to be used mainly to receive incoming calls on."

"From Akofeli," Bäckström said.

"Mainly Akofeli. I've found another pay-as-you-go cell number, but it only calls the same number as Akofeli once a week at most. And that one's been in use for several years."

"So what do we know about that one?" Bäckström said.

"Everything," Felicia said with a satisfied smile. "At least I daresay we know everything."

"Everything?" Bäckström repeated. What the hell is she saying? he thought.

"I got the list of calls for that one yesterday, so I've only just started going through it. But I'm pretty sure who it belonged to."

"So whose was it, then?" Bäckström said.

"Karl Danielsson's," Felicia said.

"What the hell are you saying?" Bäckström said.

"Bloody hell," Stigson said.

"How do you know that?" Annika Carlsson said.

"Interesting," Nadja said.

What the hell is going on? Alm thought. He was the only one who didn't say anything.

"It wasn't very hard to work out," Felicia said. "Like I said before, it was you who put me on the right track, boss."

"I'm listening," Bäckström said.

"This phone was in regular use until the day Karl Danielsson was murdered," she went on. "Since then, nothing. The last three calls were all made at around seven o'clock in the evening, just a few hours before Danielsson was killed. First a short call to a cell belonging to Roland Stålhammar. Probably to see if he was on his way to Danielsson's for a meal. Then a slightly longer call to Gunnar Gustafsson, Jockey Gunnar as he's known. Maybe to thank him for the tip about the horse. And finally a short call that ends up with the recipient's messaging service. Probably because Seppo Laurén didn't want to be disturbed when he was sitting at his computer playing games. In fact, there are loads of previous calls to Danielsson's various friends and contacts. I've only just started, so it'll be a couple days before I've got a comprehensive list."

"Let's see," Bäckström said. "So we've got three phones. They're all pay-as-you-go. One belongs to Akofeli, and one belongs to Danielsson. And they both call a third, which only seems to be used for incoming calls, owner not yet identified. And both Akofeli's and Danielsson's phones have been missing since they were murdered."

"Yes," Felicia Pettersson said.

"Next question," Bäckström said. "What about—"

"No," Felicia interrupted, shaking her head. "Danielsson and Akofeli never called each other. If that's what you're wondering, boss."

"There's no flies on you, are there, Felicia?" Bäckström said.

"Thanks, boss," Felicia said. "If you're interested, boss, I think . . ."

"Of course," Bäckström said.

" . . . that we'll have this case cracked as soon as we find the person who has the third cell."

"Definitely," Bäckström said. If you closed your eyes, you could almost believe that little Pettersson has got Russian blood in her veins, he thought.

"Hang on a minute," Alm said. "What's the connection between Danielsson and Akofeli? Apart from the fact that they were both murdered and have evidently also rung the same cell?"

"Surely that's enough?" Nadja said. The man must be a complete idiot, she thought.

"They both know the killer but they don't know each other. At least that's what I think," Felicia said.

"And who might that be?" Alm said. He suddenly felt the penny drop inside his head. "The only person who admits to knowing both of them is Seppo Laurén. If you ask me, I can very well imagine that Seppo has an extra cell, one of those pay-as-you-go phones with no recognized subscriber."

"Well, about that 'admission,'" Bäckström said with a shrug. "The unfortunate problem with most killers I've met is that they aren't usually very willing to admit anything."

"But this is unbelievable," Alm said, by now red in the face.

"Give me a straight answer. What are we going to do with Laurén?"

"Go and talk to him," Bäckström said. "Ask him if he beat Danielsson to death and strangled Akofeli."

"I've already asked him about Danielsson," Alm said.

"And what did he say?"

"He denied it," Alm said.

"Well, there you are, then," Bäckström said with a grin. "Okay, I don't think we're going to get much further sitting here talking. Let's get to work. At least that's what I'm going to do."

But only after I've had a nutritious lunch, Bäckström thought. Even a living legend needs something nice to eat, he thought.

81.

After lunch Bäckström had spent the remainder of the day granting a number of exclusive interviews, in which the recipients of this honor had a few thoughtful words bestowed upon them along the way.

For the female reporter from the Christian daily paper *Dagen,* he confessed his childhood beliefs and his faith in the Lord.

"Beaten to the ground with deadly force, I was granted the strength to get up and strike back," Bäckström said with a pious look in his eyes.

For the representatives of the two evening papers he had in turn revealed that he had long thought that the police were too reluctant to share information. Not least to the evening papers.

"How else can we hope to reach out to that great detective, the general public? We'd be lost without you and your colleagues." Bäckström sighed, nodding to the reporter from *Expressen.*

"The public interest," he said half an hour later when he was talking to the journalist from *Aftonbladet*. "It's actually the duty of the police to inform the media, so that they in turn can tell our citizens how things are going."

In the conversation with *Svenska Dagbladet* that followed he had revealed his concerns about various deficiencies in the rule of law.

"Our fight against crime must be conducted openly," Bäckström said, looking intently at the paper's representative. "Too many of my fellow officers have far too lax a view of the rule of law."

Finally, *Dagens Nyheter*, where he contented himself with agreeing with all the leading questions put to him.

"I completely agree with you," Bäckström repeated, for the umpteenth time. "I couldn't have put it better myself. It's absolutely terrible. I mean, where on earth are we heading as a constitutional state?"

On his way home he paid a visit to GeGurra for an openhearted conversation between just the two of them. GeGurra wasn't merely perplexed, he was utterly mortified now that he realized how the crooks had got hold of the keys to Bäckström's apartment.

"I can assure you, my dear Bäckström," GeGurra said. "That woman has deceived you and me alike. All I told her when she called and asked if I would like to take her out to dinner was that I was already engaged. That I was going to have dinner at Operakällaren with a very dear friend who happened to be a police officer. I had no inkling that she had questionable intentions when she appeared. As I understood it, she simply appeared to be quite captivated by you."

Right, Bäckström thought.

"So what are we going to do about the coffee table, the carpet, and all the bullet holes in the walls?" Bäckström asked.

On that point he didn't have to worry himself at all. GeGurra had all the contacts and resources necessary to put everything right. Straightaway, no less.

"I insist that you let me do that, Bäckström," GeGurra said. "The fact that I was entirely ignorant does not release me from my obligations in the slightest. After all, I was an unwitting accomplice to your being placed in mortal danger."

"The coffee table, the carpet, the walls," Bäckström said, not about to let himself be sidetracked by fine words.

"Of course, my dear friend," GeGurra said. "What do you think of that coffee table, by the way?" he asked, gesturing toward the coffee table in his own office.

"Antique, Chinese lacquerwork—the colors would match your sofa perfectly," GeGurra cajoled.

"Nice carpet," Bäckström said, nodding toward the carpet that the table was standing on.

"Another antique from China," GeGurra said. "An excellent choice, if you were to ask my opinion."

The police officers stationed at Bäckström's door had been replaced by two contracted guards from Securitas. They helped him to carry up the coffee table, the carpet, and the various packages that had arrived during the course of the day.

Bäckström had prepared a simple meal from the things in his fridge. Then he had gone through the day's haul. E-mails, letters, parcels, and presents. Everything from a knitted tea cozy in the shape of a hen and a handwritten letter containing one hundred kronor to a considerably larger amount that an anonymous benefactor had transferred into his account.

He threw the tea cozy in the bin.

He read the letter. A "Gustaf Lans, eighty-three, retired bank director" wrote, "May God protect you, Superintendent. Thank you for all your hard work."

Thanks yourself, you mean old bastard, Bäckström thought. He put the hundred-kronor note in his wallet and threw the letter in the bin.

Just as he was done with these administrative tasks there came a knock on his door.

"Hello, Bäckström," Annika Carlsson said with a smile. "I thought I'd look in on you before you went to bed."

Hello, Bäckström thought.

"Would you like a cup of coffee?" he asked.

Annika Carlsson admired his new coffee table and his new carpet. And even the bullet holes in the walls and ceiling.

"If I were you, I think I'd leave them as they are," Annika Carlsson said. "They're seriously cool. Think about all the girls you must have here. Wow, this guy's got bullet holes in his walls," Annika Carlsson said. "It even makes me—"

"Sorry, Annika," Bäckström interrupted. "A personal question?"

"Sure," Annika said with a smile. "Go for it. I'm listening."

"And you promise not to be offended?" Because who wants to get their jaw broken before they go to bed? he thought. He'd had quite enough with Talib and the other wretched prick.

"You're wondering if I'm a dyke?" Annika said, looking at him in delight.

"Yes," Bäckström said.

"There's so much talk," Annika Carlsson said, shrugging. "My most recent partner was a female police officer who worked in domestic crime in the city. That ended six months ago. But the last sex I had, if you want to know—if we're not counting the sort you make for yourself that is—was with a guy. Not even a fellow officer. He was some sort of salesman. I picked him up in a bar."

"Any good?" Bäckström asked.

"No," Annika said, shaking her head. "All mouth, no trousers. Almost exclusively mouth, actually."

A woman, talking like that. Where the hell are we heading? Bäckström thought, but contented himself with a nod.

"I like to keep an open attitude. Don't want to restrict the field, if I can put it like that," Annika Carlsson clarified. "Were you wondering anything in particular, Bäckström?"

"I was actually thinking of going to bed," Bäckström said. What the hell is happening to Sweden? he thought. To me and all the other normal, decent, hardworking men? What's going to happen to us?

82.

The first thing Bäckström did on Friday morning was to decide to disperse the last remaining cloud in his otherwise clear blue sky. He went straight to Toivonen's office and asked for a new service pistol, since his own was evidently stuck with forensics until the lazy sods in internal investigations pulled their fingers out.

"What do you want it for?" Toivonen said, glaring at Bäckström.

None of your fucking business, Bäckström thought, but contained himself. When you had to deal with complete idiots like Toivonen, it was best to stick to a formal manner of address.

"I'm a police officer," Bäckström said. "I have the right to a service weapon. It's your duty to see that I get one."

"Who were you thinking of shooting this time, Bäckström?" Toivonen said, evidently feeling a bit brighter.

"I want it for my personal protection while I'm on duty, and for other requirements in the line of duty," Bäckström said. By now he knew the routine.

"Forget it, Bäckström," Toivonen said, shaking his head. "Just be honest. You've got a taste for it. Running round and shooting people."

"I demand a new weapon," Bäckström repeated, with steely resolve in his voice.

"Okay, Bäckström," Toivonen said with a friendly smile. "I'll try to make it clear. So clear that even you can understand. I am not going to give you another service weapon. Not even if you invite me personally to shove it up your fat ass when I hand it over."

"You'll be getting a written request," Bäckström said. "Copied to management, for their files. And to the officers' association."

"Go ahead," Toivonen said. "If management wants to let you have a gun, it's up to them. But I don't want anyone else's blood on my hands."

That was as far as they got.

That evening Toivonen, Niemi, Honkamäki, Alakoski, Arooma, Salonen, and several other Finnish brothers in the force had gone to the Karelia restaurant. Even Superintendent Sommarlund was allowed to go along, even though he really only came from the Swedish-speaking Åland Islands. Men with their roots in Finnish soil, men of the right stuff, with their hearts in the right place, and, as far as Sommarlund was concerned, he could very easily have been born on the Finnish mainland. But to celebrate or to lick their wounds? Who cared? Any reason was good enough, and the intention had been the same as usual.

They had eaten cured elk snout, salmon and egg pastries, lamb with boiled turnips. They had drunk beer and vodka and sung "Rose of Kotka" with the first, second, and third drinks.

"Kotkan Ruusu," Sommarlund said with a dreamy look in his eyes. Must have been one hell of a woman, he thought.

Bäckström had taken the bull by the horns and gone to see one of the most eager of his new female admirers, one who had also attached photographs of herself when she e-mailed him. Well worth a special trip, to judge by the pictures, and since she lived in the center of the city, he could always walk out if she had passed her sell-by date.

Maybe they weren't taken recently, Bäckström thought an hour later, but there was nothing wrong with her enthusiasm. The super-salami had done its usual thorough job, and when he climbed out of the taxi outside his door, the sun had already risen in yet another cloud-free sky. Bäckström walked up to the second floor, seeing as one of his lazy neighbors had evidently forgotten to send the elevator back down, and just as he was standing in the stairwell, fumbling with his keys, he heard the sound of padding footsteps on the stairs above him.

Earlier that day one of their witnesses had got in touch with Detective Inspector Annika Carlsson.

"Lawman," Lawman said. "I don't know if you remember me. I'm the one who works for Green Carriers. Used to work with Akofeli."

"I remember. How can I help you?" Annika Carlsson asked. I wonder if they've sorted out those bikes on the pavement like I told them? she wondered.

"I want to add something to my statement," Lawman said.

"Where are you?" Annika Carlsson said. She preferred to talk where she could see the other person.

"Not far away at all," Lawman said. "I've actually just delivered a package to your police station. To that trigger-happy Bäckström. One of our crazy clients wanted to send him a gift voucher. All a bit dodgy, if you ask me as a lawyer, but . . ."

"I'll come down and get you," Annika Carlsson said, and five minutes later Lawman was sitting in her office.

The previous day a thought had struck Lawman. Something he had forgotten to tell Annika Carlsson and her colleague when they spoke at his workplace.

"You remember that Akofeli asked me about the right of self-defense? How far you could go and so on?"

"I remember," Annika said. She had already pulled out his statement.

"There was something I forgot to tell you," Lawman said. "It completely slipped my mind."

"What's that?" Annika asked.

"He asked me to give him an example of the sort of violence that would justify self-defense. I remember mentioning abuse in all its forms, right up to attempted murder. I also said something about jus necessitatis, the right to help someone else."

"I know," Annika Carlsson said. "What was it you forgot to say?"

"Mister Seven, Septimus, actually asked a concrete question as well. More or less in passing, I thought, considering the context."

"What did he ask?"

"He wanted to know about rape," Lawman said. "If someone was trying to rape you. Did you have the same right to defend yourself as you did with attempted murder?"

"And what did you make of that, then?" Annika Carlsson asked.

"I was pretty blunt," Lawman said. "I asked him if one of our weird clients had tried it on with him."

"What did he say to that?"

"He just shrugged," Lawman said. "Didn't want to talk about it."

Denial, Annika Carlsson thought. Just as she had learned in that course on sexual attacks back in the autumn. The denial of the victim, she thought. But seeing as Bäckström had evidently finished for the day, she had no one to talk to.

I'll tell him when I look in on him first thing tomorrow morning, she thought.

Footsteps on Bäckström's staircase. Little Siggy locked up by the lazy pricks in forensics, so all that was left was another Bäckström one-two, he thought. He walked forward, raised his left hand, and put the right one inside his jacket.

"Stand absolutely still or I'll blow your head off," Bäckström said.

"Take it easy, for fuck's sake," the paperboy said, waving Bäckström's own copy of *Svenska Dagbladet* at him just to make sure.

The paperboy, Bäckström thought, taking the newspaper.

"Why don't you take the elevator?" Bäckström said. "Instead of creeping around on the stairs scaring the shit out of people?"

"I didn't think you were the type to scare easily, Superintendent," the paperboy said with a grin. "Nice work, by the way. Saw you on TV the other night."

"The elevator," Bäckström repeated.

"Right," the paperboy said. "I do what everyone does. Everyone delivering papers, that is. Take the elevator to the top floor, then come down the stairs."

"Why don't you take the elevator back down?" Bäckström said. "That would save you having to walk."

"Takes too long," the paperboy said. "Think about it. Jumping in and out of the elevator, going down one floor at a time. You wouldn't get your paper before the evening."

When Bäckström walked into his own hallway and closed the door behind him he was suddenly struck by a bolt of lightning, lighting up the whole inside of his round head.

Akofeli, Bäckström thought. Number one Hasselstigen, a five-story building with a lift. Why the hell didn't you take the elevator up? he thought.

83.

"Fresh rolls, peaceful intent, interesting news," Annika Carlsson said, waving the bag from the bakery.

"Come in," Bäckström grunted. He hadn't had much sleep, since he had spent a couple hours deep in thought before he finally fainted away in his own bed.

"What time is it, anyway?"

"Ten o'clock," Annika Carlsson said. "I took it for granted that you were out carousing all night with one of your many female admirers, so I didn't come round too early."

"Kind of you," Bäckström said with a wry smile. Open to all comers, he thought. But really quite nice.

"So if you get in the shower, nice Auntie Annika will get breakfast for you."

"Pancakes, bacon?" Bäckström suggested.

"Out of the question," Annika said, and snorted.

"What do you think, Bäckström?" Annika asked half an hour later when she had told him what Lawman had told her.

"Think about what?" Bäckström said. His mind was on other things.

"Do you think Kalle Danielsson might have tried to force him to have sex with him? Seems to fit the profile of that sort of perpetrator. Slightly older, alcoholic, mostly male social circle, clearly sexually active, seeing how he had Viagra and condoms in his flat. A young man like Akofeli, black, half his size. Probably quite appealing to someone like Danielsson when he'd had a few and his inhibitions started to wobble."

"No chance," Bäckström said, shaking his head. "Danielsson wasn't the type."

"What do you mean, not the type?" Annika said.

"The type to fuck people in the ass," Bäckström said.

"What do you mean?" Annika Carlsson said. "Even someone like you would have a go if you got the chance."

"Male ass," Bäckström clarified. Open to all comers, he thought.

"If you say so," Annika Carlsson said, with a nonchalant shrug.

"Listen to this instead," Bäckström said. "Last night when I got home I suddenly realized what it is that doesn't make sense about Akofeli. You know, the thing I've been worrying about."

"Okay, okay," Annika Carlsson said a quarter of an hour later. "So he took the stairs instead of the elevator. What's the problem? Maybe he wanted some extra exercise. I do a lot of step exercises myself. It's very good for you, you know."

"Okay, here's what we're going to do," Bäckström said.

"Okay," Annika Carlsson said, her little black notebook out at the ready.

"I want to know all about Akofeli's newspaper round," Bäckström said. "What his route was, which building he started in,

327

where he finished, how many papers he delivered in total, how many he delivered in Hasselstigen, and what order he did it in. Clear?"

"Okay," Annika Carlsson said with a nod. "And how do I reach you when I'm done?"

"At work," Bäckström said. "Just need to throw some clothes on."

84.

Even though it was Saturday Bäckström was sitting at work, thinking hard. He was even thinking so hard that he forgot about lunch.

"So this is where you are," Annika Carlsson said. "I was looking for you down in the cafeteria."

"Thinking," Bäckström said.

"You were right," Annika Carlsson said. "There's something really weird about the way Akofeli delivered his papers."

Surprise, surprise, Bäckström thought. By that time he already had a fairly firm idea of what was going on.

"Tell me," Bäckström said.

Every day at three in the morning Akofeli and the other deliverers who worked the same district picked up their papers from the distribution company's collection point on Råsundavägen. In Akofeli's case, just over two hundred *Dagens Nyheter* and *Svenska Dagbladet,* and a dozen copies of *Dagens Industri.* Then he followed a fixed route that the distribution company had worked out for him, intended to stop him doing any more walking than he needed to as he delivered them.

"You can pretty much say he kept to the block to the north-west, and there were only two more buildings on his round after the building at number one Hasselstigen. The whole thing ought to take between two and a half and three hours, and the idea is that everyone should have received their paper by six o'clock at the latest."

"The last two buildings?" Bäckström asked.

"This is where it starts to get weird," Annika Carlsson said. "The last building on his round is number four Hasselstigen, and the second to last is number two Hasselstigen. Number four is down by the junction with Råsundavägen, and the underground station home to Rinkeby where he lives is a couple hundred meters farther down Råsundavägen. Instead of taking the shortest route, it looks like he rearranged the end of his route. He goes past number one Hasselstigen without delivering any papers. He goes straight to number four, which should be the last building, and delivers papers there. Then he goes back up the road to number two, the penultimate building, and hands out papers there. Then he crosses the road and finishes his round by delivering the papers in number one Hasselstigen."

"A detour of a couple hundred meters," Bäckström said. By now he was well acquainted with the geography.

"More than three hundred meters, actually," Annika Carlsson said, having checked the distances herself just a couple hours before.

"An entirely unnecessary detour that must have cost him at least five minutes," she went on. "It's a bit odd, seeing he might reasonably be expected to want to get home to Rinkeby as quickly as he can, to dump his cart and get a couple hours' sleep before he heads off to work as a courier."

"Then what?" Bäckström said. "What does he do inside number one Hasselstigen?"

"This is where it gets even weirder."

There were eleven tenants in number 1 Hasselstigen who subscribed to a morning paper: six *Dagens Nyheter* and five copies of

Svenska Dagbladet. Only ten since Karl Danielsson's murder, and because old Mrs. Holmberg had switched from *DN* to *Svenska Dagbladet,* the two media groups were evenly matched for now.

"Five *DN,* five *Svenska Dagbladet,*" Annika Carlsson summarized.

What did that have to do with anything? Bäckström thought.

"I'm listening," he said.

"The first to get her paper is Mrs. Holmberg, who lives on the ground floor. That's not so strange, since he passes her door on the way to the elevator. Then he should have taken the elevator to the top floor of the building and walked down the stairs delivering the remaining ten copies on the way. The last person in the block to get their paper ought therefore to be our murder victim, Karl Danielsson, because he lives on the second floor and is the only person on that floor to take a newspaper."

"But not that morning?" Bäckström said.

"No," Annika Carlsson said. "Because, as you pointed out when you arrived at the crime scene, Akofeli still had the papers left in his bag. According to the inventory Niemi and Hernandez took when they arrived at the scene, he had nine morning papers left in his shoulder bag. And they're both meticulous. Eleven minus the one he delivered to Mrs. Holmberg minus the one he was going to deliver to Karl Danielsson when he saw his door ajar and found Danielsson lying dead in his hall."

"The newspaper that he put down beside the door," Bäckström said.

"Exactly," Annika Carlsson said.

"Did he always do it like that?"

"Seems to have been doing for a fair while, at any rate," Annika Carlsson said. "At least that's my impression."

"What makes you think that?" Bäckström said.

"I got to the crime scene just before seven in the morning, and I agreed with Niemi that I would search the building while they carried on inside Danielsson's apartment. On the ground floor there's a room used for storing bicycles and strollers. Not many, because most of the tenants are pensioners, but there were still one stroller and several bikes in there. As well as Akofeli's cart. According to the inventory I wrote at the time, even though it didn't strike me as odd then."

"Why not leave it by the front door?" Bäckström said. "That would have been simplest for him."

"That's what I think too, although it didn't occur to me at the time. You're just smarter than me, Bäckström," Annika Carlsson said with a smile.

"Well . . . ," Bäckström said, smiling his most modest smile.

"Then, while I was busy in there, one of the tenants came down to get her bike," Annika Carlsson went on.

"In a state of extreme anxiety," Bäckström said.

"Yes, she was wondering what had happened, since there must have been at least ten of us there by that time, searching the building. I didn't go into detail. I explained that we were there because of an emergency call we'd received. I asked who she was and what she was doing down with the bicycles. She told me her name, even showed me her ID before I asked for it. She explained that she lived in the building, that she was on her way to work, and that she always took her bike if the weather was good enough. She works as a receptionist in the Scandic Hotel down by the motorway to Arlanda Airport. It's about five kilometers away, and she was due to start work at eight o'clock."

"The newspaper cart?"

"I didn't have to ask. She said it was usually in there. Had been over the past few months at least. It used to annoy her, she said, because it was always in the way when she was trying to get her bike out. She said she'd even been thinking of leaving a note on it. She realized it belonged to the paperboy. She herself didn't have a paper delivered. She got to read them for free at work."

"So she didn't have any reason to keep an eye on Akofeli's timing?"

"No," Annika Carlsson said. "She presumed their paths had crossed inside the building. And, like I said, it didn't occur to me. Not then, anyway."

"You haven't talked to anyone in the building?" Bäckström said.

"What do you take me for?" Annika Carlsson said. "How would that look?"

"A wise colleague is worth their weight in gold," Bäckström said.

"Akofeli was seeing someone who lived in the building," Annika Carlsson said.

"Obviously," Bäckström said. "I've suspected as much all along."

85.

Anna Holt had woken up around seven that morning. She had been having a vaguely erotic dream, not at all unpleasant, and when she looked up she saw Jan Lewin lying in bed next to her, looking at her. He was resting his head on his right hand while the left played with her right nipple.

"You're awake," Holt said.

"Extremely awake," Jan Lewin replied, smiling, and nodding for some reason in the direction of his own groin.

"Goodness," Holt said as she stretched her hand under the sheets to feel. "I think we have an acute problem here."

"What are we going to do about it, then?" Jan Lewin asked as he put his arm round her neck.

"Solve it," Holt said. She pulled the sheets off and sat on top of him.

It's best in the mornings, Holt thought half an hour later. And she felt energetic too. Always did afterward. In contrast, Jan seemed much more relaxed and close to falling back to sleep. Typical, she thought, just as her phone rang.

"What sort of fool calls up at this time on a Saturday?" Lewin groaned.

"I have my suspicions," Holt said, picking up the phone. The county police chief, she thought.

"I hope I didn't wake you, Anna?" the county police chief said. She sounded just as awake as Holt, and considerably angrier.

"I was already awake," Holt said. Without going into the reason and pulling a happy face at Lewin.

"Have you read the papers?" the county police chief asked.

"No," Holt said. "Which one?"

"All of them," the county police chief said. "Bäckström," she clarified. "He seems to have talked to all of them. Even that Christian rag where he takes the chance to declare his strong faith in God."

"I'll talk to him," Holt said. Say what you like about Bäckström, but he's not stupid, she thought.

"Thank you," the county police chief said, and hung up.

"Now I've got something I need to do," Holt said. "You, on the other hand, should try to get back to sleep."

"I can get breakfast," Jan Lewin said, sitting up in bed.

"You're probably wondering . . ."

"No," Lewin said, shaking his head. "I'm a police officer, have I ever mentioned that? I've already got a fairly good idea of the reason behind that call." It's always Bäckström, he thought.

Anna Holt had sat down at her computer, where she went onto the Internet to read the morning papers. It confirmed her fears. Then she called Bäckström. As usual, no answer. Then she spoke to Annika Carlsson.

If she can, then so can I, Anna Holt thought. The "she" in question was the county police chief, and the person she was calling was Toivonen.

"Toivonen," Toivonen groaned.

"Holt," Holt said.

"I'm listening, boss," Toivonen said. "I was out late," he explained.

"Bäckström," Holt said, then spent the next two minutes explaining what this was about.

"In that case, I suggest we wait until Monday," Toivonen said. "Since it's the weekend and we're talking about Bäckström here," he clarified.

"He's actually at work," Holt said. "I spoke to Annika Carlsson a short while ago. She says he's been there since early this morning."

"If he is, then he's only doing it to wind me up," Toivonen said.

86.

"What do we do now?" Annika Carlsson asked.

"Now we take it nice and slow," Bäckström said. "We don't mess it up by rushing."

"I'm listening," Carlsson said.

"That list that Alm drew up of everyone Danielsson knew," Bäckström said. "I'd like to take a look at it. Call him, tell him to get here at once and give me the list."

"No need," Carlsson said. "You can read mine. I've got a copy."

"That's a shame," Bäckström said. "I was looking forward to having a chance to wind the idiot up."

The old boys from Solna and Sundbyberg, Bäckström thought, as he read through Alm's summary of Karl Danielsson's acquaintances some fifteen minutes later. Halfy and Flash and Jockey Gunnar. Godfather Grimaldi and his former colleague Roly Stålhammar. Good old boys who'd spent the best part of fifty years drunk off their ass.

Then he called one of them.

———

"Detective Superintendent Bäckström, the nation's hero," Halfy Söderman said. "To what does a simple man such as myself owe the pleasure?"

"I need to talk to you, Söderman," Bäckström said. Already wasted, and here I am stuck behind my desk, sober, gray, and underpaid, he thought.

"My door is always open to you," Halfy said. "It will be an honor for me and my simple household. And would the Superintendent have any specific requests as far as refreshment is concerned?"

"Coffee will do fine," Bäckström said brusquely. "Black, no sugar."

Then he had gone into Nadja's office and picked up Karl Danielsson's pocket diary, then called for a taxi.

"Are you sure I can't offer to drop you off?" Halfy Söderman asked, nodding toward the bottle of cognac standing on the kitchen table between him and Bäckström.

"I'm fine," Bäckström said.

"You're not just quick on the draw," Söderman declared. "You're a man of strong character too, Bäckström," he said, pouring a decent splash into his own coffee cup.

"Ah, liqueur's good," Söderman said, sighing with pleasure. "And good for you. One million alcoholics can't be wrong."

Maybe not all of them, Bäckström thought.

"There's something I wanted to ask you about," Bäckström said, pulling out Danielsson's black pocket diary.

"Well, because it's you, just go ahead, Bäckström," Halfy said. "If it had been one of your so-called colleagues, I'd have got into a three-round scrap with them by now."

"Karl Danielsson's pocket diary," Bäckström said. "There are some notes in here that I can't quite get my head round."

"I can well imagine," Söderman grinned. "Kalle was a crafty bastard."

"There are certain notes that come up again and again. We think they mean that he was paying out money to three different people."

"I can believe that," Söderman said. "And without a stain on his character. What are their names?"

"They're abbreviations," Bäckström said. "Initials of their names, we think. Plus the amounts.

"The initials are HA, AFS, and FI. All in capital letters, take a look," Bäckström said, holding the diary out to Söderman.

"What are they supposed to mean, then? The abbreviations, I mean. What are the names?"

"Hassan Talib, Afsan Ibrahim, and Farshad Ibrahim."

"They're those fucking bastards who tried to kill you, Bäckström," Söderman said as he leafed through the diary.

"Yes," Bäckström said. "Can you remember if Danielsson ever talked about them?"

"He never talked about stuff like that. No matter how hammered he got. As to whether he was stashing money away for people like that? I can quite believe him doing it, but he wasn't stupid enough to talk about it."

"No?" Bäckström said.

"No," Halfy Söderman said emphatically. "I'm afraid you've got it wrong, Superintendent. Mind you, I'd be happy to do my bit if it would help get those camel jockeys locked up for so long that they chuck the key in a lake. But I'm sorry to have to tell you that they're probably innocent, I'm afraid."

"Really?" Bäckström said.

"Kalle Danielsson was a funny little shit," Halfy said. "These notes are about something completely different, not those date pickers from Fuckknowswhereistan."

"Tell me," Bäckström said.

"It's a good story," Halfy Söderman said, shaking his head and smiling happily at his guest.

"Are you sitting comfortably, Bäckström?" he asked.

"Yes," Bäckström said.

"Then I'll begin," Halfy said. "Hold onto your ears so they don't drop off."

87.

"What have you been up to, Bäckström?" Annika Carlsson asked when Bäckström returned to the office three hours later.

"I've eaten a nutritious lunch and solved a double murder," Bäckström said. And bought some cough drops on the way, he thought.

"What have you been up to, then?" he asked.

"I checked out what you asked me to," Annika said. "It seems to fit so far. I found the rental car you asked me to look for. Hired from the OK garage in Sundbyberg on Saturday, May seventeenth. Returned the next day."

"Really?" Bäckström said. "So what's the problem?"

"Toivonen," Carlsson said. "I'm afraid you're going to have to talk to him."

"If he wants to talk to me, he knows how to find me," Bäckström said.

"Some advice, Bäckström," Annika Carlsson said. "If I were you, I'd go and talk to him, and keep a low profile when you do. I've seen him like this once before and it wasn't pretty."

"Really?" Bäckström said. So the fucking fox is throwing his weight around, he thought.

At least Toivonen wasn't climbing the walls. On the contrary. When Bäckström came into his office he merely nodded amiably and asked him to sit down.

"Good to see you, Bäckström," Toivonen said. "I've got some nice pictures I thought I might show you."

What the hell is he sitting there saying? Bäckström thought.

"I thought we could start with these," Toivonen said, handing over a bundle of surveillance pictures. "They're from last Friday, when you were out on the town and met Tatiana Thorén. Before that I believe you had dinner with Juha Valentin Andersson-Snygg, or Gustaf Gustafsson Henning as he's known these days. So I'm guessing he was responsible for the introductions."

"What the hell is this?" Bäckström growled. "I've got an investigation that's on its knees because I haven't got enough bodies. And you waste surveillance staff harassing one of your own colleagues? I hope you've got a damn good explanation."

"You always have to exaggerate, Bäckström," Toivonen said. "We had surveillance following the Ibrahim brothers and Hassan Talib. They went off to Café Opera, and that's where you and little Miss Thorén suddenly turn up in the story. Because Farshad seemed especially interested in you, we thought it might make sense to follow up that thread as well."

"I've never met the idiot. Not until he showed up in my flat and tried to kill me," Bäckström said.

"Listen to what you're saying," Toivonen said. "In part, I believe you. I think they turned up hoping to bribe you. Get hold of someone who could tell them what was going on in our armed robbery case. Presumably they were starting to feel the heat by then. Farshad's a cunning bastard, and he clearly doesn't lack money. And presumably Thorén got hold of the keys to your flat for them. You dropped your trousers pretty quickly, I gather."

"She didn't get any keys from me."

"No," Toivonen said. "But as soon as you passed out she sorted out a copy. She's a whore, by the way. One of the expensive ones."

"If you say so, Toivonen," Bäckström said, shrugging. "I didn't have to pay a penny myself. How much did she charge you? Five hundred Finnish marks, or what?"

"You can calm down, Bäckström," Toivonen said. "I'm not going to try to get you for breaking the law on the purchase of sexual services.

"It's worse than that, I'm afraid," Toivonen went on. "We took this set of pictures the same evening you had your little shooting frenzy at home in your flat. You're sitting drinking in your local bar. Beer and a large whiskey before the food, more beer and a couple shots with the food, coffee and a large cognac after the food. A police officer, out in his free time, goes to a bar, gets intoxicated, carrying his service revolver. I understand precisely why you met our colleagues with a glass in your hand when you finally let them in. What do you think of the pictures, by the way? Damn good quality, don't you think?"

"I don't understand what you're talking about," Bäckström said, holding up the first picture. "On this one I'm sitting with a glass of low-alcohol beer with a glass of apple juice alongside. You should try it, by the way."

"Sure," Toivonen said with a grin. "And then you had some extra water in a shot glass to go with your next low-alcohol beer. And you finished off with another apple juice. In a cognac glass this time. You're very funny, Bäckström, and if it wasn't for the fact that I've already got hold of a copy of your bill, I'd probably give up and try to move on."

"What's your point?" Bäckström said.

"I have a little proposal," Toivonen said.

"I'm listening," Bäckström said.

"I don't give a damn about our so-called colleagues over in internal investigations," Toivonen said. "I'm not the sort to snitch on a fellow officer. If someone becomes too much of a problem I usually grab him by the ears. We sort that kind of thing inside the station. That's the way we've always done things out here in Solna."

"Your proposal," Bäckström said. "You were saying that you had a proposal."

"We have a growing number of colleagues who are starting to get fucking sick and tired of your comments in the media. We can probably put up with the rest of it if we have to. If you want to carry on taking a shit in the papers, I think you should change jobs. Maybe you could become a crime reporter, or replace that tired old professor on the National Police Board, that Persson bloke, the one who's on Crimewatch, droning on every Thursday. If you keep your mouth shut, we'll keep our mouths shut. But if you carry on shooting your mouth off, I'm afraid that both these pictures and the bar tab and all the other things that I and my colleagues have got in our bottom drawer will suddenly appear on the news desk of one of the really vicious newspapers. Wasn't that one of the things you wanted, by the way? Greater openness toward the media from the police?"

"I hear what you're saying," Bäckström said.

"Good," Toivonen said. "And since you're not soft in the head, I presume we have an agreement. How are things going with your investigation, by the way?"

"Fine," Bäckström said. "I anticipate that it'll be all finished by Monday."

"I'm listening," Toivonen said.

"We can take it then," Bäckström said, standing up.

"I can hardly wait," Toivonen said with a grin.

See you at the press conference, Bäckström thought. He gave a curt nod and walked out.

88.

"How did it go?" Annika Carlsson asked. "I was almost starting to worry."

"It's fine," Bäckström said.

"So what did he want? He was completely furious when he stormed in to see me. I was almost starting to worry."

"My fucking old fox," Bäckström said. "He just needed some advice and help from his old supervisor and mentor."

"Glad to hear it," Annika Carlsson said with a wry smile. "So what are we going to do with our case, then?"

"The usual," Bäckström said. "We go out hard against the suspect, telephone surveillance, the whole works, silent, invisible, untraceable. Give Nadja a call as well; she can come in and help. I'll sign for the overtime. I think we can manage without the youngsters, and I don't think we want to drag Alm into this."

"There doesn't seem to be a phone," Annika Carlsson said. "At least I can't find one."

"Oh, it's there, all right," Bäckström said. "That's the cell phone that both Danielsson and Akofeli call. The one that only ever seems to get incoming calls. If we're lucky it's still around. And there has to be a landline as well."

"I've already started on that," Annika Carlsson confirmed.

"Well, then," Bäckström said with a wry smile. "On Monday I think it'll be time to get out the handcuffs."

89.

Early on Sunday morning Hassan Talib suffered further bleeding in the brain. The doctor who saved his life less than a week before had to make another attempt. This time it didn't go so well. The operation was abandoned after just a quarter of an hour and Talib was declared dead at half past five in the morning in the neurosurgical department of the Karolinska Hospital.

It was never good when people like Talib died. There were far too many people like him who might start to get ideas. Five minutes later Superintendent Honkamäki decided to increase security. He spoke to Toivonen and Linda Martinez. Toivonen had taken the formal decision and called in another six uniformed officers and six surveillance officers.

The uniformed officers would reinforce external security. The surveillance officers would roam the hospital precinct and buildings hoping to discover suspicious vehicles and individuals in time, or simply anything that seemed out of the ordinary.

At nine o'clock that morning Frank Motoele had appeared in the orthopedic surgery department. He greeted his colleagues at the entrance, took the lift up to the seventh floor where Farshad Ibrahim lay locked in a single room with his left leg plastered from his ankle to his crotch.

"Situation?" Motoele asked, nodding to the officer who was sitting beside the entrance to the ward where Farshad Ibrahim was being looked after.

"Everything's fine," the officer said with a smile. "The patient's asleep. I spoke to the ward sister a short while ago. They say he's in a lot of pain and they keep pumping him full of painkillers, so we're just going to have to deal with that. He spends most of the time asleep. If you want to talk to his little brother, he's in the thoracic surgery department. Without a knife, this time."

"I might just take a stroll and have a look," Motoele said.

"Go ahead," the officer said. "I'm going to hit the smoking room in the meantime. I'm going crazy here. That damn nicotine gum is a complete joke."

There's something not right here, Motoele thought, even before he opened the closed door to Farshad's room.

Just to be on the safe side he pushed the door open with his foot, his hand on his pistol. The room was empty, the window was open, the bed had been dragged over to the window, and someone had tied an ordinary climbing rope to its legs.

Twenty meters to the slope seven floors below. Someone was already standing there, waiting for the man who was trying to lower himself down the rope in spite of his plastered leg. He had only got a few meters when Frank Motoele stuck his head out of the window.

Motoele grabbed the rope and started to reel it in. A simple task for a man like Motoele, one hundred kilos of muscle and bone, whereas Farshad Ibrahim on the other end of the rope scarcely weighed seventy. Besides, Farshad had made a mistake. Instead of easing his grip on the rope and just sliding down, he was clinging to it, and sliding up almost a meter before Motoele turned his gaze inward and let go of the rope. Farshad let go as well, falling helplessly and landing on his back almost twenty meters below. He died instantly. Only then did Motoele realize that Farshad's accomplice had drawn a gun and was shooting at him.

He was a poor shot as well. Motoele, on the other hand, took his time. He pulled his weapon, crouched behind the window frame, aimed high on one leg, put both hands on the gun, both eyes open. Everything according to regulations, and if he was in luck he'd manage to hit the man's femoral artery. The man below collapsed, dropping his gun and grabbing his wounded leg, screaming in a language Motoele didn't understand.

Motoele, who had turned his gaze inward, holstered his weapon and went out into the corridor to meet his fellow officers. He could already hear the sounds of shouting and running.

Superintendent Honkamäki called Toivonen within thirty minutes and gave him a short status report. Someone had helped Farshad open the window of his room. The same person had given him an ordinary climbing rope, with knots in. About twenty meters long. Motoele had tried to reel him in. Farshad had lost his grip and fell, landing on his back on the slope twenty meters below. One of his accomplices had started shooting at Motoele. Several shots. Motoele had shot back. One shot. It hit high up on the leg. Rendered him harmless. The accomplice had been arrested, identified, and taken to the ER, just a hundred meters from orthopedic surgery. And they also had a good idea of who had helped Farshad with the window and rope.

"We can't locate one of the nurses, born in Iran, if you were wondering. She disappeared in the middle of her shift about an hour ago," Honkamäki reported.

"What the fuck have you been doing?" Toivonen said, and groaned.

"Everything according to the rulebook," Honkamäki said. "What the hell would you have done?"

"The younger brother, he's still alive?" Toivonen said.

343

"Yes, he's still alive. But I can see why you might wonder," Honkamäki said with a crooked smile.

"Get him to prison," Toivonen said. "We've got to get to grips with security."

"I've already tried," Honkamäki said. "They're refusing to take him. Say they haven't got the necessary medical facilities."

"Drive him to Huddinge Hospital," Toivonen said.

"Huddinge?" Honkamäki said. "What for?"

"I don't want him in our district," Toivonen said. "Not while people are dying like flies out here, surrounded by my officers."

"Okay," Honkamäki said.

"And as far as Motoele is concerned . . ."

"It's sorted," Honkamäki said. "Forensics are already here, and the internal investigation team are on their way. The only thing we're missing is probably Bäckström," he said with a laugh.

Fucking hell. Three-zero to the Christians, Bäckström thought when he turned on the morning news on television. At last, pancakes and bacon, he thought. Seeing as his warden was evidently busy elsewhere.

"I can understand that you're in shock, Motoele," the internal investigator said.

"No," Motoele said, shaking his head. "I'm not in shock. It was all done according to the rulebook." Respect, he thought, and turned his gaze inward.

90.

After lunch on Monday Bäckström was ready to strike. First he spoke to Annika Carlsson and explained the details to her.

"Bäckström, Bäckström," Annika Carlsson said, shaking her head. "You're probably the craftiest officer I've ever worked with. I can't even count the number of evidential details you're planning to raise in your conversation with this awful person."

"Me neither," Bäckström said. "So you'll do as I say?"

"Of course, boss. What are we going to do with Felicia and young Stigson?"

"Backup," Bäckström said. "Taking Stigson along is out of the question and if the situation gets critical I don't want to have to worry about Felicia."

"That makes sense," Annika agreed.

"They can wait outside in the car, just in case, until we call them in," Bäckström said.

Then they set off for number 1 Hasselstigen in two unmarked cars. Stigson and Pettersson pulled up outside the entrance. Bäckström and Annika Carlsson took the lift up. As Annika Carlsson hid on the stairs, Bäckström knocked on the door and, since the meeting had been arranged earlier that morning, the door was opened just after his second knock.

"Welcome, Superintendent," Britt-Marie Andersson said, with a wide smile that showed off her sparkling white teeth, and for some reason she ran her left hand down the middle of her generous cleavage.

"Can I offer you anything, Superintendent?"

"A cup of coffee would be nice," Bäckström said. "Actually, I was wondering if I could borrow your loo?"

"Of course," Britt-Marie Andersson said. She tilted her head to one side and leaned forward to improve the view. "Why do we have to be so formal, anyway? I'm Britt-Marie," she said, holding out a suntanned hand.

"Bäckström," Bäckström said, responding with a half Harry Callahan.

"You're a proper old-fashioned kind of man, aren't you, Bäckström?" Britt-Marie Andersson said, smiling and shaking her head. "Make yourself at home, and I'll get us some coffee."

Bäckström went into the toilet. As soon as he heard that she was busy in the kitchen he padded out and unlocked the front door. If the situation became critical he didn't want his colleagues to have to break the door in. Then he flushed, opened the toilet door noisily, went into the living room, and sat down on his hostess's flowery sofa.

Britt-Marie Andersson had laid a whole tray. She had even got her little cockroach to be a good Little Sweetie and go and lie down in his flowery little basket. Then she sat down on her pink armchair, pulling it forward so that her suntanned knees were almost touching Bäckström's well-tailored yellow linen trousers as she poured the coffee.

"I presume that you take it black," Britt-Marie said with a contented sigh.

"Yes," Bäckström said.

"Like all real men," Britt-Marie said with another sigh.

Except when I have an espresso, because then I usually have some warm milk on the side, Bäckström thought.

"Black is fine," Bäckström said.

"And can I tempt you with a little cognac? Or perhaps a little whiskey?" Britt-Marie said, nodding toward the bottles on the tray.

"I was thinking of having a little cognac, myself," she cajoled. "Just a teeny, tiny little one."

"Go ahead," Bäckström said. "That's probably a good idea," he said, without going into the reason why.

"So tell me," Britt-Marie said, tilting her head to one side. "I'm practically dying with curiosity. On the phone you said something about wanting to pop in and thank me."

"Yes, of course," Bäckström said. "That's what I said—"

"I'm sorry to interrupt," Britt-Marie said, taking a cautious sip with pouting lips, "but I really must compliment you on your outfit. A yellow linen suit, light brown linen shirt, matching tie, dark brown Italian shoes, handmade, I'm sure. Most of the detectives I've met usually look like they slept on a park bench before going to work."

"Clothes maketh the man," Bäckström said. "Well, thank you for the compliment, and of course I came here to thank you."

"And here's me, hardly knowing how I could have helped!" Britt-Marie Andersson said.

"Me neither," Bäckström said. "But to start with, you tipped us off about my former colleague, Roly Stålhammar. The only thing you forgot to mention was that you used to go out with him some forty or so years ago and that you pretty much fucked each other's brains out back then. And when he turned out not to be good enough for us, you helped us along the way by identifying the Ibrahim brothers and their unsavory cousin.

"Mind you," Bäckström went on. "I do believe you on one point. I'm sure you did see them talking to Kalle Danielsson, and I'm absolutely convinced that the big lout standing by the car did make an obscene gesture at you. But when we still weren't happy, you managed to persuade one of my most foolish colleagues to believe your story that Seppo Laurén had been a very violent young man for years. Who also happened to hate his father, Karl Danielsson. In fact, for the past fortnight you've had my officers running round like a flock of headless chickens. There was really just one thing that you forgot to tell us."

"And what might that be?" Britt-Marie Andersson said. She was sitting up straight now, without a trace of a smile or the slightest tremble of her hand as she refilled her little cognac glass.

"That it was actually you who beat Karl Danielsson to death on that Wednesday evening with his own saucepan lid, and that you strangled him afterward with his own tie just to make sure. Before taking the briefcase containing all the money that he was stupid enough to show you just before. And that on Friday morning, just thirty hours later, you strangled your young lover Septimus Akofeli. Since he seems to have worked out more or less at once that you did it and by Thursday was under the impression that you were acting in self-defense to stop Danielsson from raping you. You must have said something about Kalle Danielsson to him before. Probably that Danielsson had tried to fuck you against your will. And when you met on Friday, you and Akofeli, he wanted you to go to the police and explain what really happened. That you were the victim, not Danielsson."

"You strangled Akofeli in your bedroom," Bäckström went on, nodding toward the closed door at the end of the living room. "After you'd fucked his brains out, so that he was suitably docile when you offered to give him a back massage. Before you both went to the police and laid your cards on the table."

"That's the most fantastic story I heard in my whole life," Britt-Marie Andersson said. "But because it's deeply insulting to me, I do hope you haven't told it to anyone else, Superintendent. Because then I'd be forced to report you for slander. Grave defamation of character, as we're supposed to call it these days. And what would that look like?"

"Don't worry. This is strictly between the two of us," Bäckström lied. "I haven't breathed a word."

"Oh, I am pleased," Britt-Marie Andersson said, her smile almost back to normal again. "Suddenly I get the impression that you and I will be able to find a solution to this. Birds of a feather flock together, isn't that what they say, Bäckström?" Bäckström's hostess said, pouring herself a third glass of cognac.

"I met your former brother-in-law the other day," Bäckström said. "He's a very interesting character."

"I find that hard to believe," Britt-Marie snorted. "He's been an alcoholic for the past fifty years, hasn't spoken a word of truth in his life."

"I thought I might tell you what he had to say anyway," Bäckström said. "And if I were in your shoes, I'd listen very carefully."

91.

"When I saw the notes in Kalle's diary I thought you wanted to talk to me about Bea," Halfy said, pouring a generous measure into his coffee cup. "Then you suddenly started going on about a load of Muslims who haven't got a thing to do with it. What is this, 9/11, or what?"

"Bea," Bäckström said. "Tell me."

"My ex-sister-in-law. Britt-Marie Andersson. An old Solna girl, biggest tits in Solna and the best fuck north of the city back in the day, when men were men and before all the fags took over. And what did we get for it? A load of fucking lesbians."

"I still don't follow."

"Bea, Britt-Marie Andersson. Known as Bea. Used to run BeA's Salon, with a capital A. BeA's Beauty Salon down in Sundbyberg. Did perms for a load of old bags, and if you turned up after hours or called and booked a time in advance, you could get a decent going-over behind the salon curtains. That was actually how my brother met her. Roly put him onto her. Mind you, Roly never had to pay, of course. Perish the thought. Swedish champion, the next Ingemar Johansson, they said in the papers. You should see his tool, Bäckström. If Roly had just dropped his shorts during a match and swung his ass, he could have knocked Ingemar out of the ring."

"But your brother ended up marrying her?"

"Yes, he was crazy about her. It was around the time that Roly was losing his edge and spent most of his time on the canvas, and Bea went and married my brother. She'd got it into her head that my dear brother, Per Adolf, had a load of money. That it made more sense to take a chance on him rather than Roly Stålhammar, who'd soon be staggering around the center of Solna telling everyone about the good old days."

"So what happened after that?" Bäckström said. "I saw that your brother died about ten years ago?"

"Yes, and it was a hell of a relief, frankly. Me and the rest of the lads had already told him to go to hell. One evening when Mario had us all round for a party he called Mario a coon. So we renamed him Råsunda Hitler and told him to fuck off. Per Adolf, you know, and the silly sod had a mustache as well. So my brother married Bea and moved into a nice house up by Råstasjön. Mortgaged up to the eaves, but Bea didn't know that when she fucked his brains out a few years later and imagined she was going to inherit the lot. But since my brother didn't have a penny, she ended up in Hasselstigen. So she traded him in for Kalle the Accountant, Kalle Danielsson."

"So he had a bit of money?"

"Things were starting to go well back then," Halfy said, nodding and pouring himself a fourth glass.

"So what happened with Kalle Danielsson, then? Between him and Bea, I mean?" Bäckström said.

"He got just as crazy about her as my brother had been," Halfy said. "Gave up on little Ritwa and her lad. Shagging Bea was the only thing in his head. It must have cost him a good few million over the years to do it. You've read his diary?"

"I still don't get it."

"HA, AFS, FI," Halfy said. "I'm starting to wonder if you're a bit thick, Bäckström," Halfy said.

"I just have a bit of trouble if I try to think," Bäckström said. "I don't suppose you feel like helping me?"

"HA, as in handjob," Halfy said, illustrating this by playing air guitar above his own crotch.

"AFS, as in Andersson's fellatio special," he went on, pursing his lips.

"And FI, of course. Full intercourse, for when you fuck like normal people do," Halfy concluded. Kalle was keeping a diary of when he had sex with Bea. It's hardly that difficult to grasp? Five hundred for a normal handjob, two thousand for a blowjob. Five thousand for an old-fashioned fuck. It even says he had to pay ten thousand the time he forgot to wear a rubber and went in bare. Kalle can't have been right in the head toward the end. Paying ten grand for a plain old fuck.

"Forget the Arabs, Bäckström," Halfy said, draining his cup in one gulp. "This is all about Kalle Danielsson shagging my ex-sister-in-law, Britt-Marie Andersson. She went back to her maiden name when she realized my brother didn't have a penny. She was a Söderman for ten years, and no one was happier than me when she changed it back to Andersson."

"Hang on a minute," Bäckström said, thinking hard. "Fellatio? No one really calls it that. What's that all about?"

"Typical Kalle," Halfy said with a grin. "He was always like that. A bit ironic. And Britt-Marie has always tried to make out that she's better than she is, if I can put it like that. If you went to her, you didn't get just any old blowjob. No, you got Andersson's fellatio special, an AFS. Typical Kalle, If you ask me."

"I see," Bäckström said, checking to see that his ears were still stuck to his round head, just in case.

92.

"Fellatio," Bäckström said, pursing his lips as he finished the summary of his conversation with Britt-Marie Andersson's ex-brother-in-law.

"Do you know what, Bäckström?" Britt-Marie Andersson said, leaning forward and displaying her undeniably impressive charms as she put her suntanned hand on the inside of Bäckström's left thigh.

"I'm starting to think that you might be rather tempted yourself," she went on as her hand made its way up Bäckström's well-cut yellow trousers.

Why the hell hasn't she rung? Bäckström thought, glancing at his watch. Fucking attack dyke, he thought, just as a cell started to bleep somewhere in the room they were sitting in.

"Yours or mine?" Bäckström said. He pulled his phone out and held it up just to be sure.

"Not mine," he said, shaking his head and putting it back in his pocket.

"Probably a wrong number," Britt-Marie Andersson said, although just for a moment her eyes looked as narrow as his colleague Annika Carlsson's. The same colleague who had just called the third cell, the one that only seemed to be used to take incoming calls from Karl Danielsson and Septimus Akofeli. At precisely the time that Bäckström told her to call.

"Do you know what, Bäckström?" Britt-Marie said, suddenly sitting down in his lap, her left hand caressing his shirt collar and chest. "I'm starting to think that maybe you and I should join forces."

"Tell me," Bäckström said. He didn't feel at all concerned, even though she had put her hand on his tie. Forewarned is forearmed, he thought.

"We're the same age," Britt-Marie Andersson said. "I could offer you one or two trips to a place you've never been before, and I'm talking about sex here, not any ordinary trips. We can share Danielsson's money. The money he stole from crooks like those awful Arabs who tried to kill you. We can—"

"How much are we talking about?" Bäckström interrupted, as cool as a cucumber even though the woman in his lap was already stroking his tie with both hands. Suntanned, strong hands, big hands for a woman, like a man's hands.

"Just curious," Bäckström clarified.

"We're talking about almost a million kronor," Britt-Marie Andersson said, as her hands stroked Bäckström's tie, blue with yellow lilies on it.

"Are you sure about that?" Bäckström said. "I spoke to the prosecutor this morning and my colleagues went down to look at your safe-deposit box in the SE Bank in Solna shopping center just a couple hours ago. They found Karl Danielsson's briefcase in the box, and inside they actually found two million. Thousand-kronor notes, in bundles of a hundred thousand each."

"That phone call, by the way," Bäckström said. "When the cell in your handbag started to ring a couple minutes ago, the call was made by one of my officers. It's the same phone that Danielsson and Akofeli used to call. Danielsson because he wanted to pay you for sex, and little Akofeli because he probably loved you."

"Do you know what, Britt-Marie Andersson?" Superintendent Evert Bäckström said. "I'm starting to think that I'm talking to a very unusual person, considering my line of business."

"And who might that be?" Britt-Marie Andersson said, her eyes now even narrower than Annika Carlsson's had been when she was considering whether to slap officer Stigson for talking about the selfsame Britt-Marie Andersson in a misogynistic way.

"A female double murderer," Bäckström said. "Right now we don't have a single woman serving a life sentence for that," he declared. "Actually, we haven't had one for forty years," he added. "The last time it was a Finnish prostitute. And this time it's her Swedish counterpart."

At that very moment she struck. Probably out of anger and as a reflex following what he had just said, and because she must have realized that the game was up. She grabbed the knot of his tie. Pulled as hard as she could and fell backward onto the floor when the little plastic clip holding it came away.

The classic police tie, he thought, even though it had cost him ten times as much as the one his alcoholic father always used to wear. Always the ready-knotted blue one on duty, to stop crooks

from being able to strangle him when he was knocking them
about and locking them up in the Maria district's old police box.
He used to wear it at home at weekends too, since he had forgotten
how to tie an ordinary knot.

"Okay, Bea," Bäckström said, pulling out the handcuffs from
his pocket and taking hold of her hands to cuff her. "Nice and
easy does it."

Not the least bit nice and easy. She spun round on the floor.
Kicked his legs out from under him, sat astride him, and took hold
of his tieless neck. And squeezed with hands that were both bigger
and stronger than his.

Her little dog had leapt out of its basket and come to the
aid of its mistress, chewing and snarling at his expensive yellow trousers. Then Britt-Marie Andersson, a woman, over sixty,
and—from a criminological perspective—an impossible criminal, grabbed the cognac bottle from the table and smashed him
in the face with it.

"Fuck, Annika!" Bäckström roared, as lightning and darkness
alternated inside his head. And he'd rather die than scream for
help even if a woman was trying to kill him.

Detective Inspector Annika Carlsson came racing into the room
with the speed of a cannonball from the olden days. She kicked
Little Sweetie, launching him across the room, then set about
his mistress with her extending baton, twice over her shoulders,
twice on her arms. Then she put a pair of handcuffs on Britt-
Marie Andersson. She grabbed her by the hair, pulling her face
up, to give her the only message that counted in a tricky situation
between women.

"Okay, bitch, behave yourself or I'll kill you," Annika Carlsson
said, sounding neither like a true sister nor a female police officer.

Then she turned her tender attentions to her boss, Superintendent
Evert Bäckström.

"I'm afraid the bitch has broken your nose, Bäckström,"

Annika Carlsson said while Felicia Pettersson and Jan O. Stigson led Britt-Marie Andersson out of her flat.

"That's okay." Bäckström sniffed as blood streamed from both nostrils. He felt beneath his shirt and pulled out the tape recorder he had taped to his stomach under his well-cut yellow linen jacket.

"That's okay, as long as the tape recorder's still working," Bäckström said. "Just get me a plaster so we can get back to the station," he said, pinching his nose between his chubby fingers.

93.

Bäckström had hardly had time to put a plaster on his broken nose and get back to his own office before his colleague Niemi came rushing in.

"What the hell happened to you, Bäckström?" Niemi said. "You look like someone's dragged you through a thornbush."

"Never mind that," Bäckström said. "What can I do for you?"

"A breakthrough in the case," Niemi said. "Our colleagues at the National Forensics Lab have just called to say that they've found DNA traces in the washing-up gloves that Polish bloke found in the trash bin. A woman's DNA," Niemi said.

"Danielsson's cleaner?" Bäckström suggested. He had known better for several days now.

"I thought that too," Niemi said.

The poor Finnish bastard must be soft in the head, Bäckström thought. He's spent several days in Danielsson's flat, and who the hell would employ a blind cleaner? he thought.

"Until we found the same DNA under Akofeli's fingernails," Niemi said. "The only problem is that we aren't getting any matches on the database. We don't know who she is."

"Yesterday's news, Niemi," Bäckström said, leaning back in

his chair even though his nose was hurting like hell. "We've got her locked up," he went on. "I'm glad you're here. Can you pop down and get a sample from her? Then I want you and your South American partner to go and examine her apartment. Because that was where she killed Akofeli. And if you have any spare time after that, the car she used to get rid of his body is down in the garage."

"What the hell are you saying, Bäckström?" Niemi said.

"I'm a police officer," Bäckström said. "So I already worked it out a fortnight ago."

And then Toivonen.

"Congratulations, Bäckström," Toivonen said. "I'm starting to think that if you can manage to keep your mouth shut, we might even be able to have a civilized relationship."

"Thanks," Bäckström said. "You should know that you're warming the cockles of an old constable's heart," he said.

"Don't mention it," Toivonen said with a grin, then walked out.

I'll kill you, you fucking little fox, Bäckström thought.

Then the prosecutor rang.

"Hello, Bäckström," the prosecutor said. "I've just heard that you picked up our perpetrator."

"Yes," Bäckström said.

"Then I spoke to Niemi," she went·on. "So I was thinking of pushing through the formal arrest procedures tomorrow morning. We've got sufficient grounds now."

"That's nice for you," Bäckström said, and hung up.

Anna Holt had even come down to his office.

"Congratulations, Bäckström," Holt said, nodding and smiling. "You've killed the dragon for me."

"Thanks," Bäckström said. "Are we doing a press conference?"

"I think we'll hold back," Anna Holt said, shaking her dark cropped hair. "There's been a bit too much of that lately. I think we'll make do with an ordinary press release. Tomorrow, after the formal arrest procedures."

Of course, Bäckström thought. First you take the honor away from me. Then you take the glory away from me. And I've got a pair of shredded linen trousers, a smashed coffee table, a blood-soaked carpet, and bullet holes in the walls and ceiling of what was once my home. As a thank-you I've been given a cut-glass vase that I've given to my alcoholic neighbor and an old police badge that's supposed to have belonged to a mad old ass bandit who wasn't even man enough to come out of the closet and was forced to wrestle other singlet-wearing trolls to stay happy.

"What do you think, Bäckström?" Anna Holt said.

"Fine with me," Bäckström said, giving her the full Sipo-wicz as she left. Run away, now, you scrawny little nightmare, he thought.

"What the hell are we going to do about Seppo Laurén?" Alm said. His face was deep red, and it was just two minutes after Holt had left the room.

"I'm glad you're here, Alm," Bäckström said. "This is what we're going to do. Now listen carefully."

"I'm listening," Alm said.

"First I want you to gather together everything you've written about little Seppo. Then I want you to roll it all up and put some elastic bands round it. And then I want you to shove it up your ass."

Not only is he soft in the head, Bäckström thought, as he watched Alm leave. The bastard hasn't even got a sense of humor.

"Respect, boss," Frank Motoele said. He turned his gaze outward and nodded to Bäckström.

"Thanks," Bäckström said. "I really appreciate that." If I had those eyes I wouldn't need little Siggy, he thought. I could just stand and stare at them while they beg for mercy.

"One left," Motoele said, turning his gaze inward again. "We'll get little Afsan after the trial. I've got friends out in the prison system. On both sides. Easy."

"I hear what you're saying," Bäckström said. One left, what the hell is he saying? he thought.

"Respect," Motoele repeated. "If we had more people like you, boss, we'd already have this sorted."

"Take care, Frank," Bäckström said. Congratulations, Evert, he thought. You've just made friends with the creepiest person ever to have become a police officer in the western hemisphere.

"So this is where you're sitting and sulking, is it, Bäckström?" Annika Carlsson said. "How's your nose, by the way?"

"Fine," Bäckström said, fingering the plaster tentatively.

"How about going and getting a beer? I'm buying, if that helps."

"Okay," Bäckström said.

94.

And with that he took his colleague Annika Carlsson to his favorite bar. Which was fine, since his blond tornado had gone home to Jyväskylä to see her family and had taken her glowering partner with her to be on the safe side.

What normal man would risk his monthly cleaning plus a decent lay once a week for a standard-issue dyke? Bäckström thought. Whether or not she claimed to be open to all comers?

In spite of everything, things had been perfectly fine until toward the end of the evening.

"Do you know what, Bäckström?" Annika Carlsson said. "I've actually never fucked in a Hästens bed. So how about it?"

Then she had suddenly grabbed his arm and squeezed with her

long, sinewy fingers. It was as if someone had put a metal clamp round it.

"Shit," Bäckström said. His nose was hurting so much that he might as well get his jaw broken before he lost consciousness in his bed at home. In the bullet-riddled flat that had once been his home.

"Well, if we're going to be completely open," Bäckström said.

"Go on," his colleague Annika Carlsson said.

"For the fucking life of me, I don't know if I'm brave enough," Bäckström said. There, it was said and his jaw was still intact, he thought.

"Like I said before, Bäckström, I keep an open mind when it comes to sex," Carlsson said. "If you like, I can be really, really sweet. But if you were to change your mind and decide you'd like to try something else, then I can be really, really mean."

"Let me think about it," Bäckström said, already feeling the sweat running down his back under his yellow linen jacket. A woman talking like that. Terrible, he thought.

"Absolutely fine," Annika Carlsson said, shrugging her broad shoulders. "As long as you make your mind up before we leave here.

"It's fine, Bäckström," she assured him, scraping her nails across his hand. "Anyway, I've already said I'm paying."

And she put her hand in her pocket and pulled out a thousand-kronor note. Strikingly similar to the ones they had been staring at a week or so before down in the vault of Handelsbanken on Valhallavägen.

Oh, so it's like that, is it? Bäckström thought. He had lost any faith in humanity more than fifty years before.

"How did you get them out of the vault?" Bäckström asked.

"The usual way, the way girls always have throughout the ages," Annika Carlsson said, smiling at him. "Besides, you were kind enough to run upstairs to call Toivonen, so it was easy. I took a bundle from the pile, rolled it up, put it inside the plastic glove, and inserted it in the usual place."

"In your snatch," Bäckström said, although he already knew the answer.

"Mind you, I got it wet with saliva first," Annika Carlsson said. "Some old advice I was once given. I worked as a prison guard in the women's unit before I got into the Police Academy. You have no idea what I found between the legs of my clients while I worked there.

"Mind you, it was a nightmare when we had to go and see Niemi," Annika Carlsson said. "I'm quite tight down there, so it was chafing badly," she clarified.

"What do you think, Bäckström?" Carlsson said. "I've got it into my head that we'd make the perfect couple," she said, running her nails along his arm once more to underline her point.

"I need to think," Bäckström said. Where's humanity heading? Where's Sweden heading? What the fuck is happening to the force? Bäckström thought.

And what the fuck happened to the princess and half the kingdom? he thought.